MINE

Blood Ties Series

A.K ROSE
ATLAS ROSE

MINE

Warnings

The Bloodties Series is part of the Cosa Nostra world which contains several interconnected series. The tone is **dark**, involves a number of romantic interests for our female main characters and reader discretion is advised.

More information on the content warnings can be found here.

Please be aware of your own triggers and limitations. This is a Mafia/Gang related world and are not heroes or heroines, they are hungry, ruthless and they do bad things to themselves and to others.

If you're okay with this, please read on. I hope you enjoy this darkly rich, forbidden series. I can't wait to bring you *so much more*....

Love Atlas, xx

Mine

Grab the playlist here on Spotify

1

Ryth

Flames reached high into the night, consuming the room on the second floor of our house with a roar. The room that had until moments ago been mine. I blinked, trying to dislodge my tears, and shivered.

"Is anyone else in there?" an officer screamed as he raced toward our home and others followed.

But mom didn't answer. She just stared blankly at what remained of our life as it went up in flames. I coughed and spluttered as I stumbled toward him as he ran to the open front door. I wanted to tell him it was useless...wanted to tell him there was nothing inside to save...*not anymore.*

Our things were already gone. Our cars, the TV's, even my laptop with all my assignments for school. All taken, even before the first lick of flames had started.

Taken by the feds for *'evidence'*. Evidence of what, I didn't know.

I looked at the few clothes in my hands, clothes that were all I had left. I hadn't even grabbed my cell phone that was lying on my dresser charging. They were all I'd had time to grab as I stumbled from the shower, threw on some jeans and a t-shirt, grabbed a handful of clothes off the bed, and raced from the house. Two shirts and a pair of ripped jeans were clutched in my hands, along with one change of panties, but no bra. Tears welled in my eyes. *What was I supposed to do with no bra?*

Movement drew my gaze to the street behind me. A black sedan with heavily tinted windows rolled past. The red and blue flashing lights from the official vehicles splashed against the gleaming paint. I'd seen cars like that, knew who drove them.

The Rossis...

"Mom?" I stared as the black car cruised past, red brake lights flaring as it drove down our street.

Her wide eyes shone with panic. She hadn't spoken to me, not said a goddamn word, even when the cops had slapped cuffs on dad and taken him away.

"What the hell happened?"

She flinched when I stepped closer and touched her arm. "Did...*did the Rossis do this?*"

Her breath caught and her eyes closed. That was all the answer I needed. *Jesus.* I wrapped my arms around my body. First they'd come for him, now they'd taken out our home, leaving us with nothing.

"Elle," a woman's voice came behind us.

Red and blue lights flashed in the dark, illuminating Stacey Cromwell's face as she stumbled over the hedge dividing our properties and came closer. She was dressed in her nightie, a satin wrap covering her modesty. A display for the emergency services, no doubt, as she headed toward us with a black plastic bag in her hand, one she held out to my mom. "For your clothes, honey."

"Go away." Mom just stared at our home without turning as it burned to the ground.

But Mrs. Cromwell didn't move, she just stared at my mom until she jerked her gaze toward our neighbor and screamed *"GET THE FUCK AWAY FROM ME!"*

She flinched and stumbled backwards, throwing the garbage bag to the ground before fleeing as fast as she could.

"You didn't need to do that," I said as her cell lit up with a message.

The same first responder who'd run into our house now coughed and spluttered as he stumbled from the door. The piercing wail of sirens filled the air as two more fire trucks pulled up to our house. But the officer just pulled his mask free and shook his head, meeting my mom's gaze. *"There's nothing...* nothing we can do. It's all gone. All—"

Boom! Something inside the house exploded. I flung myself backwards, dropping my clothes and grabbing mom, dragging her with me as the second floor of our house collapsed. But mom didn't even flinch, just looked at her cell as it lit up with a message.

"What is it?" I picked up the plastic bag and shoved our clothes inside.

God, please don't let it be dad.

"We have to leave," she announced.

"Leave to where?" I straightened and motioned to our burning house as it spewed thick smoke. "We have nowhere to go."

Headlights splashed against the living room window as it shattered. I glanced behind us to a taxi as it pulled up in our drive and stared as my mom walked toward it.

"Mom, what the hell's going on?" I followed her, thick tears sliding down my cheeks.

"Just get in the taxi, Ryth." Mom yanked open the back door and climbed in.

I caught the reflection in the back window of the taxi, my still-damp hair, my t-shirt sticking to my skin. I reached up, touching the mark on my cheek as I shivered. I'd been in the middle of a shower after straightening up the destruction the feds had left behind when mom tore into the bathroom screaming the place was on fire.

It's him! she'd screamed as I lunged from the shower and yanked on some clothes before stumbling down the stairs after her. *He knows what your father's done!*

Crack! Something in our house collapsed, flinging embers into the sky. I stared at the reflection of the inferno in the taxi window before climbing in. It was gone...*everything.* Tears filled my eyes, blurring the inside of the vehicle as I yanked the door closed behind me. We carried the stench with us, staining the already foul air. The driver rolled down his window before he shoved the car into gear and pulled out of our driveway.

"Where are we going?" I glanced toward her.

"Somewhere safe," she muttered, staring out the window.

"Safe?" The Rossis' dark sedan filled my head. "Where's safe?"

We had nowhere to go, all our friends were dad's friends, and right now they were...*dangerous.*

The word resounded as we left our world behind and headed toward the city.

"Are they going to hurt him?"

"No," she answered quietly. "They need him."

They might need him, but that didn't mean they needed us. "But that won't stop them from coming after *us*, will it?"

Silence.

That was the answer I was afraid of.

I leaned back against the seat. *Jesus, dad. What the hell have you done?* The last two days were a blur. First the argument and the sound of one of my parents' all too frequent shouting matches, before chaos...and then, the feds.

The ache in the back of my throat felt like a fist. I swallowed, watching the city lights brighten in the distance before we took the exit ramp and headed east toward the place where million-dollar homes lined the streets and where rich kids raced expensive cars for slips...and we didn't know anyone there.

Ten-foot wrought iron fences and CCTV cameras were all I saw before the driver pulled into a driveway where the black gates were open.

"Thank you." Mom reached out and handed him a fifty-dollar bill, pulled from a purse I hadn't noticed until now.

"Mom?" I murmured as she pulled back to the seat. "Where are we?"

But she didn't answer, just shoved open the door and climbed out.

I followed, finding a three-story house partially hidden from the street. A midnight Shelby Mustang sat outside, a dark blue Lamborghini beside it, leaving one other parking space empty. What kind of people had cars like that?

I stopped walking.

"It's just for a few days, honey." Mom never once looked my way. "Just until I figure this out."

A man stepped out of the door. Tall and intense, his gaze was fixed on my mom.

"Elle." He strode toward her and pulled her into a hug. "*Jesus*, I was so damn worried." He glanced my way and forced a smile. "Thank God you're both okay."

"I'm sorry, Creed." Mom looked away, discreetly brushing her tears away. "I had no one else to call."

"Sorry?" He seemed confused. "You don't need to be sorry, Elle. That's what friends are for. Come on, let's get you both inside, you're shaking like a damn leaf."

He slid his arm around mom's waist, pulling her toward the front door. But it was that empty car space that nagged me, enough to make me glance over my shoulder before I followed.

Footsteps thudded upstairs before a door closed with a bang. I flinched and jerked my gaze upwards.

"Don't worry." Creed said as he met my gaze. "You won't hear a damn thing inside. Double glazed windows."

Like everyone else, his gaze drifted to the mark on my cheek. The ugly, disgusting strawberry disfiguration I hated. Heat flared as I tugged my hair across to hide it.

"It's just for the night," Mom assured. "So I can think."

"For as long as you need a place, this is yours," he replied. "Come on, I bet you're exhausted."

I carried the plastic bag of clothes inside, acutely aware as I stepped into a stranger's house in nothing more than a damp t-shirt and dirty jeans.

"Let me get you settled," he called to me, and headed for the stairs. "Then your mom and I can have a drink and try to figure out a way out of this."

"How did you know my dad?" I asked as I followed.

His steps faltered for a second as he glanced over his shoulder. "Your dad? I don't, not really." He glanced toward mom. "Your mom and I knew each other in college."

I looked back as I climbed the stairs. She looked so lost in that moment, so utterly lost. I followed him up to the third floor and stepped forward, listening to the drone of a TV coming from a room further along the hall. "You have a son?"

"Sons..." he answered with a smile. "Three of the pains in the ass, unfortunately. But don't worry, two will be gone before long." He said as he moved ahead of me. "God knows, my damn wallet could use a break. They eat like horses."

He opened a bedroom door and flicked on the light. "The room's a bit cluttered, I'm sorry. We mostly use it as a storage room, but there's clean sheets on the bed."

At first glance, he'd looked younger in the outside lights, but standing here in the brighter glare, I caught flecks of gray amongst the black. He held my gaze, and in the connection, goosebumps raced along my arms.

"I hope you'll like it here," he murmured as I stepped into the room, automatically whispered "thank you," and closed the door behind me.

The heavy thud of his steps echoed as he left. *Like it here?* I scowled. "For the night, sure."

By morning, we'd have a plan. Mom, me, and our lawyers to figure out a way to get my dad free.

The faint sound of an engine drew my focus to the window. I rounded the bed, squeezed between some kind of machine covered with a sheet, and looked out the window as a black Jeep Cherokee drove through the open gate and pulled into the empty parking spot.

Sons...the word resounded. *Older sons...older than me, at least.* I leaned closer to the glass, trying to get a glimpse as he climbed out of the four-wheel drive and closed the door. But he was hidden, leaving me to stare at his shadow before even that disappeared.

Downstairs, the front door closed with a *thud*. I glanced toward the doorway, then moved around the machine, stubbing my damn toe as I went. "*Shit!*" I cried, shoving against the damn thing.

The sheet slipped, revealing stainless steel...a machine...a breathing machine.

I'd seen these things...*respirators*. That's right. "High five to my constant reruns of Grey's Anatomy," I muttered.

But why was it here?

I tugged at the covering, revealing more and more of the room crammed with medical equipment. New equipment, at that. There was an ID sticker on the side of one machine. Unable to help myself, I peered closer.

"Naomi Banks." I glanced at the doorway and moved around the bed, finding a pile of bereavement cards stacked in a pile and shoved underneath a stack of paperwork.

A flare of sadness moved through me as I bent and pulled them free. I knew I shouldn't be looking at something so personal. I wasn't that kind of person, not one who invaded. But I was unable to help myself as I opened the first one and started reading...

Creed,

I'm so sorry for your loss. Naomi was a breathtaking woman, alive and vibrant, especially when she spoke about you and the boys. The world will be a sadder place without her. Call me if you need anything at all.

Aulla Goldsmith.

"Aulla Goldsmith?" I whispered. "I know that name."

Then it hit me. Senator Aulla Goldsmith had been all over the news and social media, pimping his new campaign for the next electoral term, triggering a whole new wave of name mocking as he stood outside Popeye's and scarfed down a piece of chicken, like he was just one of the community. *Aulla the beluga!* The chants filled my head. It was a name no one'd forget in a hurry.

"A senator?" I opened the next card and kept reading. There was one from Sting...yeah, *that Sting.*

"Holy shit," I mumbled, and glanced at the doorway again. "This guy's kind of a big deal."

But they were all the same, all cards from very influential people...dated a month ago and all saying the same things about how his wife was loved, and how much she'd be missed.

Here I was being bitchy to the guy for helping us. "Nice one, Ry," I muttered, and leaned back against the end of the bed.

The heavy thud of footsteps stopped at the landing.

My pulse pounded harder, sending a pang across my chest, until those resounding steps started once more, only this time they came closer. I shoved the cards back together, gathered them into a pile, and pushed them back where they'd been hidden.

I didn't need to be a genius to put two and two together.

This wasn't just a bedroom, or a storeroom, for that matter, no matter how much Creed Banks wanted it to be. This room was a purgatory of grief. The last memories of a wife—I glanced at the doorway, and a mother.

2

Tobias

The stench of smoke lingered on the stairs, growing stronger near the room where we kept mom's things. I turned from the closed door and made for Caleb's room, opening the door as I stepped inside. "Who's the female?"

"Depends," he muttered, playing COD, and winced as he was killed before glancing my way. "You talking about the mother flirting with dad downstairs, or the kid in the bedroom?"

"Kid?" I glanced toward the doorway.

He just shrugged, making stupid fucking faces as he battled. "Looked like a kid to me."

"What the fuck are they doing here?"

"Hell if I know. Now piss off, I got a mission to complete."

I strode from his room, walking past his desk and tipping over a half-full can of beer as I left.

"Asshole!" My brother roared, lunging as it spilled all over his brand new console.

I didn't like this, didn't like them being here. Didn't like any female being here. We'd just buried our damn mom, for Christ's sake, and here he was, entertaining guests.

No, not guests...women.

I breathed in the bitter stench of smoke and went to my room. I yanked off my shirt, unbuttoned my jeans, and shoved them off before climbing into bed. But I couldn't sleep, still wound up from driving through the city. No matter how many hours I spent out there, I still couldn't get the image of mom out of my head. Her gaunt face and haunted eyes looked nothing like the real her. I lifted my arm, rested my head on it, and stared at my ceiling.

*Promise me...*her last words lingered in my head. They were just a whisper...one tiny plea. *Promise me you'll remember.*

As if I'd forget.

Laughter drifted through the air, coming from downstairs. My father's laughter. I should go down there, just as I am, see if he laughs then. I turned over as agony moved through me.

He didn't know what mom was like. Didn't really see her at the end...*none of them did.* No, they took the easy way, hovering in the doorway of that room we'd set up like a damn hospital downstairs. Leaving her last days to be filled with the medical staff he'd paid to keep her company...and me.

I couldn't leave her.

I'd held her hand and stroked her skin, watching while the cancer took her from us.

The deep seduction of a woman's laughter cracked through the air. I winced, my pain growing colder until it didn't sting anymore, and as I closed my eyes and willed sleep to come, I answered her. "Yeah, Mom, I'll make sure we all remember."

━━━

"WHAT THE FUCK is she still doing here?" Caleb stepped further into the bedroom.

I stood in the doorway and looked at her things scattered across the bed. Boxes. Clothes. Some with the tags still attached. "How the hell should I know?"

"He really wants us to haul this to the garage?" Caleb yanked the coverings free, exposing mom's machines.

"That's what he said." Anger seethed inside me, coiling like a snake in my chest as I moved closer and bent to shove her new jeans and iPhone case aside. Two days. That's all it had taken. I glanced at the brand new MacBook sitting on the pillow, then to the white cotton fabric edged with lace peeking out from under the sheet.

Those weren't new.

Caleb lifted the end of the machine and dragged it backwards until he smacked into me.

"You going to help, or you just going to fucking stand there?" he snarled.

I picked up the panties. *Her...panties.* Then I looked at the black plastic garbage bag still sitting on the corner of the bed. "I think you can manage."

"What the fuck are you doing?" Nick growled from the doorway behind me.

"Dad wants us to cart this out of here," Caleb grunted, and shoved past, forcing me to lean over the bed.

"And put it where?"

Soft. Worn.

"Garage," Caleb said quietly.

They were small in my hand.

"Ryth Castlemaine," I spoke her name and lifted her panties. "Seems like Dad wants them to stay."

"Tobias," Nick called my name like a warning.

I'd tried to put the sound of their laughter out of my head the other night, tried to find a little sleep, even if it was filled with memories of mom. But I couldn't sleep...not knowing a woman was downstairs, and when I left yesterday and drove through the city streets trying to find my way to somewhere I didn't even know existed, I'd come back feeling more caged than ever, like an overwound spring ready to snap. My hands had trembled. Just like I felt now.

When I'd come back home last night, I'd felt it...*the change*. The sound of her mother in the living room, the *feel* of her upstairs. The girl I'd seen outside my bedroom as she scurried toward the bathroom we now shared.

"I want them gone." I fisted her panties and lifted them to my nose. "I'll make sure of it."

"Tobias, no. She's just a kid."

"She's eighteen," I answered as that coiled serpent moved inside me. "A year younger than me."

The memory of her came back in a rush, how her eyes had widened for a second when I stepped out of my bedroom, almost slamming into her...and how she'd suddenly jerked her gaze to the floor, hiding her face from me. *A kid?* I'd raked her body with my gaze. Skinny, short. Small breasts under one of Caleb's old t-shirts.

I didn't give a shit what excuse dad gave.

I looked around the room, filled with the equipment that had kept my mom alive for a little longer, giving me one more second with her. That girl shouldn't be here...shouldn't be anywhere near here, not this room...and not our home.

Burned down house or not, she wasn't staying here. Not if I had anything to do with it.

Kid, my ass...I'd make her desperate to fucking leave.

I threw her panties on the bed, then glanced at the pretty pale green dress hanging at the end of the bed, and strode from the room.

3

Ryth

"Dad." I stood up when they brought him out. But he didn't look at me right away, just glanced my way, then lowered his head as he walked with a limp toward the barrier.

He was hurt, badly. His eye was swollen, his lips bleeding. The sight of that hit me hard. "Jesus."

He forced a smile as he sat. "It's okay, Ry." He nodded at a chair, urging me to do the same.

"Did they do that to you?" I whispered, unable to take my eyes off his face. His poor, beautiful face.

"It's nothing I can't handle," he said as tears welled in my eyes. *"Hey."* He leaned closer to the divider. "Look at me."

Through the sheen of tears, I did.

"It's nothing I can't handle. Now I need for you to do the same."

My voice trembled, still I held it in. "T-they told you? Told you about the house?"

He just nodded and licked his lips before meeting my gaze. "Your mom's gonna do her best to keep you protected until I get out of here and figure all this out."

Protected? Fear found me, so it *had* been them...*the Rossis*. Shit, this was worse than I'd thought. "When, dad? When will that be?"

"I don't know, princess." He licked his split lip, fixing me with a desperate gaze. "But I need you to know, I'd *never* do anything to put you or your mom in danger." He pulled away as pain dulled his gaze. "I just wouldn't."

"Who was it?" I clenched my fists. "Tell me, tell me and I'll..."

He saw me then, saw the way my body shook and my hatred raged, and gave a hint of a smile, even with his busted lips. "What? You gonna pay them a visit, my little lioness? You always were more like me than your mother."

And in an instant, his smile faltered and sadness consumed that flicker as the guard behind him called out. "Time, Castlemaine."

He gave a nod and rose. I followed, standing before I caught the reflection of my face in the divider, then reached up and pulled down the side of my hair.

"Be careful out there, princess," dad called, his gaze moving to the birthmark on my face. "Stay strong. I'll be out of here soon enough."

"Castle!" the guard barked. I jerked my gaze toward him and glared.

19

But it didn't matter what I wanted, in here my dad didn't exist. He was a nobody, just another inmate, one who had to obey the rules.

"Give my love to your mother, princess. Tell her I'm thinking of her," dad said before he turned and walked away, disappearing through the door, leaving me behind.

I punched my fist against the glass, drawing a savage glare from a guard, before I turned and stormed toward the door to the hallway. The sun glared, blinding me for an instant, until I saw the sleek Mercedes waiting in the parking lot. Creed Banks was a nice guy, for some kind of lawyer. He'd taken us in and given us somewhere to stay for the last two days, had even taken us shopping for clothes and necessities. But I didn't want to stay there, not in his house with his three sons I'd spied from the doorway of the bedroom where I was staying.

Not just a bedroom...*the storeroom, remember?*

That voice in my head whispered as I crossed the parking lot, yanked open the back door, and slid inside, instantly blasted by the cool air-conditioned air.

"Dad asked about you." I glared toward the passenger seat, but was met with silence.

Mom just stared straight ahead, even as Creed glanced her way, then looked over his shoulder to me. "I'm glad you got to see him. I'm sure he needed that."

"He would've liked to see his wife more."

But she said nothing, just dropped her head and cried. She wasn't the same since dad had been arrested, nonresponsive, broken. I winced. "Mom, I'm sorry."

"It's okay." She reached behind the seat for my hand. "Next time, huh?"

"Okay." I grabbed her hand and squeezed.

"That's the way." Creed gave me a wink before he put the car into gear and pulled out of the parking lot.

It was over an hour's drive back to the city. An hour when I sat back in the seat and replayed dad's words to me.

I'll get out, princess...I'll get out.

He had to. Our family depended on it. By the time he did, mom and I would be waiting, just in a different house.

"Have you found a place yet?"

She shook her head. "No."

"Seems there's a bit of a problem," Creed weighed in.

"What?" I jerked my gaze to him, then back toward her.

Mom dropped her head, her voice filled with desperation. "Our bank accounts are frozen, we have nothing left."

Nothing? But we'd just bought all new clothes...and a MacBook for school...I lifted my brand new iPhone. If we had no money, then...

I shifted my gaze to the man behind the wheel. A man who'd been a stranger less than a week ago. A man who'd just spent a small fortune on clothes and things for us.

"Then I'll get a job," I declared. "Whatever it takes."

"No, Ry, you have school."

"Fuck school, this is important."

"Your mom's right."

I jerked my gaze toward Creed, biting my lips to keep from snapping back at him. It was none of his business. But the moment my anger rose, it left just as fast. This man had just spent a lot of money on us, and never once said a word about it.

Why?

Did he think I wouldn't figure it out? Did he not want me to know about us not having any money? Shame filled me at the anger I felt. I stared at him as he drove us home...this man had gone out of his way for us...*me specifically.*

Taking me to see dad.

Getting me things I'd needed...*and some I'd just wanted, if I was honest.* There was no way my parents would've spent that much money on a damn laptop. But there wasn't even a word spoken. Mom had said, *"Pick out a laptop for school, whatever one you want."*

So I had...walking past the normal range and walked into the Apple section, where I'd found Creed staring at the brand new MacBooks. Fast, sleek...*and so damn pretty.*

He'd known.

Even then he knew we had no money, and still he'd wanted me to have something special, something that gave me a little excitement. I swallowed hard, hating myself for the anger I'd felt a second ago. "Okay, I'll stay in school."

"We'll figure it out, okay, princess?" mom said, her voice strained.

By the time we got back to the house, it was growing dark. The parking spaces out front were empty and for some reason, a wave of relief hit me. It wasn't that I didn't like his sons, I didn't really know them. They stayed mostly in their rooms. The sounds of gunfire and screams occasionally came out of one of their rooms on the same floor as mine.

Only one had really seen me.

My pulse sped as I remembered the encounter. His dark, brooding, sullen stare as he'd stepped out of his bedroom wearing nothing but cut-off gray sweats that hung low on his hips. Hate raged in his eyes the minute he saw me. I just looked at the floor and hurried past, praying to God he hadn't seen me...

I reached up and touched the mark on my cheek, praying he hadn't seen that.

He would...eventually.

I closed my eyes, knowing he'd snigger and laugh, and mentally prepared myself for the taunts that'd come.

They always did.

You look like you just got slapped, Castlemaine, obviously not hard enough.

They made fun of me. Everyone did. I swallowed hard and pressed my fingers to my cheek, wishing for the millionth time I'd been born normal. *Why couldn't I just be normal?*

"Home," Creed murmured, drawing my gaze as we turned into the driveway.

I lifted my gaze to the gorgeous house as panic raced inside me. "For now," I muttered, and released my seatbelt as we pulled into the garage.

Creed braked, then switched off the engine. "I'm feeling like a pizza tonight."

"Oh?" Mom glanced his way, a hint of a smile on her lips as she climbed out and glanced my way. "That's Ry's favorite food."

"Really?" He cut a glance my way as he closed his door. "That true?"

"Yeah." I hated how my belly tightened at the words. "It's okay."

"Just okay, huh? I know of a place that does the *best* grilled chicken and bacon. The cheese...*oh, man.* Stringy, sharp, just oozing as you lift it to your mouth."

My own watered as he spoke. I licked my lips. "Yeah. I could go for a pizza."

He smiled, then gave mom a sly wink. "How about you run upstairs and get ready and I'll order it for an hour, sound good to you?"

In an hour I could start to set up my new MacBook. Excitement hummed inside me. "Yeah, that's perfect."

He strode to the interior door and opened it, motioning me through. "Sounds like a date to me. It'll be good having you and your mom here, I won't tend to eat so much. I love pizza," he said, as he looked down and slapped his hand against his hard stomach. "Although the waistline doesn't."

I gave a shrug and slipped past. "You look fine...for an old guy."

"*Old?*" he growled as I quickened my steps, fighting the smile on my lips. "Why, you little..." he growled, playfully pretending a grab at me.

And just like that, the heaviness of the prison slipped away.

I climbed the stairs and made my way to my bedroom. Even the house felt different. Lighter, emptier. Almost like...home.

Home.

I swallowed, my fleeting smile slipping away. It was almost a betrayal. Almost like I wanted to leave it all behind, the frequent fighting...the constant worrying, the numerous lies. I'd heard it all from the cracked open door of my bedroom.

I swallowed hard and opened the door to the new bedroom, and stopped. It was empty...I glanced at the clear space now at the end of the bed. All the machines were gone. "What?" I stepped inside and closed the door behind me, moving around the room. The indentations on the carpet were still there. But apart from the bed and a dresser next to it, the room was bare.

I glanced over my shoulder. They'd done this? Came in and cleared out all their mother's things?

I didn't know how I felt about that. Sad. Happy that I could at least walk around the other side of the bed without stubbing my damn toe. I glanced at the corner where the stack of paperwork and the bereavement cards hidden underneath had been, and found they too were gone.

Like they hadn't been there at all.

Something else was different, though. I glanced at the bed, conjuring the memory of where everything had been. My gaze went to the MacBook first, on my pillow, then my clothes...and stilled at the crumpled ball of my panties. Fear coursed through me. I stepped closer, picking them up and they expanded in my hands.

Creases in the fabric.

What the hell were they doing touching my underwear?

Maybe they fell. Maybe they knocked the bed as they moved the machines out and they picked them up before tossing them onto the bed. I glanced at where I was sure they'd been buried under the pile of new clothes I'd grabbed, and pushed the thought out of my mind.

It didn't matter. I tossed them to the side and flopped down on the bed, reached for my new laptop, and spent the rest of the time pulling it out of the box, hooking it up to charge, and deciding my settings, then I loaded a pretty image of a purple butterfly on the screen before the heavy thud of footsteps drew my attention.

My pulse thundered as the sound stopped on the landing outside my room. I pushed the Mac from my lap and rose, but then a *beep* came from a cell and the heavy thud of steps drifted back down the stairs.

I stepped closer as the thump of the front door closing sounded.

"Dinner, Ryth!" Creed called.

I opened the door, my gaze moving along the landing to their rooms. The doors were closed, no sounds of gunfire. Peace. I made my way down the stairs as the heady scent of cheese and deliciousness hit me.

"Oh man, that smells..." I began as I stepped into the dining room, and froze.

They were all there...all *three* of them.

Three grown men as well as Creed...and Mom, staring at me.

"Delicious," the deep growl came from the broody one who was glaring at me.

"What?" I jerked my gaze toward him.

But he didn't answer, just glared, those dark eyes glinting.

"The pizza," one of the others stepped forward and lifted his arm over the broody asshole's shoulders. "It's Tobe's favorite." He slipped his arm free then, taking a step closer. "I'm Caleb, this is Nick." He jerked his head toward the other, who just leaned against the wall and watched with his arms crossed against his chest. "And you already know the moody one, Tobias."

I licked my lips, met each piercing gaze, and nodded as Caleb's gaze went to my cheek.

No!

Panic ripped through me as I jerked my hand up, tugged my hair low, and turned away.

"Guys," Creed murmured. "How about we sit?"

"I'll stand," Tobias declared.

I felt his stare as I moved away from them, made my way around the other side of the long dining table, and took a seat toward the end, but still close enough to reach the food.

"Ryth, honey," Mom called, and stretched over the open boxes of pizza and mountain of garlic bread, coleslaw, and sides as she reached for a plate. "Sit closer."

The two other guys sat, barely glancing my way. But I couldn't move, my cheeks burning with humiliation. A couple of growls erupted as pieces were snatched, bites were taken, and conversation filled the air. They even chattered to my mom, asking about the fire.

I lifted my head and took a plate when mom passed it to Caleb, and gestured to me. He gave me a smile and a wink as he handed it over and, for the first time since I'd stepped into the dining room, I allowed myself to breathe.

They weren't that bad.

I glanced at Nick, who watched me, then forced a smile. One I faintly returned as I grabbed a slice of pizza and bit.

"So...damn...good," Creed groaned from the head of the table, and grinned as he glanced my way. "What do you think, Rye?"

Rye?

"Good." I chewed and took another bite, tracking the movement from the corner of my eye as Tobias strode toward the table, yanked out a chair next to me, and sat.

They all tried not to look his way, even as mom smiled at the others and helped herself to more food than I'd ever seen her eat before.

All of a sudden, it felt almost normal. Food, friends...apart from the glaring asshole who dragged his focus from my breasts to my eyes as he took a massive bite of his pizza and chewed.

4

Tobias

She had no idea. None at all. I watched her eat with her downcast gaze, staring at that ugly fucking birthmark on her cheek, until Nick kicked me under the table. I shot the bastard a glare as he gave a small shake of his head.

She was just a kid, right? I glanced at those perky little tits. No, not a kid. My cock grew hard as my anger grew. Hate I understood. But seeing her like this, so damn small and meek, taking tiny bites of her pizza like she was a goddamn mouse, incited something dangerous inside me. *Squeak, squeak,* little thing.

"Tobias."

The sound of my name on her lips made me jerk. I lifted my gaze to the woman who sat next to dad. "Yeah?"

"I was just asking if you're enjoying Clarence. Business major, right?" she asked like it was every day conversation.

"I'm not, actually," I answered. "Dropped out about two months ago."

"What?" Dad's head shot up, a smear of cheese grease on his lips as he scowled. "Since when did you make that decision?"

"When I decided the last days I had with my mother were more important."

Conversation halted.

Caleb and Nick froze, then slowly looked from me to dad as the bastard had the gall to blanch, then swallowed *hard*.

"You know..." I continued, holding his gaze. "*Before she died.*"

"Tobe..." Nick started.

"Suddenly, I'm not feeling fucking hungry." I shoved up from the table and turned away, catching the little bitch's gaze as I left.

But it wasn't a sick smear of sympathy I saw in her eyes. No, it was something more like sadness...like she almost *understood my pain*. Which was a damn lie. She didn't know a goddamn thing about me.

I strode from the dining room, leaving a void behind me. I'd sucked the joy from dad's moment and the blossoming friendship that fucking woman wanted to have with us, then took the stairs two at a time, leaving them behind.

"I'm sorry about that..." dad murmured, his words barely reaching me.

"There's no need," Elle Castlemaine answered. "None at all."

I slammed my boots against the stairs until I reached my floor, glancing at her room. *Her fucking room.* I glanced over my shoulder and headed toward it, throwing open the door. Christ, it even smelled different. Gone was the biting scent of hospital antiseptic and the faint smell of death I couldn't fucking shake, no matter how deeply I exhaled.

It smelled like...vanilla.

Fucking vanilla.

I glanced at the small bottle of perfume on the dresser. *Pure,* the gold label stated. I swallowed hard as heat raced to my cock. *Pure?* Fuck, I wanted to smell it...wanted to search her bed for those panties and spray the shit on them, too. I stepped closer, pawing through the mess of her clothes, ones she'd torn the tags from, and found her underwear hidden beneath ripped black jeans.

I crossed the room, grabbed the perfume bottle, and lifted it to my nose. Anger drove me to pump the mist across her underwear before placing the bottle back. I balled the panties in my hand, then shoved them into my pocket before striding from the room.

The door closed quietly behind me, leaving the heady scent of that perfume behind. I didn't know why I'd done it, why I hated her. Her white cotton fucking panties and the bottle of *Pure* burning into my mind. But I took them...*I took them like she'd taken from me.*

"Get the fuck out of my house," I muttered as I stepped inside my room and closed the door.

Darkness swallowed me. The blackout blinds were drawn, the walls were painted dark steel gray. I didn't want light in my world. I pulled the panties free. I didn't want women, or vanilla...and I sure as hell didn't want her.

I closed my eyes and lifted them, inhaling deep.

The scent invaded me.

In my head, I saw her naked, those tight little peaks of her breasts puckered tight. I swallowed as I grew hard. I wanted to lick them, wanted to open her legs and see just how pure she was. She couldn't be too pure, no eighteen-year-old stayed a virgin for long.

But that ugly fucking mark on her cheek said she probably was. I bet it drove her to run and hide anytime a guy looked her way. I bet because of it, she'd never been kissed...or touched.

Fuck. Me.

I reached down, unzipped my jeans and took out my cock. An ache pulsed deep as I took myself in my hand and looked down. The head was red, flushed and hungry. I hadn't been this hard in...

Forever.

I squeezed my fist and pressed the white cotton to my face and in my head, she squirmed under my hold.

You a fucking mouse? I roared at her.

In my fantasy, those little tits bounced and trembled as she bucked her hips under me. Her dusky pink nipples grew even tighter as she fought.

You a fucking mouse in my goddamn house, bitch?

Get off me! she screamed, those washed-out gray eyes glaring into mine. *Sadness. Sadness and fucking desperation.* That's what I'd seen downstairs. That's how she'd fucking looked at me, like she gave a shit. Like she *cared!*

I gave a low, harsh grunt, coming hard in my fucking hand. My cock twitched, the vein underneath pulsing as I drew in deep gasps and croaked, "What the fuck was that?"

I lowered her panties as a tremor of disgust rolled through me.

What the fuck was I doing? I shoved my cock back into my jeans and crossed the room, tossing her panties onto the bed before grabbing some Kleenex. This wasn't right. She was just a kid. I turned to my desk, yanked my headset on, and opened up a game, trying to force my attention on anything else.

But my gaze drifted to the white cotton ball now resting against my pillow. The scent lingered, filling me, taking up space that the bitter scent of antiseptic had occupied before. I didn't know which one was worse.

A knock came at my door before it opened. I tugged my headset down as Caleb walked in carrying a plate of pizza and garlic bread. "Figured you'd get hungry sometime."

"Thanks." I stared at the screen, not even remembering what game this was.

He closed the door, placed the plate on the desk in front of me, and took a seat on the end of my bed. "Why the fuck are they here?"

I just gave a shrug, acting like I didn't care.

"Dad's actually smiling."

I winced at the words.

"Haven't seen him smile in—"

I cut him a glare, my pulse pounding in my head. *Say it...say the words and I'll punch you in the fucking mouth.* But Caleb

33

flinched as though he actually realized what he was saying. "Anyway. Food, fucker, and give dad a break, yeah? He's just being a good guy to a friend, nothing more."

I glanced back to my game. "Since when is he *ever* a good guy?"

"That was the past, T. Don't you think it's time you moved on?"

"It wasn't *you* he fed to the dogs though, was it?" I muttered.

He stepped closer, kicking the bottom of my chair. "You were the stupid fuck who went after Lazarus Rossi, so let's just leave it at that, okay?"

Anger roared through me, searing just as hot in that minute as it had a year ago. "He fucking trashed my car, then sent his goons to pay me a visit at school, what the fuck was I supposed to do?"

Caleb just shook his head. "You made a move on his woman. I think his response was justified, don't you?"

"It wasn't even his woman. He didn't love her, he barely even looked at her. She was fair game."

"You didn't want her either, T. You were only an asshole whose mom had just been diagnosed with cancer. Look, you were acting out, I get that. All I'm saying is, how about we let bygones be bygones? Dad's doing a good thing here, helping these people out by giving them a place to stay and figuring out a way to get the girl's dad out of jail."

My lips curled, I stared at my brother as though he was a stranger. Because in that moment, he might as well be. He didn't see dad like I did, didn't see that this wasn't him being a 'good guy', because men like my father didn't fucking change.

He was a shark, feeding in the water, moving from one target to the next, always hungry...and fucking cold.

34

"Thanks for the pizza," I muttered, and turned back to my game.

"I saw the way you looked at her," Caleb murmured carefully, not taking the goddamn hint. His gaze went to the other end of the bed, and I knew the moment he saw them...saw her white cotton panties. He scowled for a second, until he realized whose they were. But he never said a word, just kept fucking talking. "And Nick did, as well. Don't mess with her, Tobias. She's...sweet."

The corner of my lips twitched. *Sweet.*

"I mean it, stay away from her...and check your damn attitude."

"Get the fuck out, Caleb," I growled, and glared at the TV.

He stayed there for a second longer, then left. I wanted to throw that fucking plate after him...wanted to hit dad and that little bitch downstairs, too, just to prove a point. Instead, I strode toward the door, grabbed my keys off the dresser as I went, and slammed the door behind me.

Fuck him...

Fuck her...

And fuck the Rossis.

I strode down the stairs and through the front door, my face burning, as I left them all behind. No doubt dad would be making some bullshit excuse.

Remember me...

Mom's words resounded as I pressed the remote, then climbed into the car. I was backing out of the driveway before I knew it, braking the moment I was out on the street, then shoved the Jeep into gear before punching the accelerator.

The tires squealed before they caught and I shot forward. I drove the same damn streets I'd been driving for weeks now, ever since Caleb and Nick moved back home for a while. They came under the pretense of being together as a family, but the truth was, we felt more disconnected than ever before.

They didn't bring me food, not before today. They barely even spoke to me, content with sitting in their rooms and having everything done for them. None of them spoke to me about Mom, and they sure as hell didn't go near that room..

Stay away from her. Caleb's warning rang in my head as headlights burned through the night. Headlights flared behind me, making me clench my fists around the steering wheel and head toward the city.

And as always, my thoughts returned to her.

That ache filled my chest, like it was my heart. I couldn't breathe, couldn't catch my—

I yanked the wheel and braked, pulling over. My pulse thundered, until it was all I could hear. I leaned over the wheel and closed my eyes while I shook and shuddered. *What the fuck was wrong with me?*

I was coming apart.

Becoming the failure dad always knew I was.

And the one person who'd always believed in me was gone...

*Remember me...*she whispered as that ache in my chest balled into a fist and rammed into the back of my throat. *Remember...*

I wrenched my eyes open, let out a wounded fucking moan, and forced that agony back down, down in the pit inside me, where it belonged. I would not let it out, would not let them see me like this. I sucked in hard breaths until that wave passed, then glanced into the side mirror and pulled back out.

I drove through the streets, making my way to the lookout high above the city, and parked. Bright lights glittered and sparkled like jewels below me. I tried to think about something other than that churning abyss of grief inside me and slowly my thoughts turned to her...

The kid who wasn't a kid.

Ryth Castlemaine.

I pulled up my phone and searched her name. The usual social media; Facebook, TikTok, an Instagram that hadn't been touched in months. I searched her profiles and went through her photos. "Too trusting, aren't you, Ryth?" Her photos were all there, for anyone to see.

In an instant, the memory of her panties came roaring back to me, and that fucking scent. "Pure, right?"

I hated the way I thought about her. I wasn't like this, wasn't so fucking *cruel* around other women. I stopped on an image of her, one where she was at the beach with her parents...a video. I hit play and listened to her laugh. "We come to the beach and here I am, left all alone. Where the hell are my parents?"

I leaned forward, watching the smile falter on her face.

The camera panned outwards, catching the two figures further along the beach. The way they faced each other, hands flailing in the air, it wasn't hard to realize what was happening. They were arguing. She pulled the camera away.

"Looks like they're busy," she breathed, her words panicky and rushed. "But yeah guys, this is Castlemaine Beach, named after my father's family, pretty cool, huh?"

"Cool," I muttered as the video ended, freezing on her face in the frame.

That ugly fucking birthmark front and center in the camera's view.

I bet she was bullied at school for that, bet all the kids made fun of her. Something inside me clenched with the thought. My breaths deepened and my body came alive. There was something about her that triggered something in me. Something about the splattering of freckles across her nose and those washed-out-looking gray eyes. What kind of fucking color were they supposed to be?

I licked my lips, remembering the way she'd looked at me as I strode from the dining room, as though she wanted to like me... as though she needed a friend.

I wasn't her fucking friend.

I was the *furthest thing from a friend.*

Especially for her.

I scrolled through her photos, letting myself get carried away, until I glanced at the time. Fuck. I'd been here for hours, hours looking at her goddamn social media. I leaned forward, started the four-wheel drive, and pulled out, making my way back home.

By the time I pulled into the driveway, the house was dark. I glanced at the clock as I killed the engine. It was almost eleven...still early enough. Double-glazed windows smothered the sounds from outside. They wouldn't even hear me. Movement came from above as I climbed out and closed the door.

I lifted my gaze to the shadow in the window on the third floor. In the same room that'd once housed my mother's medical equipment, and now her...

I stilled, staring at her as she watched me. She had to see me, had to know I saw her, too. Maybe she didn't care...maybe little Ryth Castlemaine wasn't a mouse at all. The idea of that sent a shudder through me. My fucking pulse raced. I swallowed hard and turned away, watching from the corner of my eye as the blinds fell back into place.

My keys slid into the lock and I twisted, slipping into the house without a sound. Silence greeted me, low creaks of the house all that reached me as I closed the door behind me, locked it, activated the alarm system and slid the chain into place. My steps were soundless as I climbed the stairs all the way to the third floor, then stopped in the hallway outside her room.

I wanted to go in there, wanted to see her curled up in bed, wanted to see those eyes once more...until a sound drifted up through the darkness.

A moan.

Low...demanding...and coming from the second floor.

I glanced over my shoulder as the sound came again.

Only this time, the moan was feminine.

And coming from my dad's bedroom.

5

Ryth

I clenched my jaw, willing the ache in my bladder to ease as I tossed and turned on the bed, wrestling the sheets. I'd taken too long trying to pretend I didn't need to go and now it was all I could think of. That and the sound of *his* steps as they quieted outside my bedroom.

Not my bedroom.

Theirs.

This wasn't my house. Wasn't my family. Wasn't anything other than a place to stay while we figured this all out. I turned my head, and tried to listen for movement. Had he gone to bed already? Had I missed the thud of his bedroom door? I had to pee *soon*.

That pressure in my belly grew, shooting agony deep inside me. I winced and curled my knees to my chest. *Don't think about it...don't...think about peeing.* I shouldn't have had that second cola, no matter how much Nick urged me to take it. But I wanted to fit in...wanted them to like me. And look where that had gotten me now.

In agony.

My insides clenched, clamping around the heavy weight in my abdomen. I couldn't wait, not any longer, or I'd wet myself. I opened my eyes and rose from the bed, wincing with the agony as I took a step toward the door and listened.

Silence.

That's all I heard. He had to have gone. I reached for the handle and cracked open the door before waiting again. But he wasn't out there, not standing at the entrance to the stairs watching me, or glaring at me from outside his bedroom. So I opened the door wider and tiptoed hurriedly for the bathroom just past his bedroom. My pulse boomed, filling my head with thunder as I closed the bathroom door and hurried to pee.

Relief made me shudder as I leaned forward and emptied my bladder. I wiped, then rose, panic filling me as I turned. Should I flush and risk them hearing? I couldn't leave it all night. No way. They'd know it was me. I closed the lid quietly, praying the sound wasn't loud, and pressed the handle, wincing as the rush filled the air.

But it wasn't loud, just a muffled roar that was over in a second. "Thank God." I moved to the sink and washed my hands before drying them on my towel and left.

Half of me was expecting him to be waiting outside. But he wasn't. He wasn't anywhere. I smiled and walked past his bedroom, slower this time. No doubt he'd be in bed, or sulking, his hearing muffled by those gaming headphones I'd seen yesterday when I walked past the open door to his room.

Tobias was an asshole, unlike his brothers, who'd actually gone out of their way at dinner to be nice to me. They understood this was only temporary. By tomorrow, or the day after, mom would be able to access her accounts, then we'd be out of here. I licked my dry lips and glanced toward the open door to my room, my body still aching a bit from needing to pee. A glass of milk, then I'd be able to settle. It had always worked at home.

I eased down the stairs, until a muffled sound made me still. But it was gone in an instant. Probably nothing...until it came again...low...tortured.

"Fuck, you feel good," a male voice growled. I jerked my gaze to the closed, darkened door and realized the bedroom was Creed's.

Heat raced to my cheeks. I carefully turned away, until a woman's voice followed. "Harder, Creed...for God's sake, fuck me harder."

I jerked my gaze to the door as an icy wave of shock slammed into me, punctured by the loud sounds of flesh on flesh.

"Creed..." Mom moaned.

I flinched, jerking my gaze to movement as it came from the shadows. I was frozen as Tobias stepped out from the shadows in the hallway outside their bedroom, those dark, unflinching eyes finding mine.

He was there...listening.

To the two of them.

"Elle," Creed growled from that room.

And my mom cried out. The sound was muffled just as fast. But I knew...I knew what they were doing, and Tobias knew as well.

Revulsion hit me like a slap to the face. Tears sprang to my eyes as I stumbled backwards. Tobias just watched me as I scurried away, my feet almost slipping on the stairs as I lunged for my room, closing the door with a slight *thump* behind me.

No...

NO!

I clenched my fists as rage bubbled up to the surface.

The slow, methodical...*thud...thud...thud* of his steps grew closer as Tobias followed me up the stairs.

I spun, staring at the closed door to my bedroom.

I'd hit him if he opened it.

I'd scream and hurl myself at him, clawing out his eyes and slamming his head against the wall. I'd hurt him, hurt him any way I could. A whimper tore from my lips as the sound of my mother's moans filled my head. The tears that threatened to fall blurred the door in front of me before I spun and threw myself on the bed, sinking into the soft mattress and the messed up sheets.

No...Mom. No.

Those sounds haunted me as I squeezed my eyes closed. A scream was trapped in the back of my throat. I slammed my hand over my mouth and shoved my face into the pillow. *She... she fucked him.*

She fucked a stranger in his own house while his kids were sleeping.

No.

Not sleeping.

Not all of them, at least.

And not a stranger.

I knew your mother back in college. I squeezed my eyes closed as Creed's words came back to me. They knew each other. Of course they knew each other. *They were lovers.* I clenched my fists as that smothering scream of rage rammed itself down my throat.

I couldn't breathe...couldn't—I pressed my face harder into the pillow.

Tobias' dark eyes haunted me as he'd stood outside his father's bedroom, listening to them. Revulsion hit me, finally tearing that savage sound from my chest. I had to leave this place...and I needed to take mom with me.

6

Tobias

I listened to her pathetic little sounds as she cried and whimpered, hating how part of me actually ached the same. But we weren't the same. Not even close. I went to my room and closed the door behind me.

Hate filled me as I threw my keys on the dresser and kicked off my boots. This was just the last fucking betrayal I'd known was coming. I was actually surprised he'd waited this long. I bet he couldn't wait for mom to die, couldn't wait to move on and fuck other women, out in the open at least. I knew damn well he didn't give a shit when she was still alive. But why did it have to be her?

Why did it have to be that little bitch's mother?

I yanked my shirt free as the sound of her sobs reached me, making me clench my fists and turn to glare at the door. "Shut the fuck up or I'll give you something to cry about," I muttered under my breath.

The sounds grew quieter, leaving me to turn back to my bed. I unbuttoned my jeans, kicked them off, and climbed between the sheets. But I didn't close my eyes. Instead, I stared at the ceiling in the darkness, their grunts and moans taking up space inside my head.

But it was her haunted eyes that burned through those fucking sounds.

The whites almost neon in the dark.

The way she'd jerked her gaze toward me as I'd stepped into her view. I didn't know why I'd wanted her to see me, why I'd wanted her to feel as betrayed as I felt. Why I wanted to share that moment, that brutal fucking moment. I closed my eyes and turned to my side as a wave of perfume hit me.

Vanilla.

I opened my eyes, finding the pale blur in the dark. Her panties. Soft, worn, cotton fucking panties only a good girl wore. I licked my lips, panic taking flight inside me as I drew them close. In my head, those sounds of our parents became ours.

My tiny, tight little mouse.

Christ, I grew hard at the fantasy.

But she wasn't so compliant...no, in my head, she bucked and writhed, fighting to hold onto her virtue. I clenched my fist around the fabric as my balls grew tight and became hard. There was something about her that made me like this...

Like a blinding light for my darkness.

And I was darkness...*desperate to consume.*

But I didn't reach for my cock this time. Instead, I let the fantasy play in my mind, and the more vibrant it became, the more I realized I wanted her. I wanted that tiny little mouse. To see her squirm, to watch her cheeks redden. To stare into the reflection of my own pain in her eyes.

I wanted her to feel like I felt; hurt...abandoned...*betrayed.* I wanted to make her fucking buck and cry. I wanted her humiliated. A pang tore through my chest at the savagery. I closed my eyes and inhaled deep, letting her ruin play out in my head...and finally slept.

MY EYES BURNED when I woke. My heart hammered, panic moving through me as I wrenched open my eyes and shoved upright. I glanced around my darkened room, finding nothing but the murky gloom. *What the fuck?* I clenched my fist around something soft and looked down.

White.

I blinked, fighting the blur, and looked again.

White panties...

And all of a sudden, it hit me...last night...the sounds coming out of my father's bedroom. That fist in my gut returned as revulsion slammed into me, then changed...becoming harder, colder...I glanced at the doorway, then looked down at my fist. Turning into something that scared me...and excited me all at the same time.

I kicked off the sheets and rose, made my way out of my room, and headed for the bathroom to take a piss. When I was done, I turned and headed for Nick's, shoved open the door and stepped inside, kicking a pair of black lace panties as I went. He was still asleep, one arm wrapped around Natalie...who was naked and sprawled out beside him.

Her big tits splayed to the side, the dark brown nipples soft and smooth. I stepped closer, dragging my gaze from her breasts to her round stomach and her shaved mound. Still there was nothing, no surge of desire, not even a twitch of my cock. She may as well have been a dude.

"Hey." I jerked my gaze to my brother. "Get the fuck up."

"Piss off," he muttered without even opening his eyes.

I kicked the side of the bed, drawing a moan from my brother's girlfriend. "We need to fucking talk."

"Nick," she moaned, and rolled over. "Make the bad man go away."

The bad man? I glared at Natalie as Nick cracked open his eyes. "What the fuck is it?"

I just glanced at the bitch next to him, then met his glare once more.

"Fine..." he groaned and gave her a shove. "Nat...time to go."

"Jesus, *really?*" she bitched, then gave a long, deep groan and opened her eyes, stabbing me with a glare as she pushed up from the bed. "You know, you really suck all the happiness out of the world."

"Nice to see you too, Natalie," I muttered. "Give my best to Derek."

A pillow sailed through the air, hitting me in the stomach. Natalie just snarled as she swiped her clothes from the floor before yanking them on in a huff. I paid her no mind. Instead, I stared at my brother, who watched her with zero fucking interest until she yanked open his bedroom door and stormed out.

"Well done," Nick grumbled. "Now I'll have her bitching at me for the next goddamn week over you being a fucking prick."

"Why was she here in the first place? She cheated on you..."

"It was a mistake," he mumbled as he looked away.

"Which time?"

Sparks of rage burned in his glare. "Fuck you, Tobias."

The problem was, he was angry at the wrong person. I'd heard the way she'd begged him to take her back, telling him it was all a misunderstanding...at first, until the truth came out. Then there were the tears. Like the doormat he was, Nick had taken her back.

But it was only a matter of time before she did it again. If not with Derek Carmichael, then some other fucking schmuck. The front door slammed shut with a *boom*. "You can do better."

"And you can shut the fuck up," he barked, and shoved the sheets aside. "What the fuck do you know about love, anyway?"

"You love her, really?"

He just curled his lips and flipped me off as he hunted around for his boxers. "What the fuck was so goddamn important that you had to ruin my sleep, anyway?"

"Dad is fucking someone."

He stilled, then shot a surprised glare my way. "What? *Who?*"

"Who the fuck do you think, dickhead?"

It took him a whole second before it dawned. "The woman downstairs?"

I just nodded.

"No way." He yanked on his boxers and ran his fingers through his hair. "You're lying."

"I heard them last night."

He swallowed, searched my eyes for the truth, then rocked backwards. "Jesus...*her?*"

"Her," I answered carefully. "And I wasn't the only one who heard them, either."

"Caleb heard as well?"

I shook my head. "No, not Caleb."

It dawned on him then. I saw the connection, that *wince* before he stalled hard, and when he spoke again, his voice was husky. "She heard her mom and our dad?"

I nodded.

He tried to fight it, tried to drive away the image that rose, me... her...standing there listening to our parents fucking.

"What'd she do?" he asked, slowly looking my way.

"The stupid little bitch didn't know what it was, not at first. I caught the moans on my way to my bedroom...before I heard her coming from the bathroom and down the stairs. She stopped when her mom told dad to fuck her harder."

"Jesus." He licked his lips. "She heard that?"

"She did..." A charge of excitement raced through me, pulsing, *shivering*. I didn't need to look to know I liked it, and by the way he swallowed and sucked in a hard breath, I knew he liked it too.

"She's just a kid."

"She's eighteen."

"A. Kid..."

"I bet she's never been fucked."

He closed his eyes. "Tobias, don't, you sick fuck," he moaned.

"I saw her wearing one of Caleb's t-shirts, those little tits perky and hard."

He shook his head and lowered it. "No."

"Her mom is fucking our dad not even a month after ours died." I stated the facts. "You think he's just going to move her out now?"

"He's a good guy," my brother growled, and lifted his head, meeting my gaze.

"You keep saying that and one day you might believe it." I strode closer. "Fresh young pussy," I continued. "I bet she's never even been licked. I bet she tastes...*perfect.*"

Purer than Natalie...and I'd occupied the room next to my brother long enough to know he not only liked to fuck, but he liked to eat, as well.

"Have you touched her?" he asked. But this time, there was no hint of disgust. This time, excitement raged in his eyes.

"Not yet," I answered, desire and anger bleeding into one. "But I will..."

"If dad catches you, he'll kick you out."

"Not the first time, would it be?" I met his stare. "Besides, I won't do anything unless he does. If they move out, then I'll never look at Ryth again."

"But if they don't, what then?"

"Then I guess I'll have to take my anger out on her sweet young body, won't I?"

"You're sick," he muttered.

"And you're just as excited. The only difference is, you're too fucking weak to do anything about it. You'll just keep fucking the same bitch who cheats on you with other guys and pretend it's love."

"Get the fuck out, Tobias," my brother warned. "Before I forget we're blood and beat the living shit out of you."

He'd do it, too...I'd seen him angry.

Seen him drive his fist through a car window.

And I'd seen him walk away, as well.

But I'd never seen him so tortured as he was right now as he licked his lips and looked toward the doorway. He was thinking about it. *Oh yeah, he was.* His body was craving something his mind knew was wrong. It was only a matter of time before one would win...the only question was, *which one?*

7

Ryth

"I was thinking you might be able to put that laptop to good use."

I stared at the butter as it spilled onto the plate.

"Ryth?"

I hated her. Hated the way she stood in front of me. Hated the way I couldn't get *those* sounds out of my head.

"*Ryth?*"

I jerked my gaze up. "*What?*"

Mom flinched as though I'd slapped her. "What the hell has gotten into you today?"

What the hell has gotten into YOU? I wanted to scream. *Oh, that's right...another man's cock!* I jerked my gaze to Creed, sitting at the far end of the island, his reading glasses in one hand and his iPad in the other, staring at me with surprise.

But they shouldn't be goddamn surprised. They should be *fucking embarrassed.*

She'd smiled at me when I gathered enough courage to walk downstairs and face her. Pretending like it was just another day staying in a stranger's house, and for a second there, I could've believed her. I could've talked myself into believing what I'd heard last night was all a bad dream...until Creed walked downstairs and mom smiled at him, smiled like she'd never smiled at my dad...my dad who was sitting in prison.

There was no mistaking the truth anymore. I'd heard them last night. Heard them *together.* She didn't even have the nerve to look embarrassed. "What's going on with you this morning?"

"I could ask you the same thing," I said carefully, my pulse hammering.

I wanted to tell her that I knew about them, but the words were stuck in my chest, balled up tight, unable to be dislodged. I couldn't do it. Couldn't say the words, because once I did, everything would change.

The heavy thud of steps came from the stairs behind me. The hairs rose on my arms as Tobias sauntered into the kitchen bare chested, his hair still damp from the shower, the scent of something masculine hitting me as he walked past.

"Dad." He grabbed a cup from the overhead cupboard and slid it under the spout of the coffee machine before pressing start and turning. "Elle," he greeted my mom.

"Tobias," she said carefully, her attention no longer on me.

"Sorry about last night."

She stiffened, then glanced at Creed, who lifted a brow in surprise.

"The outburst," Tobias added, walking slowly past me.

"That's fine," she said slowly as a look of relief washed over her. "I understand."

He just lifted those dark eyes to me. "That doesn't excuse my outburst. I know dad's only trying to help you get your home back. So I'll keep myself in check in the future."

But there was something else sparking in that glare, some kind of danger only I saw.

"T-thank you," she replied, oblivious to the fact he was playing her, and licked her lips, desperate for a way to keep the conversation going.

"You could ask Tobe about Duke," Creed suggested. "He finished up there a couple of years ago."

Duke? As in Duke High?

"Oh, you thinking about going?" he asked carefully...turning to me.

"What?" Panic rushed in as I tore my gaze from him to my mom.

"That's what I've been trying to say." She glanced at Creed. "We were thinking you could transfer schools?"

We? Since when did this become a we?

Since last night. A pang tore across my chest. I shook my head. "I'm in my last year."

"Then it'll be a simple process." She smiled, knowing damn well what she was doing to me. "You'll attend maybe, what? A few classes, then take your exams, and you'll be done."

They'd discussed this? Discussed it between the two of them? Heat rushed to my cheeks. "No, Mom."

"If it's transportation you're worried about..." Creed started. "I'm sure Tobias will be happy to drive you."

Anger flared in Tobias' gaze as coffee trickled into his cup.

"See," mom beamed. "Tobias will be only too happy to drive you, honey."

But he didn't look happy about it at all. The muscles of his jaw flexed as he clenched, then lifted the cup from the machine to his lips, never once taking his eyes off me.

She didn't see it, the savage hatred that lingered inside him. The kind that made my belly clench.

"Of course," he answered carefully. "If you want me to."

"I thought we were going home," I said quietly, looking at mom. *Please, mom...no.*

"Ryth, the fire took everything. There's nothing to go home to." She stepped around the island toward me. "Anyway, once I get my accounts back, I figured we could get a place around here."

She's still working on getting us out of here. That's one thing, I guess. Maybe this thing with Creed was just a *mistake*. I bet she was drunk. I bet they both were. Guilt filled me.

"Which might take a while," Creed added. "The damn feds seem to have shown a particular interest in your mom. Until then, consider this place home. Do whatever you want to the room. Hell, we can even get you a desk and a chair, maybe even a small bookshelf. What do you think, kid?" He gave me a wink.

Tobias stilled mid swallow. There was a twitch at the corner of his eye, his throat muscles clenching before he finished. The muscles of his jaw tightened as those sparks in his eyes grew colder...until they reminded me of shards.

Shards of glass...

All of a sudden, it felt like battle lines were being drawn. That cold stare pinned me to the spot, and my mom...my mom *fucking smiled,* oblivious to how that *asshole* was staring at me. I wanted to lift my hand and hide my cheek. I wanted to back away slowly, until I hit the stairs, then I wanted to run.

I wanted to get out of this house and far away from the chilling way that asshole looked at me, and I wanted that panicked rush swirling inside me to stop. I just wanted it all to stop. Him. Them.

But I had no home to run to, and no other way to get to school halfway across the city to the friends who protected me from the bullying of others. *Look at her face. Jesus Christ, you need a paper bag for that! Anyone got a paper bag for Ryth Castlemaine?*

The taunts rose in my head. Taunts I knew would come. In a new school, I'd be alone...and vulnerable. In a new school, I'd be fair game. *God, please don't do—*

"That's settled then," Mom beamed, glancing at Creed, who rose from his stool and motioned toward her.

"Looks like we have a few things to organize, we'll leave you guys alone." He gave a wink to Tobias as they left, leaving the two of us behind.

"They want us to be friends." I swallowed hard.

He placed his coffee cup on the edge of the island and took a step toward me. "I'm sure they do."

I swallowed hard as the memory of last night returned. The way he looked at me now was just like then. Cold. Savage. Hate rippled from him as he lowered his gaze to my breasts.

I flinched, curling my shoulders as I tried my best to draw away from that stare, and glanced toward the stairs. The thud of my mother's steps now faded.

"You want me to drive you to school, Ryth?"

My name on his lips sounded...*wrong*. I flinched and jerked my gaze back to him.

"Stop looking at me like that." I crossed my arms over my chest.

"Like what?" He took a step, forcing me backwards.

"L-like *that*."

There was a twitch in the corner of his mouth. His perfect, full lips curling. "I have no idea what you're talking about."

But that same savage glare was in his eyes. The same one I'd seen last night when he stood outside his father's bedroom.

"You want me to be your fucking chauffeur?" he said quietly, his gaze raking down my body once more.

I swallowed hard, taking another step back, then he moved until I hit the counter at the end of the room. *Stop it...stop...it...*I glanced toward the entrance of the kitchen.

"You looking for someone to save you?" He lifted his other hand and braced it against the cabinet bedside me.

I flinched and jerked my gaze to him. "No."

"No?"

"No," I forced the words, but inside I was panicking.

"I'll drive you, Ryth. On the end of my cock."

I flinched at the words as heat raced to my face. Shock moved in. "W-what did you say to me?"

I'd heard wrong, *very...very...wrong.*

"You heard me." He lifted his other hand to the counter at my side, boxing me in. "After all, that's what you want, right? You... and your fucking mom. You want to be fucked, little mouse? I bet you've never had a cock between your legs, have you? I'll take your virginity for you. But I won't be kind about it...in fact, I'll be a fucking mongrel."

Virginity? He knows I'm a virgin? A feeling of dread washed through me. I glanced toward the entrance of the kitchen, desperate for one of the others to walk through.

"They won't save you."

I jerked my gaze to his. "I'll scream."

He just smiled. "I was hoping you would."

He'd hurt me, tear my clothes, paw at my body. He'd ram himself inside me and he wouldn't be nice. He'd fuck me like they did on those sites. Heat bloomed inside me with the thought and I swallowed hard.

Move! Fear kicked inside me. I stepped to the side, but he shifted his body, blocking me. Panic made me flinch when he brushed a few strands of my hair to the side. His gaze fixed on that ugly mark on my cheek, before he lowered his hand and placed it over my breast.

"No!" I punched out, but he grabbed my wrist, pushing it behind me. "Get the fuck *off me!*"

But he didn't. He just drove his body against mine, grinding my breast, his cruel fingers pinching until more than fear tore through me.

"They won't help you, *Ryth,* because you're mine. Mine to play with, mine to have any fucking way I want. You move into my home, take over the fucking bedroom with my mom's things... while *your* mom fucks my dad. *This* is what you get when you try to ruin my family."

His ugly face blurred under the sheen of tears as they rushed to the surface. "I didn't *try* to ruin anything. I don't want to be here as much as you don't want me here." Tears blurred his cruel face.

"You gonna cry, little mouse?" He pushed, driving me against the end of the counter.

Pain flared as he leaned down, his breath hot against my cheek as he stared at my birthmark. "That makes you mine to do whatever I want with."

You're a fighter, Ryth. Dad's words filled me as I pushed forward, slamming into him. *"Fuck you!"* I tore free, stumbling to the side, then backwards as I headed for salvation. "Come near me again and I'll..."

"You'll what?" His smile was daring.

Ugly. Fucking. Grin.

"I'll make you regret it," I whispered.

"We'll see," he answered before I turned and ran, lunging for the stairs.

Movement blurred coming from the doorway as I hit the top of the stairs. I smacked into a wall...one that grabbed me before I fell backwards.

"*Whoa.*" Nicholas steadied me, concern flashing in his eyes as he glanced behind me, then settled his gaze on mine. "What's happened?"

He...he fucking touched me! The words were a roar inside my head, until that sickening feeling washed over me once more. The feeling that pushed through with the pain. Heat. Shame. I lifted my gaze to Nick as it hit me. *It wasn't just fear I'd felt when he'd touched me.* It wasn't just disgust that welled in the dark pit of my stomach when I'd seen him standing outside his father's door last night...*listening to them.*

"What did he do?" Nicholas asked, his voice husky.

Heat raced to my cheeks as I shook my head. I couldn't tell him, couldn't say the words. Shame filled me as I shoved away from him, ran for my room, and closed the door behind me with a *thud.*

No...no, this can't be happening.

I'll drive you, Ryth. On the end of my cock.

Those words resounded as the sick feeling and the shame filled me. I closed my eyes and leaned my head against the wood.

"*Ryth...*" Nicholas called through the door.

I closed my eyes as the thunder in my chest gave way to a burn. "Go away."

Silence came from the other side of the door. I swallowed the throb in the back of my throat and pressed my hand over my breast. My nipple was hard, poking in the middle of my palm. Pain coursed through me, tearing all the way between my thighs as I dragged my finger across the peak.

Mine to play with, mine to have any fucking way I want.

He didn't mean that. He was just trying to scare me...trying to rattle my cage. I squeezed my eyes shut tighter, rolled my nipple between my fingers, and stoked the flames. I'd seen men like him on those sites, seen how they bullied and manhandled those women...like the kids did at my school. Heat flared in my cheeks, drawing my attention to the mark on my face.

Just like the kids at school did to me.

But this wasn't school...

This was where I was living.

For now.

I waited until the soft thud of Nick's steps faded before I risked opening the door. The place was quiet...*too quiet.* I stepped out and hurried to the bathroom before closing and locking the door behind me. Hard breaths tore from my chest and I stumbled for the basin and turned on the taps.

He was a bully...just a fucking awful bully.

Just like the ones I'd dealt with.

I gathered the water and splashed it to my face.

But he wasn't...*he was worse.*

I needed to get out of here, out of this house and away from these people. If mom wasn't going to help me, then I'd leave on my own. I twisted off the tap, dried my face, and made my way out of the bathroom and down to the second floor. My gaze went to Creed's bedroom door and a sickening wave of dread hit me.

I tried to push the memory of last night out of my mind and instead, went to his study door, where I knocked. "Creed." And waited.

But there was no answer. I knocked again, only this time louder, then opened the door. "Creed?"

The study was empty, no one was inside. Where were they? Curious, I stepped inside. The room was nice, black bookshelves packed with expensive looking books ran the length of the wall. I moved closer, finding burgundy hardbacks etched with gold. *Criminal Justice for the Guilty.*

"The guilty?" I murmured, running my fingers along the edges before I turned my attention to the desk.

Who the hell was this guy, anyway?

A lawyer, I got that. Someone who'd known mom years ago. Papers were splayed out on the desktop. I glanced over my shoulder at the door and stepped closer, peering at things I really shouldn't be. But right then, I didn't care. I wanted out of here, away from his asshole son...

Bank of Phoenix...

Our bank.

I grabbed one of the statements and lifted it.

Assets frozen from the IRS.

"What the hell?"

So they were telling the truth. There was more. All our bank accounts, all our money...*gone.* He really was helping us.

"Ryth?"

I spun, the statement still in my hand and watched as Creed narrowed his gaze. He glanced around the room, then stopped on me once more. "Everything okay?"

Mom followed him inside, her eyes shining and red like she'd been crying. The floor seemed to open up and swallow me whole. He had been trying to help us. He'd bought me things with his own money, *expensive things.*

Things he hadn't needed to buy.

He'd gone out of his way to help us, giving us a place to stay. I was an asshole for charging in here demanding...*what?* That we leave? I clenched my grip around the truth and glanced at Mom, finally understanding. *We literally had nowhere else to go.*

"Ryth...I—" Mom started.

"I'll go." I cut her off, my words slipping free as I met Creed's gaze. "I'll go to Dukes, whatever you need."

Mom's eyes widened with surprise as a look of utter relief washed over her.

But Creed grinned and crossed the room to take the statement from my hand, and pulled me into a hug. "I knew you'd come around. Thank you, Ryth, that means a lot to me and your mom."

I let him hug me, then slowly pulled away. "But on one condition. I want Nick to drive me..."

Creed nodded, that smile growing wider. "Deal."

8

Ryth

"You want me to come in," Nick asked as he stared at the entrance to the school. "Or are you good from here?"

My pulse was thundering, my panic out of control. But I just swallowed, clutched my MacBook to my chest, and yanked the door handle. "Thanks, I got it."

My cheeks burned, even as I dropped my gaze and nervously tugged my hair lower. *Don't look at me...please, don't look at me.* I passed a group of girls as they crowded the sidewalk. But they didn't laugh at me...they didn't even see me.

"Holy shit, is that Nick Banks?" one of them muttered, staring.

The midnight Mustang idled heavily, throbbing, growling, drawing every female gaze in the vicinity. Of course they knew him, especially the girls. I mean, why wouldn't they? Broody, dangerous...*intensely good looking.*

I'd notice, too...if I wasn't living with them. Notice, and what...*panic.* Tobias crept into my mind, his cruel pinch of my breast, the way he'd trapped me with that savage stare. *You want me to drive you, Ryth?* I hugged the laptop tighter against me, shoving the memory of him down, until it left that throbbing sound of the Mustang to push in.

I half expected Nick to pop the clutch and roar past the school like every other rich hot-head did. But he didn't. Instead, he idled the car, slowly crawling behind me.

"Hey, Ryth!" he called out as he lowered the passenger's window.

Fire lashed deeper as I jerked my gaze over my shoulder.

There was concern in his eyes as he motioned his head at the drop-off point. "I'll meet you here later, okay?"

I just nodded, turned, and scurried, feeling the heat of attention as I hurried for the admin building. It'd been days since I'd agreed to come here. Just enough time to try to forget what an asshole Tobias had been in the kitchen, and just enough time for the storm of panic to build at the thought of starting a brand new school halfway through my last year.

Creed Banks had called ahead and, of course, everyone was more than accommodating. Why wouldn't they be? Rich and powerful. What he wanted, he seemed to get. All I wanted was my dad out of prison and my family back together. I shoved through the doors, my sneakers squeaking on the vinyl floor as I scanned the entrance, caught the sign, and headed for the office.

When I pushed through the doors, it was quiet. A few younger kids were sitting on a bench and one guy was standing idly by a display loaded with pamphlets.

"Help you?" an older woman called over the counter.

I licked my lips, tugged my hair lower, holding my hand over my face, and stepped closer. "Ryth Castlemaine. I'm here to start classes."

"Oh, Ryth. Yes, we've been expecting you," she smiled, then lifted her hand, motioning to someone behind me.

I glanced over my shoulder at the guy standing beside the pamphlets, then jerked my gaze away. He was gorgeous, with dark brown eyes and dimples when he turned to me and smiled. Panic rose inside me as I turned back to the woman. "What...what are you doing?"

She smiled carefully, then frowned. "Getting you an escort. Gio here has offered to show you to your classes."

"I don't need that," I muttered as the sound of his steps grew closer. "I just need a schedule and a map."

"Nonsense." She met Gio's gaze and smiled at him. "It's good to make friends, especially on your first day."

I didn't want a first day.

I didn't want friends.

I just wanted a class schedule. How fucking hard was it to give me a damn schedule?

She reached to the side, grabbed something from behind the counter and handed it toward me. "Welcome to Duke's, Ryth. I hope you'll enjoy it here."

I forced a smile, took the paperwork, and turned away, wanting to sink into the floor or the wall and hide.

"Hey," he smiled nervously, then looked away, giving a slight shrug. "Giovani, most call me Gio."

"Ryth," I muttered.

"Yeah, I figured that already," he smiled, and nodded toward the door.

I wanted to run, and when I say run, I wanted to haul ass out of this place and keep on going. I waited for the look as I stepped outside and into the corridor. Heat rose, finding its way along my neck to pool in my face. The wince would be next when he settled his gaze on the mark on my cheek, then would come the questions...and finally, when he was amongst his friends, the taunts.

"O-okay," he stuttered, then stopped, his voice quieting. "Your c-cl-asses."

He stuttered.

Like, actually stuttered.

He glanced at my shocked expression, then looked away. "It's fine most of the t-time, just comes out wh-when I'm nervous."

"You stutter when you're nervous?"

He licked his lips and nodded. "Yeah."

"Why the hell are you nervous around me?"

His cheeks reddened as he looked away. Oh shit...okay. That need to flee froze inside me as I focused on the guy. He was tall, muscled, obviously popular. *But was he? Would a popular guy escort someone around on their first day? Someone they didn't even know?*

"So, looks like you have Harkins with me first up." He tried to change the subject. "She can be a hardass, especially if you're late, so we better get going."

I just followed, feeling that storm inside me slip away. Maybe it wasn't so bad here. Maybe I could do the last six months of school and finish, I dunno...*normal, like everyone else?* The thought of that excited me.

I followed him to the first class, sliding in behind his seat after he sat at a desk. Others glanced my way, but they quickly turned their attention back to getting through the build-up to exams and hardly anyone paid me any mind.

By the time the day was half over, I was basically invisible...but still awkward as hell when the bell rang for lunch. I glanced at Gio, then to the loud roar in the hallway as it filled in an instant.

"Thanks for showing me around," I smiled, stumbling out of the way as a girl shoved passed in a huff. I glanced his way, waiting for him to just turn and leave me behind. After all, he had other friends to sit with, right?

"You hungry?" He glanced my way and motioned toward the cafeteria.

Sitting amongst a group of assholes who basically picked you apart? Not my idea of a good time. I shook my head. "Thanks, but no."

"Good. I'm grabbing something from the vending machine and heading outside, you want in?"

"Yes." Relief washed over me. "Thank you."

He gave me a hint of a smile, then strode to where a bank of vending machines lined the wall. I grabbed my card from the wallet of my phone case and pressed it against the reader. He glanced my way, his brow rising. "What, you gonna buy me lunch, Ryth?"

I just shrugged. "Figured it was the least I could do."

His grin grew wider, showing teeth, before he turned back and cracked his knuckles. "Well alright, in that case..."

I let out a bark of laughter, catching him grin and glance my way. He grabbed a sandwich and a cola and stepped to the side, waiting for me. I followed suit as he waited, then grabbed my food and motioned toward the exit.

It was a relief to get outside. We found a secluded table and sat, and while we chatted about classes and the start of our lives in less than six months, I actually felt...*happy*.

"So, you moved in with the Banks', huh?" he asked, then took a gulp of his cola.

My happiness dulled as I nodded. "It's only temporary."

"Those guys can be real assholes," he muttered, casting me a cautious gaze. "You want to be careful of them."

Careful?

Tobias pushed into my mind. *You're mine, Ryth.* "Yeah," I muttered, forcing my mind to focus on Nick and Caleb instead. "Like I said, it's just temporary until we get on our feet."

He glanced my way and I could tell he wanted to say more. But instead, he just drained his cola as the bell rang. "Looks like the party's over. Speaking of a party, Hanna Kresler's throwing one this weekend. Hers are pretty notorious, if you wanna go?"

My stomach dropped. "Like on a date?"

He just gave a shrug and pushed off from sitting on top of the table. "Date, no date, I don't care."

Date or no date? As in my first ever. My pulse sped at the thought. I wanted to say *why me?* Or even look in the mirror to see if that hideous mark that didn't fade under foundation had somehow disappeared. But I knew it hadn't. Even with the stutter, other girls would be clamoring over him, so why ask me?

You gonna cry, little mouse? Tobias pushed into my head. I couldn't get him out...not his words or the feel of his goddamn hand on my body. "Sure." The word slipped free as I met his gaze. "Why the hell not?"

"Really?" he looked shocked, then slowly smiled. "Fuck yeah."

I had no idea how I was going to get there and even though I'd had my license for months now, I was betting taking Creed's Mercedes was out of the question. I felt bolder as I strode to class beside Gio. Hell, I might even take Tobias' Jeep...swipe his keys from his room while he was showering. I'd be gone before he knew it was missing. *Let him see how much of a mouse I was then...*

That thought stayed with me all through the afternoon periods, and when the last bell rang, I was almost sad to leave. We made our way through the stampede to the front doors of the building, then outside to the bright blue skies and fresh air.

"Same time tomorrow?" Gio cast a glance my way as we headed for the drop-off point.

The deep rumble of the Mustang overpowered every other engine noise, drawing my gaze...and Gio's. He scowled when he saw the car and I swore I saw a flicker of annoyance. But he turned his gaze toward me and in an instant, that flare was gone, turning into a smile for me again.

Maybe for once I actually *had* met a real friend. "Sure."

He gave me a wink, one that sent a flutter through my chest, and strode away, leaving me alone. I watched him for a second before turning back to the chick magnet. Nick waved his hand from behind the wheel, drawing my attention. As if I could miss him. I didn't even care others stared as I opened the passenger door and climbed in.

"You're smiling." Nick glanced my way as I pulled the door closed. "That's a little troubling, considering it's your first day."

The corner of my lip twitched higher. But he wasn't putting the car into gear, not yet.

"That guy you were with, who was he?"

I shrugged as annoyance flared. "No one."

Possessiveness burst inside me. Why did he have to know? Couldn't I keep anything to myself? "I didn't get his name."

"Just be careful, Ry, okay?" he muttered, and shoved the car into gear, pulling out of the waiting zone with a roar...for attention.

My pulse kicked hard as I grabbed the armrest and we turned sharply before surging forward. *Ry?* I glanced at Nick as he watched the street, his black t-shirt molding against his hard body. Ripped black-jeans rode low on his hips and Gio's warning came back to me. *Those guys can be real assholes. You want to be careful of them.*

I'd been at their house just over a week. A week occupying the same space. Tobias was an asshole for sure, a goddamn bully. But Nick...Nick was nice and Caleb, too, when I saw him.

Nick must've felt my focus and glanced my way. "What?"

"Nothing." Heat raced to my cheeks.

He hadn't made fun of me, hadn't even once looked at my cheek. That intense gaze that looked eerily like Tobias' fixed on mine, then glanced away.

"You up for a shake? I know a place."

"A shake?" I smiled. "You know I'm not a kid, right?"

He chuckled, muttered something under his breath, and jerked the wheel hard to the right, tearing across the street to somewhere else. "Yeah, I know," he grinned and reached across the seat to jab me in the ribs.

I laughed. He was actually a really good guy.

He drove to some small cafe and pulled into an alley, plunging us into dimness before muttering, "Wait here." And climbed out.

He commanded me.

Like I was his to boss around.

I should be pissed at that. Should be doing the opposite. I glanced at the handle, almost seeing myself yanking the damn thing and doing whatever the hell I wanted. *Defying him.*

My breaths turned shallow as I watched Nick disappear in the side mirror. That's what I wanted. I wanted to defy him...defy mom...*and Tobias.*

A surge of something dangerous tore through me, making me wiggle in the seat in an attempt to find relief. I reached up, brushed my fingers against my breasts, and pretended to fix my hair. But I was hard...tight and *excited.*

I risked a glance into the rear-view mirror as a flush of shame came over me. My heart was booming, sitting there in Nick's car with his growl still ringing in my ears, waiting for him to come back any moment. Still that heat lingered, unwanted and unneeded, drawing my focus. I looked at the mirror once more and reached down, sliding my hand between my thighs.

Tight black shirt.

Ripped jeans.

That dark, dangerous stare.

You want me to drive you, Ryth? I pressed my fingers against my crease, drawing in the deep rich scent of the leather. I didn't understand this...this hunger. That burn moved deeper as I grew wet. I didn't normally do this, not out in the open, only in private under the glare of the laptop screen in the dark.

Dark...dirty. The seduction consumed me like a fantasy.

I'll drive you on the end of my cock...

I closed my eyes and curled my fingers, pressing harder. My breaths deepened, tearing from my chest as that need roared... almost...almost...*alm—*

The snap of the door handle wrenched me out of the moment. I jerked my hand out from between my legs, my cheeks growing brighter as the door opened and Nick sank in behind the wheel, his hands laden with two massive shakes and a brown paper bag with grease darkening the bottom clutched in his teeth.

God...had he seen me?

He handed me a shake, then pulled the bag from his mouth. "I hope you're hungry," he muttered, his tone deep and husky.

75

He wouldn't meet my eyes when he dropped the bag in between us. He just stared straight ahead and scowled, then leaned forward, starting the car before shoving it into reverse.

"Thanks," I murmured when he braked to a stop at the end of the alley, checked the traffic, and drove away.

Silence filled the car as I took a sip. I snuck glances, trying to get a bead on his state of mind as a heartbeat pounded in my head. He didn't see me...he couldn't have, not over the bag in his mouth. I took another draw on the thick, malted-chocolate shake and glanced his way again.

"Stop staring, Ryth," he murmured, his gaze fixed on the road.

I expected us to go somewhere, some kind of park, or lookout, somewhere we could enjoy the food and the drinks. But we didn't. We headed home...*their home.*

When we pulled up to the driveway, there was an expensive looking gold Lexus parked just outside the closed gates. "We have a visitor?" I couldn't help but ask.

"Dad, not us." He stopped at the gate and rolled down his window, then punched in the code on the box and pulled back in. "Lawyers meeting with him and your mom all damn day."

"Oh?" My brows shot upwards as I glanced at the car, excitement coursing through my veins.

It was the first sign of progress I'd seen. Hope hummed as we pulled up and parked next to the black Jeep. I didn't even think about Tobias or what had happened in Nick's car as I pawed at the door handle and climbed out.

"Ryth!" Nick called behind me. *"I got you damn fries!"*

Food was the last thing on my mind. I gripped the shake and my laptop and charged to the door, turned the handle, and shoved it wide. The place was quiet. It was always quiet. I lifted my gaze to the study on the second floor and climbed the stairs.

The thud of the front door sounded before Nick's heavy footsteps thudded behind me. "I'll eat them all if you're not careful."

"Go ahead," I threw over my shoulder as I caught the sound of voices from the study.

I stopped in front of the closed study door, my heart hammering.

"I wouldn't go in there if I were you." Nick stopped behind me. "Lawyer talk is boring anyways. Come on, come to my room and we can discuss your first damn day at Dukes."

I licked my lips, listening to their muffled words drifting through the door. I wanted to cross the hall and open it, wanted to know what was going on. Were they finally getting dad out? Was that why the other lawyers had been there all day?

"Ryth." Nick urged.

I stepped away and followed him, even as my mind raced. What had happened between mom and Creed had been real, but it didn't have to be a deal breaker...marriages survived all the time even if one of them had been unfaithful. Mom and dad hadn't been happy in a long time, but this could be our fresh start, a way to make things better...*I'll be better.*

I followed Nick, my mind fixed on the image of us being one big happy family once more, and stepped into his room.

9

Tobias

Nick: Eating fries. She won't stop talking about her mom and dad getting back together.

I stared at the text on my cell, texts from my brother in the next room, and clenched my jaw.

Nick: But you should've seen her in the car, man. Eyes closed, head back, rubbing her goddamn pussy. I wanted to fucking come all over her goddamn milkshake. I wanted to climb into that car and—

"Sonofa*bitch*," I growled, then lifted my gaze and cast the cell onto the bed.

The faint sound of their muffled voices drifted through the wall. I clenched my fists as my cell went *beep*.

I wasn't going to read them...wasn't going to look. But I couldn't stop thinking about her, the way that pink fucking mark on her cheek blushed when I'd cornered her in the kitchen. The way her breath had hitched when I'd told her what I'd do to her.

Christ, I wanted to do that to her.

Her mom and the lawyers had been in dad's office all fucking day. They were there when I came back from the gym, and they'd stayed there ever since.

Beep.

Don't look...

Don't fucking look.

Beep.

"Fuck." I reached over and grabbed it from the bed.

Nick: She just got a message from her mom. Apparently there's a special dinner tonight. She's talking about wearing a fucking dress, for Christ's sake.

A special dinner?

Something savage moved through me. My mind raced, searching all the possible threads it could be. Maybe they were moving out? Maybe Nick had been right and this was just a friend helping out a friend...and our life would go back to normal.

Me hating dad.

Nick and Caleb running interference.

That was the only reason they stayed, because they didn't trust I wouldn't kill him after what he'd done...they were smart to stay. There was a lot of unspoken truths between us. The kind of shit that sticks...the kind of shit I wanted to ram down his fucking throat.

I'm just the fucking messenger. Lazarus Rossi's last words to me still fucking haunted me.

The words he'd uttered before I threw him to the ground and beat the shit out of him. He'd had no fucking goons then, no, it had been just him and me.

Because he'd trusted me.

I winced at the words. He'd been my fucking friend...the guy I'd thought of as blood. Now we were fucking enemies...and it was all dad's fault.

Beep.

I jerked my gaze to the cell.

Nick: She's fucking excited, man. You should see her, she fucking hugged me, pressing those little tits against my chest.

My cock grew hard as I took in a deep breath, my rage and hunger fusing. It was good they were leaving...good they left this place and the fucking rage and stench of death behind.

Run, little mouse. Run as fast and as far as you can.

I didn't know what'd happen if she didn't. I licked my lips, imagining them in Nick's room. She thought he was a friend, thought he was the *'good guy'*. But he wasn't. He was just as fucking excited about having her here as I was. He just needed a little...*push.*

Nick: She's going to shower and get ready. I wonder if she needs some company?

A twitch came in the corner of my cheek as I jerked my gaze to the wall separating our rooms.

He wouldn't fucking dare.

Would he?

I grabbed my cell and punched out a reply. *You fucking touch her first and I'll kill you,* and hit send.

She was *mine*, mine if her mom didn't move the fuck out.

She lingered in my head as I pushed to stand up. I needed to go for a run, needed to somehow get clear of her. This hunger in me wasn't right. I yanked on my sneakers and pulled on a shirt before heading out the door. I raced down the stairs, listening to my dad as he chuckled. I was halfway down when the study door opened and he stepped out.

Our gazes met and surprise lifted his brows. "Tobias."

"I'm heading out for a run," I muttered, catching sight of Elle Castlemaine as she smiled and reached out, placing her hand on his arm.

She saw me then, her eyes widened, and her hand slipped from my father's arm as she forced a smile. I didn't wait any longer, just turned my focus to the stairs and left them behind. My damn head was booming as I yanked open the front door and stormed out. By the time I hit the front of my car, I was striding out, making my way to the gate.

The way she fucking touched him...the way he'd fucking smiled.

He hadn't smiled that way with mom. I punched in the code and slipped around the gate as it opened. Then I was gone, lengthening my strides and pushing into a run. I'd already been at the gym for three hours this morning, but still it wasn't enough.

I couldn't stop thinking about her, about her tight little tit under my hand and the way her nipple tightened when I'd pinched it. I pushed harder, forcing myself faster as the fantasy returned. It wasn't my fingers that grazed her flesh.

I wanted my tongue there, too. My teeth, as well.

Pure...

The scent of vanilla drew deep with every breath. I focused on the road and the houses. I focused on the kids on the swings that I raced past and the sun as it dimmed in the sky. I focused on anything else and by the time I turned into my street once more and slowed at the gates, I was spent.

Hard, sawing breaths consumed me. My shirt was soaked and stuck against my skin. I punched the code into the gate box with trembling fingers and yanked my shirt over my head.

When I opened the front door, I could hear them. Music piped through the speakers in the house, something old and...*happy.*

"Another bottle of champagne," Elle Castlemaine called as I strode toward the stairs.

From the corner of my eye, I caught it as my father chuckled and strode to the kitchen. He didn't see me, not this time. But there was something different about him, something I didn't like. He seemed too happy to be moving Elle Castlemaine and her daughter out. *Far too fucking happy.*

My mouth twitched with a snarl as I climbed the stairs and headed for the bathroom. The scent of vanilla hit me like a fist to my gut as I stepped in and closed the door. *Jesus.* I closed my eyes and reached out, bracing my hands against the vanity.

My body was trembling, but my mind was still hungry, ravenous with a cruel fucking need. I yanked my clothes off and tossed them into the hamper before stepping into the shower and hitting the taps. Heat ran down my neck and my shoulders. Under the blur of the water falling in my eyes, I saw her things, her damn shampoo and conditioner. I reached and picked up a pink bottle of her bodywash and cracked open the lid.

Ylang Ylang.

Fuck, that shit smelled nice, real nice. I squeezed some out, rubbed my hands together, and ran them over my body. I was already fucking hard, too goddamn hard. It didn't matter how many times I jerked off to the smell of her panties and her perfume, I still craved more.

More of her body.

More of her fucking soul.

I washed and rinsed, using my own shampoo before I stepped out and grabbed a towel. A *thud* came from the other side of the door before it opened. Nick stepped in, wearing clean jeans and an open-collared white shirt with the sleeves rolled up. "Dad wants you downstairs, apparently there's an important dinner."

"Good for him, enjoy that dinner."

"Tobe."

"Fuck off, Nick."

He scowled, those golden-brown eyes darkening. "What the fuck has gotten into you?"

I clenched my jaw and wound the towel around my waist before smacking my shoulder into him on my way out. "I dunno, what do you fucking think?"

He stilled for a second, then strode after me. "You're seriously pissed about that?"

I twisted the door handle and stepped into my room. "Get out of my face, brother," I snarled before closing the door in his face.

I half expected him to come after me. If he did, there was no way I'd look him in the eyes without laying one on his nose. *Did he touch her?* The thought rose. *Did he pull her close when she hugged him?* Did he smell her fucking hair and press his cock against her body?

"Come downstairs, we're all down there," Nick said from the other side of the door.

I just jerked a glare toward the sound and unwrapped the towel, listening as he walked away. *Come down there...why, so I could see them get fucking drunk and look happy?*

That room rose in my mind, the room that had had my mom's machines in it. Machines he'd made us haul to the garage and store in the dark. I lifted my gaze to the door and the sound of their voices. *Come down there?*

To what, see how fucking happy they were?

To see Ryth in her pretty green dress?

A dress I wanted to tear from her body...

With a growl, I strode to the dresser and yanked open the drawer, pulling on boxers, jeans, and a t-shirt. I'd fucking come to their dinner and see what they had to say. I'd give my father and Elle an ultimatum, move the fuck out and leave us alone, or else.

They just didn't know it. So it'd better be good fucking news.

Her daughter's virginity was on the goddamn line.

10

Ryth

She was happy...like really happy. Whatever the lawyers had told her had turned her into a woman I barely knew, a woman who threw her head back and unleashed a throaty laugh at something Creed said to her...a slightly intoxicated laugh.

"Sit...*sit,*" she gushed, coming back to reality and remembering we were actually in the room, motioning to the massive dining table.

I didn't look, just pulled out a chair and sank, smoothing my dress under my ass as I went.

"What's going on?" Nick muttered, glancing at his dad, who grinned and lifted a half-filled glass of Scotch in the air.

"We've got some important news," Creed announced through his grin.

It was the money...and dad. He was getting out of prison, *he was coming home.* My mind raced, thinking about the kind of new life we'd have. I didn't care if it involved the feds or court cases. I just wanted him home and with us.

Nick pulled out a chair and sat on my left, his confused stare taking in the display. The table was beautiful, silver plates gleamed, shining against the long black table cloth that skimmed my lap. The sight only heightened my excitement more. I could barely see mom in the dim candlelight as she leaned over, wobbling, and struck a match to light the third candle in the middle of the table.

Caleb sat at the end of the table and scowled at them as though this was strange to him. "Want to tell us what's going on?"

My chest tightened with excitement, my breath barely moving as Creed glanced around the table. He was looking for Tobias, hoping that he'd take part in the celebration. I licked my lips, the words on the end of my tongue. I wanted to tell him that it didn't matter about Tobias. We didn't really need him. I was excited for all of us.

Dad's getting released.

That's all I thought about, all that consumed me. I barely saw the movement, not until it was too late, as Tobias dragged the chair out on my right and sank down beside me. I glanced his way, my pulse hammering, but he didn't look at me, just glared at his father with that same moody look.

I'd seen him leave before, seen him from the window in Nick's room. The fries sat heavy in my stomach, oily and hard against the cold chocolate shake I'd downed.

Poor Nick.

I glanced his way as he shot me a careful smile, then glanced back to his dad as Creed cleared his throat, standing next to my mom. Nick had been nice to me, taking me to school, getting me food. My cheeks burned at the memory of what I'd done in his car, but I quickly shoved it to the side. I was almost sad not to talk to him again.

"So, we've had a pretty major development today," Creed started.

Mom's eyes twinkled, riveting me to the spot.

"We wanted you all here to be the first to know." Creed glanced at mom, then back to us again. "Elle and I..."

"We're getting married," mom smiled, her gaze fixed on me.

My stomach lurched. The booming in my ears muffled their words.

"What the fuck did you say?" Caleb growled.

But Creed just smiled. "I know it must seem like a bit of a shock." He lifted his glass and drained the contents.

"You can't." My words were hollow as I glanced at mom. "You're already married."

The intoxicated sparkle in her eye grew bolder. "No, not anymore. Your father signed the divorce papers today." She swallowed hard. "We're still working on getting him out, Ry, but we wanted a stable home for you...and your new brothers."

My new brothers?

No...*no*...*no*...*no*...I closed my eyes, trying to understand.

"You're marrying her?" Nick snarled, glaring at mom. "Barely two months after mom died?! Her body is barely cold !"

"Still think he's a good guy, brother?" Tobias murmured.

I clenched my eyes shut tighter. This wasn't happening...*this wasn't happening*. The tablecloth brushed my lap before a hand landed on my thigh.

For a second, I didn't understand what was happening. My mind was frantic and dull all at the same time, like a muffled scream consuming me, as that hand gripped tighter and pulled...

I yanked my eyes open, that scream in my head growing clearer. Tobias stared across the table to where Creed and mom stood, the glint of broken glass in his eyes. "Married..."

Panic roared as he shoved my dress high and pressed his fingers against my sex.

What the fuck...stop! I flinched with the contact and jerked my gaze to mom.

"We want you guys to be happy," Mom's words turned throaty as that intoxicated gleam shimmered with tears. "We realize this is sudden..."

His fingers slid against me, driving deep. That trapped scream in my head had nowhere to go...howling and shrieking in the void. *Stop this...stop it now!*

"Ryth, having stepbrothers will be good for you," Mom insisted, smiling.

"And having a little stepsister will be good for all three of you, too." Creed looked at Tobias.

But they didn't see what he was doing...didn't see his fingers sliding against me, fingers curling as he found my clit, his voice hollow and strange when he answered. "I think so, too."

Mom's eyes still shimmered with tears, her smile wide as she turned to Creed. "I knew this was a good idea."

Tobias yanked the elastic of my panties aside. I clenched my fists and shoved upwards...until I was stopped by Nick's hand on my arm.

Nick turned his gaze toward me, those golden-brown eyes darkening to the same stony stare.

"*What?*" I whispered. "No."

"We're in love," Mom declared as she stared into Creed's eyes.

I tried to shove against the table, but Nick held my arm down, trapping me. "Step-sister," he growled as Tobias' fingers found my clit, rubbing and sliding, stoking that heat inside me.

Heat strangled with revulsion.

Coated with humiliation.

"Nick...*please,*" I whispered, shaking my head.

I didn't need to lift my gaze to see my mother and Creed kissing, oblivious to what Tobias was doing to me. Heat moved deeper as he slid his fingers deeper inside me. Nick clenched his grip tighter around my arm. From across the table, the act would be seen as comfort...but here...it was anything but.

My belly clenched, those oily fries burning in the pit of my stomach as Nick dragged my hand from the table and moved the tablecloth aside.

I didn't understand at first...until he lowered his gaze.

Those ravenous eyes fixed on the movement between my thighs. He wanted to see...see what his brother was doing. Nick tugged my dress higher, bunching it against my hip, until all he saw was his brother's glistening fingers as they slid in and out of my pussy.

"We know it's soon," Mom cooed, staring into Creed eyes. "But this feels right."

"It does," Tobias urged. "Very right."

I closed my eyes, hating how under the shame, need grew inside me. My body moved against his invasion, rocking, desperate for more. I knew I was slick. I was going to come... right here in front of everyone...*under the hand of my soon-to-be-stepbrother*.

That thought ignited the panic inside me. *"No!"* I shoved my chair backwards, tearing Tobias' hand from inside my panties and stumbled away, ripping from Nick's hold.

My face burned, that heat consuming me as the tears came.

Mom glanced my way as my dress fell...settling around my thighs.

"Ryth," pain coursed through her voice.

"You *bitch*," I spat, hate fueling me. "You *fucking bitch!*"

"Ryth!" Creed bellowed, his happiness darkening with anger. "That's no way to talk to your mother!"

But I didn't care. I *didn't fucking give a shit*.

I jerked a glare at Tobias, then Nick. Both of them looked at me with merciless need. I was just a game to them, a cruel, fucking game. I wasn't safe in this house...*I was the prey*.

I turned and lunged, hurling myself out of that dining room and toward the stairs. My legs didn't work right, my knees buckling as I hit the first stair. I grasped the banister, holding on as I found my footing and shoved upwards.

The stairs were a blur through my tears. I hit the third floor before I knew it, and made for my room, slamming the door behind me before I threw myself onto the bed.

She'd betrayed him...

She'd betrayed him...

She'd betrayed my dad.

Tears came hard and fast, soaking into the pillow. I fisted the sheets and screamed. *"I FUCKING HATE YOU!"*

The words burned, ripping from the middle of my chest. But even as the heat of them pressed against my face, I knew they were a lie. I didn't hate her. I *couldn't* hate her, and that's what hurt the most.

The light thud of footsteps came.

"Ryth," mom called from the other side of the door.

"Go away!"

"Ryth, honey, I know this is hard for you to hear."

She wouldn't go away. No matter how tight my fists clenched and that burning pit inside me raged, she wouldn't leave. Instead, the sound of her sobs came through the door. "You think this was easy for me? Your father and I haven't been good for a very long time. But I stayed...*I stayed for you.*"

I shook my head. I didn't want to hear this.

"Your father's a bad man, Ryth. He's done terrible things...*dangerous things*. Things that put us in danger...things that got our house burned down."

I lifted my head, my breaths coming hard and brutal.

"We're *still* in danger," she whispered close to the door. "And this is me doing what I have to do. This is me protecting us."

I shoved from the bed and stumbled, making my way to the door. I yanked it open, to find my mom's tearstained, tortured expression. She took one look at me and burst into sobs again, stumbling forward to throw her arms around me. "Oh, Ryth. I wanted to tell you for so long. I *needed* to tell you. But you were so young, and so innocent."

Innocent.

Like I was last night?

My body clenched, the feel of his fingers still so real. I swallowed and held her, winding my arms around her and burying my head into her neck. She still smelled like mom, soft and warm and perfect.

"Mom..." I blubbered.

"I'm happy, Ryth." She managed to stop crying, and pulled away to stare into my eyes. "For the first time in a very long time, I'm actually happy. I just need you to be happy for me."

But how could I?

How could I, when just hours ago...she was married to my dad.

And unhappy....

Slick, warm tears slipped down my cheeks. My mind was at war. I knew they were always fighting, knew dad was always away. I knew the men dad worked for, dangerous men. The memory surfaced of that sleek black Rossi sedan driving past our house as it burned to the ground.

My pulse boomed as she stroked my hair. "I'm doing this for the both of us. I need you, Ry...I can't do this on my own."

Desperation swelled inside me as I met her tearstained gaze.

"Can you do that?" she whispered. "Can you please just try?"

Try with the feel of Tobias' fingers inside me.

Not Tobias. Stepbrother. The word resounded inside me.

That thunder inside me grew as mom waited for an answer. I wanted to tell her about what had happened, but the desperation in her eyes stopped the words cold. "I'll try, mom," I answered. "I'll try."

She burst into tears again, with relief this time, yanking me hard against her chest. "I knew you would...I just knew it. I love you so much, honey."

"I love you too, Mom," my tone was dull as I stared through the open doorway at the hall as Tobias sauntered up the stairs, glancing my way as he rounded the newel post, the cruel smirk on his mouth growing.

She squeezed me tighter, then pulled back. "I know this is too much...and I know it's really soon. But I was wondering if you wanted to be my bridesmaid?"

I flinched, meeting her excitement.

"Creed and I said we wanted this to be small, keep it in the family, what do you say?"

I swallowed...

Those words resounding inside me as I nodded.

Keep it in the family...

If only she knew.

11

Ryth

It all felt like a bad dream when I woke up the next morning. My head was full and throbbing, my eyes grainy and raw, reminding me that what had happened last night was real. My mom and Creed were getting married, and she wanted me to be her bridesmaid...

But that wasn't the only thing my mind had trouble understanding.

The memory of what Tobias had done to me rose like a storm, destructive and dangerous. I closed my eyes, my pulse triggered by the memory of his hand on my thigh, pulling my legs open.

God, his fingers...

Were inside me.

I slid my hand under the sheets and reached down. I was already wet...wet at the thought of him. Those dark, broody eyes, that pouty fucking mouth. *You want me to drive you, Ryth? I'll drive you...on the end of my cock.*

Oh...*God.*

I slid my finger inside, then around my clit, dancing on that slick flesh.

"Ryth, honey," Mom called from the other side of the door, tearing me from the moment.

"Yeah?" I kept my eyes closed, my finger still sliding in.

"You going to school today?"

I wrenched my eyes open as reality hit hard. Tobias...*and Nick*...

Nick, who I'd *thought* was a friend. But he was no friend, he was just as dangerous as his brother. "No. I'm not going."

"Ah...honey, you might want to tell Nick that. He's downstairs waiting to drive you."

Heat tore through me in an instant. I shoved upwards and scrambled from the bed. "He's what?"

"He's waiting to drive you to school, honey," mom murmured. "He's been incredibly nice."

My insides clenched, that need pulsing between my thighs. He can't possibly...I stumbled over to the window and peered out. He was leaning against the Mustang, his muscled arms were crossed over his chest, bare from his cut-off sleeves.

As though he knew I was watching, he slowly lifted his gaze to my window. Those intense dark eyes daring me...

No. This can't be happening. There's no way I can go down there, no way I can get in his car and pretend like last night never happened. *No. Fucking. Way.*

"I don't think it's a good idea for you to miss school on your second day. Besides, you said you had a friend now, didn't you?"

Gio...

His face pushed to the surface. He'd be waiting...standing outside the classroom. I unleashed a moan and closed my eyes.

"Good girl, honey." Mom's voice drifted through the door. "I'll let Nick know you're on your way down."

I swallowed hard, listening to her steps fade from outside my door. I didn't understand this world, this battleground I found myself in. I didn't understand it at all.

But I had to...because this was now my life.

A life living here, with the three of them.

My new stepbrothers.

I made my way to my dresser. My fingers brushed the white formal shirt Duke's insisted you wear before tossing it onto the bed. My underwear was next, then my knee-length navy-blue skirt. Of all the schools to send me to, they chose the one that had a damn uniform.

I grabbed my things and hurried for the bathroom, casting a glare toward Tobias' room as I went. I hurried, locking the door behind me. I had to be smarter now, Had to be more careful around them. I closed my eyes, swaying with the memory of Nick's ravenous stare as he'd watched Tobias do that to me last night.

Then I opened my eyes, undressed, and raced for the shower. By the time I was done and dressed, Nick was scowling. I strode out, clutching my laptop to my chest like a barrier.

"You want to make me wait, Ryth?" Nick cast me a pissed off look as he shoved off the car and strode to the driver's door, motioning with his head. "Get in and don't be an idiot, your mom's watching."

I glanced over my shoulder to where my mom stood in the open doorway. She gave me a careful smile and a wave of her hand, standing there still dressed in her black negligee and matching satin gown. I waved back, my anger prickly and hot against my cheeks, before making my way around the car and climbing in.

Nick reached forward and started the engine. I wanted to snap at him, wanted to unleash the tirade that shrieked in my head as I pressed myself as hard as I could against the door. But he never said a word, just threw the Mustang in reverse, gripped the back of my seat, and punched the accelerator.

I swallowed, trying not to let my attention creep to the way his arm was almost around me. But my gaze went to the corded muscles of his arms anyway. Muscles that flexed as I stared. He was strong...*and built*. Chiseled pecs tightened as my gaze drifted.

We drove through the gate and out onto the street, pulling away from the house in no time. That thunder in my head rumbled as the tension between us grew. I forced my gaze to the dashboard, then found myself moving it back to his hands...remembering the way he'd grabbed my arm, holding me down as Tobias touched me.

I swallowed hard, swaying as the car pulled hard across the street and accelerated. I jerked my focus to where we were headed, and found unfamiliar streets. "Where are we?"

He didn't answer, just glared with a broody stare, his hard jaw flexing before he turned again.

"*Nick!*" Panic filled me as trees gave way to buildings and the entrance to a park appeared ahead.

He braked, then pulled the Mustang in, heading to a parking spot that faced the trees. I scanned the area, finding us all alone, no kids played on the playground, nobody walked their dog. Nick killed the engine, then turned to me.

"You want to look at me, Ryth?"

Fire lashed my cheeks as I stared straight ahead.

He just shifted, gripped the back of my seat, and leaned across, getting in my space. "You want to talk about last night, then?"

I shook my head as my panic surged.

I felt his gaze then, drifting down my body, taking in the white shirt and pleated navy-blue skirt. "Christ," he muttered, and looked away.

He was angry. I didn't know who he was angry at, himself or me.

"I thought you were a friend." The words slipped out.

I hated that they had, was desperate to swallow them back down. But it was too late. They were free, lingering between us. He drew in a hard, deep breath, then glanced back at me. "You want me to be your friend, Ryth?"

I didn't know what to say. "At least an ally."

"An *ally?*" he growled, then shifted his gaze to my lap. My body responded, warming and throbbing.

I didn't understand why I was so affected by them, why they seemed to tap into that dark, aching place inside me. He reached out, brushed his fingers along my thigh, and drew my skirt higher. "I'm not your friend...you're family now," he murmured, his gaze riveted to my thigh as he exposed it inch by inch.

I grabbed the skirt, yanking the hem down.

"I saw you, you know?"

My hand stilled, fisted against my leg.

He lifted his gaze to mine. "Yesterday in the car."

Heat raced to my cheeks as shame rioted. "I...I was fixing my jeans."

"Liar." His golden eyes darkened to amber.

My breaths deepened and I fought the need to lick my lips.

"You were touching yourself." My body throbbed as he searched my gaze. "You're our little sister now."

"Stepsister," I snapped. *"And not yet, anyway."*

He gave a shrug. "It'll happen. My dad is different with Elle. He likes her...a lot."

I shook my head and glanced around the park, desperate to find a way out of this. But there was no one...

"And being our stepsister, we want to make sure you're taken care of." Nick tugged my skirt once more, forcing the fabric from under my grip. "We want to make sure you're getting what you need."

Throb...

My body betrayed me. I closed my eyes. "Please, Nick..."

"I want to make sure you're doing yourself right."

I flinched and jerked my gazed to his. He wasn't a friend. None of them were. They were...I didn't know what they were.

He licked his lips, his gaze moving to my thigh again. "So I want you to show me."

"You *what?*"

"Show...me..."

Throb...

Fear and excitement stole my breath. I couldn't keep up, not with the rush of air or the thunder in my head.

"You're a virgin, right?"

Shame swallowed me. I couldn't answer, couldn't think. I glanced outside the car once more.

"No one comes here," he assured. "It's just you and me...no different from yesterday. You can pretend I'm not even here."

I clenched my jaw, that heat rising with his words.

"Are you...a virgin?"

"Yes."

His breath stilled before a pained look swept across his face. When he spoke again, his voice was husky. "Then show me, show me how you take care of yourself."

He wasn't letting me go. He wasn't letting *this* go. Not until I gave him what he wanted.

The battle of right and wrong consumed me. Everything had changed in one night. Mom would be married to Creed soon enough and I'd have to call these men brothers.

But they weren't brothers, not by blood.

And the way they looked at me...

Throb.

I dragged my teeth across my lip and widened my thighs, slowly sliding my hand between them.

"That's the way," he urged. "I need to make sure my little sister is satisfied."

I pushed my hand over my panties and closed my eyes with embarrassment before I pulled away. "I can't."

"You can." He tugged my skirt higher. "It's just you and me, no one else. I won't even touch you...not unless you want me to."

Lightning tore through me. I jerked my eyes open and met his gaze.

"Angle your body toward me, Ryth." he demanded.

Muscles quivered as I lifted my knee and turned. I held his gaze, my own desperate need roaring to the surface as I slipped my hand between my thighs once more.

"Are those Hello Kitty panties?"

I swallowed and nodded. Pink hearts against the white. I slid my hand along my crease and let out a moan.

He froze, unable to breathe, riveted by the way my hand moved against my body, until he murmured. "Lift your leg higher."

I did, pressing my spine against the armrest of the door, dropping my thighs wider until he saw all of me. I could just touch myself a few times and moan a little. He'd think I was done...then this'd be over.

I tried to focus, deepening my breaths, this time keeping my eyes open. God, if anyone saw us, if anyone saw me. I slid my finger deeper, finding that hollow of my body. My panties were already wet and warm.

"Jesus Christ, Ryth."

My hand trembled as I fought my body's desire and quickened my breaths, forced a moan and closed my eyes, stilling my hand, before I tugged my skirt back down.

He moved fast, grabbing my hand. "What the fuck are you doing?"

I opened my eyes, the mark on my cheek burning. "What do you mean? I'm done."

His anger lashed deep. "The hell you are."

He knew...one look in his eyes, and I realized he knew. I lowered my gaze to where his cock bulged against his jeans, then I found that savage glare once more.

"Do it again," he demanded. "This time properly."

I started to shake my head, but the curl of his lips stopped me.

"I'm not moving this car until you do, Ryth."

The hard edge in this tone told me the truth. He wouldn't...not until I gave him what he wanted. So I slowly lowered my hand, my fingers finding the burn between my thighs. I started moving, rubbing.

"Slower."

I did, easing down until I found that damp patch of my panties.

"I want to see you." He met my gaze. "Pull them aside."

My belly trembled, but I did as he told me, sliding my finger under the elastic and slid them to the side.

"Jesus...*motherfucking Christ.*"

My pussy clenched and my clit pulsed as I slid my fingers along the sensitive flesh.

"Deeper."

I sank in, sliding two fingers into the center of me, and they came away wet.

"So goddamn beautiful." He licked his lips and I was caught by the movement.

His lips. His mouth...

His tongue sliding into me.

I unleashed a moan as the world fell away, taking the shame along with it. The end was coming closer as my body rocked, driving against my own touch. I sank deeper, sliding out to rub, only to return again.

Tiny pulses grew, clenching around my fingers.

In my mind, they were his fingers.

Nick's...Caleb's...*Tobias'*...

That wave crashed over me, squeezing, quivering...*and releasing.*

I dropped my head backward and cried out.

Blackness...ate away at the edges of my vision.

My pussy trembled against my fingers as I slid them out and went to wipe them on my skirt.

"No."

I flinched at the demand, having forgotten for a second that he was there, and opened my eyes. Nick reached over, those dark amber eyes glinting in a strange, dangerous way as he grasped my wrist and pulled it closer. He opened his mouth and slid my fingers inside.

Warmth consumed me as he sucked, sliding his tongue between them, taking all he could. When he was done, he let me go, then turned around, started the car, and pulled out of the parking lot.

He never said a word to me, just drove as I straightened and tugged my skirt down. Desperation rose in the wake of what I'd just done. I didn't know what to say when he pulled up at the school's drop-off point.

"I'll meet you here." He sounded well and truly pissed off. "And don't be talking to any boys this time."

"They're not boys." I fought back.

"Oh?" He directed that animalistic glare my way. "Believe me, Ryth. They're only after one thing from you...*so they're boys.*"

And you don't? I wanted to snap. But I couldn't, all I could do was yank the handle and climb from his car, slamming the door behind me and hurrying away.

12

Nick

I watched her walk away, fighting the damn urge to shove open the door and drag her back into the car. But the moment I leaned forward to kill the engine and climb out of the car, my damn phone gave a *beep*. I looked down.

Natalie: I miss you baby, when can I come over again?

The corner of my eye twitched. The moment I thought of her, Tobias' fucking words roared to the surface of my mind. *You can do better.* I lifted my gaze from the cell to Ryth as she reached Duke's main building. Do better? Better, because I fucking knew deep down she was playin' me. I knew she hooked up with other guys. I knew, and still I took her back when she begged me to.

I lifted my cell, hit the finder for her phone, and waited for her location to load. Streets narrowed in, then the flashing icon hovered above an address I didn't fucking know. It sure as hell wasn't hers.

That twitch came once more in the corner of my eye.

Not her place...

So she was fucking around again.

"Goddamn stupid whore," I growled, and shoved the car into gear, but the moment I did, darkness caught my eye.

A black Audi idled across the road from the drop-off point, but no teenagers shoved out of the rear seat and strode toward their classes...no, none got out at all. The hairs on the nape of my neck rose the longer I stared at that car. It was familiar. *Real fucking familiar.* I pulled the Mustang out and jerked the wheel, turning the car hard, but the moment I neared alongside the Audi, I slowed.

A guy sat behind the wheel, his dark, hooded eyes threatening as he turned his head slowly to meet my gaze. I knew him instantly...*Freddy Sloane.* What the fuck was he doing here? My gut tightened and I instantly thought of the gun in the glove compartment of my car. If he started...

Dude, if Freddy started, I was fucked.

Even I knew that.

But he didn't climb out of his car, and he didn't lift his piece. Instead, he looked away from me, and turned his gaze to the main building of the school. *He wasn't here for me...*

He. Wasn't. Here. For. Me.

Panic punched through my chest as I turned my head and searched for Ryth. But she was already gone, probably striding through the hallways of the damn school now. So why the fuck was Freddy watching her? I braked hard, staring at the Audi in the rear-view mirror.

Turn around.

Turn around and force the asshole to tell you.

In a gunfight, the savage bulldog would have it all over me. But hand to hand...I licked my lips. Hand to hand, I'd hold my own. But then the Audi pulled forward and turned hard, the engine snarling as it blew past me and headed down the street.

I didn't have to follow to know where he was heading. Back to the Rossis'. He might work for his father, but his loyalty was to Lazarus, the Stidda Mafia Prince. The kid who'd grown up hard the last few years, alongside my brother.

I hit the accelerator, only slowing at the end of the street. But the Audi was gone...

Why the fuck was he watching the kid?

Was it retribution?

I pulled over and glanced into the rear-view mirror. Did I follow him into the city and demand a meeting with Laz? Or did I go home...

Beep.

Tobias: Where the fuck are you?

I scowled and punched out a reply: *Taking Ryth to school, why?*

Tobias: You know why. What kind of fucking game are you playing at?

What kind of fucking game? What did the fucking little prick think...that Ryth was his? If only he knew. I glanced at the passenger seat, remembering how her sweet body had looked angled toward me on the seat, her thin fingers slipping in deep. My cock hardened with the memory.

I gripped the bulge, and massaged. Fuck, I wanted more... wanted to taste her. I licked my lips, my tongue seeking her scent. But it was gone...leaving me fucking craving. I bet if I went down on her, I'd blow her fucking mind.

The thought of that tore something savage from my chest...until my damn phone *beeped* again.

Tobias: Stay the fuck away from her, Nick.

"Stay away? Who the fuck does he think he is?" I snarled out loud, my anger seething. I grabbed my phone. *You listen here, the kid doesn't belong to you.*

Because...she was mine.

The thought hit me out of nowhere. Hard and heavy, like brass knuckles to my chest. I sucked in a hard breath and tried to leash my anger. But it was savage when it came to T. The little fucking punk thought he was the only one hurting after mom died.

But she was my mom, too.

My mom, who I'd loved more than anyone...I just couldn't cope with seeing her at the end. Remorse waited for me in that deep, dark pit of despair. I'd tried to push it out of my mind, tried to bury myself in Natalie's cunt. But that only made me feel worse.

Because she was a cheating bitch. And I'd allowed it.

"Not anymore. I'm done," I muttered, hitting my texts.

But it wasn't Tobias I answered. It was the past. I should've done it a long time ago, when I'd found out the first time.

Nick: Don't bother me, we're done and hit send.

I could've ghosted her, it was what she deserved. No, what she deserved was to find me cock-deep in another bitch's pussy. Now that would've evened the score. But that didn't sit well with me, not the part about fucking someone else...just who that someone was.

But Ryth wasn't just a bitch, was she?

And the more I thought about her living in the same house, two bedrooms down from mine, it pushed me closer to the edge. That perfect pink pussy, slick, gleaming. I wanted to lick and suck and never come up for air.

Would she take my cock?

Christ, I hoped so.

The throb in my fucking pants turned savage. I looked down, the teeth of my zipper gleaming like fucking lights as I strained against my jeans. I hadn't been this hard in...forever.

Because of her.

My fucking stepsister.

Ryth.

Now, if only Tobias knew to back the fuck off...

I lifted my cell at Natalie's reply. I caught the *Nick, what?!? NOOO! PLEASE NICK! PLE—*

"Fuck that." I swiped and opened Tobias' text. *Nick: I watched her fuck herself this morning in my car, her pussy on full fucking display. I want it. So I'm telling you, T. Back the fuck off* and hit send.

A smile tugged at the corners of my mouth as I shoved the car into drive and pulled away. For the first time in forever, I felt good. Real fucking good.

Until the memory of that Audi pushed in.

I'd need to keep more of an eye on Ryth, make sure I was here the moment the fucking bell rang, to take her to our special park. At first, I'd thought it was a fucking joke, driving her... now I wouldn't have it any other way.

13

Ryth

I strode along the hallway and lifted my gaze to the towering guy waiting outside the door of AP class.

"Took your time." Gio gave me a wink. "Didn't think you were coming for a while there."

I looked away as heat rushed to my cheeks. "Sorry, got held up."

"Oh, yeah?" he followed me in, taking the seat behind me. "Anything interesting?"

"Okay, settle down everyone," the teacher called out, and motioned for the voices to settle.

For once, I didn't hear them. I didn't notice anything. Not the laughter or the chatter, or the way that heavy feeling grew on the back of my neck under Gio's stare. I was still back in that car, with excitement and shame moving through me. I couldn't believe I'd just done that...

Oh, fuck...what have I done?

"Hey."

I snapped back to reality and turned my head.

"You okay?" Gio scowled, his gaze serious. "You seem k-kinda out of it."

I forced a smile and nodded. "Sure."

But that was a lie...just like my entire life, it seemed. I tried to focus on the class, but I was still back there, my body quaking as I came under Nick's stare. I hadn't wanted to do that. I shouldn't have done that. *That wasn't me*...the good girl everyone saw. I lifted my gaze to the class, felt the weight of Gio's stare, and tugged my hair down to cover my face. In the wake of desire, fear pushed in.

I needed to stop it, whatever this was with Creed's sons. My pulse sped at the thought. It was *wrong*.

My mind was heavy, weighed down by the desperate need to figure this out.

Gio met my stare, giving me a confused smile before I turned away. My mom had divorced my dad without me even knowing...and now was marrying a man I barely knew, a man whose sons wanted nothing more than to torment and play with me. I needed to get out, needed to stop this before whatever this game they were playing was got further out of hand.

The bell rang before I knew it. Chairs scraped against the floor as the other students rushed out. I followed, my heart thundering...until the crash. *I wanted them.* That's why I was so conflicted. I wanted them and I liked what they did to me...a little too much.

"You want to walk to History?" Gio asked, his tone low and careful.

I pulled my thoughts away from them and glanced at him. "Sure."

"You're not pissed at me or anything, are y-you?"

I met his gaze as we walked out of the classroom and along the hall, following the herd. "No, of course not. Sorry, my...my mom told me she was divorcing my dad last night."

One brow lifted in surprise. "Whoa, that's heavy."

I nodded. "Yeah."

"No wonder you're distracted. I thought it was me for a moment, thought those Banks assholes had said something about us standing together yesterday."

"No." My mind was trapped by the *D word*. "They don't even know."

"Oh?" He flinched and glanced my way. "I just figured—"

"Figured what?"

"That you'd do whatever those assholes told you."

*Open your legs, show me...*Nick's demands rose in my head. *I need to make sure my little sister is satisfied.* "No," I answered. "Not everything."

"Good. 'Cause I was hoping you'd still want to go to Hanna's party this weekend."

I stepped around a group of others and thought about it. It'd be a way to break away from this hold they had over me. A way to make some friends. I glanced toward Gio. Maybe even more than friends.

Gio caught me looking, and a spark brightened in his gaze as he motioned to the class-room up ahead. "What?"

"Nothing," I muttered.

"You checking me out, Ryth?"

I flinched. "No."

His green eyes grew wider. "Yeah, you w-were. It's o-okay."

His stutter grew worse when he was embarrassed. Maybe I *was* checking him out, maybe I was a little desperate, desperate to get away from Creed and his sons. I stepped into the classroom, only this time Gio sat beside me.

I barely heard the chatter in the class, capturing just enough of the teacher's lecture to take notes on the laptop Creed had bought me. I guess I had to expect that now...him being my stepfather and all.

"So I want a three-thousand word paper on my desk by Monday on this." The teacher's words wrenched me from my thoughts. I jerked my gaze to the gray-haired professor wannabe with his glasses perched on the end of his nose.

"What?" I muttered.

"What?" Gio snapped, then the entire class groaned.

"Don't *ohhh me,*" the teacher snapped. "You all knew this was coming. I gave an entire lecture on this last week."

"But I wasn't here last week." I searched the faces of my other classmates.

But it didn't matter, they didn't hear me. No one did under the muttered swearing and pissed-off groans.

"I don't care..." The teacher shook his head. "Three thousand words on legislative social reform of the nineteen twenties," he called out as the bell rang and we all rose and shoved our chairs back. *"And it better be well researched, it's going to make up twenty percent of your overall grade!"*

Twenty percent?

Twenty goddamn percent? The classroom seemed to blur under the weight of my panic.

"Ms. Castlemaine."

I froze at the sound of my name, halfway to the door, and turned. Heads turned toward me and I caught a glimpse of snarls from a few of the girls, and in an instant, that mark on my cheek started to burn.

"Yes?"

"I expect you to be able to catch up," Davidson, or whatever his name was, said. "I won't be giving any special favors, even under the circumstances."

"Yeah, that she lives with the fucking Banks. Stuck-up bitch," someone called out.

I jerked my gaze around the room, scanning those who were looking at me. But they just stared...until Gio stepped in. "Enough. Come on." He motioned me forward.

"What the hell was that?" I glanced his way, unable to comprehend what had just happened. "What were they saying?"

"Nothing." He didn't meet my gaze, just ushered me out of the room.

Something was happening though. There was a shift...a dark, hateful shift happening all around me. I hadn't noticed it before, maybe I wasn't looking. But I felt it now, felt the anger and their stares. I glanced over my shoulder as they glared. The moment I stepped through the door and into the hallway, I was hit from behind.

"Get out of the fucking way, you traitorous cunt."

The impact slammed me off balance. I stumbled sideways and glanced toward them. But they were gone, striding through the crowded hallway filled with students.

"Jesus." Gio grabbed my arm, pulling me toward him. "You okay?"

"Fine," I answered. "What the hell was that about?"

"Nothing. Come on." He tried to pull me forward again, until I jerked from his hold.

"You keep saying nothing, but there's clearly *something*. What's going on here, Gio?"

A tortured look rose in his eyes before he pulled me gently, guiding me through the students toward our next class. The moment we were inside the classroom, he stepped in front of me. "Look, some of the students here are friends with the Rossis."

The Rossis?

The blood drained from my face.

Dad...*that's what this was all about.* It was about dad betraying them. I slowly shook my head. "But that's got nothing to do with me."

"Doesn't matter," he muttered, and glanced over his shoulder. "Not to them. Which is why you need to stay with me, okay?"

I glanced around his body. "All of them hate me?"

"Not all." He met my gaze.

I knew then, knew why he was so insistent for me to sit with him in class and at lunch. But what I didn't understand was why him...*and why me?*

"Okay, let's settle down," the female teacher called out.

She glanced my way as I turned, my fingers pressed against the throbbing ache in my forehead, one that was starting to grow. I sat there, catching glances my way from the other students and feeling like the entire world was against me...

Until finally, the last bell rang.

"Come on." Gio rose from his seat beside me. "Let's get you out of here."

But once I'd seen their hate the first time, it was all I could see. Not everyone looked at me, but there were enough. I grabbed my laptop, lingered long enough to stay out of the rush, then made my way to the front of the school.

Rumble...rumble...rumble...

I glanced up, finding that dark, midnight beast waiting for me at the curb. *I'll meet you here...and don't be talking to any boys this time.* Nick's warning filled my head.

"I'll walk with you for a bit," Gio offered.

I just shook my head, scattering that pounding roar throughout my head. "No, thanks, I got it."

I left Gio behind and strode toward the waiting Mustang, feeling that throb in my head grow barbs. Nick was watching the other cars when I yanked open the door and climbed in.

He wasn't chatty this afternoon, not demanding and snarly. Thank Christ for that. He shoved the car into gear before I had a chance to grab the seatbelt. And before I knew it, I was thrown hard against the door as we turned. Agony roared through my head as I slammed into the door, then clawed for the seatbelt and snapped it closed around me.

I waited for the snarl...

Waited for demands and the degradation.

I waited for *him*.

But he was silent all the way back home. The moment he pulled into the driveway and killed the engine, he turned to me. "Ryth..."

"Just leave it," I muttered, and shoved the door open. I couldn't deal with this, not any of this. Not dad, or mom...or my new predatory stepbrothers and now the kids at Duke who hated me. Nothing ever changed for me. *Nothing*. I clenched my fists, fighting the overwhelming urge to lash out or run, and I gripped the laptop to my chest and strode toward the house.

"Wait," Nick barked.

But I didn't, just shoved through the front door and made for the stairs.

I barely registered that the rest of the house was silent as I hit the top of the stairs.

"Ryth!" Nick roared, yanking me around to face him. "What the fuck is your problem?"

A bedroom door opened beyond me...the thud of heavy steps followed as Tobias stepped out. "What the fuck is going on, Nick?"

A chill rose along my spine as Tobias glared at Nick. "Brother. You and I need to talk."

14

Tobias

She fucking ran from us, barely glancing toward me before scurrying to her room. She should. She should lock herself in there and never come out. If she knew what was inside my head, she would. The moment she was gone, I turned to him...*my brother.*

"Look at me like that, T, and I'll lay you out."

"Look at *her* like that, brother, and I'll do more than lay *you* out."

His lips curled into a snarl. "You gonna do this here?"

"It's my house."

"Our fucking house, Tobias! And it's about time you remember that."

Caleb's door opened and he strode out. "Remember what?"

"That little brother here has had long enough to get rid of that chip on his goddamn shoulder."

"Nick," Caleb cautioned.

"No," my brother snapped, turning his pissed off glare my way. "It's about time we had this out."

"I'm not doing this," I forced the words through clenched teeth.

"Fine, walk away, go and hide in your goddamn room like you're so damn good at. But this shit *has* to stop, Tobias. Mom wouldn't..."

He didn't have time to finish. I lunged across the landing and swung, hitting the bastard on the jaw...then we went to the floor when he swung back.

"Tobias!" Caleb roared as I straddled Nick.

But I didn't hear him.

MINE...that word roared inside my head as I swung, connecting with my brother's cheek. His head snapped sideways, turning that hot, pissed off look in his eyes to cold, hard rage.

I swung again, unleashing a tirade of blows until my rage became all I cloud see. Some connected, some missed, driving through the air an inch from his nose. It didn't matter who I hit. I just needed to get it out. Get it all out. All the pain and the hurt...all the fucking loneliness. *God, I missed mom.*

"T, for fuck's sake!" Nick unleashed a hard blow, catching me right on the nose.

Stars erupted behind my eyes as I rocked backwards. The bastard didn't waste the opportunity, grabbing me around the throat with both hands and shoving me off him.

"Calm the fuck down!" he yelled as the sound of dad's car drifted in from outside.

The engine of his Mercedes only infuriated me more. *He was out there...out there with another fucking woman...*I swung again, even as Nick's grip around my throat clenched tighter.

The blow landed on his cheek once more, in the same spot as the last one. His cheek was already red, his eyes wild and teeth bared as laughter came from the doorway and spilled through the house.

"We're back, boys!" Dad called.

"Ryth, honey!" That bitch summoned her own...

In an instant, my rage was consumed into a vacuum, and my world along with it. I shoved away from my brother's grip on my neck, sucking in hard gulps of air.

"You're fucking losing it!" Nick stabbed his finger at me as he shoved up to stand, the corner of his lip bloody.

I didn't care that he was bleeding...didn't care about anything—movement came from the corner of my eye. I turned my head, finding her standing in her doorway, eyes wide...watching us in horror. The way she stood there, so fucking small...*so fucking insignificant.* A reminder of everything I'd lost.

My gaze went to that ugly fucking mark on her cheek as I strode closer. *"What the fuck are you looking at?"*

She flinched and took a step back, her eyes darting to my brothers behind me. I couldn't stop it...couldn't stop from grasping *her* around the throat with one hand, my thumb grazing her pulse, barely hard enough to hurt her, and forced her against the wall, dropping my mouth to her ear. "You think

I don't know what you did?" Hard breaths burned deeper. "So, you'll show him and not me? We'll see about that, Ryth...*we'll fucking see.*"

"Fuck you," she gasped under my grip and forced her gaze to mine. Tears shimmered in her eyes, but under that was something else. *Pain.* That's what it was.

"We have wedding cake to try!" that fucking whore downstairs called.

That ugly mark turned even darker on Ryth's cheek. I curled my lips at the sight before shoving away. She gasped and coughed, touching the red mark I'd left behind.

"You're losing it, T," Caleb snarled beside me, closing in so they wouldn't hear downstairs. "Leash it...*or else.*"

"Or else what?" I jerked my gaze to him. *"Or else* what, Caleb?"

"Boys?" our father called out.

I just held my brother's stare. I wanted to punch the fuck out of him, too. I wanted to hit them all and keep hitting them. I turned my focus back to Ryth. *All but her. I didn't want to hit her...I wanted to* own *her.* I sucked in a hard breath, and that faint, unmistakable scent of vanilla plunged inside me, invading my nose and my senses.

Until I turned and strode for my bedroom, slamming the door behind me with a *boom.*

Goddamn fucking bitch!

I stood there in the middle of my room, listening to their muffled words as they tried to console her. A door slammed a second later. I didn't need a goddamn map to know whose it was. My chest rose and fell as that savagery inside me calmed to wounded-fucking-lion level.

Fuck you, her choked words resurfaced. *Fuck me?*

The little bitch didn't know who she was playing with. I clenched my jaw and glanced toward the bed, my gaze seeking out the corner of her white cotton panties as they peeked out from under the spare pillow.

Fuck you.

There'd been fire in her eyes when she'd said that. *Real fucking fire.* The knowledge of that moved deeper...so my little mouse was growing some teeth. My cock twitched, even as the damn side of my face throbbed. I touched my tender jaw and winced, but still that hunger rose inside me.

The little fucking mouse.

I strode to the bed, grabbed her panties, and lifted them to my nose. *Fucking vanilla.* I reached for the zipper of my pants, then grabbed my cell from beside the pillow and brought up Nick's message. *I watched her fuck herself this morning in my car, her pussy on full fucking display. I want it. So I'm telling you, T. Back the fuck off.*

She'd showed Nick her cunt...

I reached inside my pants and gripped my cock. Christ, I was already hard.

She'd showed Nick her pretty little virgin cunt.

I closed my eyes. She'd fuck him. I just knew it. She'd fuck Caleb, too.

All three of us...taking turns with her.

126

The way we fucked, we'd ruin her by morning. I'd barely fisted myself before my balls tightened. *All three of us, taking turns over and over and over again.* She'd be our little secret, our own private fucking whore. She'd do anything we wanted...

Anything at all.

My ass tightened and the vein under my cock kicked as I came hard...and fast...and empty.

I opened my eyes. The thought of that resounding inside the darkness. I barely felt the ache in my jaw anymore. All I felt was that hunger, and the image of all three of us riding her into oblivion. My fingers shook as I dropped my cock and grabbed my cell, opening up Nick's message once more.

T: You want her? Well, so do I and pressed send.

A second was all it took for him to reply.

Nick: What the fuck are you saying?

I lifted my gaze from the message. That image of her underneath me while my brothers fucked her mouth and her ass rose inside me.

T: We all have her.

Nick: What do you mean 'all'?

T: You figure it out.

Silence. Silence while I waited for him to get it together. He was never the sharpest tool in the shed. Or maybe he didn't have the balls. Maybe he was comfortable fucking a bitch who he knew cheated on him.

Beep.

I looked down.

Nick: You're a sick fuck, brother, almost as sick as C. But I like it...I like it a fucking lot. I'm in.

"Yes," I murmured, my face hurting as I smiled. "We all are, brother. Now..." I glanced toward my door. "How to convince Caleb he wants this as much as we do."

I didn't know how to do it.

But I knew I wanted it.

I wanted to see her as she bucked and screamed, pleading with us to stop.

And I wanted to see her finally give in, give in to what her body craved...to us...I opened my texts and started typing.

15

Ryth

"Come down, guys!" mom called, oblivious to what had just happened. "We need help with this."

I glanced at the other two, then raced for the stairs.

You think I don't know what you did? Tobias' words bounced around in my head. *So, you'll show him and not me? We'll see about that, Ryth...we'll fucking see.* Heavy steps came from the others behind me as I hit the last step and made for the kitchen.

Cakes were displayed on the large island in the kitchen. I stared at the small mini versions and fought the need to throw up.

"The chocolate mud isn't my favorite." Mom scowled at the tasters, then lifted her gaze. "So I need your opinion, Ry." Then she glanced at Nick and Caleb behind me. "And both of you, as well."

"Seeing as how you'll probably be eating most of the damn thing," Creed muttered, pouring himself a Scotch.

They didn't notice a damn thing, just lived in their own private world, a world made up of wedding plans and secret, consuming love. Love that showed through when mom turned to Creed with a beaming smile and swatted him. They played, they laughed until Creed pulled her into his arms for a long, consuming kiss.

And I just stood there with the feel of Tobias' grip on my throat as a cell went *beep*. Nick grabbed his phone and scowled at the message.

His cheek was red and swelling and the small cut on his lip was beading with blood.

"So," mom urged, stepping out of Creed's arms to grab a fork from the counter and pushed it toward me. "Taste them and tell me which one you prefer."

I forced myself toward her, taking the utensil from her hand. But as I stabbed the first cake and tore a chunk from the side, I caught Nick lifting his gaze to me.

"I don't think the kids really care, hon," Creed murmured, pulling mom into his arms once more.

Revulsion swam in my belly as I placed the cake into my mouth and chewed. They didn't notice, not when Nick lifted his phone to Caleb and showed him the message. Goosebumps raced along my arms as they both looked at me.

My pulse quickened and the cake in my mouth turned into a hard wad that I swallowed. Nick turned back to his phone, his fingers flying across the keyboard as he replied. But it was Caleb who watched me now, Caleb's dark, unfathomable stare that made me shift my weight and stab the next cake.

I tried all four cakes, pointed to the plain vanilla one, and murmured, "That one."

Mom grinned, then shifted her attention to the two guys. "What do you think?"

Nick strode toward me, his lips tugging at the corners. The moment I met his gaze, I was back there in his car, with my hand stroking my core and his gaze riveted to the movement.

"I can get you a clean fork," Mom started as he took mine from my hand.

"This is fine. I don't mind swapping germs with my little sister," he winked at her and turned his attention to the display in front of him, lifted the fork in with one hand, and dropped the other to the front of his jeans, out of view from the other side of the counter.

I knew what he was thinking.

Knew what he was remembering as he clenched his fist around the bulge.

He took extra care and time, savoring each mouthful, and mom seemed to lap it up, her eyes sparkling as he moaned and took a bite of the next cake. "Yeah, the vanilla. I love it. C?" He held up the fork to the eldest of the three. "Want to share?"

There was something about Nick's words and the intensity in his voice.

Something about Caleb's stare, too, as he stepped closer and took the fork from his brother without saying a word. My pulse stuttered and my breath caught as Caleb casually sauntered over and stabbed one cake, then lifted some into his mouth, chewed twice, and swallowed.

"That one," he said, placing the fork down on the island before turning and striding from the kitchen.

He didn't look at me once as he left. But those heavy steps on the stairs hit a little harder.

"Excellent," Mom grinned and turned. "Did Tobias want to try?"

"No," Nick answered for him. "He's all in anyway, just now messaged me about it."

Mom fucking beamed and turned to Creed. "I told you. I told you they'd be into this. We just needed to give them a chance."

Creed glanced my way with a careful look on his face. He wasn't as convinced as mom hugged him, giggling like a damn schoolgirl. "You did." He wrapped his arms around her, his gaze still on me as Nick turned and strode from the kitchen.

⊏⊐

I WOKE EARLY the next morning, too damn early. The moment I surfaced, I thought of them. *Tobias, Nick...and now Caleb.* Their fixated attention. Their dark, hungry stares. I shoved the sheets away and climbed from my bed. It was still dark when I cracked open the door and listened to the silence before hurrying to the bathroom. This place had become a battleground. One I needed to learn how to navigate...if I was going to survive.

Cold tiles kissed my feet as I stepped in and closed the door quietly before using the toilet, then winced, holding my breath as I flushed. By the time I was racing back to my room, my pulse was out of control. I closed my door behind me and switched on the light, grabbed my laptop from the end of my bed, and set to work at my desk.

Stepbrothers or not, I had an assignment due by Monday, one I wasn't prepared for. I logged into the school portal and brought up the details before opening up a new document and started outlining my proposal.

By the time I lifted my head and noticed the sky was growing light outside, I was deep into the complexities of the nineteen twenties. I glanced at the scribbles on the paper in front of me and all the ideas I'd started then crossed out, and closed my eyes. The way I was going, I'd never find something substantial to write on.

I was going to fail.

My last year of school and I was going to fail.

I reached up, touching the birthmark on my cheek, and shoved upward. My back howled and my ass felt flat and sore. I massaged it, grabbed my school clothes, and hurried for the shower.

It was bliss being up this early in the morning. I showered, knowing those three assholes were still sound asleep, and for the first time in ages, I took my time. I shaved, scrubbed, and stepped out, glowing and red and feeling more alive than I had in weeks. My tortured thoughts returned to them, to their broody stares that seemed to gravitate toward me.

I wanted to know what that message Nick got last night had said. I wanted to know what was so interesting that he had to show Caleb...and that seemed to mention me. Why else would they look at me the way they had...

Why else would Nick have gotten hard?

He'd gotten hard. I froze, my grip clenched around the comb embedded in my hair. Through the misted mirror, I found that ugly red mark on my cheek. He'd gotten hard...and he'd looked at me. I shook my head. "No, it wasn't me."

Still, that nagging feeling remained.

Wasn't it?

He'd been hard in the car when he'd demanded I touch myself. He'd been hard when he looked at me. I closed my eyes at the thought. No guy had ever looked at me like that before. No one had barely given me a passing glance, let alone the kind of intensity that burned in their gazes.

First it was Tobias...

Then it was Nick.

Now it was Caleb.

I forced my eyes open and hurried, dragging my hair down to cover my face, and left the bathroom behind. My bare feet padded lightly, but a surge of panic still rose as I raced to my bedroom. *My bedroom*...the words repeated in my mind. I deserved to be here as much as they did. So why was I the one in fear, trying not to wake them?

Why was I the one scared at all?

I glanced at the mess of scribbles on my writing pad as I pulled on socks and shoved my feet into the ugly goddamn shoes. I didn't want to hide here anymore. I didn't want to cower from their anger. I didn't want to cower at all. The soft *thud* of a door echoed somewhere downstairs. I hurried, lunging to grab my laptop, and tore from my room to race for the stairs.

"Creed!" I called out as loudly as I dared.

He stopped with his hand on the door, dressed in navy blue business pants and an open-collared white shirt, and turned toward me. "Ryth, everything okay, honey?"

"Yeah," I smiled. "I was hoping I could get a lift to school with you, if that's okay?"

"It's a little early, but sure," he smiled, and gave a jerk of his head. "Come on, kid."

Kid.

The word felt almost alien as I followed him, walking past Nick's Mustang on the way. I let out a pent-up breath, my gaze drawn to that shiny black beast as I closed the door to Creed's Mercedes and snapped the seatbelt closed around me.

"I'm kinda glad for these few minutes alone, if I'm honest." He started the engine and hit the button on the gate sensor before backing out of the driveway.

His shirt pulled taut as he glanced over his shoulder and backed out, gripping the back of my seat. It was easy to see where his sons got their good looks and sex appeal. Creed might be a father, but he was toned and handsome, especially when he was dressed like that.

I tried not to look at him, forcing my gaze to the road as we braked and drove forward.

"Are you enjoying living with us?"

I clenched my jaw at the question, my heart pounding in the back of my throat. *Am I enjoying it?* Heat raced as I remembered the way Tobias had touched me under the table, and the way Nick had licked my fingers, slick with my own pleasure. Was I enjoying it? A surge of adrenaline hit me between the thighs as I opened my mouth to speak.

"I'm really hoping you are, because to be honest, Ry, I really like your mom."

His words were a splash of cold water to that uncontrollable desire.

"Like, really like her."

I glanced his way, catching the slight scowl, and something stilled inside me. "You do?"

"Yeah." He looked at me, then turned back to the road. "I do, which is why I'm hoping you're fitting in. The boys seem to be looking after you well, driving you to school and everything."

Looking after me? Sure, they were looking after me, if you called fingering me under the table and licking my cum from my fingers. Looking after me, the way they looked at me, the way they touched me. Their cruel hands on my breasts and wrapped around my throat.

Just like the men on the websites...

I swallowed, trying my best to push the panic down as Creed glanced my way. There was a flare of concern, of something akin to panic. But he loved my mom...he loved my mom, and this was the first time I'd seen her happy in years.

I'd ruin it...one word and I'd ruin it all.

"Yes," I answered, the word hollow and empty. "They're looking after me."

Relief swept through his gaze. "Oh, good...that's so good. They can be demanding at times and a goddamn pain in my ass, especially when all three are at home. But Nick and Caleb will be going soon and it'll be just you and Tobias."

A shudder ripped through me as the school appeared in the distance.

I didn't know which I dreaded more, the thought of all three of them after me...or Tobias on his own.

"Well, you're a little early, but I'm sure the study lab is open." He pulled the car over to the empty drop-off point. I reached for the door handle, yanked it open, and climbed out. "And Ry..."

He stopped me as I stepped out of the car, making me turn and bend back in. "Yeah?"

"I'm really enjoying having you as my stepdaughter. I just want you to know that, and by no means do I mean to take away from your real father. It's just, I always wanted a girl. So I'm glad I have you now."

The universe couldn't be any crueler, even if it tried.

I gave him a nod and the ghost of a smile before I muttered, "Me, too."

His smile grew as I closed the door and stepped away. I waited, feeling like the biggest goddamn failure in the world as he turned the car around and drove away. "Me, too?" I muttered. "Your one fucking chance to end this and that's all you have? *Me...too?*"

With a sigh, I turned and headed for the study lab, which was surprisingly busy when I entered. The teacher smiled at me, motioning toward a row of empty seats. I'd pulled out my laptop and logged into the school's wi-fi when my phone *beeped.*

I grabbed it out and glanced at the message.

Nick: Where the fuck are you, Ryth?

Fear ripped through me as I reread the message. But that fear was quickly replaced by something else, something deeper... something that didn't make me cower. Instead, I smiled as I punched out a reply.

Ryth: At school.

And I hit send. Barely a second later...

Nick: I drive you to goddamn school.

My smile grew wider. "Not anymore, asshole," I whispered.

"*Shh...*" another student hissed at me.

Even that didn't dampen the excitement inside me. Nick and the others might've thought they had me all figured out. They might've thought that somehow, I'd do exactly what they wanted....

They might've thought I was meek and pathetic. I tugged my hair across my cheek. *You gonna pay them a visit, my little lioness? You always were more like me than your mother.*

Dad's words filled me as I slipped my phone back into my pocket. A mouse...isn't that what Tobias had called me?

A mouse.

Beep.

My phone vibrated, but I ignored it.

And when it beeped again...and again, I turned the notifications to silent.

A mouse, huh?

I'd show them just how much of a mouse I really was.

16

Ryth

I worked on my assignment, finally nailing down what I was going to write before the bell sounded. Everyone else packed up in a hurry, so I followed, glancing at my schedule and the map as I found my way to my classroom. As usual, Gio was standing outside waiting.

"I looked for you this morning," he grumbled.

"Oh, you did? I came early." I strode past him and into the room, taking a seat off to the side.

"Yeah," he said as he slid into a seat behind me. "Don't tell me. Nick Banks had more important things to do?"

"No," I answered, trying to ignore that nagging annoyance. "You ask a lot of questions where they're concerned."

I caught the shrug over my shoulder. "Just curious."

About me or the guys I live with?

Stepbrothers, remember? I tried not to, shoving them from my mind as I focused on the class in front of me. But it didn't matter how much I wanted to ignore the fact my mom was getting married to Creed, it still pushed in.

She'd brought home wedding cakes, for God's sake. I winced at the thought, my heart aching for my dad. I wanted to see him, or at least talk to him. More importantly, I wanted to know what the lawyers were doing to bring him home.

The class passed in a blur, as well as the next one. I tried to think about my assignment due on Monday, and even though I had an idea of what I'd write my assignment on, getting it together in my head would require a serious amount of work. The bell rang for lunch, leaving me to push out my chair and grab my laptop. The moment I turned to Gio, he looked at me with a hurt expression.

"What?" I asked.

"You're different today." He shook his head. "I don't like it."

"Different how?"

"I dunno." He gave a shrug. "Colder toward me. Is there something I've done?"

"You worry about that a lot, don't you?" I grabbed his arm and dragged him with me toward the door.

"Fucking traitor," came the call the moment I stepped into the hall.

Eyes darted toward me. They all stared. My cheeks burned under the outburst, but this time I didn't run and hide. This time, I met each gaze. "Who said that?"

No one answered. Instead, they shuffled past, pretending it hadn't happened.

But I couldn't pretend, not anymore. I may as well stand there and let them hurt me.

"I'm not a fucking *traitor!*" I screamed. *"I'M NOT MY DAD!"*

Hard breaths tore from me as I seethed.

"Hey, you okay?" Gio touched my arm, making me flinch and pull away. But he didn't mean it as anything other than comfort.

"Sorry," I muttered, watching as everyone walked past.

"It's fine." He smiled. "Why don't we get something to eat and sit outside, my treat this time."

I nodded, followed him to the vending machines, and took the sandwich and cola when it was offered, then accompanied him outside. The sun was warm, caressing my body as I sat on top of the table next to Gio and closed my eyes.

"Hanna's party is going to be awesome."

I vaguely caught the tail end of his chatter and opened my eyes, instantly remembering something about the wedding. "Not sure I can make it."

"What?"

"The party." I glanced his way. "Mom has dress fittings this weekend and something about a party. I guess I'll be expected to attend."

Panic crossed his eyes and for a second, I was confused, why would he panic about that? Then he moved, leaned across the table and kissed me.

"Gio!" I shoved him away, my face burning. "What the hell was that?"

He looked shocked, confused. His brow furrowed as he looked around to see if anyone had seen me rebuke him. "I thought...I mean, I like you, Ryth."

"You like me? You barely know me." I fought the need to wipe the feel of his lips from my mouth.

At least Tobias and Nick never tried to kiss me...

The unwanted thought surfaced before I shoved it away. Gross...I didn't know why I thought that, why that would even come into my mind, yet it had...and it brought with it the image of Nick as he'd gripped my wrist and guided my slick fingers into his mouth.

I knew what he'd wanted, knew what that meant, and I knew what came after. I closed my legs, trying to will that sick desire away.

"I'm sorry," Gio muttered, and looked away, embarrassed, making me feel like a real bitch.

"No, I'm sorry. I just got scared, okay? I wasn't expecting it."

He looked at me, a spark of hope igniting in his eyes. "I get it. I came on too strong."

"Yeah, kinda." I gave him a smile.

"But that's not a no..."

God save me. "No, that's not a no."

He grinned, cracked open his cola, and drank hard and long before giving me a nod. "Next time, I'll give you fair warning."

Next time...

I smothered my panic by grabbing my sandwich, watching for movement in the corner of my eye as I opened the packet and took a bite. He wouldn't kiss me with a mouthful of ham and rye...*surely*. If he did, what then?

Then I'd have to tell my stepbrothers, wouldn't I?

The thought of that filled me. *"Someone kissed me today at school."* I could almost see the thunder in their eyes.

They were possessive.

And controlling.

And utterly disgusting.

That heat rose inside me.

"You're smiling."

I jerked away from the thought and felt the curl on my lips, killing it instantly. "Just thinking about the wedding."

"Oh? You're all for it now, are you?"

"If it makes mom happy."

"*Is* she happy?" he asked as the bell rang for class.

I grabbed my trash and slid from the table. "Yeah, you know, I think she really is."

Which made living there with those assholes all the more like Hell. Why couldn't they be normal instead of gorgeous and rich and driving seriously hot cars? Why couldn't I, just for once, slink away into the shadows.

I followed Gio as we made our way to class. Just before I stepped inside, my cell vibrated in my pocket. I pulled it out and looked at the five missed calls and ten texts from Nick. He was pissed...more than pissed.

Nick: I'm warning you, Ryth. You won't like playing this game with me...

"Won't I?" I murmured, switching my phone off before sliding it back into my pocket. "We'll see about that."

"Won't what?" Gio asked, taking the seat next to me.

"Nothing." I shook my head and focused on the class.

I thought about him all during the lecture, until my mind turned to mom. The cakes were just the start of it. She was different, freer around Creed...*she was in love.* Was that what love looked like? Like you were blind to everyone and everything else?

The last bell rang suddenly, making me jolt. Gio was up, reaching for my arm before I glanced up at him.

He looked at me as though I'd slapped him. "It's fine, Ryth. I'm not going to try to kiss you in class."

"No," I answered with a smile "I didn't think that."

I walked with him along the hallways and stepped outside into the warm sunshine once more...before I was grabbed and hauled backwards. Panic reared, and I was fighting as I spun. Nick's glare was venomous as he manhandled me, shoving me toward the drop-off point where his car waited.

"Get your fucking hands off me!" I screamed, tearing my arm from his hold.

But he was back beside me in an instant, crowding me until he was all I saw. "This isn't what you think, Ry. Now get in the goddamn car."

I shook my head, lurching away from him. I felt them now, all the shocked stares as the entire school watched Nick's possessive rage, then in an instant, Nick lunged and grabbed me around my waist to haul me into the air. I barely held onto my laptop, clamping my fingers around the edge as I landed hard on his shoulder. My feet dangled, my ass up in the air as he strode toward the Mustang, then dumped me on my feet.

He yanked open the passenger door and forced me down with a hand on top of my head. "Stay," he commanded, his voice low and hostile. "You run from me, and so help me God, Ryth, I'll tackle you to the goddamn ground in front of everyone, and I'll make damn sure your skirt rides high enough to show everyone what's mine."

My heart pounded. My face burned as I glanced toward the entire school as they watched. And Gio was there, standing in the middle, his gaze fixed on me.

"You want that?" Nick demanded.

I shook my head, tears blurring their faces. "Good, now put your goddamn seatbelt on."

The door closed with a *thud*. One that made me jolt, but I couldn't move, couldn't look away from Gio's scowl as he fixed his glare on Nick, his lips curling in a sneer. The driver's door opened, then slammed closed.

A snarl came from Nick before he reached across me, his hand brushing my breast as he yanked the seatbelt over me and clasped it into place. The engine started in a burst of noise and we were peeling away from the drop-off point, tires squealing as we went.

Now he shows off...

Now, when the road in front of me shimmered through my tears.

Now, while everyone stared.

Nick glared at me as he drove, stealing quick glances at the road, his hands fisted around the steering wheel, his foot heavy on the gas. I hated him...*I hated him...I HATED HIM!*

"You want to go to our park?"

My breath caught with the words. But I didn't dare meet his gaze.

"You want to yell and scream and hit me?"

I clenched my jaw. "No."

"No?"

I jerked my gaze to his. *"I SAID NO!"*

"Well, too fucking bad, Ryth." He jerked the wheel, tearing us through a yield sign and toward oncoming traffic.

I slammed into the door and clamped down on a scream as he steadied the car, downshifted, and roared along the streets until a familiar place came into view. The moment he braked and slowed the Mustang, I risked a glance around the parking lot.

It was empty. Just like he'd said it was always empty. I hit the seatbelt release, clawed the door handle, and shoved open the door before he had a chance to fully stop.

"Fuck!" he roared behind me as I lunged, tore across the parking lot, and headed for the empty swings.

The heavy thud of his steps came barely a second later, the car left idling. He was fast, faster than I could ever be.

He grabbed me around the waist and lifted. Only this time, I turned on him and fought back, but I stumbled and lost my balance. He barely caught me, pulling me against him as we both fell and hit the ground.

The impact knocked the air from my lungs in a *whoosh*. I tried to breathe and get out from under him, but he grabbed my wrists and pinned them to the ground above my head.

"Stop," he demanded as I coughed and choked, fighting with all I had. *"Ryth, stop."*

I sucked in a breath. *"Get off me!"*

"No."

I bucked my hips, driving against him as hard as I could, as those menacing eyes glared down at me. I knew the instant anger shifted to something else in him, something just as hungry and just as dangerous...*for me.*

"You want to fight me, Ryth?" He ground his cock against me.

I could tell he was already hard.

"You don't want to answer my goddamn calls...or reply to my fucking texts? You don't want me to drive you to school so you can see your little friends?"

"No," I spat, glaring at him. "No, I don't."

"You think you have a goddamn choice here?"

He lowered his gaze to my shirt as it rode up, then moved my hands until he clasped them in one. "You have the most perfect fucking pussy I've ever seen." He reached between my thighs, his fingers brushing against my panties. "I want to look into your eyes as you come, want to hear your breath catch. I want to see that slow slide into oblivion when you give yourself to us."

US??

I shook my head and squeezed my eyes closed. "No...you're my stepbrother."

"Who else will treat you right, little sister?"

I threw my head to the side as his thumb slid along my crease, finding my clit. "Who else is going to give you what this body craves?" he demanded.

"Not...*you*." I jerked my gaze to his, letting him see the savage in me. "Go to fucking Hell, Nick...*and take your goddamn brother with you.*"

17

Ryth

I shoved him away and scrambled to my feet.

"Okay." Nick pushed up to stand, holding his hands out. "Easy."

My breaths were hard and sharp, tearing from my body as I lifted my hand to the twigs and leaves in my hair. "You want to take me home, Nick? Then take me home *right now*. But I swear to God, you do that to me again, I'll tell mom...*everything*."

Defiance was a lit match in his gaze. "You won't, or you would've by now. You liked it, Ryth. You can deny it to yourself all you want, but don't try to lie to me."

I started to shake my head.

"You gonna stand there and tell me you're not wet? I bet if I parted your legs right now, I could prove you a liar."

I froze, unable to say another word.

But I didn't need to. Nick just nodded. "I drive you, Ryth, you got it? You want to go somewhere, *anywhere*, you come to me."

Come to him...he smiled with those words. I bet he'd like it, too, bet he'd like me needing him. But the truth was, I did need him, unless... "I could always dr—"

"Fat chance." He cut me off with a glare before he turned. "And don't even think about taking my goddamn keys, the car's fitted with a kill switch. I'd call up and kill the engine in an instant, leave you stranded on the side of the road just to prove a goddamn point."

He would, too...I just knew it. He motioned me forward. "Come on, Ryth. I'll take you home."

The tension seemed to ease between us when I climbed back in the idling car. I yanked my seatbelt closed as he gave me a sideways glare, then reached across and brushed the dirt from my knees. "Can't have anyone thinking we just rolled around in the dirt, now can we?"

"But that's exactly what we just did," I replied.

He smiled, giving me a wink. "Next time, answer my fucking texts, Ryth."

So I was theirs to command now? They'd say jump and I asked how goddamn high, and if I didn't do what they wanted, they'd what...*make me?*

I forced myself to focus straight ahead as Nick shoved the Mustang into gear and pulled out of the parking lot. It didn't sit right, them *making* me. But there was something inside me that writhed under the knowledge. Something that wanted them. I glanced across at Nick.

"Told you before, Ryth," he muttered without looking my way. "All you gotta do is ask, you can look at whatever you want."

Oh...my...God...

I bet he would, bet he'd pull the car over right now if I asked him. I bet he'd lay me down and take care of that constant ache between my thighs, the one that'd started the night he held me still so his brother could touch me. But I didn't ask. I bit the insides of my cheeks as I clamped my mouth shut as Nick pulled into our driveway.

"Ryth," Nick called as I shoved open the door.

I froze, my hand gripping the handle, but didn't turn around.

"Whatever you need, princess."

I swallowed hard, closed the door behind me, and strode to the front door, my steps hurried. I clutched my laptop and raced upstairs, taking comfort in the only thing I could right now...*the fact that both Nick and Caleb were leaving.*

I closed my bedroom door and pressed my spine back against it. Footsteps thudded up the stairs, lingering outside my door before they continued. I tracked the sound all the way to his bedroom.

Beep.

My cell vibrated. I grabbed it from my pocket, finding a message from Gio.

Gio: You okay?

I winced, hating how he and the rest of the entire school saw what had happened.

Yeah, pain in the ass big brothers. I'm home now, and fine.

I waited for the response. I didn't have to wait long.

Gio: Didn't look like a big brother kind of thing, Ryth. More like a jealous boyfriend kind of thing.

I stared at the message and didn't know what to say. In the end, I hedged.

All good, I'll talk to you tomorrow Gio.

But the truth was, I didn't want to talk to him. I didn't want to talk to anyone. They didn't understand what it was like living in this house. *They didn't understand me.* I wasn't afraid of them, not anymore. Whatever had shaken free when I first came here was now something else. Something just as ungrateful damaged...*and out of control.* I glanced at my door, just like they were.

But I understood something now, something I hadn't understood before.

Something about me triggered something in them. I didn't understand it. I didn't like it, but I sure as hell felt it. I'd seen it in Nick's eyes today and seen it in Tobias' last night when he had his hand around my throat. They were drowning in pain... swept away by grief, and for some reason, they were clawing me, tearing me apart, desperate to feel something.

I made them feel.

Desperation.

Anger.

Lust.

All of it.

I glance at Gio's message as I made my way to the desk, looking at the *more like a jealous boyfriend kind of thing.*

A boyfriend. Is that how they saw themselves? I thought of Tobias and the hate and rage in those dark eyes. A boyfriend... maybe with Nick, but not with him. I didn't think Tobias saw himself as anything but the bad guy. Maybe he just needed someone to show him he was wrong?

I set up my laptop, then cracked open my bedroom door and checked the hall before making my way downstairs to the kitchen. I made myself something to eat and grabbed a glass of orange juice before making my way upstairs once more. The grunts and groans of sex echoed from under Tobias' door.

I stopped, listening. For a second, I thought he had someone in there, until I realized there wasn't anyone else...just Tobias...*watching porn.* My cheeks burned as I made my way to my room and closed the door behind me.

I tried to settle, tried to focus on my assignment, but my gaze kept moving to the door. I wanted to know what he looked at, wanted to know what made him excited. I wanted to step onto his room and touch his things.

I wanted to touch him.

I swallowed hard, bit down on the sandwich, and took a gulp of juice to wash it down, then I forced myself to work. I worked until it was dark and I finally heard the sound of an engine before I rose from my seat and stretched. I was making headway in small steps, gathering the information I needed to plead my case.

If I had a solid day to get the rest of this together...

I glanced toward the door. If I had a day or two at home, I'd finish this and maybe...maybe I'd be able to see dad. I stepped out of my room and quietly made my way past Tobias' room, knocking gently on Nick's door.

"Yeah?" he called.

I opened the door and stepped in, closing it softly behind me. He was hunched over the keyboard, watching some kind of stock exchange I'd never seen before.

"You need something, princess?" he murmured, not even looking my way.

"You said you'd drive me, so I want to go somewhere."

"Now?" He glanced up.

"No." I shook my head. "Tomorrow."

He turned toward me then and leaned back in his seat. "I'm all ears."

"Mitchelton Prison."

One brow rose. "Your dad?"

I gave a quiet nod.

"What time?"

"Ten? That okay?"

"Consider it a date." He turned back to the screen, his fingers flying across the keyboard as he punched in numbers and hit buttons. "You need anything else, Ryth?"

The way he said it made my pulse race. "No," I answered quickly and left, closed the door behind me, and headed for the stairs. Creed was pouring himself a Scotch when I walked into the kitchen. I glanced around. "Mom's not with you?"

"No." He gave me a smile. "Apparently she's at a wine and cheese night, so it's just us to fend for ourselves."

"She went alone?"

He glanced at me and frowned. "No, why would you say that?"

Because my mom didn't have any friends, none that I knew of, anyway...until Creed.

"She went with some of the wives of my friends." He rounded the counter and pulled me into a hug. "Don't worry, sweetheart, your mom's well taken care of now."

I winced at his words. *She was taken care of before...well, I'd thought she was, at least.* It seemed like she was desperate to leave that old life behind, but at least she was taking me with her. Creed pulled back and looked down at me. "You know what, fuck it. Let the boys fend for themselves, how about it's just you and me, what do you say, kid?"

I'd say I'd had enough of his sons for one day. "Sounds amazing," I smiled.

He gave a deep chuckle and hugged me a little harder before stepping away, and for the first time, I felt a deep yearning. I watched Creed as he made his way around the counter, opened a drawer, and pulled out a handful of menus. "Now, just decide what food you want."

He was being nice to me and he looked like he really liked my mom. This...whatever this was, it felt *good*.

I wondered what she'd been like, Creed's wife. I wondered what kind of wife she'd been and if she'd been a good mom.

Sadness gripped my heart at the thought. Tobias was hurting, the kind of hurt that didn't come from an empty well. She'd loved them, and she'd loved them well.

I rounded the counter, feeling the aching loss the woman I hadn't known had left behind and this time, I was the one who hugged Creed. I wrapped my arms around his waist. He stiffened for a second, then melted, pulling me against him.

God, I'd missed this.

I missed dad, even if he'd never really been like this, never been so affectionate, and had seldom even been home. Tears welled in my eyes and slid free. Creed seemed to understand and without speaking, held me as I sobbed.

I didn't know why I cried. But I knew some of my tears weren't for me. They were for the assholes upstairs. The assholes I was starting to care about. I found myself falling for them...them and this dysfunctional, damaged family.

"You okay?" Creed broke the spell.

I dropped my arms, wiped my cheeks, and nodded. "Sure, just tired I think."

"Everything okay today?"

I met his gaze and those dark gray-blue eyes seemed to darken. His eyes narrowed as I looked away.

"They know...know about dad. The kids at school, I mean."

He grabbed my arm gently, forcing my gaze to his. "Did they say something to you?" His tone turned cold. "Did they...hurt you?"

That shove came back to me, but I shook my head. "It's fine."

"It's not fine if they hurt you, Ry."

That ache inside me that already felt too much for this man and this family swelled inside me. "It's nothing I can't handle, put it that way."

"Okay," he gave a sigh. "I respect that. But *if* it does ever get too much, I want you to come to me."

I gave the ghost of a smile and nodded.

"Promise?"

My smile grew wider. He just didn't leave well enough alone, did he? It was easy to see where his sons got their tenacity. "And if you're not comfortable telling me, then I want you to talk to the boys. They know the school and will help. Besides," he gave a chuckle. "They seem to have taken an instant liking to you. I haven't seen Nick away from his damn games like this for ages."

My body clenched tight, remembering the way he'd hauled me over his shoulder like I was a brat and carried me to the car in front of everyone.

"Now, about this food." Creed slid the menus my way. "It's your night, so your choice."

I settled on my favorite, Chinese with soup dumplings, and when the food came, we sat in the living room, trying our best to impress each other with our pathetic skills using chopsticks. I found myself laughing when he grew frustrated and stabbed the thing and ate it, caveman style.

By the time mom came home, I was happy and stuffed. Creed's sleeves were rolled up and he wore this kind of goofy grin on his face when she walked in, slightly intoxicated. Mom took one look at the two of us giggling like idiots on the sofa and chuckled. "Looks like you guys had a better night than I did."

Good food.

Good company.

Sitting at home.

What more could I ask for?

Mom laughed again, kicked off her heels, and went to the kitchen. "I need water."

I watched her leave, my gaze drifting to the shadowed outline behind Creed's shoulder on the stairs, a shadow that moved when I stared longer, a shadow that stepped forward, glaring at me with betrayal.

A shadow which was going to be my stepbrother...

Tobias.

18

Ryth

"You ready, princess?"

I lifted my gaze from the keyboard, the scowl still trapped on my face. "Yeah."

"Something bothering you?" He stepped closer, peering at the mess of information scribbled across a hundred different colored sticky notes attached to the wall behind my desk. "Looks complicated."

"It is." I shoved upwards, stepped around him, and grabbed my bag. "I think I'm going to die of old age before I get it finished."

"At least you have some extra time," he said carefully. "Seeing as how you're staying home the next couple of days."

My cheeks burned with the memory. Last night Creed had told mom that I'd had some trouble at school and that it seemed to be taking a toll on me. I hadn't meant to break down and cry in front of him. I hadn't meant to cry in front of anyone. It had just happened.

But mom just nodded and brushed her fingers along my cheek and over my mark before pulling me close. I think it was the alcohol more than anything that made her hug me. But still, I took it. This was the mom I remembered, the one grounded in reality and not distant and cold.

She didn't have a problem with me staying home, didn't even cause a fuss when I said I wanted to visit dad, just nodded carefully. But she couldn't hide her relief when I told her Nick was taking me. Instead, she seemed overjoyed, gushing about how the boys were taking care of me.

If only she knew.

I suppressed a shudder

"I'll just grab my bag and some snacks." I stepped around him, reaching for my shoulder bag and jacket.

"Snacks," Nick muttered, and shook his head. "What do you think this is, Ryth, a damn school trip?"

I shot him a glare. "I can't have you spending all your money on food as well as fuel."

He looked at me with a deadpan expression, then let out a bark of laughter. "All my money, huh?" He stepped close, capturing my gaze. All I saw was gold in his eyes. "You'd have to eat your bodyweight in food for the next hundred years to come close to tapping me dry, little sister. So, thanks for the concern, but I think I can manage."

A hundred years? I looked at him, bewildered.

"You think I sit in there playing games all damn day?" He lifted his hand to brush the hair from the side of my face, his gaze boring into mine. "Little sister, I have enough money in Bitcoin to make sure I never have to lift a finger again...and my wife, or my damn kids, for that matter."

My breath stilled.

Wife...

Kids...

My heart clenched tight with the words as the room around me swayed. I felt myself falling. Falling onto him, and for him...for this sick, hungry need that seemed to control me when I was around them, a need I knew wasn't right, but that didn't change what it was.

"You okay, princess? Kinda looking at me strange now." Nick let his fingers trail down my neck, knowing exactly what kind of force he was exerting on me.

"Fine," I mumbled, and swallowed.

He smiled, that cockiness rising before he dropped his hand and stepped away. "So that settled it, yeah?" he threw over his shoulder as he strode from my bedroom. "No goddamn snacks in the car."

I gave a huff. That's all he cared about, wasn't it? His precious damn Mustang.

I followed, grumbling the entire away as we walked outside and climbed into the midnight beast. We backed out and were on the road before I knew it, passing the green view of the surrounding forest this side of the city and heading for the highway.

The last time I'd taken this drive, I was with Creed and mom, the day before they...

Before they...

Got together.

I winced and stared out the window. "How long do you think it was going on?"

Nick glanced my way and shifted gears, overtaking other cars at a steady pace. They whipped past us in a blur, or maybe it was the other way around. I was too scared to look.

"Your mom and my dad, you mean?"

I nodded and turned his way.

He clenched his jaw. Maybe he'd never thought about it, or maybe he had and he didn't like the answer. Either way, it didn't really matter.

"Long enough, how's that?" he said finally, shutting the conversation down.

But I wasn't done with the heavy questions, and now that I had Nick trapped with me for the next few hours at least, I wanted to find out all I could. "What was she like, your mom, I mean?"

"Jesus, Ryth," he muttered, surging toward the on-ramp that'd take us west. Silence filled the space for a while until he started talking. "You know how a storm can smother the sun, how it can get so dark that you'd swear it was night, and you stand there, waiting for that first clap of thunder and the downpour... then all of a sudden the storm changes. It breaks up and through the cracks of the storm, the sun that'd always been there shines through?" He stilled, then glanced my way, his words trembling. "She was that sun. She was everyone's sun. That's who she was."

Naomi Banks.

I still saw her name printed on that sticker wrapped around the stainless medical equipment.

"She was warm, loving. She loved Tobias hard and he loved her back just as hard."

Did I hear an echo of sorrow? Like he wasn't jealous of that love, but had still been left wanting.

"How did she love you?"

His smile was instant. "That was easy. She taught me to be independent. Sky diving, motocross racing, she even took me to get the shit beaten out of me learning MMA fighting."

"Sounds gruesome."

His grin grew wider. "I loved every second of it. More importantly, she taught me about cryptocurrency and how to be a trader."

"Oh, that's what that was...the stock exchange I saw you working on yesterday."

He nodded. "Yeah, sold a heap, bought a heap more. She taught me what to look out for, a small company with solid groundwork and the ability to expand within their means. That's what I do, I buy and trade."

So that's why he didn't have a job to go to.

"Mom taught me that, all those hours sitting in board meetings and listening to her as she broke companies down and rebuilt them better from the ground up."

I flinched and jerked my gaze to his. "Board meetings? But I thought..."

He met my gaze and scowled. "You thought what? You thought dad was the one with the money? That he was the one everyone looked up to?"

But all those cards, addressed to Creed. I'd just assumed he was the driving force in their family...it seemed I'd assumed wrong.

"Mom said they met at Harvard and that for her it was love at first sight. Dad, however, took a little convincing. But she'd never met a challenge she didn't give her all to, so eventually they started dating and became engaged. When she graduated, she graduated with honors. It didn't take her long to get snatched up by some big corporation, which she stayed with for a while, until she became pregnant with Caleb and went out on her own."

"She sounds impressive," I said in awe.

"She was...still is."

I glanced toward the road. "No wonder Tobias hates us."

"T is just T. He took her death hard, harder than the rest of us. Don't take it personally."

I shot him a look filled with daggers. It was easy for him to say. It wasn't *his* body his brother had violated under the table as our parents announced their engagement. An engagement that was coming to an end...and soon.

What then...

What happens after the wedding, when there was no way I could avoid Tobias, or Nick for that matter? I glanced across the seat to his black jeans and his thick boots and the silver rings he wore on his fingers, then to the hard muscles under his shirt. Muscles I knew he honed daily in the gym on the first floor of the house. I'd seen him come back, striding up the stairs to head to the bathroom, his shirt soaked and stuck to his skin.

Tobias I hadn't seen. He preferred to leave, tearing out of the driveway early in the morning, to come home hours later and, when he was really pissed, strapped on his sneakers and headed out running. Caleb, too, although he left at night. Every time I tried to catch glances at him from the doorway of my bedroom, I wasn't fast enough. No, Caleb liked the night, coming home at the first break of day.

I heard him, heard his light steps in the stairwell, heard when he lingered in the hall outside my door and finally left. I heard all of that lying in bed with my breath trapped in my chest and my pulse throbbing between my thighs.

I clenched my knees together and watched the landscape change as we left the city behind and headed for Mitchelton. It wasn't too far out of the city, but far enough for me to watch Nick as he drove with expert skill. The longer I watched him, the more I saw.

I saw the years of sheer adrenaline recklessness, saw the way he drove hard and fast, how he didn't give a fuck what anyone else thought of him. I remembered how he'd pounced on me, hauling me over his shoulder the moment I'd stepped outside of school.

As though he read my mind, he muttered. "Still pissed at me for yesterday?"

"Yes," I snapped. "I am, actually."

He smiled. "Good. I liked you with a little bite."

I lashed out, slapping his shoulder. "I'll give you a bite."

"I wish you fucking would," he answered, his gaze drifting down my body before turning back to the road. "Bite, lick, swallow. All in that order."

Heat rose to my cheeks, forcing my gaze away.

"I fucking love it when you blush like that, Ryth. It does things to me...dangerous things. Things that make me want to take a goddamn detour and find us another secluded park."

His words only made me blush harder. "Not funny," I muttered, and tried to keep my breathing under control.

"Not a damn thing funny about the bulge in my fucking jeans."

I tried not to look...I really did. But he turned his head, glancing over his shoulder, and I did. My gaze fixed on that thick round ridge, wondering just how *big* he really was...until he caught me looking.

His low chuckle echoed through the car, then quieted as he signaled and turned onto the road marked by signs for Mitchelton Prison. The sun was shining, bouncing off the rooftops of cars in the parking lot.

The Mustang carved through the spaces, finding a spot up close to the entrance before Nick killed the engine. "You want me to come in with you?"

I stared at the towering fences and the cold, ugly brick building and shook my head. "Thanks, but I got this."

I didn't wait, just shoved open the door.

"I'll be right here," Nick said as I started to close the door.

Those words stayed with me as I headed for the entrance. It was as though he knew I needed something to hold onto as I stepped through the automatic door and was stopped by the guards. I gave my name and details, then a brisk search and a check of the visitor records, and I was allowed into the room to see dad.

I waited, my knee bouncing with nervous tension that stopped dead when the door opened. But it wasn't dad who came through. I waited...and the longer I waited, the more upset I became. What was taking so long? *Didn't he want to see me?*

The words hit me like a stab to the chest, until the doors finally opened and an old man shuffled out. It took me a second to realize it was dad. He was hunched, walking with a slow, limping gait and it wasn't until he was close to the plexiglass barrier that he lifted his head and looked at me.

He was bad...real bad. One eyeball was black and bulging, the side of his face was grazed and bloody, his lips were swollen, and he was missing a tooth.

"Dad?"

There was no smile this time, no, *I'm fine, Ry. I'm fine.*

There was just a wince and an achingly slow descent to the chair in front of him. Tears filled my eyes at the sight of him.

"Ryth, honey...don't. Don't cry."

"W-who did this to you?"

There was a tiny shake of his head. Those swollen lips parted.

Slick warmth spilled down my cheeks. I made no move to brush the tears away. "And don't tell me you have it under control."

"It's just a misunderstanding, that's all."

"The *Rossis?*

He flinched and jerked his gaze around, panic flaring for a second. "Ryth, *no.*"

I clenched my fist and leaned close to the barrier. "Then tell me? Who?"

"I don't know," he murmured, holding my gaze. "And that's the God's honest truth. Someone out there has set me up. I don't know who or why. But I've got people working to find out."

"You mean Creed Banks?"

Dad gave a nod. "He's a good guy, Ry. He'll treat your mom well, better than I ever did."

"Don't say that," I whispered. But I saw the truth in his eyes. He believed it and that was dangerous.

A man with no hope was a man drowning, and that's what I saw when I looked at him.

He wasn't even reaching for a rope.

"Dad, I need you to keep fighting. I *need* you to come home."

"What home, kid?"

I shoved up, standing to press against the barrier. "Me...*I'm home, aren't I?*"

"Sit down!" the guard called.

I sank to the chair once more. There was a flare of anger in dad's eyes as he glared at the guard. I held onto that glare. He hadn't given up completely, not yet. I still had a chance.

"I hear the wedding is soon," he said quietly. "I need you to do whatever your mom needs, Ry. Do that for me, because I can't. I can't give her happiness, but you can."

"I will...if you promise me you'll keep fighting."

"Time, Castlemaine!" the guard called.

I shook my head. "But we haven't had our hour."

Dad just shook his head and rose cautiously, without even a fuss.

"Dad, we haven't had our hour."

He gave me a smile and stepped away. "It's okay, honey," he said carefully. "We'll have plenty of time once I'm out."

He shimmered as fresh tears filled my eyes. I watched helplessly as he shuffled away. With a nod to the guard, he stepped through the open door and was gone. I understood then.

Understood what had taken him so long.

Understood why the visit was cut short.

He didn't want to see me.

A moan bubbled up from inside me and tore free. I clasped my around my waist and rocked under the weight of it. But it wasn't enough...nothing was enough to ease the agony inside. I shoved up from the chair, and in a haze of agony, I stumbled out of the visiting room and along the hall.

I hardly heard the guards when they spoke to me, barely saw my hand move across the page when I signed my name. By the time I stumbled out into the sunshine, that agony bubbling inside me was turning into a scream. I stumbled forward, unable to see a thing through my tears.

I was going to break down...

Going to crack.

Going to fall...

"I got you." Arms wrapped around me. "I got you, Ryth. *Hold on to me.*"

I dropped my head against him as the shudders tore free.

He was all I had to hold onto.

My anchor in a turbulent sea.

Shudders overtook me. Nick eased me back along the walkway to the Mustang. "Get in, princess. I'm getting you the fuck out of here."

I didn't fight him this time, just let him open the door and ease me inside before buckling the seatbelt across me. I flinched with the *thud* of the passenger door, then he was striding around the front of the car in a blur of black and climbed in behind the wheel.

The car started with a roar and the tires howled as we tore out of the parking lot and were gone.

"Hey." He reached across the seat to grip my hand.

I stared at his fingers, my head dropped low. Tears fell to splatter on his arm, but he didn't move, just steered the car with one hand, driving away from there as fast as he could.

I closed my eyes, my fingers clenched around his. By the time he slowed the car, making me lift my head, we were nowhere near the prison. We'd turned off somewhere and now were heading toward a diner in the middle of nowhere.

Nick pulled the car into the parking lot and stopped in a space shaded by a large oak tree, away from everyone else. The spot reminded me of our park where he'd tackled me to the ground.

He killed the engine, but made no move to get out. Instead, he turned to me and held my watery gaze. "That bad, huh?"

I nodded, the words stuck in the back of my throat.

The leaves on the tree moved above us, captured by the wind.

"I couldn't speak either, the first time I saw mom strapped to those machines. I just froze, like a fucking kid, then walked out. I went to the nearest bar, drank myself stupid, then got into a fight." His anguish hurt me, just as much as it still hurt him. "Still haven't been able to say a fucking word to anyone. I'd rather a broken bone than to talk about it. You're the only person I've ever told, the only one who knows what I did. But it fucking hurt, worse than anything I'd ever felt. I'm telling you this because I know what that kind of thing does to you. I know what loneliness feels like, even living in a house filled with family."

This time, I was the one who reached for his hand.

His big, beautiful hand. I stared at the rings on his fingers as the damn wall inside me cracked, then crumbled. "He didn't want to see me."

"Fuck, he said that?"

I shook my head. "Didn't need to. I waited for ages, then at the last minute, he came in. I didn't even recognize him at first.

They'd beaten him before, but this time it was different. This time, the beating wasn't just to hurt him, it was to kill."

"Jesus, Ryth."

"His eyeball was black, the entire side of his face was scraped and bloody. He was missing a tooth and he walked with a limp, holding his arm against his body."

Nick was silent.

"He's giving up on me."

"You don't know that."

I smiled, but it was full of sorrow. "Yeah, I do. He told me to make mom happy, that Creed will do a better job as a husband than he ever had." I sniffled, releasing his hand to swipe the mess away.

"Everything's going to be okay. Dad won't give up fighting and neither will your mom. There has to be someone who knows something."

"They set him up." I didn't care how ugly I looked right then. I needed him to understand. "Because there's no way he wasn't loyal. He's more loyal than anyone I know."

"For a drug dealer."

My breath caught. Deep down, I knew...*maybe I always had.* "Yes, for a drug dealer."

Nick nodded. If nothing else, he was forcing me to be honest, to tell it like it was. No pretense, no lies. The ugly, violent truth. Just like that tainted desire between us.

"They're going to get married," Nick said quietly. "There's no escaping it, Ryth." He brushed his thumb across the back of my hand. "You need to be ready for that."

I was ready for that...I thought I was, anyway.

But was I really ready for them?

I didn't know...

But I had a feeling I was about to find out.

And soon.

19

Ryth

They're going to get married...you need to be ready for that.

Nick's words haunted me as we walked into that little diner, ate cheeseburgers and drank colas, then drove home. I spent the rest of the day trying to focus on my assignment, feeling numb and empty after seeing dad, until the thud of the front door sounded and mom's voice rang out.

"RY! RY, HONEY!"

I shoved my chair backward and raced downstairs, to find the kitchen island loaded with bags.

Mom spun, her eyes shining with elation as she held out her hand. "Dresses."

I stepped closer, confused.

"For you, as my bridesmaid." She rushed forward. "Now these are all from the same place that has my dress, so when we settle on a design you like, we can get you fitted with me on Saturday."

"Saturday?" I glanced her way, mentally calculating how much work I still had on that damn paper to get the passing grade.

"Yes, Saturday. The wedding is a week away."

I swallowed hard. Of course it was. This was really happening...

"So, Saturday." Mom stepped closer to grip my shoulders. "You're okay with this, right? You haven't changed your mind?"

"Changed her mind about what?"

I flinched at the sound of his voice, turning to watch Tobias saunter into the kitchen, wearing nothing more than tight black jeans. Mom's gaze widened as she took in his hard stomach and muscled chest before looking away, a slight red blush rising to her cheeks. "The wedding, of course."

Tobias grabbed a glass from the cabinet and slowly made his way to the sink to hit the tap. He didn't need to do that. I knew he had a small refrigerator in his room, knew he kept it well stocked, too...so why the display?

He switched off the tap and turned, his gaze fixed on me. "Now why on earth would someone want to stand in the way of true love, right, Ryth?"

"Right," I answered carefully, watching the glint shine a little bit brighter in his eyes.

"Oh, shoot, I forgot the shoes!" Mom yelled as she raced from the kitchen to the door.

Tobias just casually placed his glass on the counter behind him and sauntered toward me. "I heard your little drive with my brother was...*interesting.*" He glanced toward the front door and my pulse stuttered as he stepped closer, leaning down to murmur in my ear. "This is your last warning, pack your gold-digging whore of a mom up and get out of my house."

His words burned like acid in the pit of my stomach. My mom might be a number of things...but a whore wasn't one of them. I turned my head, meeting his gaze. "Or else?"

His lips curled, revealing a chilling smile. "Or else all bets are off. I'm giving you until the wedding, Ryth...then you're *mine*."

He expected me to cower from him, expected me to scurry away like the little mouse he thought I was. He thought he could scare me. I straightened my spine, looked him dead in the eyes, and answered. "I think you're nothing more than a hurt little boy and you miss your mom. I get that. But taking out your anger and pain on me or my mom isn't the right way."

There was a twitch in the corner of his eye, one tiny tell. "You think I'm in pain? Oh, how cute. I'll show you fucking pain, little mouse."

Mom's rushed steps drew my gaze.

He moved before I knew it, pinching my nipple *hard* until I flinched and cried out. Then he was gone, leaving me to hide the agony as mom hurried in, her cheeks flushed, breaths panting. "Oh, has T gone?"

His heavy steps thudded on the stairs. I fought the need to scream at him, to fight and kick...and cry. He was a *bastard!* A cruel, manipulative bastard who thought he could bully me into breaking my mom's heart.

I'm giving you until the wedding...

I fisted my hands, fighting the urge to stride up those stairs, bang on his door, and scream in his goddamn face, *"Fuck you! And fuck your ultimatums!"*

My nipple throbbed like hell, aching and swollen. I hated how it echoed between my thighs. I hated how he *hated* me, and how he thought putting his hands on me was okay. I squirmed at the discomfort and fought the need to rub my breast.

He wanted a goddamn battle?

He wanted a war?

Well, two could play at that game.

"The dresses," Mom said hopefully, drawing my gaze.

I forced a smile. "Let's do it."

She clapped her hands like an excited schoolgirl, her eyes shining and bright as she laughed. *"I knew you'd be excited."*

She pulled out pink chiffon and gold satin, handing them to me one after another. I grabbed them, walked up the stairs to try them on one after another and parade them in front of her, and every time I stepped down the stairs, I looked at Tobias' door.

We settled on a rose colored strapless dress that accentuated my waist and off-white heels.

"Amazing," Mom beamed as I walked toward her.

The front door opened right as I stepped into the hallway.

"Wow," Nick murmured, drawing mom's gaze.

"I know, right? Doesn't she look beautiful?" Mom stepped closer, grabbed my hair, and drew it away from the ugly birthmark, then coiled the strands on top of my head.

"Mom." I yanked my hair from her hold, embarrassed.

"I think you look beautiful, Ryth," Nick said, his tone careful.

"I think so, too, Nick." Mom rested her hands on her hips and stared at me. "Thank you for noticing. My daughter is always so incredibly shy."

She didn't see the way his gaze drifted over my body, lingering on my breasts, before dropping to below my waist as though he was remembering what I'd done in his car. "I'd better leave you ladies to it." His voice was husky as he turned toward the stairs.

I followed him as he took the stairs two at a time, leaving us in a rush, like it affected him seeing me like this. I scowled, then forced my gaze back to mom, who was packing the rest of the dresses into their bags.

"Saturday," she said with a smile.

"Mom." I stepped closer, still hearing Tobias' warning in my head. "Are you sure you want to do this so soon? I mean, I get you wanting security. But you don't have to marry to get it."

Mom straightened, then turned to me with a look of pained confusion. "Marry to get it?" She came closer. "Honey, this isn't a marriage of convenience and I'm not marrying Creed because of some misguided sense of appreciation. I'm marrying him because I love him and he loves me."

But why so soon? I wanted to ask her, but the moment I opened my mouth to speak, the front door opened and Creed walked in. He took one look at me in my dress, then smiled as he made his way to mom. "You two look like you're having fun."

She kissed him hard, making me turn my head away, embarrassed.

"How about you ladies get dressed up and I'll take you out for dinner?" Creed suggested cheerfully.

"Yes, I'd love that," Mom agreed, then glanced my way. "I'll just get dressed."

"Honey, you're perfect as you are." Creed only had eyes for her.

Mom glance toward me. "What do you say, kid?"

"I can't, I've got that assignment I have to get done, but you guys go ahead. Have a nice night," I smiled, wincing with the ache in my breast, and stepped backwards.

"Then I'll just grab my purse." Mom headed for her bag, hidden underneath the bags of dresses, glancing my way as I crossed my arms over my chest. "Don't wait up!"

"Oh, I won't."

I waited for them to leave, waited for the click of the front door closing and the echo of the Mercedes engine before I turned and strode for the stairs. I wanted to bang on his door, I wanted to scream in his face. I wanted to slap him and keep on slapping him until he felt the kind of pain I felt. I didn't know why he hated me so much. I couldn't comprehend hating somebody like he did.

His rage was fixated on me, like it was all he saw and all he wanted to see. I slapped my feet on the stairs as I climbed. What I needed to do was channel my anger into getting that assignment finished. I need to pass this year, needed to figure out what my next step was...now that my life had turned upside down. I needed a plan. Because staying here wasn't an option.

That stayed with me, blending with the throb in my chest as I headed to my room. The moment I stepped inside and closed the door, I knew something was wrong. I spun, looking to the desk. My laptop was gone. Panic roared to the surface. I raced around the side of the bed, trying to remember where I'd had it. But my focus kept coming back to the desk. I'd been there, only moments ago.

Tobias...

It had to be. My rage bubbled up to the surface. I'd had enough of his taunts. I'd had enough of his cruelty. I'd had enough of him! Yanking open my door, the heat of anger seared inside me as I strode along the hall to his door.

"Tobias!" I screamed, and slammed my fist on his door. "I know it was you! Give me back my laptop, *right now!*"

But there was no answer, no thud of his steps, no yanking open his door, no smug fucking grin on his goddamn face. I leaned closer, I could hear the TV was on inside and the familiar, sickening slaps of flesh on flesh were punctuated with deep, guttural groans.

He was watching porn...*again.*

My pulse pounded, the heat that had consumed me seconds ago now cooling.

But he had my laptop.

And I wanted it back.

I moved without thinking, knowing Mom and Creed weren't here. I twisted the handle and shoved open his door, stepping inside. My gaze went to the TV, and the sight of a man sliding his cock inside a woman as she lay on her back, her feet high in the air.

Fire found my cheeks as I tore my gaze away. *Goddamn bastard...*

I saw his room, his PlayStation and his controllers, and his cell phone. If his phone was here, then he wasn't far away. My gaze darted around the room, frantically searching. I stepped closer to his desk, but I couldn't see it anywhere. *Where the fuck was it?*

I turned, looking at his bed in the middle of the room, then glanced toward the open door of his walk-in closet. But there was no movement inside. His bed was made, even if the comforter was crinkled where he'd been lying. I glanced over my shoulder as his porn played out on the screen in front of me.

I stepped closer to the side of his bed, maybe my laptop was hidden...and caught sight of something white peeking out from under his pillow. My breath stuck in my lungs, I was drawn closer. Was that...*my panties?*

I reached down, grabbed them from under his pillow, and tugged them free. They *were* my panties, the ones I'd had when I ran from our burning home. I knew they were, because they were all I'd had left. But the question was, what are they doing in *his* room?

"What the fuck are you doing in here?"

I spun at the sound, coming face-to-face with my hated brand new stepbrother. "My laptop, give it back."

His lips curled as he stepped closer, those dark, menacing eyes moving to the panties in my hand. "What makes you think I have your fucking laptop, Ryth?"

I took a step forward. "Because I know you do. Give it back to me now."

"Or?" He threw the same word I'd used down in the kitchen at me now.

But I wasn't having it. Desperation forced me even closer. "Or I'll tell Creed everything you've been doing, from the way you touched me under the table, to the threats and the intimidation you seem to enjoy directing my way. I'll burn your little world down, and I'll fucking enjoy it."

Hate raged in his eyes, sparkling with an intensity I'd never seen before, one that made me tremble. But I was too far gone now, too far beyond anything I'd ever felt before. He triggered something inside me, something dangerous.

There was a second when he sniggered, then smiled before he lunged to grasp me around the throat and drive me backwards until I slammed against the wall. "Did you think you could come in here, throwing your pathetic little tantrums, threatening me, and I'd just take it?"

I tried to speak, gasping for air as I wheezed. "Give it back."

His grip tightened as he looked down, taking in the bridesmaid's dress I still wore. "You look like a slut."

I hated the tears that came to my eyes. I hated that his words hurt me. My hand trembled as I lifted my panties. "Why are you so obsessed with me?"

He was quiet for a second, rage shimmering in his eyes, before he lunged and shoved his face against mine. "I don't want to be, can't you see that?" he yelled, his voice etched with desperation. "You come in here and take over *my* life, *my* house, and *my* mom's memory, and I want to hate you for it. *I do hate you*. But there's more. I found an outlet for my anger and my grief, and it's you, Ryth. What better way to let my mom go than to fill the void with an obsession, like hating you."

He leaned closer, pressing his body against me, and I could feel how hard he was. I closed my eyes as his grip clenched, then eased. Anger...rage. It was laser focused at me. So help me God, something inside me welcomed it, some sick desire inside me screamed her own desperate howls of pain.

But he didn't hear any of that. He just clenched his grip tighter, hard enough to choke off my air just a little, and whispered in my ear. "Now get on the goddamn bed."

20

Tobias

I yanked her from the wall and shoved her backwards. She coughed and spluttered, grasping her throat as the red mark of my handprint darkened. "You, you *bastard*."

I smiled, that's the least of what I was. I lowered my gaze to the panties in her hand. "Get on the fucking bed, Ryth."

"Fuck you, Tobias," she snarled. "Now give me back my fucking laptop."

At least this time the little mouse wasn't looking for someone to save her. No, she was getting feisty, her anger triggering that savage desire. I looked at her, standing there in her pretty bridesmaid's dress, and all I wanted to do was rip it off her pathetically thin body. My fingers twitched as I lowered my gaze to her breasts. "Either get on the bed or I'll force you down."

"What's going on?" Nick growled behind me.

I didn't bother to turn around, I couldn't stand to see the concern in my brother's eyes as he came closer, holding her goddamn laptop in his hand.

"You?" Ryth looked at him. "*You* had my laptop?"

"Yeah, you looked stressed and I wanted to see if there was a way I could help you." He took another step, and his gaze moved to the panties in her hand.

But I wasn't letting this go, I wasn't letting him have feelings for the little bitch. I wasn't letting him see her as anything other than an invader. "Either get on the bed, or I'll make you."

Nick looked my way. I waited for my brother to say something. I waited for him to shake his head and be the white fucking knight she needed, but all he did was stare her way. "You did it for me before, you can do it again."

Her eyes widened as it hit her. She knew what Nick wanted her to do and her breath caught.

All I could see were his texts in my head, telling me how perfect she was. I wanted that... I wanted that now.

"Nick, no," she whispered, and shook her head. "Please."

"It's just us." He placed her laptop on my desk. "Your mom and our dad are gone."

She looked at me, that ugly fucking birthmark burning on her cheek. Nick moved, grasped her by her shoulders, and eased her down onto the bed. She turned those wide, scared fucking eyes my way. Christ, if it didn't excite me. My cock twitched, growing hard. I reached down and rubbed my hand along the heat, and her gaze followed the movement.

"You liked it," Nick urged. "I fucking liked it. You want this to change between us...then give Tobias what he wants and he'll leave you alone. We can all be one happy family."

My brother threw a look over his shoulder at me. The bastard was even more into this than me. I bet he was already rock fucking hard. He leaned down, pushed her gently back against the pillows, then bent, grasped her feet, and lifted them to my bed...*my fucking bed.*

My eyes drifted along her pale legs as Nick kept talking, soothing her. "It can be just like it was before, remember how wet you were, how much you enjoyed it? Show him, show him how beautiful you are." He slid his hand between her knees and parted her legs.

Pretty pink panties were revealed between her legs. Her gaze was riveted on me, finding the movement of my hand as I rubbed my cock, before she lifted her gaze to mine. "You hate me."

"So much, it fucking hurts," I answered.

Her fingers trembled, moving toward Nick as he pushed her dress up her thighs. "Touch yourself, make yourself feel good."

She looked at him, like he was...everything.

Her hand moved closer, the tips of her fingers grazing her crease. She was so fucking nervous, so utterly fucking scared, but there was something in her eyes that told me she liked this. She wanted this...almost as much as we did.

"That's it." Nick straightened, watching her hand.

But it wasn't Nick she stared at as she rubbed herself, it was me. Her lips parted, her fingers finding a rhythm as she stroked the outside of her panties. I unbuttoned my jeans and pulled down my zipper, releasing my cock. Her eyes widened and her fingers stopped for a second as a tiny wet patch bloomed on her panties. Fuck...

My pulse boomed at that sight.

It was the hottest thing I'd ever seen, hotter than any hardcore fucking porn.

My little virgin stepsister liked looking at me.

Nick let out a groan, his hand moving to his own erection. "That's the way," he urged, yanking down his zipper. "Pull them aside, let Tobias see you."

The vein along my cock throbbed, shooting sparks through me. I ground my teeth and fisted my length, hating how I needed this more than I'd ever needed anything in my fucking life. I lowered my gaze as she grasped the elastic of her panties and all I could think about was I'd had my fingers in there.

She pulled those soaked pink panties to the side, showing me what my touch had caused, until I almost came in my fucking hand.

"Take them off," I demanded, making her eyes widen. "Before I rip them off you and use them right fucking now."

"Have you ever been licked?" Nick growled.

She tore her gaze from mine to his and shook her head, sliding her fingers inside.

"You want to be, princess?" Nick leaned down and slid his finger along hers, almost touching her pussy.

She didn't answer, too fucking scared to give into what her body craved. Christ, I'd never wanted to fuck so bad in my life. I wanted to see this little bitch writhing under me. I wanted to hear my name on her lips, *needed* to see her tears as I slid inside her, taking her for the first time.

Nick glanced my way, meeting my gaze. He knew...he fucking knew.

Her first time was mine.

Still he stroked her, his finger moving down as hers slowed, dancing around her clit before he slipped inside. I was hooked on that movement, his big finger sliding into her, coming away glistening. She let out a moan, a trapped, choked sound. It triggered me. I jerked my gaze to her cunt. "Do that again."

My brother slid inside her again, only this time inserting two fingers. He curled them, grazing the inside, stoking that need. She closed her eyes, her hips driving off the bed against his touch.

"Fuck me, you're gonna fuck so well, aren't you, princess?" He murmured. "I bet you're gonna ride us all fucking night and beg for more."

I fisted my cock, bearing down harder. I was going to come... watching my brother fuck our brand new stepsister.

"What the fuck is going on?" Caleb growled as he stepped into the room behind me.

Ryth let out a low moan, her legs opening wider, giving Nick all the freedom he wanted.

"What the fuck does it look like," my brother snapped. "Welcoming Ryth into the family."

He leaned over, pulled her leg to the side and licked her cunt.

She bucked and cried out, her hands falling to the bed.

"Jesus fucking Christ," Caleb snapped. "Her mom is about to marry our fucking dad."

"I know." I licked my lips as Nick tongued her, sucking on that tiny clit until she reached for the back of his head, pulling his mouth harder against her.

"Fuck me." Caleb watched as she lifted her leg, the dusty pink hole of her ass puckering.

But Caleb didn't reach for his cock, even when he grew hard at the sight.

"Fuck, you taste so goddamn good," Nick murmured, sliding his fingers inside her dripping wet pussy.

She was swollen, aching, thrashing her head side to side. I wanted her to come in my bed...all over my sheets, all over my fingers. But I couldn't move, just stared as her hips rose on the bed and a plea ripped from her whore mouth. "Please...oh, God, *please.*"

"You need more, princess?" Nick lifted his gaze to her. "You want Tobias to fuck you? Slide his cock all the way inside, make you feel good?"

She lifted her head from the pillow, hate mingled with need in her eyes. *"Yes!"*

My cock twitched, jolting and spasming in my hand as I came hard and fast, all over my goddamn fingers.

"Looks like you're too late, princess." Nick lowered his head to her slit once more. "Maybe next time."

She held my gaze as my brother licked and sucked, driving her closer to the edge. I stared at the red mark around her neck, the remnant of my hand. "I fucking hate you," I growled.

"*Oh!*" she cried out as though my words drove her even closer.

I tucked my cock back into my jeans, moved around my brother as he licked her, and slipped my cum-coated fingers between her lips. "I fucking hate you, you pathetic little bitch."

She bucked and her teeth clamped around my fingers, but her tongue followed, licking my fingers as she came against my brother's mouth.

21

Ryth

No...*God, no.* Not him...*not them.* I knew this was wrong. But I was helpless to stop it. My fist clenched in Nick's hair as I lifted my other hand to Tobias' fingers and pushed them deeper into my mouth.

Warm. Salty.

God, he tasted so good. I licked and moaned as that acute surge of desire slammed into me, making me cry out and shudder. Nick's tongue probed deeper, dragging every twitch of my body to the surface. I closed my eyes and dropped my hand from Tobias', letting out a deep, guttural moan. I'd never felt like this. Not with my own fingers watching porn on the internet.

This was more than I'd ever imagined. Hunger hummed inside me. And as I came down from the high, I became breathtakingly aware of what had happened.

I'd crossed the line.

No, *we'd* crossed the line, diving headlong into something I knew was wrong. I sucked in hard breaths and opened my eyes as Nick lifted his head. His lips glistened and his honey-brown eyes were so dark they were almost amber as he smiled. "How was that, princess?"

How was that?

"If they find out, we are so fucked. You get that, right?" Caleb moved closer.

But it wasn't his brothers he stared at as he spoke, it was me. He lowered his gaze between my legs, and there was something unholy shimmering beneath the surface as he met my eyes. "Are you going to tell them about this?"

What was he asking? Did he think I was going to run and tell my mom what my stepbrother had done to me?

No, not what they had done...what I'd let them do.

I was the one who let Nick push me to the bed. I was the one who took my panties off. I glanced beside me to the bed where they lay soaked and discarded...*I was the one who'd spread my legs for them.*

"Or are you going to keep this our little secret?"

I glanced back at Caleb as he dragged his teeth along his lower lip, his focus lingering between my thighs once more.

"I don't know." Excitement coursed through me with the lie.

I knew I wasn't going to say anything. So did Tobias and Nick. If I was going to say something, then I would have long before now.

"You going to tell, Ryth?" Caleb came closer, causing Nick to step aside. He leaned down, fisted a handful of my hair and yanked it backwards hard enough to tear a cry from my lips. "Or are you going to be our good little girl and keep our dirty secret?"

My heart hammered. I was caught in this trap, confused and scared, but a big part of me wanted this. I liked their attention, I liked the hunt...I liked to be prey. I looked at Tobias, remembering the way he'd clenched my jaw, looking at me like he wanted to choke the life from me and fuck me all at the same time. "I might...I might tell them everything. Are you going to hurt me?"

"Yes," Tobias answered. "You say a word and I'll pull you down to the floor in front of everyone and fuck you senseless."

My pulse raced with the words as Caleb's grip tightened on my hair until I felt the burn. "Is that what you want, Ryth? You want to be punished? You want Tobias to strip your clothes from your body and fuck you?"

Oh God...

Oh God...

I gave a slow, numb nod.

The slow curl of Tobias' lips said it all. He hated me...*and he knew I liked it.*

"You going to beg?" Caleb murmured.

Heat bloomed between my legs.

I closed my eyes as that heartbeat between my legs came alive again.

"Jesus," Nick's voice was husky. "She's gonna make me come."

I opened my eyes, unable to hide my shame any longer.

Then Caleb let my hair go and pushed my legs wider. "Good girl." He slipped his finger along my crease, then inside me. "You're going to be a very good girl indeed."

First Tobias.

Then Nick.

Now Caleb helped himself to my body.

"The wedding..." Tobias warned. "You have until then to get out of this."

Then he turned and strode from the room, leaving Caleb to slide his finger free. I looked up into his gaze. He was the eldest...he was the one who was supposed to control everyone else, and here he was...*controlling me.*

"Best be careful." Caleb rose, clenching his wet finger into his fist, then stepped away, bending at the last minute to grab my wet panties from the bed. "I don't think you realize what you're in for."

He walked out, leaving Nick to stare down at me.

"I...I just came for my laptop." The words were dull as I met his gaze.

He just nodded to where it sat on the desk. "If it's any consolation. I think your paper is written well."

It's written well? Nick left me behind, striding out of Tobias' room after his brothers. Heavy footsteps thudded on the stairs. A second later the *boom* of the front door sounded before the Jeep's engine came to life with a growl and Tobias left. I closed my legs and slid my feet over the side of his bed before I rose, grabbed my laptop, and left Tobias' room with my legs shaking and my pussy bare.

Written well? Nick's words resounded in my head. *Written fucking well?*

I made my way into my room and closed the door quietly behind me, my mind racing with what had just happened. *What did just happen?*

Tobias wanted me gone...

But did he?

You come in here and take over my life, my house, and my mom's memory, and I want to hate you for it. His words resounded inside me. *I do hate you. But there's more. I found an outlet for all my anger and my grief, and it's you, Ryth. What better way to let my mom go than to fill the void with an obsession, like hating you.*

He hated me....

And I liked it.

I sat down on the bed, wondering what the hell had happened to make me this way? I wasn't beaten as a kid, I wasn't hated by my own parents. The taunts of all the kids resounded in my head from school. I lifted my hand and touched the mark on my cheek, remembering how their cruel words had hurt me.

But this...this was different.

This was calculated and controlled. This single-minded focus wasn't directed at the birthmark on my cheek, but on me. On my body and the way they wanted to claim me.

I stayed like that until my knees stopped shaking and I could move. Then I rose from the bed and eased my mom's bridesmaid's dress free, hanging it neatly on the hanger and hooked it on the back of my door. I dressed, sliding clean panties on, remembering my white cotton underwear Tobias had taken from my bedroom.

I thought I'd misplaced them days ago...but it seemed that he'd been in here, rifling through my things, taking what he wanted. I closed my eyes and dropped my head, thinking about that. Him...taking...what...he wanted.

What better way to let my mom go than to fill the void with an obsession, like hating you.

I was coming apart under his obsession...losing myself to his hate, and I didn't know how to stop it. When the heat of desire left me, I made my way to my desk and opened my laptop once more. *He hadn't taken it. It had all been Nick.* Something about that made me think of dad. I sat at my desk, with my mom's dress hanging behind me, and started to work.

I worked for hours, until the sound of Creed's Mercedes outside drew me away from my paper. Then I rose and made my way over to the window, watching him and my mom climb out. He moved around the front of the car, the headlights splashing over them as he lunged, grasping her hand and pulled her hard against him. Guilt swelled inside me as I watched them.

I was ruining it all...

Mom's happiness...Creed's, too. If they ever found out what had happened...it'd be over. The headlights of the car died and I watched them make their way to the house until I lost sight of them. My belly snarled and I realized I hadn't eaten in hours, had missed dinner. But I wasn't about to go down now. I moved to the door, listening to mom's schoolgirl giggles as they made their way to their bedroom.

Their bedroom...how quickly mom and I had become part of something new...

I waited for their door to close before I stepped out and quietly made my way to the kitchen and opened the refrigerator door. In the glaring light, I helped myself to a small plate of leftover turkey, some cheese, butter, and mayo, and placed them onto the counter.

"Hungry?"

Caleb's voice came from behind me, startling a shriek from my lips. His hand clamped over my mouth in an instant and I was dragged backwards, into the expansive walk-in pantry. The doors closed in an instant, confining us in the small space.

His voice was deep, husky in my ear. "I just want to make sure we're on the same page here, Ryth." He grasped a handful of my hair, tugging it back hard enough for me to whimper against his mouth. My pulse stuttered, then raced as panic tore through me.

I fought against his hold, but it was useless. He was too big for me to fight. His grip tightened in my hair, his hand clamped over my mouth. "You going to scream?"

My eyes watered, the fear was choking. Still, I shook my head.

"Good...*very good.*" He slid his hand from my mouth.

And cupped my breast, fingers kneading, as outside the pantry the kitchen light flicked on and mom's happy humming slipped between the slats of the pantry door.

"Shh..." Caleb whispered as his hand moved lower, slid under my t-shirt, and tugged down my bra.

"Really?" mom sighed, her voice coming from near the refrigerator, where I'd stood just seconds ago. "You boys, always pulling food out and never putting it away," she muttered.

"Tsk...*tsk,*" Caleb whispered in my ear as his fingers found my nipple. But his touch wasn't cruel, not like Tobias'. Instead, he kneaded gently, dancing the tips of his fingers around my nipple until my body responded, tightening and puckering it. He tugged my hair, forcing my spine to bow backwards until I stared into those dark, ravenous eyes.

The feel of his hand...

The humming of my mom not more than a few feet away.

One wrong move...one wrong sound, and she'd find us. He knew...*he knew and he liked it.* His hand left my breast as a cold, calculated smile curled his lips and slipped under the waistband of my boxers. My pulse raced as mom's humming grew louder and she stowed the food I'd only just pulled put back into the refrigerator.

Caleb's eyes bored into mine as his finger found my crease. My body was still buzzing from what we'd done before, yet it seemed like he wanted more.

You have no idea what you're in for...

The warning filled my head as his fingers found my clit. A moan rose in the back of my throat. Caleb's smile grew bolder as he gently shook his head. I clamped my teeth down, biting the inside of my cheek as mom poured herself a glass of water...

Hurry the fuck up! Oh God, hurry up, please, mom...please...

Caleb's fingers moved inside me, stroking with an expert touch, moving to dance around my clit, stoking that fire inside me. My hips moved on their own, thrusting against his touch. Caleb lowered his head until his breath blew against my ear. "I want to fuck you. I want to slide my cock deep inside you. I want to ride you until you give over to me." His grip tightened in my hair. "I want you to be my good girl. Are you going to do that, Ryth?"

His fingers moved deeper.

Mom still hummed, taking her sweet ass fucking time placing the bottle back into the refrigerator.

"You coming, Elle?" Creed called from outside the kitchen.

Still Caleb's fingers never stopped thrusting inside me.

"Yep, just putting the food away one of the kids left out," she called. "It was still cold though, so maybe they..."

My orgasm barreled toward me like a freight train. I clawed Caleb's arm as my body jerked and shuddered. *"Please..."* He was cruel...so fucking cruel.

"You're doing so good" he murmured against my ear. "Just like that...*just...like...that.*"

My body trembled at his words. I was out of control, coming apart at the seams as mom closed the refrigerator door and muttered, "Never mind."

I fixated on the soft thud of her steps, tracking the movement as Caleb's fingers sucked and squelched, making me thrust my hips against his fingers.

"When I take you, Ryth...I'm going to take you all fucking night. You're going to be my favorite fucking toy...my wet,

200

perfect plaything, aren't you?"

The moment my mom's footsteps faded on the stairs, I whimpered, coming hard against his hand.

"You're going to learn. Fuck me, you're going to learn," Caleb whispered, sliding his fingers from inside me. "I'm going to think about fucking this beautiful mouth tonight...I'm going to come tasting you on my fingers."

He released my hair and smoothed down the strands, then leaned forward and kissed the top of my head. Then he straightened, opened the pantry door, and stepped out, leaving me shaking and weak...wondering what the hell just happened. My belly wasn't howling anymore. Instead, I felt exhausted, my body humming and throbbing, still feeling their fingers and Nick's mouth.

I'd only ever had my own fingers...and the urgent thrust as I came in the darkness of my own bedroom. But this. This was consuming. I pushed against a shelf to stand straight, then slowly stepped out, making my way out of the kitchen as the front door of the house opened and Tobias came in.

He took one look at me, then turned his head, catching the fading thud of his brother's steps before Caleb's bedroom door opened and closed. But he said nothing, just watched me with that seething anger that both wanted to hurt and consume me all at the same time, before I quietly hurried back to my room.

I flicked off my bedroom lights and climbed under the covers.

I had to be careful now...

And it wasn't just Tobias I needed to watch out for...

It was all of them.

22

Ryth

"That looks wonderful. What do you think?" Mom stood back, looking at the dress now that it'd been tucked and pinned. "Will you have it ready in time?"

"Of course, Mrs. Banks," the seamstress nodded and smiled.

"Mrs. Banks," I repeated. "Already?" I turned to her, finding darkness creeping in outside over her shoulder.

It was getting late, and the bridal shop was staying open, just for us. I guess it was just another one of the perks of being Mrs. Banks. And she loved it, loved her new friends, loved her new lifestyle. One so completely different from the one she'd had with me. Her phone *beeped* again for the eighth time in the last five minutes.

"Just trying it on," Mom shrugged, laughing at some message from one of her new friends, who were actually the wives of Creed's friends. "I'll be using it for good in another week."

I ground my teeth at the words. She even looked different. Gone was her natural brown hair, the same shade as mine. Now she was a honey-ash blonde with highlights. Even her clothes were different. I stared at her nude-colored, mid-thigh, strapless dress and heels that drew your attention to her long legs and small waist. She was dressed to party. I guessed that was her life now. Parties and a brand new husband. The only thing that stayed the same was me. I opened my mouth to ask about dad and the lawyers, but she looked so happy in that moment...and I didn't want to ruin that.

"You like him, right?" Mom narrowed in on the flare of my jaw. "I mean, he's been kind."

"Yeah." I stared away, avoiding her gaze. "Creed has been cool."

"And you like living there, in the house?"

My stomach was in knots as I reached up to the zipper at my back before the seamstress hurried forward and tugged, pulling it down. "I like the house just fine, mom."

"And the boys seem to have taken a liking to you. Creed said how proud he was how they've taken you under their wing."

And into their bed. The words resounded in my head.

"Which is why I'm not so worried about leaving you for the week."

I stopped, then spun to face her. "Leaving? Why?"

She smiled, letting out a small bark of laughter as she lifted her third glass of champagne. "Ryth...for my honeymoon, silly. You didn't think I was going to get married and not want to celebrate it, did you?"

Her honeymoon...

Her goddamn honeymoon.

Blood rushed from my face as my pulse spiked. I hadn't thought about that. I'd been so busy. *You have until the wedding, Ryth.* Tobias' warning pushed into my head.

"You're okay with that, right?" Mom asked as my phone went *beep.*

I didn't answer, I couldn't speak. My heart was in the back of my throat as I picked up my phone and stared at the message from Gio. *Hey, just seeing if you're still keen on our date?*

"A date?" mom asked over my shoulder. "Gio, huh? Someone from school?"

I flinched and went to pull the phone away, but then I stopped. Gio...Gio could be my way out of this. I could use him, pretend he was my boyfriend. It'd give me time to figure this out. That's all I needed. Time...to figure out what the fuck I was going to do. "Yeah," I answered as I typed out a reply to him. *I can't tonight. Next time?*

I waited for an answer.

Gio: Your mom?

I smiled and typed. *Yeah. Hen's night.* He sent back a thumbs up, which made me wince. Christ, I hated those. Three little dots appeared when he started typing. I waited for the message as mom drained her glass behind me. "This is really nice, Clarissa."

"Another, Mrs. Banks?" she asked as I still waited for Gio's reply.

"Sure," Mom responded. "Why the hell not? I'm going to be Mrs. Goddamn Banks in a week."

I stared at the screen as those dots scrolled over and over. *Hurry the fuck up, Gio.*

Then the dots faded, leaving me staring at an empty screen as the door to the bridal shop opened and a piercing female squeal sounded. "There you are!"

I winced at the sound and headed for the dressing rooms, swiping a glass of champagne from the tray as I went.

"Oh my God, this place is *sttuuunnnnning!*" mom's new friend groaned.

I downed the champagne as I stepped into the dressing room, then I stopped and lifted my gaze. And as always, I found that ugly mark on my cheek...it wouldn't matter how my life changed, that would always be the constant.

The one thing that reminded me exactly who I was...*ugly*...

My chest rose hard and fell even harder as the piercing shrieks from the showroom tore through my head. *Honeymoon...why the fuck hadn't I realized?* I flinched, then stepped out of the dressing room. Mom didn't even see me. Not anymore. I placed my empty glass on the tray and took two more. I'd barely touched a drink in my entire life. I'd sneaked a sip of dad's Scotch when I was ten, then spent the next hour gagging and gasping from the burn. I swore I'd never touch alcohol again... but now...now I needed to not feel.

I drained a glass, then placed it back down, taking the second one into the dressing room as I shrugged off the pinned dress and put my own jeans and t-shirt back on.

"Honey," mom called outside the dressing room. "Do me a favor and try this on, just for size. You need a party dress."

She plopped a black strip of cloth over the door.

"Mom...*no.*" I stared at the thing.

"Just to get the sizing. You're always wearing those ugly jeans. You're a young woman now, Ryth, and Gio...well, you might like to go out sometime. Just *sayin'*."

Who the fuck was this woman?

This wasn't my mom. I lifted the glass and swallowed the slightly bitter swill. My head buzzed, moving my panic to the back. I put down the empty glass. *Just for sizing.*

"That's right, honey," mom answered.

I hadn't even realized I'd spoken out loud. I grabbed the dress mom had hung over the door and tried to find the damn opening. The tiny cubicle swayed, making me slam my hand against the mirror to stop from falling. Laughter and giggles outside masked the thud, and for that I was grateful.

I tried to concentrate while my head spun, and tugged down the zipper. I slipped it on, working it over the revealing white lace bra and panties mom had made me wear. My gaze slipped down, finding the blush of my nipple through the almost sheer fabric, and I remembered Nick's hands on me.

Heat flushed through me as the *ding* of the bridal shop door opening sounded. I tugged the dress up, black over white. The dress was tight, skintight. The thigh split gapped as I turned, looking at the gaping zipper.

"Show me," mom urged as her friends erupted in a wave of giggles and chatter, drowning out everything else.

I opened the dressing room door and stepped out, and the room spun a little as I turned. "I don't think I can wear this."

"Of course you can," mom answered slowly. "Ryth, you look…"

I lifted my gaze to the floor-length mirror at the end of the dressing rooms…and found Creed and his sons staring at me.

"Stunning," Creed finished, meeting my gaze in the reflection.

My heart lunged as I spun, my gaze moving to Tobias and Nick as they stood next to him.

"We came to check on you," Creed smiled. "The boys offered to drive you home, seeing as how your mom is about to be…*wasted.*"

"Hell, *yes she is!*" one of her new friends squealed.

I winced at the sound, glancing at the three women gushing over mom and Creed. One of the women navigated to Nick, opening her arms, quite obviously intoxicated already. "Nicky *boy!*"

She pulled him into a hug, one that he didn't fight. Instead, he smiled and hugged her back, laughing. "Jess, you're such a cheap drunk."

"I know," she groaned, and stumbled a little.

But when Nick turned his gaze back, it was directed at me. "The dress looks good on you, Ryth." He said carefully, hiding his real emotions as he gave a shrug. "You should wear it."

I shook my head. "I wasn't going to—"

"Elle, we're gonna *be laaattteee,*" Jess moaned, jealousy flashing in her eyes as she glanced from Nick to me.

"Okay," Creed chuckled, motioning with his hand. "You ladies go. *Go on.*"

Mom turned to Creed, wrapping her arms around his neck. "Will we see you out?"

He laughed. "Not where you're going. I don't plan on swimming across the harbor to crash your stripper party on the damn boat, Elle."

Stripper party?

No wonder she didn't want me to come.

"Leeetttssss gooooo!" Jess howled and the two others added to the chorus until the entire shop was filled with whiny, intoxicated calls for partying.

"Okay...*okay,*" mom laughed as her newfound friends pulled her from Creed and dragged her toward the door.

"Have a good time!" Creed laughed. "I don't want to see you home until tomorrow! *Late!*"

She blew him a kiss and flashed me a smile before she was gone out the door, taking the deafening squeals of her friends with her. Creed laughed and shook his head, his gaze moving to mine before he took in the dress. "Buy it, honey. It looks beautiful on you. *You* look beautiful in it."

I shook my head. "I—"

Tobias hadn't said a damn thing since walking in, he hadn't even smiled, just scowled that moody goddamn scowl that seemed to be fixed on me, until he turned and strode away. Humiliation mingled with the cheap champagne, making my cheeks flush bright red until I caught Tobias swiping his card across the scanner attached to the cash register.

Nick glanced at his brother, then chuckled. "Looks like you're getting the dress, little sister."

Tobias glanced over his shoulder, meeting my stare. It wasn't disgust in his eyes as he took in my body. *It was hunger.*

Creed's phone gave a *beep,* drawing my focus as he winced, staring at the message. "Shit. I'm late, too. You guys okay to take Ryth home?" He glanced at Nick.

"Sure," he smiled. "Go, Dad. Have a good time yourself."

I was starting to understand their dynamic now, starting to find out where they all fit. Nick was the good guy, the smiling assassin, the one who drew you in like a rattlesnake, until he pounced, and Tobias...Tobias was the wounded beast, the one caught in his own trap, staring at his own heart like it was a limb he needed to gnaw off to save himself.

And Caleb?

*You're such a good girl, Ryth...*those words resounded, making my pulse race and my body tremble.

"Go," Tobias murmured as he headed my way. "We'll take care of her."

Creed strode forward and pulled me into a hug, planting a fatherly kiss on my forehead. "The dress is beautiful, honey. The boys will take care of you. I'll see you tomorrow, okay?"

"Tomorrow?" I glanced up into his eyes.

He smiled and stepped away. "Who knows, once these guys start drinking. You know what lawyers are like."

Then he was gone, clapping Nick on the shoulder and giving Tobias a nod before he opened the bridal shop door and strode off. Leaving us alone...

The lights in the rear of the shop flickered and plunged into darkness.

"I think that's our cue to leave," Nick murmured, glancing toward the dressing rooms. "Grab your clothes, Ryth. Let's go."

"I can't leave wearing this." I shook my head.

"Can and are," Tobias growled, striding toward me to push into the dressing room. He grabbed my jeans, t-shirt, and boots before coming back out.

I looked ridiculous, leaving in the tight black party dress and the heels mom had bought for the wedding. But as the seamstress appeared from the rear of the shop, giving us a desperate smile, I found myself following Nick toward the door.

"*See you next week!*" she called behind us.

Cool air hit me as I hit the sidewalk, making me sway a little.

"Whoa." Nick grabbed my arm, steadying me. "Have you had something to drink, Ryth?"

"A little," I answered, meeting his gaze. *God, he was pretty...how had I not seen how pretty Nick was?* I glanced at Tobias, with his gaze like a thundercloud. *Christ, they were both pretty.* I swallowed hard and looked away.

"Your mom know?" Nick asked.

I shook my head. "Took the glasses when she wasn't watching. She wouldn't know anyway, had her new friends to distract her." The words sounded snarly. I didn't mean them to be snarly.

Beep.

My phone vibrated in Tobias' hand. He glanced down and read the message. My pulse spiked as his brows narrowed. "Who the fuck is Gio and why the hell does he think you're going on a date with him?"

Nick stopped dead on the sidewalk. They both turned their attention to me.

"Ryth?" Nick called my name. "Who the fuck is he?"

The black Mustang waited, parked against the curb a little further along.

"Ryth?" Tobias took a step closer, lifting my phone, his gaze savage. "Who the fuck is this *punk?*"

"No one," I answered, the words a rush under the effect of the alcohol. "Just a friend."

Tobias lifted my phone. "Seems like a lot more than a goddamn friend. Unlock your phone. I want to read the texts he's sent you."

"What? *No.* I'm not going to do that."

He came for me with a look of rage, striding closer in the blink of an eye. I stumbled backwards until I hit the glass front window of a darkened shop.

"Can and will," he growled, shoving my phone at me. "Now unlock the damn thing before I smash it on the ground."

I flinched. "You wouldn't."

The curl of his lips was chilling. Midnight sparkled in his eyes. "Try me."

"Ryth," Nick warned, glancing over his shoulder to look for bystanders noticing. As though he knew what this looked like.

Two men pushing me up against the glass. No one would believe this was nothing more than a little sibling spat...*because it was more than that.*

They were jealous and controlling. Two older supposed brothers that looked nothing like me, because we weren't family by blood. That panicked thrumming in my chest grew bolder as I stared into the pit of jealousy in Tobias' eyes. Nick turned back, his gaze just as terrifying. "Unlock the phone, Ryth. We want to know what this prick has been sending you."

"You think...you think he's sent me a dick pic?"

Tobias' lips curled. "*Has* he?"

*Oh God...oh God...*heat bloomed between my thighs as Tobias lifted his hand, bracing it against the glass, blocking me in. "You looked at his cock, Ryth?"

And there was that look again.

The look that said he wanted to choke the life from me and fuck me all at the same time. Power rushed to my head, carving through the effects of the alcohol. "If he did?" God, I felt powerful in that moment, watching how badly they were affected. I needed this...needed to know how they felt about me. Because the truth was buried under the lies I kept telling myself. Lies I'd been whispering louder and louder the more time I spent with them. I wanted them just as much.

"If you did, then he's fucking dead," Tobias warned.

I flinched.

"Tell us the truth." Nick dragged his fingers through his hair, then curled them into a fist. "Tell us the truth and we can work it out."

He looked desperate, strung out, licking his lips before glancing at the phone's screen. *Did he feel something for me?* My breath caught in my chest and that same need flared inside me.

Did they both feel the same as I did?

I reached up and slowly entered the code, unlocking my phone. Tobias stepped away, opening up Gio's text. "He thinks you're fucking dating?" he snarled, scrolling through the few pages of texts Gio had sent me. "What's this about a goddamn party? You planning on going, Ryth?" My brother met my gaze. "Was that it? You think you can sneak off and meet up with this fucking punk?"

"You planning on fucking this guy?" Nick asked carefully.

"What?" I flinched. *"No."*

But he wasn't having it. He shook his head, moving closer to take Tobias' place. But he wasn't hot, cruel rage like his younger brother. No, Nick was cold and careful, his vengeance calculated. "You planning on losing your virginity tonight, little sister?"

Jesus, the way he said those words. *Little sister*...the words resounded as he pressed his body against mine, driving my spine against the glass. "Because if it's that much of a burden..."

"Mine..." Tobias growled, his eyes flashing with rage as he came closer, sliding my phone into his pocket. "You get that? You... belong...to...*me.*"

Desire slammed into me with the words, even as a tiny part of myself made me shake my head. "No."

"Oh yes." Tobias strode closer and grabbed my arm. "Now get your ass in the car, Ryth. We're taking you home."

He pulled me toward Nick's car, opened the door, then got in himself and pulled me down into his lap and slammed the door as Nick got in behind the wheel and started the car.

"Wait," I barked, fighting him. *"Tobias, stop!"*

"Settle down, or so help me God, Ryth. You don't know what I'm capable of right now."

His grip left me as he clasped his arms around my waist, since we couldn't fasten the seatbelt over both of us.

"Fuck, try and run." Tobias glared at me in the dark. *"I dare you."*

His words were a warning, one I didn't want to push.

"Get us home, Nick," Tobias demanded, his ravenous gaze riveted on me. "Now."

23

Nick

I shoved the car into gear and surged out of the parking space, tearing past the goddamn bridal shop, and headed for home. She was going to meet with that fucking kid? Was she...

Christ, my pulse sounded like a goddamn hurricane, thrashing in my head. Focus...*focus*. But my gaze drifted to her pale, goddamn beautiful face and her dark, innocent eyes. Didn't she know what punks like that...*Gio* wanted from her? God, if we hadn't found the message...if she'd gone there...

In my head, I could see it. Her drunk, in that goddamn black dress that looked far too sexy to be legal, sitting on the end of some random asshole's bed, a plastic cup filled with spiked punch in her hand and his fucking tongue down her goddamn throat.

His tongue down her throat and his thoughts up in her...

"*Nick!*" Tobias yelled behind me.

I jerked the wheel, swerving us across the street, the oncoming headlights blinding, and still all I could see was her.

All I could see was her.

Fuck, I'd never had it this bad...not even with...*Christ, what was her name?* Natalie. That's right. Jesus, I'd been with her for over a fucking year and I'd just forgotten her name. In the blinding glare of Ryth, I'd forgotten everything. I swallowed as my cock hardened. "Tell me," my voice was husky and raw. "Tell me what he means to you, Ryth."

"Nothing!" she screamed. "He means nothing!"

I could tell she was close to tears, her eyes wide, that mark on her cheek red and practically glowing.

"Do you like him more than a friend?" I had to know, *I* had *to fucking know.*

"No." She turned her head away.

Why the fuck did she turn away?

"Look at me," I demanded, dividing my focus between her and the road as I raced through the city streets. *"Ryth...I said look...at...me."*

She jerked her gaze back, and cold anger seethed in her eyes. I remembered the girl that had stumbled from the prison just yesterday. The one who'd basically fallen into my goddamn arms. The one who'd made me open myself up to her and tell her things I'd never told anyone—I glanced at Tobias sitting with her in his lap—not even my own blood. But she was different. She was...*mine.* The word echoed in my mind as I glanced at the street, then back at her again, and repeated the question, only this time my voice was cold...and dangerous. "Do you like that fucking punk more than a friend?"

"No."

She said no. She said fucking no. But could I believe her? I glared at the road as my phone starting to ring and the stereo flashed with Caleb's number. I stabbed the screen. "Yeah?"

"You might want to get here," he slurred into the phone.

I flinched for a second...

"Where the fuck are you, and why the hell are you drunk? You barely fucking drink."

"Never mind about that," he snarled as something crashed in the background. "Just get here...Razers."

Razers? My voice was careful. "You know you're not allowed there."

He gave a small bark of laughter. "Not allowed to want to fuck my goddamn stepsister either, but apparently I'm breaking all the fucking rules tonight."

Ryth jerked her gaze to me. In the background, a man spoke, probably a bouncer. "Get the fuck out of here, Caleb. You know what Lazarus said last time. Don't make me hurt you."

"He didn't mean it," a woman's cry came through. One of the dancers, I assumed. *"Caleb!"* she screamed as a grunt was wrenched from my brother.

I strangled the fucking wheel, scanned the traffic behind me, and spun the wheel. "Tell that motherfucker he lays a hand on you and I'll feed him his own fucking teeth. *I'm on my way.*"

The tires squealed as I punched the Mustang, and Tobias said the one fucking name he shouldn't, "Lazarus."

I fought the wheel, slipping through the traffic. "You don't know that."

His savage glare blazed. "Don't I?"

I jerked the wheel, spearing the car toward the exclusive bar downtown owned by the Rossis. The one place Caleb had sworn he'd stay away from...I glanced at Ryth again. Looked like we were all kinds of fucked up tonight.

Her goddamn messages were stuck in my head. I braked hard, then pulled into the alley. Darkness concealed the beast, the headlights splashing against the pitch-black building hidden in the back as I turned around. I scanned the parking lot as I crawled past, searching for familiar cars.

But there was no black Audi, which hopefully meant no Freddy. But if Caleb was inside, I'd bet my left fucking nut he wouldn't be far away...and waiting for Lazarus' command. *Shit.*

The very last thing I needed was my hothead fucking brother and Lazarus throwing goddamn hands...*again.*

The last time had resulted in goddamn threats that neither side wanted to have to uphold. I pulled the Mustang into the parking lot, shoved the car into park, and threw open the door. "Stay in the car, Tobias."

"Brother." The little shit was already climbing out as I flung the door closed, giving me a goddamn look as he muttered. "You and I know that's not going to happen."

But then Ryth was climbing out after him, her dress riding high as she struggled up from the heap he'd dumped her in. "I'm coming too."

"Like hell you are!" Both of us spun on her, making her flinch.

But that spark of defiance had ignited in her eyes. "You want me to stand out here all alone?" She threw open her arms, drawing my gaze to the tiny skintight dress that did things to me that weren't fucking legal.

Tobias stared...just like I did.

"Stay by our side," I warned. "Do not leave."

She said nothing as I turned and headed for the back door of the goddamn club. Blood red neon lights with the club's name flickered and glowed against the black building. I stared at the color and hoped to Christ it wasn't a damn omen. The last thing I wanted for any of us tonight was to get shot. I stopped at the door, rapped my knuckles on the painted metal, and waited for it to open.

The door opened, and a mountain stood in the way. Grievous glared, looking from me to Tobias, then to Ryth. I clenched my jaw, knowing full well what he was thinking. "We're not here to party," I forced the words through gritted teeth. "She's our goddamn sister."

One brow rose on the big bastard before he stepped to the side. "He's out the back."

I shoved past. "Of course he is."

It was fairly early, but here within the black painted walls and the sparkling lights of this upmarket stripclub, it was an endless fucking party. One we were no longer invited to. "Find him and let's get the fuck out of here," I ordered and headed toward the back of the club.

But Tobias was already scanning the filled tables and searching the bar, then he headed off toward the other side of the goddamn club. *"T!"* I barked.

But he didn't answer, just fucking strode away with that same cocky fucking gait that was gonna get us in trouble. I shot Ryth a look. "Stay with me."

Her eyes were wide, taking in the plush midnight interior of the club, then the dancers illuminated and on full display as I strode forward. I knew what she saw, the tits and fucking pussy. Christ, I didn't want her anywhere near this.

I glanced at her over my shoulder, at her wide eyes and her parted lips, before I forced my gaze forward. My fists clenched as I headed for the back area. *Goddamn you, Caleb.*

I wanted just one fucking untainted thing, was that too much to ask? Or did everything that touched our name have to be fucking ruined? A *crash* came from across the club. Heads of the men watching the dancers turned. I didn't have to follow the movement to know who it was.

"Where the fuck is he?" Tobias' rage cut through the deep throb of the music.

"Goddammit!" I strode toward the door to the back, until I was stopped by the bouncer standing there. He lifted his hand and shook his head.

"Let me through, I'm here for Caleb Banks," I demanded.

But the asshole didn't move, didn't lower his fucking hand. "Don't care."

I stepped closer. "You know who the fuck I am?"

He held my gaze. "Like I said, buddy. *I don't care.*"

A roar came from behind that door...*my brother's roar.* I jerked my gaze to the bouncer, catching a tiny twitch in the corner of his mouth. He knew...*the fucking bastard knew who we were...*

I shook my head and turned, taking a step away, catching the smug fucking chuckle from the piece of shit in my way...*then I spun and lunged.*

I dropped my shoulders, then drove upwards, swinging with a brutal jab to his sternum. The bouncer slammed backwards and crashing against the door, that smirk dying in an instant as he crumpled to the floor.

"Like I said," I stepped closer, drawing in a hard breath as he choked and gasped, his face turning a shade of gray. "You're in my fucking way."

He tried to lift his hand as I reached over him and opened the door. *Crash!* The sound of breaking furniture exploded in the room. I charged forward, to find Caleb in some bastard's grip, his face bloody, his eyes wild as four of the motherfuckers surrounded him. One leaned in, driving brass fucking knuckles into my brother's side.

He bowed, unleashing a howl of agony.

All I saw was red.

I threw myself forward and grabbed one around the throat as he cocked his fist back to swing at Caleb...he swung alright—*his entire fucking body*—as I pivoted, cocked my hip, and slammed the gutless bastard to the floor.

My body came alive.

All I felt was the fight, my years of training kicking in. I went after them one by one as the *crack* of a gunshot rang out somewhere else in the club. Caleb and I stopped fighting, his eyes widening.

"Tobias?" Caleb cried as it hit me, and I scanned the empty room around me.

Ryth...Ryth wasn't here...so where the fuck was she?

24

Ryth

"Easy." The bouncer came from nowhere, cutting me off from Nick as he charged between the tables and leaped at the group of bouncers who were beating Caleb.

"You're not supposed to be back here. It's exclusive only." He took one look at me, his gaze lingering for a second on the mark on my face, before he stepped closer.

I shook my head, stepping to the side. "Get out of my way."

"Not so fast." He moved in, grabbed my arm, and shoved, forcing me backwards.

I jerked my gaze to Nick, a scream trapped in my throat, watching as Nick slammed one of the assholes to the floor and swung his fist at another.

"Pretty little thing like you." The bouncer forced me backwards, through the door and out into the main club, pulling the door to the back room closed behind him.

"Get off me!" I shouted, wrenching my arm free. I spun, searching the tables full of of men, seeing the barely clothed dancers in front of them.

"Need help?" Another bouncer came from my left as a deafening *crash* came from the back room.

I lunged, shoving the first bouncer aside to get to the door. They needed me...*they needed me.* "Caleb! Ni—"

A hand clamped over my mouth, smothering my scream.

"This the Banks bitch?" the second bouncer growled at my back. I fought against his hold, opened my mouth as wide as I could, and bit down. *"Owww! Fucking bitch bit me!"*

I thrashed my arms, tearing from his hold to stumble backwards. "Stay...the fuck away from me."

Men sat at tables not ten feet away, but they did nothing as the two big bouncers flanked my sides and inched in.

"Gonna pay for that, Banks bitch," the handsy asshole snarled.

"Hey." Came from behind the bouncer.

He turned automatically. I caught the flash of rage in Tobias' eyes before he unleashed, punching the jerk right in the nose. The towering male stumbled backwards and lifted his hand as blood spurted from his nostrils and ran down his lips.

"Get your hands off her," Tobias roared.

My pulse raced as he stepped closer and turned that savage gaze to me, searching my eyes. "You okay?"

I nodded, my heart in my throat.

But then the other bouncer reached into his pocket and pulled out a knife. "Should've stayed away, Tobias. Now I'm gonna wreck that pretty face of yours." He lashed out, driving the blade through the air dangerously close to Tobias' face.

"*No!*" I let out a scream and lunged, clawing his cheeks from behind as the other guard tore me off him, lifting my feet from the ground.

"*ENOUGH!*"

The attack stopped dead with the roar. The bouncers turned, finding a blond guy, flanked with his own dangerous-looking bodyguards, striding toward us. He glanced my way, scowled, then turned to Tobias. "You know better than to come here."

"Yeah, well, not like I'd planned on it." Tobias yanked his arm free, shooting the bouncer a glare. "I came for my brother, and I'd already be out of here if your fucking attack dogs had let me."

The bouncer with the bloody nose growled and stepped forward.

"Ryth?"

I spun at the voice, trying to tear out of the bouncer's vise-like grip as Gio stepped out from behind the bullies. "Gio?"

I caught the flinch from Tobias, then a low, menacing chuckle. "Of course. It's just like you, isn't it, Lazarus?"

Lazarus? As in...Lazarus Rossi? I froze.

"Let her go, James," Lazarus muttered, and the asshole at my back released his hold.

"Jesus." Gio came closer, his wide eyes fixed on me. "What the fuck are you doing here?"

I adjusted my dress, rage simmering close to the surface as I stared at Gio. "I could ask you the same thing."

He glanced at Tobias as he answered. "I decided the party wasn't worth attending. So, I came here instead."

I glanced at the nearest dancer, who spun around the pole and spread her legs for all to see. "To a stripclub?"

"To *my* club," Lazarus muttered, before directing those intense eyes my way. "Ryth."

I focused on the *punk* with his fucking attack dogs. When I looked at him, all I saw was my father's bruised and beaten face. I hated him for that...for the fucking men he had behind the prison walls, men who obeyed their commands. The Rossis. I took a step forward, drawing a flinch from one of one Lazarus' men, until he waved his attack dog back.

"I know what you did," I murmured, glaring right into his eyes. "To my house and my father."

There was an explosive glint in his eyes as Lazarus regarded me carefully. "Oh yeah? And what's that?"

I flinched, then looked around the club. He was calling my bluff, seeing if I was really going to spell it out for everyone to hear. He was seeing if I was going to be...*stupid.* I stilled, my mind racing. I faltered, caught in a trap of my own making. Was I making things worse for dad, just by being here?

It's okay, Ry...I'm going to get out of here...

Dad's words echoed in my head as I stared into Lazarus Rossi's clear blue eyes and tried to think. Was I one step away from making things worse...?

First, dad's arrest...

Then, our home...

Where would it end? *Not with me being stupid, that's for sure.* I swallowed hard, the hate in me cooling just a bit.

"Well done," Lazarus murmured. "Looks like you're not as stupid as the company you keep. There might be hope for you yet, Ryth."

He looked at Tobias when he said it, triggering him to lunge.

"Uh-uh." The towering, musclebound guy next to Laz shook his head. "You and I know you don't want to do that, T."

Another *crash* came from the back room, echoing through the door.

"Yeah? How about you tell them to let my brothers go, Logan?" Tobias demanded.

Lazarus glanced toward the door and motioned him forward. In the blink of an eye, the massive bodyguard left his side and disappeared through the door.

Gio stepped closer and reached for my arm. "Come on, Ryth, let's leave these two to piss it out."

He was trying to drag me away...so they could *what?* Hurt him? I shook my head and took a step toward Tobias, my voice shaking. "Get the fuck away from me, Gio."

"It's not what you think," he grumbled, his kind eyes flashing with desperation.

"Isn't it?" Tobias moved closer, so close I felt the warmth of him against my back. "You came on to Ryth, tried to fucking poison her against us."

Gio stiffened. But it was Lazarus who spoke. "Not poison..." he denied, glancing my way. "Keep an eye on."

Rage rippled at my back as Tobias reached around, sliding his hand along my stomach and cupped my breast, pressing me against him. The move couldn't be any more primal.

Mine. It said and something inside me howled with satisfaction.

Gio flinched, his gaze moving to Tobias' warm hand kneading my breast. He licked his lips, then met my gaze.

"I knew you were a cold, ruthless bastard, but this is a new fucking low, even for you," Lazarus growled. "She's a kid, Tobias."

"She's *family,*" Nick spat as he came through the door.

His mouth was bleeding and one eye was weepy and swelling. "Nick!" I tore from Tobias' possessive hold and rushed forward, touching his forehead above eye before I turned on the leader of this pathetic fucking club. "You *fucking piece of shit!*"

Nick just smiled over my shoulder. "Looks like she's got your number, Lazarus."

"Fuck you, Nick," Lazarus growled. "Fuck your goddamn brothers, too."

I reached toward the corner of Nick's eye and saw him flinch. God, if the bone was broken...

"Ryth." Lazarus held Nick's glare. "Why don't you come to the bar? I can get ice for your...*for Nick.* It'll give us time to talk."

That same possessive glint shone in Nick's eyes.

"You want to talk to her," Caleb sneered as he tore his arm away from a bouncer and strode through the door. "Then you talk in front of us."

There was no ice to be found, not for Nick's face, or for the searing rage that burned between these two warring sides. There were no strained fences to be mended. Lazarus saw that now as he met my gaze. I swore there was a flicker of disappointment mingled with...*fear.*

He nodded toward Gio. "You ever want to talk to me, Gio will make that happen, until then..." he glanced at Tobias and the others. "Watch your back."

"Watch her back?" Tobias snapped as Lazarus turned and strode away. *"Watch her fucking back, Laz? Come back here! Come back, you fucking backstabbing bastard!"*

My pulse spiked with the roar.

Fear punched through me as the rest of the club came into focus. They all stared, every asshole who'd refused to help me... and every dancer on stage. There was no twirling around the poles in this second, not until the other guy at Lazarus' side snapped. *"Get back to dancing!"*

Tobias clenched his fists.

Nick seethed with anger.

But Caleb...Caleb looked at me with tormented need as he licked his bloodied lips and muttered, "Let's get out of here."

I followed all three as we made our way through the tables. Caleb reached out and grabbed a bottle from one of the tables as he passed.

"Hey!" the asshole seated there roared, and shoved to his feet.

"*Forget it!*" Lazarus barked. "Let them go."

It seemed everyone always did as he ordered. The asshole quieted as we made our way out through the black door and into the blacker night, all four of us bruised and shaken.

Caleb lifted the bottle to his lips and took a swallow.

"You're a real fucking asshole, you know that?" Tobias snapped as we strode toward the car.

Caleb glanced my way, then held out the bottle, his focus fixed on me as I took it and drank. Heat burned all the way down, making me splutter.

"Yeah," Caleb answered. "I know."

Nick limped as he walked toward the car, but Caleb slid his arm around my shoulders and pulled me closer. "You think I'm an asshole?" he slurred, taking the bottle and drinking again.

"I don't know what to think." I sucked in a breath that tuned icy in the back of my throat as Tobias yanked open the Mustang's passenger's door, and climbed into the rear, leaving the door open behind him like a summons.

Nick slid in behind the wheel and started the Mustang.

"Maybe I can change your mind, then?" Caleb handed me the bottle, then strode forward, leaving me to trail behind.

I took another swallow, trying to stop the shaking of my hands, and followed Tobias inside. His glare was instant as he snatched the bottle from my hand. "Next time you want to meet up with your fucking boyfriend, Ryth, just fucking say."

He swallowed some Scotch as Nick shoved the car into gear and pulled out of the parking lot, then accelerated hard.

"I need a goddamn drink," Nick snapped, then winced.

I caught the lick of his lip in the rear-view mirror as he headed for home. But it was Tobias' words that stung. I reached out and snatched the bottle back from him as he lifted it to his lips again. "For the last goddamn time, he's not my boyfriend."

"Yeah?" He moved, pushing himself across the seat to drive me backwards, and snarled in my face. "Maybe someone might wanna tell him that."

My pulse leaped. The bottle in my hand drove into his side. My nerves were frayed and the Scotch mingled with the cheap champagne. But I was past the point of caring now...past the point of playing his goddamn games.

I leaned forward, tilted my head upwards, and kissed him.

He stiffened above me. His hate tasted so fucking good on his lips...until he let out a wounded sound. His hand was in my hair in an instant, fisting the strands until my scalp burned as he shoved his body harder against mine.

Not my boyfriend.

The words resounded in my head as the kiss deepened. *Not my goddamn boyfriend.*

Because the truth was...I wanted Tobias...

I wanted all of them.

I opened my mouth, my hunger greedy. An acute surge of desire ignited that fire inside me before he broke the kiss and pulled away.

He hated me.

I saw it in his eyes.

He hated me for invading his home and ruining his family. But he wanted me more. That torment was tearing him apart...*and I wanted it, too.*

He lowered his gaze to my dress, then slid his hand up the inside of my thigh, bunching my dress under his touch.

He was careful but unhinged as he met my gaze. "What the fuck are you doing to me?"

The answer was simple...*the same thing he was doing to me.*

Bringing me undone...

25

Tobias

No...don't do this. A tiny voice sounded in the back of my mind as she lifted her head from the backseat of the car and kissed me. I fisted her hair and consumed her mouth. I wanted her moaning, wanted her whimpering. I wanted her bruised and breathless underneath me...

But was that the right thing for her?

I ended the kiss and pushed her toward the window.

She lay there, need shining in her eyes. Streetlights flashed against her as we drove. I looked down, my hands moving before I knew it, sliding her dress upwards until I could see her white panties...only this time, they were lace. White lace, almost sheer...sheer enough for me to see her pussy.

"I can't stop." I pushed her dress higher. "And I don't want to." I lifted my focus, meeting her gaze. "What the fuck are you doing to me, little sister?"

Caleb turned, looking around the edge of the seat as Nick adjusted the rear-view mirror, tilting it down as he punched the accelerator. She lifted her knee, shifting it to the side. "The same thing you're doing to me...*all of you.*"

I shook my head and pushed backward, my voice raw. "This is wrong." But my eyes drifted down her body, from that mark on her cheek to her perfect fucking breasts, then to her pussy.

"Get us home, Nick," Caleb demanded.

The car took a corner hard. "What the fuck do you think I'm doing?"

That dangerous hunger inside me was fading, turning into something more, something desperate and urgent. Something that made me think way too much. I shook my head, trying to cast the demons out, but all I saw was *him,* fucking Gio. My cock twitched, remembering the way he'd looked at her. Like he...*wanted to save her.*

She deserved someone like him.

Someone good.

Someone honest.

Someone who wasn't going to ruin her for the rest of her goddamn life. Because when I looked at her sweet goddamn face and smelled that faint scent of her *pure* perfume, that's what I wanted to do.

I wanted to ruin her.

And make her mine.

"I would've let him," she whispered.

I wrenched my eyes toward her as a *"Fuck,"* came from Nick.

"You what?" I asked, my voice devoid of emotion.

She looked at me like she knew that I was thinking, like she could see the change inside me. *Like she could feel my fear.* "I would've let Gio kiss me."

The car swerved and braked hard to pull over to the side of the road outside someone's damn house, headlights cutting through the darkness. *"Goddamn bastard."* Nick clenched the wheel. "I'm going back there...I'll rip his fucking cock off."

But all I saw was that daring gleam in her eyes as I repeated. "You would've let him kiss you?"

She nodded slowly. But I could see it was a lie. It was all a seething fucking lie, one designed to push me to the goddamn brink...*and it was working.*

"Home, Nick," I demanded. "If our sister wants to be kissed so badly, I'm sure we can help her out with that."

He seemed to understand, accelerating hard to pull out into the street once more, leaving her bathed in the flickering streetlights until he pulled the Mustang into the driveway, hitting the button for the gates to close behind us.

My father wouldn't be home tonight, and neither would her mom.

It would be just us...all night long.

We jerked to a stop. I was already climbing between the seats as Caleb shoved the door and stepped out. But I just stood there, outside the car, not helping her, watching as she scooted her ass along the seat, catching glimpses of her pussy, and fought the overwhelming need to take her right here and now.

The driver's door closed with a *bang*. Nick was quickly there beside me, watching as she stepped out of the car and stopped, unable to get around me.

"T?" Nick called me cautiously.

Lights came on inside the house. I hadn't even noticed Caleb leave.

"Get inside, Ryth..." I stepped aside. "Now."

She hurried toward the house, her damn heels clacking on the driveway, inciting in me the need to take her down to the ground. *Fuck, I felt like a beast around her.* Maybe that's who I was now? First mom, then Lazarus, now Ryth and the goddamn wedding.

A beast...raging with emotions.

I raked my fingers through my hair and glanced over my shoulder at the street. I didn't know what I expected to find, Lazarus or Freddy in their fucking Audis, so I could redirect my anger. But they weren't there. The street was as quiet as it always was. Leaving only her in my fucking path.

I strode after her, stepped inside the house, and locked the door behind me.

Soft steps came from the stairs, then disappeared at the top into the hallway. Nick's voice murmured, then silence, before a tiny moan came from feminine lips. I headed for the stairs and climbed up. Ryth wasn't like other women. She was innocent. She was familiar. *She was mine.*

Ours...

I saw the way my brothers looked at her, and the way she looked at them. I lengthened my stride, taking the stairs two at a time until I stopped on our floor. Nick's fingers were in her hair, his mouth on hers. *My brother.* I bit my lip as Caleb stepped out of his bedroom door, now missing a shirt, a fresh bottle of Scotch in his hand.

I glanced his way, finding those dark eyes fixed on her. "You okay?"

He was drunk...and hungry. I'd never seen him this out of control. I glanced at my soon-to-be sister as she slid her hands along Nick's biceps and took his mouth, and I realized that, when it came to her, we were all out of control.

And I welcomed it. "Get her into the bedroom, Nick," I commanded.

Hate, hurt, and hunger lashed inside me like a tornado, tearing apart everything in their path as Nick bent, grabbed her around the waist, and carried her into my room.

Caleb followed, right behind me. Ryth let out a moan. Whatever Nick was doing in her mouth excited her. Excitement tore through me, too, racing to the head of my cock. I didn't need to reach down to know I was hard as we crowded into my bedroom.

Nick moaned into her mouth, his hand between her legs, fingers stroking her pussy as he lowered her to the bed. That dress...that goddamn dress was bunched around her fucking waist.

Caleb stepped beside me, his gaze fixed on our brother as Nick broke away from her mouth and moved lower, tugging those sheer panties to the side to find her pussy with his mouth.

"You'd let that fucking Gio kiss you?" I stepped forward, rounding the side of the bed as she let out another moan.

But she wasn't getting away from my question so easily. I scrambled inside my head, desperately clawing for that burn of hate as I leaned over, grabbed a handful of her hair, and tugged her head backward to stare into her eyes. *"Answer me."*

Panic filled her eyes, swallowed by the slow, sweet torture of my brother's mouth as he tongued her pussy.

"Y-yes," she whispered.

Lie...

The word was a slap. *She was fucking lying.* My cock pulsed, thickening in vengeance. I clenched my fist in her hair hard enough to make her eyes widen. "You'd let him put his mouth on you."

I glanced at Nick, watching his tongue delve into her pussy around the elastic of her panties. She lifted her hips, arched her back, and widened her legs for him. For his mouth and his fingers. Thunder boomed in my head as I met her glazed eyes. "You'd let that piece of shit stick his tongue inside you?"

Nick pushed deeper, then sucked her clit. Her eyelids fluttered, and her skin was pale. Still, she fought, my little fucking mouse, to gasp. "Yes...yes, I'd let him stick his tongue in me."

Nick lifted his head, his lips glistening. He was too far gone, even I saw that. I glanced at Caleb, whose gaze was fixed on her. She was so fucked. I don't know if she had any idea how far this had already gone.

"T..." Nick reached up and grasped the edge of her panties as she lifted her hips from the bed.

I looked at Caleb, then to the bottle in his hand. He stepped forward, shoving it against my chest. "She wants this, don't you, Ryth?" he asked, returning his stare her way.

I took the damn bottle from his grasp and downed a long swallow as her panties were pulled off and flung to my bedroom floor. *I'm getting a collection.* The words came out of nowhere. A goddamn collection of her panties. Fuck if that didn't make the beast inside me howl with pride.

Nick reached up, rolled her to the side, and tugged down the zipper of her dress. Then that too was gone under the slide of my brother's big hands, leaving her in her white lace bra and heels.

She reached for the bottle in my hands, and the movement triggered something inside me. I grabbed it just as the rim reached her lips. "Need to drink for courage, little mouse?"

Desperation burned in her eyes as I dragged the bottle from her hand and tilted it, pouring the heat into my own mouth. Nick slid his hand along her body and reached under her back, releasing the hooks of her bra before pulling it free. The greedy little bitch opened her mouth as I leaned closer, as though she knew exactly what I was going to do...

I spat.

Scotch splashed her mouth, some shooting inside, leaving the rest to dribble down her cheeks. Nick moved in, licking the remnants from her skin.

"More?" I asked as she swallowed, then nodded.

I lifted the bottle, taking a smaller draw, and leaned over again, kissing her hard. The burn consumed us, numbing our lips and claiming our mouths. Movement came from the corner of my eye as Caleb ran his hand up the inside of her leg and parted her thighs.

"Fuck her, T," Nick urged.

"Do it." Caleb dragged his finger along her slit and slid it inside, right where I wanted to be. "I want to stare into her eyes when she has her first taste of cock."

"It won't be her last," Nick declared as he reached for his zipper.

"You said until the wedding," she whispered, her face flushed from all the goddamn alcohol.

I leaned over and stared into her eyes, making sure she understood what was happening. "You want me to stop, little mouse?"

Silence...silence while she searched my eyes and I did the same. *Tell me...tell me to fucking stop and I will...so help me fucking God, I will.*

My heart was pounding as my world shifted.

This moment was suspended in time.

Another plane.

Another existence.

Where there was just the four of us.

Caleb's finger in her pussy.

Nick reaching for his fucking phone and hitting record. "Fuck her, T, or I will, brother."

"Tell me, Ryth," I demanded, unable to hold on a second longer. "Tell me what you want me to do..."

26

Ryth

"Tell me, Ryth," Tobias demanded. "Tell me what you want me to do."

They're my brothers. That's all I could think of with the Scotch muddling my head. I opened my mouth to say *no...no more* as Tobias reached for the button on his jeans and slid down his zipper.

He hated me, *fucking loathed me.*

But he wanted me just as much...*probably even more.* "Do it," I whispered. "I want to feel you inside me."

"Jesus..." Nick muttered, moving in the corner of my eye. I could still feel his tongue inside me, still feel my body swollen and tingling from his mouth. His hand lingered in the air, something in his grasp. But I didn't care at that moment. The alcohol burned it all away, every fear, every thought. It was all about them right then and that hunger I could no longer hide... not anymore.

Tobias gripped the bottle and kicked off his boots before tearing his shirt off. It felt good being naked in front of them, bare to their gazes. My pussy was desperate for their brazen fingers. I let my gaze trail down to the *bastard* who'd made my life hell from the moment I'd arrived.

"I would've let Gio fuck me, too," I whispered.

Tobias froze, his eyes growing colder and more dangerous before he bared his teeth. I grabbed the bottle from Tobias and took another swallow, then handed the rest to Caleb as he rounded the bottom of the bed, still staring down at my pussy.

I opened my thighs wider and dropped my hand, then slipped a finger inside. "I bet he would've been good, bet he would've taken care of my every need."

With a snarl, Tobias lashed out, grasped my ankle, and yanked me down to the end of the bed. "Is that right?" His tone guttural and dangerous.

I shifted against the bed, then kicked out and tried to turn. But he pounced, grasping me around the waist and with a savage roar, flipped me onto my back. He was between my thighs before I knew it, pressing his thick arousal against me. Panic seared through me for an instant as I cried out, "Condom."

"No protection," Tobias growled. "Not for you, little mouse. I'm fucking you bare." He stilled for a second, that glint of hate dulling as he met my gaze. "This is going to hurt, okay?"

"Just do it." I closed my eyes. "Get it over with."

I waited, my body trembling, but there was nothing.

"Open your eyes, Ryth," Tobias demanded. "Open your eyes and look at me."

My panting breaths were all I heard as I did as he told me, cracked open my eyes and watched him.

He looked down between us before he bucked his hips forward, hard and brutal. Fire carved through me with the force, consuming, plunging, making panicked breaths catch in my chest.

Through the blur of alcohol, Caleb was there, naked and standing above me, his fingers in my hair, his voice in my ears. "That's it, princess." He moved closer. "Such a good fucking girl. *Breathe...*"

Tobias withdrew, then plunged back in, only this time driving deeper. "Fuck, she's tight," he grunted, thrusting once more.

"So fucking tight." Caleb turned my head toward him. He stood there, his naked cock huge and hard in front of me. I opened my mouth as Tobias' invasion came once more, making me clench my eyes shut and cry out.

"Easy," Tobias soothed, his thrusts slower now, driving deeper inside me.

"That her blood?" Nick's voice came from my side.

"Yeah."

My body surged downward with the words as the pain ebbed, and in its place came that hunger that had waited under the surface, the one that didn't care my brand new brother was fucking me.

"You okay, princess?" Caleb asked, his face blurring as I nodded. "Good girl, now open your pretty mouth."

I did as he said, licking my arid lips just before they slipped around the head of his cock. Those dark eyes stayed on me, shimmering, as the merciless thrusts jolted my body against the bed.

"Pull out, Tobias," Caleb growled above me.

Nick moved closer, the phone in his hand angled down between my legs. "Pull the fuck out, T."

"No."

"*T, pull the fuck out now!*" Caleb grunted, and drove his cock deeper into my mouth. I couldn't breathe my lips were stretched so wide, just like my pussy as Tobias drove deeper.

Fucking me.

This was what it felt like to be owned...to be used...to be *nothing more than pleasure.* Pleasure. The word resounded through my head as heat built between my thighs. Delicious, throbbing heat that built with every thrust now. Until with a grunt, Tobias rammed all the way inside and stilled, spilling warmth.

"Christ." Caleb pulled out of my mouth. I sucked in hard breaths, then looked down to where Tobias watched me as he slowly withdrew his cock from my body.

But there wasn't fear in his eyes now.

They were endless dark pits of obsession as he looked at the mess he'd made.

I reached down, my fingers finding his slick warmth. He came inside me. *Oh shit...he came inside me.*

Tobias stepped away, the bright mark of my blood on his cock. He gripped the length and massaged the smear, rubbing it along his shaft. "Gio comes near you now and I'll fucking end him. You understand that? You belong to us now. You... are...*mine.*"

"You fucking came inside her," Nick barked, striding forward to punch Tobias in the shoulder. *"What the fuck, T!"*

But Tobias smiled, like that had been his plan all along.

"She hasn't come." Tobias met Nick's gaze. "You gonna leave her aching, brother?"

"You fucking bastard." Nick shook his head, then looked back at me, the phone still in his hand as his gaze went to my pussy again.

"Didn't think so," Tobias said behind his back as Nick stepped forward and lifted his gaze to me.

"You want me to..." Nick asked, watching my fingers.

I slid them deep and closed my eyes. I needed...I *needed.* "Nick," I whispered.

"Yeah, princess?" he moved even closer, his voice husky. "I'm right here."

His fingers replaced mine. I opened my eyes, floating as he pressed his body between my thighs. I lost myself when his cock slid inside. I writhed and moaned, then lowered my gaze to watch him. He was looking down, angling his phone as he stretched me wide. My legs spread even further apart. I couldn't take him...I couldn't...take all of him.

I lifted my head, seeing him...thrusting deeper, gliding with the slick Tobias had left behind, his bare cock driving to the hilt.

"Fuck, you feel so good," Nick groaned. "Fuck, Ryth, you feel so goddamn good."

I watched as he pulled out, his shaft glistening, before he drove back in. I cried out and arched my back as that delicious wave of euphoria hit me.

"That's the way, princess," Caleb urged as my body moved on its own, driving down, stoking the flames. "Fuck him."

The sight of Nick sliding inside me, the shimmering slick of Tobias' cum, and Caleb's deep voice in my head pushed me higher than I'd ever been before. Slick sounds filled my ears. "Open your eyes, look at him when you come, princess," Caleb demanded.

He took me over, demanding, controlling...*dominating* my every move. I was helpless to stop it, opening my eyes, which I hadn't even realized I'd closed, to watch Nick. His hands were on my hips and that look of primal hunger, more desperate than ever before, sent me flying over the edge. My body quivered before it clenched, *clenched*...and I was blown apart.

Caleb's thumb stroked my cheek, urging me to turn my head. I did as he wanted and opened my mouth. It was too late to fight them, even if I'd wanted to. My mouth stretched, that same familiar burn as he slid his cock in and thrust slowly, looking down to meet my gaze.

"Such a good little mouse." He stoked my cheek and thrust. Panic surged as my lips closed around him and he smiled softly. "We're going to have so much fun with you."

27

Tobias

Her little body tightened as Caleb thrust into her mouth, and Nick pulled free from her pussy, aiming his phone down to follow the movement. He fucking loved to watch, I'd bet he'd replay this night over and over. Christ, the image of her lying there, her cunt dripping, her mouth wide, taking as much of my brother as she could. *This was my deepest fantasy come to life.*

I just never imaged it'd be with someone who was going to be our goddamn sister. Maybe that was why this felt so damn good.

"Ours," I demanded, my voice husky. "You get that, Ryth?"

She moaned as Caleb gently gripped her head, guiding himself deeper. His ass clenched and his big cock stretched her mouth wider until she gagged and spluttered.

"Ours," Caleb murmured, his balls tightening as he thrust harder, then stilled, forcing her head backward as he came down her throat. "All *ours.*"

She bucked, then sucked in hard breaths as he pulled out and stroked her hair. "You did so well, princess. *So...very well.*"

Her chest rose with the consuming breaths and her breasts trembled after what we'd just done to her. Two of us...on her first night. "I'll take care of her."

Caleb glanced my way, surprised. "You sure?"

I didn't answer, just rounded the bed and knelt beside her. "It's okay." I slid down next to her, pulling her close. She resisted at first, shoving her hand against my chest to push me away. Maybe it was because I was such a fucking asshole. I didn't want to be. But she triggered me, driving me over that brink to be that fucking beast.

"Easy," I murmured, my movements slow, fingers sliding over her hips, drawing her against me.

Memories flickered in my head as Ryth stopped fighting and lifted her gaze to mine. I wasn't always like this, wasn't so fuck hard...or unkind. "I'm not going to hurt you," I said carefully as I pulled her close.

Her breasts pressed against my chest. That warmth felt so fucking good. Almost as good as the hate. I closed my eyes and lowered my head, nestled my face against her neck, and breathed in that perfect scent of vanilla. "I've got you, little mouse," I whispered in her ear.

And in the echoes of my mind, I told my mom I'd take care of her, too.

All those months I washed her face and brushed her hair.

All those nights I'd sat by her side, holding her hand as the realization hit home that this was real, this was happening, she was dying and there wasn't a fucking thing we could do to stop it.

Ryth relaxed, sliding her arm around my waist. "Tobias..."

"Shhh..." I turned my head and kissed her mouth. "It's going to be good now, you just wait and see..."

She closed her eyes, letting me kiss along her neck and take her mouth, and after a while she relaxed. I looked over at Nick, who'd just lowered his damn phone, and glared at him, letting the warning spill through my eyes. *Show anyone else and I'll fucking end you, blood or not. She was ours to keep secret and there wasn't a goddamn thing I wouldn't do to protect that.*

He nodded, slipping his phone back onto his damn pocket as slow, soft snores came from the woman in my arms. Nick jerked his gaze to the sound. I flattened my hand against her back, pulling her closer against me. The act was possessive, even amongst my brothers. But I didn't care. I didn't care, because it was her—I looked down, finding that birthmark on her cheek, and felt something inside me shift.

I leaned over, brushing my lips along that mark she hated so damn much. But I didn't hate it...in fact, I felt all kinds of things about it. I scowled as I dragged my finger along it, then glanced at my hand and the shape of her mark. I tilted my palm and pressed my fingers against the outline again.

Jesus...

"T," Nick murmured.

But I couldn't look away. I was transfixed at how the mark wasn't just a blob of redness...*but it was the exact fucking outline of my fingers.* The same height, same crook on my middle finger where I'd broken it on some asshole's cheek.

I shifted my focus to her closed eyes. She'd been made for me. Even if she didn't know it...she would. I'd never felt this way about someone, had never *wanted* to feel it. Not in the wake of mom's death...and not in the wake of the fight with Lazarus Rossi.

The other bastard who'd seemed to take a fucking interest in her.

I needed to keep her away from him...him and that asshole Gio.

"Nick, can you find out where that fucking Gio lives?" I asked, staring at her in my arms.

"I can ask around."

I nodded, rocking her gently. "Good. I feel a proper introduction is in his goddamn future."

Caleb bent, grabbed the blanket which had been shoved to the bottom of the bed, and dragged it up over us. Ryth let out a sweet goddamn murmur and shifted harder against me. My brothers watched her for a second, then glanced at me, with a dangerous knowing burning in their eyes.

We couldn't let her go.

Not even if we wanted to.

Not anymore.

"Clothes." I jerked my gaze to the dresser.

The last thing I wanted was for her to wake up naked in her own damn bed. That would freak her out. Nick yanked open the drawer, then froze and threw a glance over his shoulder at her still asleep in my arms, then proceeded, quieter that damn time.

Our little mouse needed sleep and to process. I prayed to God she didn't freak out. I looked down at her, and as gently as I could, slid my hand under her neck and eased her head to the pillow.

"Do you want me to..." Nick started, holding out one of my t-shirts and a pair of my boxers.

"He's got it" Caleb answered for me.

I lifted my gaze, finding his. And all of a sudden, I was thrown from this moment and we were back there, to that room downstairs near the basement. The room we never went to now. The room that was once used as a hospital room.

Nick looked from Caleb to me, and stilled.

"Go on, brother." Caleb motioned and leaned down, gently pulling the blanket from her body.

Nick seemed to understand, holding out the boxers to me. All three of us worked in silence. It was the kind of comfort they couldn't give our mom, the kind they'd turned their backs on, but now...now they were here. I eased one of her perfect goddamn feet through the leg of my underwear, dragging the elastic waistband up her legs then over her thighs.

Her pussy glistened, some with my cum, some with her own desire. I slid the boxers higher, gently sliding them under her hips, and settled them around her waist.

They were too big, way too big, bunching around her hips, but still the sight made me feel weightless, like the burden I'd been carrying for the last few months had somehow lightened a little. *She* lightened it a little.

Nick held out my favorite shirt, his gaze meeting mine before he looked away. I took it, slid my hands through the neck, and reached for her head. She mumbled as I slid it over and her eyelids fluttered, then her lips parted with a tiny snore that was too fucking cute.

I moved on impulse, leaned down and kissed her mouth like it was the most natural thing in the world before I froze. That wasn't me. I didn't dress my women, and I sure as hell didn't kiss them while they slept, half worried I'd wake them.

I was moving into new territory here.

Way out of my depth. I gently eased her arm into the sleeve of my shirt, grateful when Caleb tugged the other side down. "You want me to carry her?" he asked.

I shook my head. "No, I got it."

Both my brothers held back as I bent, slid one arm under her knees and the other around her shoulder blades, and lifted. Nick moved to open the door, making sure the house was still empty as I carried her gently to her own room.

I hated leaving her, part of me wanted her to stay in the warmth and the familiarity of my bed. But that might be too much, especially when she woke up, and the last thing I wanted to do right now was make her regret what had happened.

Little mouse...

My words repeated in my mind as I carried her into her room and placed her down on the bed. Nick pulled her bedding up and for some strange reason, I glanced at the space at the foot of her bed, a space that'd been crowded with the machines that had kept mom alive until the end. Machines I'd hated and yet I couldn't get rid of them. Machines that'd taken over this room, a constant reminder of what I'd lost. *What we'd all lost.*

But this room didn't feel like that anymore. Now it was filled with the smell of vanilla and crowded with a messy desk and some godawful Hello Kitty plush toy that sat in the corner.

She mumbled as I straightened. Nick leaned down and kissed her lips.

The sight sent a tremor through my chest.

Familiar.

God, that's what this felt like.

Family...

28

Ryth

I surfaced, my breaths easing...a snore trapped in the back of my throat as I opened my eyes. I blinked and shifted, then let out a moan at the brutal thumping in my head. *What...the... fuck...happened?* My mouth tasted bitter and strange. The corners of my lips were tender as I licked them. I shifted in the bed, trying to remember.

An ache pulsed between my thighs, not painful...just *there*. Then it all came flooding back. The dress, the alcohol. *Oh God, the stripclub.* And Lazarus Rossi burning neon bright in my head.

I know what you did. My own savage tone drifted from that throbbing inside my head. God, I couldn't believe I'd said that... and to him, of all people.

But that wasn't the only thing I'd done, was it?

That nagging tenderness between my thighs pulled me toward the truth. I closed my eyes, trying my best to back away from the realization of what I'd done last night.

Memories flickered. Tobias...Nick...Caleb with his hand fisted in my hair. *Good girl, that's the way, fuck him.*

"Noooo," I moaned, and shook my head as faint sounds of movement came from somewhere downstairs in the house.

This wasn't happening. *That* hadn't happened. But I didn't need to dig too deep to know it had...I'd fucked my soon-to-be stepbrothers, *all three of them.*

The ache between my thighs turned into something else, something sick and not quite normal. I didn't need to touch myself to know I was wet with the memory.

Pull out, Tobias. My pussy throbbed as Nick's voice came roaring to the surface. *Pull the fuck out, T.*

I could still feel his cock inside me, that dark, merciless gaze fixed on me as he thrust deeper, harder, and growled, *No.*

He came inside me...*Oh God*...my own stepbrother came inside me. I reached down, my lips plump and swollen, sending an ache deeper as I slipped my finger inside. *Gio comes near you now, little sister, and I'll fucking end him,* Tobias reminded me. *You understand that?* I bit my lip, the ache giving away to that sick desire inside me. *You belong to us now. You...are...mine.*

I danced my fingers around my clit, slow circles dancing around that oh-so-sensitive flesh. I ached, and hurt, and fucking came alive.

My orgasm hit me hard, flooding through me like a tsunami of molten desire. I shuddered, slid my fingers free, and clamped my thighs together, riding that wave of euphoria until I crashed back down.

Would they hate me now? Tobias' rage was seared fresh in my memory. He'd be meaner, maybe more than he'd been before. *God, what the fuck have I done?* My bladder ached, reminding me I had to get out of bed. *My bed...*

I'd been in Tobias'...so how had I gotten here? The answer was a blur of darkness as I pushed up, climbed out of bed, and looked down. I was wearing Tobias' t-shirt...and his boxers. I winced and pulled the shirt over my head, not knowing how to feel about that.

He just wanted you out of his room...that's all, that nagging whisper said. *Don't read anything into it.* I shoved the boxers down, grabbed them both, and waded them up tight. I'd leave them in the hamper in the bathroom, no one would know.

I hurried, slipping on panties and a pair of cutoff sweats, before pulling on a bra and t-shirt and left my room with Tobias' clothes in my hand. I couldn't stop my gaze from traveling to his door, and my body clenched in response.

The low hiss from the automatic coffee machine came from the kitchen downstairs, drawing me back to the night mom and I had arrived. It seemed like forever ago now. Forever since I'd been here, trapped in this hell with three men who wouldn't leave me alone. I stepped inside the bathroom and closed the door behind me, then marched to the hamper and tossed Tobias' dirty clothes in.

"Getting rid of the evidence, I see."

I flinched and spun, coming face to face with Tobias as he closed the door quietly behind himself and hit the lock. "You need to be careful now, Ryth. Don't you know, locking the bathroom door is a must when you live on the same floor with three insatiable men."

He came closer, gripping a small white bottle in his hand. I flinched when he reached for the strand of hair on my face, brushing it to the side. "Last night," he started, and for a second, I thought I saw longing in those dark eyes. "Was what I wanted, but it wasn't right for you. So, I need you to take this."

He opened the bottle and shook out a small white pill. I lifted my gaze from his hand. "What is that?"

"Something to counter what I did last night." He came closer, placing it in the center of my palm before moving to the sink. He turned on the tap and came back to me, a half-filled cup in his hands. "Do you regret it?"

I met his stare, seeing fear. Did I regret having sex? A good girl would be appalled, even sickened, especially by who they were soon to be. But I'd known for a long time there was a darkness in me, a hunger handed down through my bloodline.

You always were more like me than your mom, dad's words resounded as I stared into Tobias' gaze. "No."

The corners of his lips curled with a smile. "Good. Take this pill, Ryth, and we'll get you an appointment with a doctor we know for the regular pills."

The pill.

There was no way I'd even thought about that, Seeing as how I hadn't even come close to having a steady boyfriend before. Now...now it seemed like I had three. *Don't get ahead of yourself.*

I took the pill, placed it in my mouth, and swallowed it with a gulp of water. Tobias took the cup, placed it on the counter, and turned, grasping me around the waist. "Can I trust you to keep your head about this?"

My mind was a blur, but he wasn't, nor was the memory of what we'd done last night. He was telling me I could have it again if I kept my mouth shut. Was that what I wanted? My body knew the answer, sending my panicked pulse skyrocketing. "Yes."

"Good." He moved his hand to the back of my head. "Very good."

Then he kissed me, taking my mouth until that familiar ache came again. But this time there was no alcohol to dull my emotions. No, this time I was breathtakingly aware of how much I wanted him. I melted into his forceful mouth, giving into him before he broke away.

"Get dressed, Ryth. Nick will take you to see the doctor within the hour. You're to take the pills she gives you regularly, because if you don't...I'm going to put a baby in that belly of yours."

Oh God...

My knees shook as he turned and went to the door, stopping with his hand on the handle, his voice low and forceful. "We're giving you time to heal after last night, but don't take too long, little sister. Because knowing you're two doors down from me is going to be pure fucking torture. I can't wait to fuck you again."

He opened the door and I caught sight of Nick standing in the hallway before Tobias was gone, closing the door carefully, leaving nothing but the frantic pounding in my chest behind.

"Oh shit." I stumbled forward and grabbed the vanity. *Did that just happen?* I lifted my gaze to the mirror, finding my lips flushed and my eyes wide. *It did...Oh God, it did.*

I couldn't stop the heat roaring through my body, and the way he'd made me feel like nothing else existed. I pressed my lips together, feeling that dull, throbbing ache, remembering Nick and Caleb last night. They'd all looked at me like that, like I was the most important thing in the world to them. Like I...I stared at my reflection, lingering on the mark on my face and my messy bed-head, *this me,* was an opiate they couldn't kick.

Because they didn't want to.

They wanted me...

All three of them.

Trembles coursed through me once more, until Tobias' instruction resurfaced. *Get dressed, Ryth...Nick will take you to see the doctor.* I turned and used the toilet, then stripped and hurriedly hit the lever for the shower and stepped in, wanting to obey my stepbrother's commands.

I washed and rinsed, and by the time I raced from the bathroom wrapped in a towel, I was almost humming with excitement. I threw on underwear and dressed, pulling on jeans and a soft pink top before I yanked on my boots and hurried downstairs.

Mom was sitting at the island, her head in her hands, while Creed moved, slowly cooking eggs on the stove, barefoot and still dressed in last night's very wrinkled clothes. He turned and slid a plate along the island to her.

"Do you have to breathe so damn loud?" Mom grumbled.

Creed just stood still, then slowly lifted his gaze to me and winked. I couldn't help but burst out laughing, which earned me a bleary-eyed glare from my mom. "Shouldn't you be at school?"

"Honey," Creed whispered. "It's Sunday."

Mom just looked at him like she didn't understand the concept of no school on the weekends.

"It's okay," Nick said, striding toward me from somewhere deeper in the house. "I'm taking Ryth out anyway."

"Go." Mom waved me away and closed her eyes, leaning over her plate of eggs. "Everyone...just go."

Creed smiled and motioned to the door. "I think it's best you guys are busy, at least until I can get her into her bed with some damn Advil."

"Good luck with that. I don't think I've ever seen mom that hungover before."

"Apparently the night went well." He glanced over his shoulder at her moaning in the kitchen and chuckled. "Maybe a little too well."

Nick just jiggled his keys, which made Mom groan even louder, and grabbed my arm...in a brotherly way. "Good luck with that," he smiled. "Looks like you and me, kid."

I didn't have time for coffee, didn't have time to even say goodbye. Creed just opened the front door and ushered us out.

"Ever get the feeling you're not wanted?" Nick chuckled, and pulled me with him.

"Just not for the next...say three to five days, that sound good to you?" Creed whispered, smiling and waving us out.

I left, following Nick, and laughed, like actually fucking laughed. Which felt alien and so damn good. He unlocked the Mustang and opened the passenger door. "Princess."

That name sent a shiver along my spine as I climbed in, leaving him to close the door behind me. Everything had changed now, and yet as he climbed in behind the wheel and gave me a wink, I realised nothing really had.

He was still the same gorgeous bad boy...and I was still the naive girl he'd driven to school on my first day. *Except he'd fucked me...last night, his cock stretching me wide. Christ, he was big...*

I clamped my thighs closed and raised my gaze to Creed standing in the front door.

"Smile, princess, and wave, like nothing has changed."

I did as he said, lifting my hand, giving a flicker of a smile as Nick started the car.

"Good girl," he murmured.

Heat surged inside me, pooling between my thighs. God, I was permanently wet around them, fixated on every glance and every damn sigh. He braked, then shoved the car into gear and slowly accelerated, reaching over to rest his hand on my thigh. "You okay?"

I swallowed hard and nodded. "Yeah."

"You did well. T wasn't sure if you'd unravel."

I jerked my gaze his way. "And you?"

He gave a sly smile and gripped my thigh. "I knew you'd do just fine."

His praise made something in my chest flutter.

"Now, how about we see to this doctor, yeah?" He pulled his hand away and drove, taking us toward the city.

My body craved his fingers, and his lips. Sitting there across from him, knowing what we'd done, was both awkward and consuming. "Did you...did you like doing that with me?"

He cut me a look. "Last night?"

"Yeah." I swallowed, my face burning.

"Let's put it this way. I've jacked off three times thinking about it this morning and I'm still fighting the urge to take you to the goddamn playground."

Adrenaline raced through me at the thought. *Our playground.* I imagined it differently now. I envisioned the way he'd tackled me to the ground, imagined the way he'd demanded I turn in this very seat and face him while I touched myself.

I fixed my gaze on his lips, imagining his mouth between my thighs, and let out a tiny, tortured sound.

"You doing okay, princess?"

The way he said the words, he knew I wasn't. I wasn't doing okay at all.

I forced my focus back to the road and answered. "How much longer until we're alone?"

He just laughed, then punched the accelerator and drove faster.

29

Ryth

I walked out of the doctor's office with a prescription and a month's supply of birth control pills and climbed back into the Mustang, letting it all sink in.

"Everything okay?"

I nodded and lifted the box that was already opened, with one of the pills gone. "Yep. She said we need to use protection for the first few weeks."

"Good," he nodded, then reached over and took the prescription from my hand before starting the engine. "We don't want you getting pregnant, do we?"

You're to take the pills she gives you regularly. Tobias' warning echoed from earlier. *Because if you don't...I'm going to put a baby in that belly of yours.*

The way Tobias had spoken, I wasn't so sure about that. I glanced over at Nick as he pulled out into the traffic, making his way further into the city. The thought of being pregnant was

263

terrifying, especially at my age. But the thought of my belly big and round, carrying their baby, made me a little giddy.

But I didn't need to worry about that. Not now.

Nick drove me to some busy looking diner on the south side and pulled the car into the lot. "Ready to eat?"

My belly let out a savage snarl and that dull throb in the back of my head echoed in kind. "More than ready."

He led me in, found us a booth in the back, and ordered pancakes and bacon, as well as juice and coffee. It was enough to feed a family, but the moment the waitress left, leaving us alone, he fixed those dark, molten eyes on me. "Do you want to ask me anything?"

I glanced around. "Here?"

He shrugged, barely caring. "Why not?"

He was testing me. That's what this was...a damn test. Would I be stupid and blurt out something without thinking, or would I be careful? I smiled as the waitress neared, carrying the coffee and juice, then waited for her to leave, grabbing my coffee and lifting it almost to my lips. "Do you share everything with your brothers?"

Nick just grinned, grabbing his own. "It depends..."

"Have you shared everything before?" I was intrigued now. Was there no rivalry?

"No." His eyes glinted, capturing mine as he spoke. "But then again, we hadn't had something we all wanted badly enough...*until now*."

"Oh," I whispered. My blood felt warm, *too warm* as I remembered that first night Tobias cornered me in the bathroom. "I thought Tobias said you did."

"If he did, then he was scaring you." He narrowed that carnal gaze on me. "We decided in this instance we could all be winners, *if that was on the table.*"

Electricity hummed between my legs. I clamped my knees together as the waitress neared again, carrying two plates piled high. "Here you go, you two, out for a breakfast date?"

"She's my sister," Nick growled, meeting her nosy stare.

"Oh," she winced, then covered it with, "How nice of you to take care of her like that. I don't see much of sibling love like this."

"I bet you don't," Nick answered, and my face burned.

He glared at her until she turned and awkwardly left.

"Nosy bitch," he muttered, then grabbed his cutlery and attacked the food on his plate, stopping to look over at me, his fork halfway to his mouth. "Eat, Ryth."

I grabbed my fork before I knew it. How easy it was to now follow his every command. *Eat, Ryth...get dressed, Ryth...that's the way, fuck him, Ryth.* My hand trembled. I licked my lips and met his stare. It wasn't food I wanted...now that I was sober and every much aware of every glance and every touch, I wanted to feel him in other ways.

He just grinned and clucked his tongue. "There'll be plenty of time for that, princess. Right now, you need to eat to keep up your energy."

When he said it like that...

I shoved a forkful in my mouth. Pride gleamed in his eyes as Nick watched me take every bite until I leaned back and moaned. "I'm done. I can't eat another thing."

His smile grew wider and God, if that small thing didn't make me feel alive.

He leaned across, grabbed my plate still piled with bacon, and scraped it onto his own, then set to demolishing the whole thing. I sat back, watching him with amusement, wondering how someone could eat like a damn horse and still look like him. Memories came back to me, the club, the fight, the way he'd charged into that back room, lunging after the men who had Caleb...and the way he'd thrown that bouncer to the floor.

I'd never seen anything so aggressive. Sitting there watching him, knowing what we'd done last night, only made me want him more.

"You're staring," he muttered, carving into the last pancake before shoving it into his mouth.

"Sorry."

He lifted his head and his movements stilled, the fork halfway to his lips. I caught the flicker of his eyes as he quickly scanned the diner around us, his voice deepening. "Told you before, princess. You can look all you want, all you have to do is say the words."

I looked away, flushing. But inside, I was racing, breathless with his intense focus. Then he ate, consuming the rest of everything else. "You gonna drink the rest of your juice?" he asked, drawing my attention.

I shook my head and slid the glass toward him, watching him give me a cocky smile and grab it, draining the contents in three massive gulps. How many years had I spent wondering what it'd be like to have brothers? To have a house that was loud and boisterous, to have my food eaten for me, and to have someone to watch out for me, to protect me no matter what. To have something that wasn't just born from blood, but carved out of soul. My soul. Now I knew.

Nick stilled, the back of his hand chasing the remnants of the juice on his lips. Stars sparkled in his eyes and inside me, I ignited. He saw me, the real me, and he wanted more. We might not be tied by blood or the impending marriage of both our parents, but this moment, right now, felt different...*it felt more.* It felt more real than anything else I'd ever had before.

More real than the love of my parents.

More than the love of myself.

And as that glint in his eyes grew deeper, I knew he felt it too. Whatever this was between us was growing, taking on a life of its own...and we were helpless to stop it.

"Everything okay over here?" The waitress neared the table, shattering the moment.

But Nick didn't let her steal everything. "Go away," he growled. "You can clear the table when we're done."

She stiffened and jerked her glare from me to Nick before turning on her heels, muttering something under her breath as she stormed away. I was speechless. The way he'd turned on her, the way he'd gone from that charge of excitement to pure unmistakable dominance left me giddy.

"Are you done, Ryth?" he asked carefully as he threw enough cash to cover our bill onto the table, and added a generous tip.

Unable to think properly, I just nodded. He slid out of the booth then, offering his hand. "Little sister." I took it, catching my breath at the connection as his hand clasped around mine.

Then together we strode out of the diner and headed for the car.

I expected him to take me to the park, to make good on what his eyes had promised. God, if I wasn't ready. But he didn't. Instead, he drove home and pulled into the driveway.

The Jeep was back.

My pulse raced at the sight. Tobias and Caleb had left before us, and now they were back. My gaze went to Creed's gunmetal gray Mercedes with the trunk open. Nick pulled up and killed the Mustang's engine as Creed strode out of the house, looking very different from how he'd looked before.

He was freshly showered and dressed in his usual dark gray slacks and crisp white shirt with the sleeves rolled up. He carried an overnight bag and a suit in a garment bag.

"Going somewhere?" Nick asked as we neared.

It was easy to see where his sons got their looks from...and their dangerous magnetism. Creed scowled, looking pissed as hell as he placed his bags into the trunk. "Something's come up."

"How many times have I heard that?" Nick muttered.

"It's a quick one. I should be home tomorrow, but in case I'm not," he continued, glancing my way. "You might want to check on your mom later tonight. She was feeling pretty lousy, so she's taken something that will help her sleep it off. Just don't expect her to surface anytime soon, okay?"

I nodded, my pulse spiking as Nick turned his head, directing that hunger my way. A fierce flare of yearning slammed into me like a locomotive as Creed slammed the trunk closed and rounded the car, yanking open the driver's door before climbing in without another word to his son.

Nick grabbed my hand, pulling me out of the way as Creed started the Mercedes, then backed down the driveway.

"That was..." I started, watching the Mercedes reverse through the open gate, then brake and accelerate away.

"Him," Nick finished for me. "In his usual stay-out-of-my-way fashion." His hand still gripped mine, but it shifted, warming, turning from a touch of necessity to one of wanting. "Come on."

He pulled me toward the front door of the house. *It'd be our house in less than a week,* our family house. The thought lingered as Nick locked the door behind us. Silence waited, the thud of our steps echoing. The kitchen was clean and back to its usual pristine condition.

There was no cleaner today...and now, no Creed.

"I guess we better look in on your mom." Nick tightened his grip around my hand and tugged me to the stairs.

I followed, climbing behind him until we stopped at the second floor, outside the bedroom my mom now shared with Creed, her soon-to-be new husband. Nick slipped his hand from mine and motioned his head to the door.

I stepped close, calling softly, "Mom?"

There was no answer, so I cracked open the door, listening. Deep snores came from the darkened room. I opened the door wider and stepped in. Nick followed, coming close behind me.

Through the murky gloom, I caught the outline of her body under the covers. "Mom?" I called again.

Her answer was a snore that resounded through the room. A bottle lay on her nightstand, the cap off...I crossed the space and picked it up.

"She's out cold," Nick murmured behind me.

I stepped closer, gripped her shoulder, and have her a shake. "Mom?"

But there was no answer, no fluttering of her eyelids, no indication she heard me at all.

"Come on." Nick tugged on my hand. "She's not surfacing anytime soon."

I let him pull me away, taking a look over my shoulder as I neared the door. She snored as she slept, passed out and hung over. That woman who looked like my mom was a stranger to me. Maybe I was a stranger to her, too...

I stepped through the door, letting Nick close it behind me. He stopped, his gaze capturing mine before he stepped closer, grazed my jaw with his finger, and tilted my head. His kiss was insistent and warm, the faint taste of the juice still lingering in his mouth. I let out a moan before I realized where I was.

Panic filled me, booming in my chest, as I broke free from his mouth and glanced at mom's bedroom door.

Nick just chuckled. "She's not waking, Ryth. Those tablets she took? They're the ones they gave my mom. You won't see her for a solid twelve hours."

Twelve hours? I looked away.

He smiled, those devilish eyes glinting as he gripped my chin, turning me back to him. "Wonder what we can do to fill the time?"

Oh God...

30

Ryth

He leaned down, kissing me with the kind of hunger that was consuming. But there was a difference this time. A change I felt in the brush of the back of his finger along my cheek, and the way he stared into my eyes as he towered above me.

He moved, driving me back against my mom's door, and cupped my breast. "I've been desperate to do this all morning," he murmured too loud.

Panic raced through me. I tore my gaze to the door. "Nick," I whispered. "She'll hear."

His slow, wicked smile made my pulse race as he lifted my shirt. "Then I guess you're gonna need to be quiet, princess."

My blood hummed in my veins as his crooked finger found my nipple. I dropped my head back and closed my eyes. The feel of those big hands on me sent a delicious warmth through me. I felt him move, brushing my shirt up to tug on the cup of my bra, my pathetically plain cotton bra.

Mine

"Christ, I love it when you wear this," he whispered, lowering his head to take my warming peak in his mouth.

Warmth surged through me, dancing around the sensitive flesh until my knees shook and my will wavered. I speared my fingers through his hair, sliding deep in the length, driving him harder, which only spurred him on.

He gripped me around the waist and lifted my feet from the floor before he sank to his knees, laying me down carefully, right in the doorway of my mother's bedroom.

Quiet now, princess, his smirk warned as he reached for the button of my jeans. I shook my head, my eyes wide as my gaze turned helplessly to the door. But no matter how hard I pushed his hands away, he wasn't stopping. The slow slide of my zipper had me shivering in fear.

I couldn't think over the booming of my heart. My gaze was riveted on the handle of my mom's door as Nick peeled my jeans lower, growling as he found the same Hello Kitty panties I'd worn in the car that first time he'd taken me to our park.

Our park...

That's what it was now. Ours...his...mine. He yanked off my boots and tugged my jeans down before discarding them in one brutal jerk. Movement came from the corner of my eye. I tilted my head, to see Tobias and Caleb approaching along the hall and watching the display.

"I see you found your mom out cold," Tobias said to me with a hint of amusement. "Couldn't wait, brother?"

Nick's answer was the solid slide of his finger along my crease. "What the fuck do you think?"

I looked down, eyeing the enormous bulge in his jeans. He was hard...already he was hard. Oh God, the memory of him last night had me trembling.

"That's the way." He pushed my legs wider and leaned down.

His big fingers captured the elastic of my panties. The same warmth that was cooling on my breast now found my pussy. I lifted my head, my fingers entwined in his hair as I guided him where I wanted him.

I was already wet, already aching, already desperate to come against his mouth. He sucked my clit, sending shivers along my spine.

"Such a greedy princess," Caleb murmured, drawing my focus.

I looked up, finding them watching Nick licking between my legs in the doorway of our parents' bedroom.

"Muffle that cry, Ryth," Tobias warned as Nick slid his hands under my ass and tilted my pussy to his mouth.

I bit down on my lip, hard enough to send a spear of pain to collide with the pleasure.

I was going to come...

I was going to come.

I was...

Nick pulled away, leaving me shaking...and panicked. I jerked my gaze to him, my throbbing lips curling against my teeth. "What?"

He just smiled, his mouth glistening as he swiped the back of his hand along his lips. "Nothing." He lifted his head, but movement rushed toward me.

"Our turn." Tobias bent, grabbed me with both arms, and lifted me from the floor.

I reached out, grabbing him as I landed bareassed and squirming in his arms.

"Easy, Ryth," he ordered, those dark eyes flashing with promise. "Unless you want me to hang you over this railing...*and rail you*."

My body clenched.

The image of that came alive in my mind, the hard railing pressed against my hips, my legs splayed wide, my pussy bare for all to see. I closed my eyes, biting the inside of my cheek and squirmed once more in his arms, only this time it was for a whole different reason.

I tightened my grip, lifted my gaze to Tobias', and whispered. "I'm...*I'm going to come.*"

"Not yet you aren't, little mouse," he forced through gritted teeth and took the stairs faster, then headed for Nick's room. Footsteps echoed behind us before the door closed.

Then it was just them and me...

The only difference was, this time I was sober.

"Protection this time." Caleb shot Tobias a glare.

"You okay with this, princess?" Nick stepped closer, gripped his shirt and peeled it free.

My pulse was out of control. I wanted to crawl into the corner and hide. But there would be no more hiding, no more denying what my body craved.

"Say now," Caleb urged. "Tell us what you want, and it'll happen."

I jerked my gaze to him. "You mean, no sex?"

He shrugged. "If that's what you want. Or if you just want Nick to go down on you, or if you just want one of us to take care of you. It's up to you."

The three of them waited. I lowered my gaze. They were ready, hard...and oh so greedy. "I...I want." I glanced at Tobias, finding that cruel spark shimmering under the surface. "One at a time. I want to feel you, want to know you." My cheeks burned. "I want to see you."

The corners of Tobias' lips curled as he yanked his shirt off.

"That's our girl," Caleb grinned.

I came alive under the praise, that pulse between my legs throbbing as Tobias shoved down his jeans. His cock was thick and hard, bouncing against his abdomen as he neared. But the moment he leaned forward and slid his hands along my thighs, I caught sight of his bloodied knuckles.

Panicked snatched me away from desire. I grabbed his thumb, lifted his hand, and met his gaze. "What the hell happened?"

"Nothing," he answered, giving nothing away. "Just a minor disagreement."

I winced, staring at the split, raw skin. "Doesn't look minor to me."

"You haven't seen the other guy," Caleb disagreed coldly.

God, these men were pure testosterone, from the muscle cars, to the looks of ravenous desire they fixed on me, to bare-knuckle fistfights with God knows who. I lowered my head, lifted his hand, and kissed the torn, bloody skin.

He was in pain...

If not now, then he had been then. I didn't like that, not at all. A sudden flare of rage tore through me as I stared at his injured hand. "Did you beat him..." I met his gaze. "Did you hurt him?"

"Yeah." That deadly shine shone brighter. "I did."

"Good." I lowered those poor hurt fingers to my breast, and watched his thumb brush my nipple, drawing a ragged breath free. "Good."

He bent low and kissed me, pushing me back on the bed, pride so close to that threatening trait I knew in him.

"You still hate me?" I had to know.

"Do you want me to?" he asked, leaning over me, caging me in.

Part of me wanted him to. It needed him to, like there was a role we all played here, and this...this cruel, predatory mask was his. "Yes," I whispered.

He grinned, then his fingers on my breast pinched, hard enough to draw a sharp gasp. "Then I do, more than ever, little mouse."

That longing in me came alive with his words.

"And I'm going to take out my anger on your body. I'm going to fuck you, little sister. Whenever and however I want, you got that?"

I shivered...*hard.*

"I'm going to punish you, going to use you." He leaned close...so close his breath became mine. "You're mine, little mouse...*and I'm the goddamn viper.*"

His hand moved against the bed as promise glowed in his eyes. He needed this, almost as much as I did. He needed it to *feel*. I moved upwards, desperate to kiss him...until he pulled away with a smug smile.

Bastard.

A crinkle came from his hand. He lifted the wrapper to his teeth, never once taking his gaze from me, and tore it open. This was happening...*really...really happening.* My body came alive, adrenaline surging through me as he held the sheath over his cock. "Soon, little mouse. Soon I'm going to fill you."

My gaze trailed down his chest and hard stomach. He was toned and firm from all those mornings spent in the gym and the afternoons pounding the pavement. I wondered what drove him...what consumed him. He slid the condom over the head of his cock, those dark eyes fixed on mine. Whatever had driven him before was now replaced with something else...*me.*

He shoved my leg aside cruelly and leaned closer, pressing his cock at my entrance. I held my breath, waiting for that initial rush, but there was nothing. Pressure built, the slick of the condom slid against me...until with a growl, Tobias plunged in.

I closed my eyes, shaking with the invasion. My senses exploded with the brutal thrust.

He snarled and slid out slowly, only to drive back in even harder. The movement shoved me into the mattress and he rode my hips as he thrust again...and again, stretching me until I couldn't breathe.

"I fucking hate you," he grunted with the brutality. "Look at me."

I wanted to panic. *I fought to panic,* but still I obeyed, opening my eyes to watch him. His lips were curled, that endless stare shone with frenzied compulsion. "I hate you, Ryth," he growled, sliding out.

Only I didn't see hate, I didn't *feel* hate, not when he rammed back in and lunged forward, bracing his arms on each side of me. No, it wasn't hate that shone back at me as he bucked his hips, driving that thickness inside me.

I slid my arms up his back and his body shivered with the touch. There was a flare of panic in his stare. A tremor I felt in my soul. Heat spilled through me, stoked by his desperate need.

"I know you do," I whispered as he fucked me, sliding my hands along his strong back, feeling the corded muscles.

"Hate her, brother," Caleb urged softly. "Hate her all you want."

Tobias lowered his head as his hard breaths against my cheek stoked the flames. He was all I felt, his brutal invasion, his breath searing that mark on my cheek. His consuming agony that seemed to have no end as he fucked harder and faster...and I wanted more.

"I love you," I moaned as that heat raged, pulsing in my pussy.

Slick.

Hard.

Hated.

I cried out as he thrust deep, giving into that surrender. His mouth found mine and his cruel fingers gripped my ass as he grunted. The sound invaded my mouth, and he stilled. He spasmed inside me, drawing the last tiny shudders from deep in my core.

His lips burned and his hunger was consuming. Suddenly, I was standing on the driveway of my old house once more, watching my world burn to the ground. Only that was a world I'd never felt part of,. a world where I'd never once belonged... *but here...with them...here, I'd found my space.*

His mouth grew softer, moving to the corner of my lips. "My little mouse," he whispered, still inside me. And I knew in that moment there was no going back...for the both of us.

My little mouse. The words branded me.

He lifted his head. Need and pain danced together in the glint of his eyes as he slowly withdrew. "Got that, Ryth?"

I sucked in deep breaths, unable to look away as I watched him push off the bed and slowly stand. I knew what he was saying. I slowly nodded, my gaze trailing down the shine of sweat on his chest.

I wasn't just his...*he was now mine.*

"You okay?" Nick stepped forward, drawing my gaze.

I gave him a small smile, coming back into my body. "Yeah."

Tobias slid his hand along his cock, dislodging the condom with a swipe. The surge of desire I felt for him compounded as Nick moved to kneel on the bed. "You did so well, princess." He slid his hand under my neck.

For a second, panic found me. I looked at Tobias, searching his gaze for a hint of jealousy or anger...and found *pride*. He watched me, then his gaze moved to his brother.

"Do you feel alright?" Nick drew my focus.

I turned my head as he trailed a finger along my core. Aftershocks followed his touch, drawing that ebbing heat back once more. "Yes."

"You're not sore?" He met my gaze. "My brother fucked you hard, princess."

Oh God...

Fire licked deeper with the words. His fingers followed that flare of heat, the lightest trace of his fingers circling my clit, dancing around the tender flesh.

"Yeah," he whispered, dipping a finger inside. "He fucked you real hard."

I closed my eyes, my body trembling.

"You still want to feel me inside you?"

My body bloomed. I opened my eyes and nodded as his finger slid deeper. Tobias tossed a foil packet his way, hitting him in the chest. He slid his finger from me and grabbed it, pushing up on the bed to work the button of his jeans.

This moment had been coming since the second we'd stepped into that diner. He'd bought me food and driven me in his car. Nick took care of me in ways the others didn't...and I *craved that.*

He stilled, those honey-brown eyes deepening to amber. I opened my legs, showing him exactly what I wanted. His breath caught with the movement before he lifted the wrapper to his mouth and tore it open. One long slide of his hand along his cock and he'd sheathed himself. I froze with the movement. He was big...bigger than Tobias, bigger even than I remembered. That thick, angry vein pulsed along the shaft under his hand. "You like this?"

I nodded. "I like you." I glanced at Caleb, then Tobias. "I like all of you."

Nick just grinned and stepped out of his jeans. "That's good, princess. We like you too..." He climbed onto the bed, his finger finding my aching pussy as he looked down. "Very...very much."

Faint memories of last night came to me as he leaned closer and slipped his hand free to guide his cock. That big head probed my entrance. Panic burned for a second as he pushed in, stretching me, before he slid out.

"Breathe, Ryth," he urged, guiding himself back in once more.

He went down...a lot. Now I knew why.

"She's fucking new," Tobias snarled, glaring at his brother. "Don't hurt her."

"This hurt, princess?" Nick asked, sliding the head inside again, pushing me, straining me.

I opened my legs wider, my pussy clenching for more. Hunger licked deep inside me. I shook my head.

"That's my girl," he grunted, driving a little deeper, sliding that thick knob inside.

Inch by inch, he moved further in, forcing my thighs to tremble with the invasion. He tilted his hips, stroking that part of me that made me cry out. I clutched his shoulders and drew him closer.

His arms caged me in until his body was all I could feel, invading, consuming, and I was nothing more than that slow, powerful thrust.

"Fuck, you feel perfect," he moaned, bucking his hips. "Goddamn perfect, princess. You're gonna make me..." He lowered his gaze, the word shining bright in his stare. "Gonna make me fall for you."

"Then fall." I gripped his shoulders and drove my body down, meeting his surge. I wanted more, more of him, more of them. I wanted him crowding my every move. I wanted not a second of my life without them. I wanted the heat of their bodies to never leave. "Fall for *me*."

Nick scowled, driving deeper. That delicious heat slammed into me once more as my pussy trembled, clenching around his cock. I bowed my spine, smashing my breasts against his chest, and cried out.

Over and over...

My body spilled and tightened, tiny pulses quaking around Nick as he lowered his head, his breath hot against my neck. His low moan filled my ear.

"Fuck...*me*," he groaned, stilling deep inside me.

Hard breaths came to me in stereo, filling my ears, rushing in my head. Nick's breaths were a blowtorch against my neck before he lifted his head and looked at me. "You okay?"

I couldn't speak, only nod. He pulled away from me, but I wasn't ready. "No," I croaked, pulling him back against me. "Not yet."

He stayed, pressing his weight against me even as he slipped free. My body throbbed, aching and clenching. I was overloaded, overwhelmed, but I still needed the warmth.

The bed dipped beside me and warmth pressed against my side. The sultry scent of Caleb washed over me. But there was no touch, no demands, just his *presence*.

"Relax, Ryth," Caleb murmured. "You need to rest, princess. There's plenty of time."

I exhaled hard and slow, opening my eyes to turn toward him. "I still..." I searched his gaze. "I still want to see you."

Nick moved slowly, rolling to the far side, leaving Caleb to rise. "You want to see me?"

I nodded, my body trembling. He rose from the bed, sleek and powerful, with barely more than a small dip to the mattress. His dark eyes glinted as he worked the buttons of his black shirt, opening them slowly as he turned. His knuckles were grazed and red, but not as bad as Tobias'. Whatever had gone down...they'd been there together.

Because they did everything together.

Caleb dropped his shirt to the floor. Powerful muscles flexed as he moved, working the tongue of his belt through the buckle. "This what you want, Ryth?"

My body shivered as he pushed his pants to the floor, leaving him standing in soft black boxer briefs, his cock straining against the fabric.

So precise.

So controlled.

The real him shimmering under the surface.

There was a lie about Caleb, a pretense where he lived. Everyone knew it. Everyone saw it, but no one acknowledged it. No one stepped into his darkened room and threw open the blinds, exploring his desires...*except for me.*

He survived in that lie, shrouded by mystery. Keeping himself hidden away. I pushed up in the bed, my arms trembling, my body spent. "Show me," I whispered, my core clenching.

He pushed his briefs down, releasing his cock. I saw his face from last night, the way his fingers had tangled in my hair as he'd guided my mouth there. My tongue skimmed my lips as my mouth grew wet. I wanted him inside me, even if my body shivered at the thought.

His hand worked his length, the red, marred knuckles turning white as he fisted the girth. A tiny tortured sound tore free as he stood there, just inches away. I swallowed, and lifted my gaze to his.

"There's plenty of time, Ryth," he reassured again, his clenched fingers sliding all the way to the head.

A tear glistened at the tip, until it was captured by his fingers and rubbed into the skin. I moved against the bed.

"Uh-uh." He stepped out of reach. "You want to watch, princess...*so watch.*"

I focused on the husky tone of his voice, and the way he worked his cock, the movement hypnotic and powerful. His stomach tightened. "Lie back," he demanded.

I dropped my weight, bracing on my elbows.

"Spread your legs for me, princess."

My core quivered at the command and my knees shook as I widened my thighs.

"You like my brothers fucking you?"

I let out a guttural moan, my cheeks burning.

"No need to be shy." Caleb took a step closer, his hand still moving, sliding up and down the shaft. "Not around us, little sister. After all, family takes care of each other...isn't that right?"

He moved closer, so close now I could reach up and touch him, the heat of his body touching mine.

"I want to tie you down." He stared into my eyes. "I want to take you into my room and leash you to my bed. I want to do things that will make sure you can't walk tomorrow." That animalistic gaze swept down my body. "I want to push that sweet little body to its limits. I want to stretch that pretty little cunt of yours wide. I want to fuck you, and keep fucking you, until even when I'm not inside you, you'll still feel me."

An orgasm hit me, vibrating deep, spilling through my body. Caleb smiled and reached down, grasping my knees to widen my legs further. "You like the idea of that, don't you?"

Even after Tobias and Nick, I was ready.

"Maybe I'll take your ass," Caleb murmured, those dark eyes alive. "How does that sound, sister?"

I reached down, my pussy pulsing, wet and aching. I pressed my palm against the hot flesh and closed my legs, turned my knees, and rolled, giving him access to where he wanted.

"That's my sweet angel," Caleb approved as he moved.

The slick heat of his cock trailed down my back as he lowered himself to the bottom of the bed. "Just a taste, little sister," he whispered, his finger gentle against my hot core, skimming the tight pucker of my ass.

Pressure built, but I had no time to feel shame, no time to feel anything but his touch working against the ring, pushing in, only to slide out.

"So brand fucking new," he muttered, pushing his finger into my ass. "Christ, I can't wait."

I lowered my head, my body clenching around the invasion, making that heat push nearer to the surface. The slick sounds of his hand on his cock came once more, the movement making him moan. I curled tighter, opening myself for his touch.

Hard thrusts of his hand came faster, working against the gentle probe of my ass as he slid his other finger deeper.

"I'm going to stretch you so wide, princess," Caleb growled, his voice filled with darkness and hunger.

I trembled, listening to the sounds behind me. The fact I couldn't see him or touch him only seemed to heighten my desire. I pushed against the conquering of my body...until, with a savage grunt, warmth spilled over my ass, sliding down into the crevice.

Caleb slid his finger free, leaving me gaping, until he rubbed his cum over my ass and inside. "Soon, little sister," he promised. "Soon."

31

Ryth

I trembled as that delicious warmth of Caleb's fingers marked me. They branded me as theirs with every touch and every kiss, with every look...God, even with their scent. The tang of sweat and sex was heavy in the air, staining every inch of my memory.

The crack of the small refrigerator in Nick's room came before footsteps. "Drink, Ryth," Tobias directed as he cracked open a bottle of electrolytes. "You need to stay hydrated."

I slowly pushed up, my body feeling battered as I reached for the bottle in Tobias' hand and took a swallow. Tobias dressed, yanking on his jeans, boots, and shirt. Nick followed, but it was Caleb who grabbed my clothes from the floor. "You're going to feel a bit sensitive for a while, until your body gets used to it." He lifted my panties, letting me slip my feet through the openings.

He did his best not to touch me, letting me slide my underwear up before he handed me my bra. "And I know you have that assignment due tomorrow," he continued. "So we're setting your desk up in here."

Nick was already moving to his desk, making room...*for me.*

I hooked my bra, then took my jeans from Caleb and slid them on. "Okay, why?" I wasn't sure about this.

"Just in case you need something," Tobias murmured, watching me.

"In case *I* need something, huh?" I rose from the bed on shaking legs. Caleb was right, my body trembled, even with the weight of my shirt as I slid it over my head.

"Let us take care of you, Ryth," Tobias added as Nick moved to the door, crackled it open, and stepped out. "After all, that's what big brothers do, right?"

Big brothers...the words collided with what we'd just done. I tracked the thud of Nick's footsteps to my room, then he returned moments later, carrying my laptop and notepad.

"You were having a little trouble, referencing." Caleb met my gaze. "You know I could help you with that?"

"I'm getting us food," Tobias muttered and strode toward the door.

In a heartbeat, the room was filled with movement. A space was made for me, sitting next to Nick. I drank the drink they gave me and stepped forward, sitting as Caleb motioned. It felt awkward, being in their room, and yet part of me wanted it. Part of me ached for it, no longer on the outside.

No...now I *belonged.*

I opened up my laptop and found my assignment. Caleb was right, the referencing was a hot mess. It was one of my most hated parts. Caleb left, then returned moments later with his own laptop. He sank to the floor at the bottom of Nick's bed, barefoot, sleeves rolled up, then opened a screen. "Send me the links and I'll reference for you."

"Isn't that cheating?" I gave a sigh, glancing over my shoulder.

His cocky smile was instant. "I won't tell if you don't, little sister."

My cheeks flushed at the wicked wink, making my chest flutter. *Thank God.* I smiled, pulled up the email draft I'd had the forethought to copy, and pasted the details. "What's your email?"

I sent it to him as Tobias strode in, placing a plate in front of me with a ham, cheese, and mayo sandwich. My stomach howled, even though I'd only just had breakfast. I glanced at the clock and stiffened. "It's two in the afternoon?"

Caleb chuckled.

"Yeah, it is." Tobias looked down at me, those coal eyes glittering with pride. "Time flies when you're having fun, right, little mouse?"

"Where's mine?" Nick muttered.

"Kitchen," Tobias growled as he strode past. "I'm not your fucking maid."

Caleb roared with laughter behind me as Nick turned and gave Tobias a shove, then the next minute, Tobias' sandwich went flying as they wrestled right behind me.

Grunts and growls, strength against training. Neither of them won. But by the time they were finished, Nick had taken a huge bite out of half of T's sandwich, earning him a threatening snarl. "Brothers," Caleb warned, his focus on the screen in front of him. Nick sank to his chair as I broke my half in two, handing one piece over.

"Thanks, sis," Nick said, and gave me a wink.

Jesus, I couldn't keep up with this. One minute Nick had his head between my legs, his tongue deep inside me, and the next he was calling me *sis*. Heat flushed in my cheeks as I forced myself back to my laptop. Caleb was right, I had only a few hours to finish this damn assignment and make sure it was compelling.

We lost track of time. I re-wrote chunks based on Caleb's input. Nick worked on his laptop on some kind of Bitcoin trade site, and Tobias just lay back on Nick's bed with his EarPods in, as he played a game on his phone. It all felt...*totally normal.*

We worked until the sun dimmed outside and night closed in.

"Food?" Tobias muttered.

"I swear, you're like a bottomless stomach, T." Caleb muttered.

"I'm fucking starving, too," Nick announced as he tossed his headphones aside and rose, stretching cramped muscles.

I lifted my head, but all I saw were passages I needed to rewrite before morning. But my body ached and my head felt fuzzy. "I think I need a break, too."

"Food it is then." Tobias shoved up from the bed. "This time someone else is cooking."

"You didn't cook last time," Nick glared. "A sandwich isn't cooking."

Tobias gave a shrug. "Bite me." He strode from the room, heading for his bedroom.

"Come on," Caleb said as he pushed up from the floor and moaned, stretching. "Looks like it's you and me, kid."

I glanced at Nick, who grinned and urged me onwards. I followed Caleb down to the kitchen, moving to the panty. "Right, what can you cook?"

"Whatever you feel like." He yanked open the refrigerator door and peered inside. "I make a mean omelet, how about that?"

"Sounds delicious," I said, my mouth watering. "It just so happens, I make a mean buttered toast."

He shot me a grin over his shoulder, his face brightened by the refrigerator lights. "Sounds like a match made in heaven."

That fluttering in my chest came once again as he pulled out cartons of eggs and butter, placing them on the counter. We worked silently. He plundered the fridge while I pulled out a bowl and whisk and started cracking eggs. One careful look toward the stairs, and Caleb grabbed my hips as he moved around me, kissing me on the shoulder.

I froze at the brush of his lips, my pulse stuttering and fear punching high as I jerked my own gaze to the stairs. "You still feel my cum on your skin, princess?" came the low murmur at my back.

Shivers tore along my spine as my body responded. "Yes," I answered.

"Good."

He moved away, grabbing one of the heavy pans and setting it on the stove. *Good? That's it?* I swallowed hard and tried to control the shake in my hand. He lit the burner, shifting the pan, and I was drawn to those hands, thick fingers clenched around the handle. I knew what was under that shirt, knew what lay under all his clothes, and knew what he tasted like.

"You're staring into space again," he murmured, and then turned.

Faint amusement shone like stars in his eyes, and the tight curl of his lips told me he liked the attention. "I forgot what we were doing," I answered.

He crossed the space toward me.

"Cooking dinner, by the looks of it," Mom groaned from the doorway, the faint *thud* of her steps finally registering. "Really, Ryth, you'd forget your head most days if it wasn't attached."

I flinched at the bite in her tone, watching her come toward us. She looked like hell, barely glancing at Caleb. No, instead, her bleary glare seemed to be fixed on me. "Where have you been?"

"Here," I answered, my tone cold.

"All day?" She yanked out a seat at the island and slumped down hard.

"All day." Caleb turned, sliding butter in the bottom of the pan before he grabbed the bowl of cracked eggs. "Ryth has been working hard on her assignment."

"Working," mom gave a huff and closed her eyes. "Just like her damn father, no doubt."

I froze, pain cutting through me at the words. Anger darkened Caleb's eyes as he turned on her, striding forward to brace his arms on the island in front of her. "You know, if you paid a little more attention, you'd actually see her for who she was, and not just an extension of you or her father."

She opened her eyes, finding Caleb right there, and gave a ghost of a smile. She seemed to notice him then, noticed his open shirt and the rolled-up sleeves, noticed the way he exuded seductive control. Her breaths deepened and a look of molten desire seemed to melt the ice she had for me. "I didn't mean..." she started.

"Didn't mean what?" Tobias growled, striding into the kitchen.

He rounded the corner, peered into the pan on the stove, and headed my way, reaching over my shoulder to snag a piece of cheese and plop it into his mouth, then turned toward her, standing at my back.

"Elle was just saying that Ryth—"

"That Ryth *what?*" Nick strode toward us as he, too, entered the kitchen, and headed to the fridge, grabbing out a beer before he cracked it open and took a step closer to me, peering at Mom.

The moves couldn't have been more deliberate, Caleb on one side, Nick on the other, and Tobias...Tobias standing at my back. She glanced from one to the other, and gave a small smile. "Nothing." She turned that smile to me. "Nothing, honey. Don't mind me, I'm just tired."

"Then maybe you should take your pissy attitude back to bed?" Tobias growled.

Mom flinched, glancing at Caleb. Did she see Creed in him? Did she think he'd turn on his own brother to take her side?

"You look tired, Elle," Caleb murmured.

"Those sleeping pills are hell," Nick added.

I glanced away, this was all my fault, if I hadn't...Tobias reached over me once more, grasping a piece of ham, his arm brushing mine with the movement. His chest was warm pressed against my back.

"I think you're right," Mom muttered, sliding from the chair. "I can't seem to shake this damn throbbing."

"Night," Caleb finished as the slow hiss of the butter melting filled the air.

Nick turned toward the stove. "I'm fucking starving, don't burn it, brother."

Dismissed, just like that. She never even looked at me before she slowly made her way back to the stairs and climbed. I tried to find a fragment of the mom I'd once known in the curve of her back and the slump of her shoulders.

But the truth was, she was as much a stranger to me now as she'd been then. I never really knew her, had never known her love. It was so hard, trying to find the feeling when it had never really existed at all. Mom gave only what she wanted, like a leaky faucet, and I'd clung to every drop, waiting for it with a ravenous thirst.

Pain coursed through me as her steps faded. Scrape, whisk, mumble, even the low brotherly jabs from Nick didn't invade the fog of my memories.

"You wait for her, and you'll be waiting a lifetime," Tobias said at my back. "Believe me...I should know."

He was right, I knew that. Still, it didn't ease the sting, nothing did. But as the scents and the sounds of my brothers closed in, they soothed the wound, pulling me away, until the ache of her was replaced by something else.

Something I'd never had in my entire life...a sense of belonging.

32

Ryth

I woke, cracking open my eyes. But this time, there were no vague memories of my soon-to-be stepbrothers, no murky darkness to hide the truth. No, this time, it came through neon bright. My heart sped even before they moved in.

One by one...

Tobias...

Nick...

Caleb.

I closed my eyes again and rolled over in the bed, tugging up the comforter. Mom's wedding was less than a week away. Then they'd be family...*for-real family.* Not blood, but still. Shame filled me, pulling me down a deep, dark hole.

The kitchen pushed into my thoughts, the way they'd stood at my side while Mom glared at me. It wasn't right, what I was feeling, wasn't what good girls did.

Maybe you should take your pissy attitude back to bed?

Tobias' growl rose inside me and that racing in my chest only grew bolder. I was starting to feel things for them, starting to find myself falling...and that was wrong. I shoved the bedding aside and sat up, lowering my head into my hands. *What the fuck was I going to do now?*

I lifted my gaze to where my laptop sat. I'd spent the next few hours after dinner alone in my room, submitting the assignment late last night. Nick had come in to check on me and Caleb had sent me a message along with the most perfect referencing I'd ever seen.

In the space of a day, they'd given me more than my parents ever had in my entire life. I rose from the bed, catching the bright glare of the morning sun. I needed to hurry, shower, and get ready. Nick would want to drive me to school, maybe we could stop at the park on the way?

The idea of that excited me.

I grabbed out my uniform and my stupid cotton underwear. *Christ, I love it when you wear this.* Nick's words filled me, stopping my embarrassment cold. I lifted the white Hello Kitty panties. Anyone else would hate them, think of them as childish. But not him...it looked like my stepbrother had a thing for the schoolgirl look.

I scanned the drawer and pulled out my white knee-high socks. God, I'd never have been caught dead wearing these before. I could only imagine the ridicule. But Nick...he'd *love* them. That was good enough for me. I tossed them onto the bed, grabbed my clothes, and hurried to the bathroom.

I showered, washing my hair and rubbing my hands down my body, taking my time to cup my breasts. My body was different now, a slow burning ache hidden under the surface. I closed my eyes and tilted my head under the spray, touching my nipples.

That's the way, princess, Caleb's voice sounded in my head. I rolled the tender flesh and my body responded. I wanted to stand here, exploring the way they made me feel. Maybe another morning. I turned, switched off the spray, and stepped out, grabbing the towel as the sight of Tobias' clothes drew my gaze. They were messy, leaving everything where it landed around them.

Brothers...

The word made me smile as I towel dried my hair and moved to the vanity, tugging on my panties. The door opened with no warning. I flinched, throwing my hands across my breasts.

"Seen them, licked them...*and will lick them again, little mouse.*" Tobias grumbled and yawned, striding past me to use the toilet.

"Tobias," I hissed, jerking my gaze to the open bathroom door. "You can't just barge in when I'm in here."

"Why not?" He yanked down his boxers and a steady stream hit the bowl. "You seem to forget...I hate you, *remember?*"

"Fuck you, Tobias," I snarled, grabbing my clothes and hurrying from the bathroom.

But underneath the burn of anger hummed a sensation that went straight to my core. I stepped into my room, muttering under my breath, and dressed for school, tugging the socks all the way to my knees.

I grabbed my laptop and strode out of my room, finding Tobias' bedroom door now closed. I wanted to beat my fists against it. I wanted to rattle his cage like he seemed to rattle mine...*every damn day.* My gaze went to my mom's door as I made my way downstairs. But instead of caring about how mom was...I was transfixed by the floor in front of the doorway.

Nick, no...what if she hears?

My own words echoed in my head as I made my way down the stairs, expecting Nick to be waiting for me...but he wasn't. Creed was, standing in the middle of the foyer.

His shirt was wrinkled, with dirt smeared across his side, and as he turned to me, I caught the dark splatter of dried blood.

"Creed?" I stepped closer. "What's going on?"

This was bad...whatever it was.

He raked his fingers through his hair, agony flaring in his eyes. "Ryth." He started forward, then stopped, glancing at the laptop in my hand. "I'll drive you to school."

I shook my head. "No, it's okay, I'll—"

"I said I'll drive you to damn school," he snapped, then stopped and took in a trembling breath before muttering, "I'm sorry. Look...*I'm sorry, okay?*"

I took a step closer, unable to look away from the blood. "Is everything okay?"

He wasn't okay, that was easy to see. He was...frantic. I'd never seen him like this, not unraveled, not *scared.* Memories of home came flooding back, the home I'd had with dad before he went to prison.

Creed forced a smile, his focus on me. "It's fine, Ryth. I just want to drive you, okay? Will you at least let me do that?"

I wanted Nick and fought the need to call out to him.

"Please, Ryth," emotion choked his voice as that pain-filled stare seized mine.

I stepped forward, nodding before I knew it. "Sure...sure, Creed."

He took a step closer, his shaking hand clenching to a fist before he glanced at the laptop. "I'll...I'll take you now."

I'd seen people in shock, seen them do some crazy shit. I'd even seen some act like they never remembered a thing. Was that Creed? I didn't follow as he turned for the door, just glanced over my shoulder, fighting the urge to call for Nick and tell him I was leaving.

"Ryth?" Creed opened the door and waited. "It's just to school, honey."

I tore my gaze from the stairs and walked out. The sun was glaring, causing me to lift my hand to shield my eyes before I yanked open the passenger door of his Mercedes. I leaned forward, stowed my things on the floor, and turned to scan the windows of my brothers' bedrooms.

The engine started and we were moving down the driveway when the blinds shifted at Nick's room. We drove a little too fast, hitting the asphalt with a jolt before Creed braked hard. My phone went *beep.*

I gripped the seatbelt, hanging on as Creed punched the accelerator, his hold on the steering wheel heavy, jerking the car hard.

"Looks like the meeting didn't go so well." I tried to make conversation as I grabbed my phone.

Nick: What the fuck, princess?

I gripped the phone, trying my best not to cry out as Creed spun the wheel and cut across the traffic.

"No," he said. "Not as well as I'd hoped, anyway." He jerked his gaze to me, something unhinged coming to life in his eyes. "But there's always more than one solution to a problem, wouldn't you agree?"

I didn't know what to say, so I just gave a small nod and opened up the messages, typing out a quick reply. *Creed made me get in his car. He's driving erratically. Nick, I'm scared.*

Cars flew past almost in a blur. I grabbed the seatbelt and looked at the speedometer. "Creed, please slow down. You're starting to scare me."

He didn't seem to hear me. His hands clenched around the wheel as he muttered, "More than one solution...*more than one solution...more than one—*"

Creed's phone started to ring, the number splashed on the screen between us. *Nick.* But Creed didn't answer. He acted like he didn't hear it at all. I leaned forward and, with shaking fingers, swiped answer.

"Dad?" Nick's voice came through the stereo.

I glanced at Creed, catching his lips moving as he muttered the same thing over and over again, only there was no sound.

"Hey, I think there's a problem with Tobias," Nick declared, his words falling on deaf ears. "Hey, can you hear me?"

"N-Nick," I spoke. "I don't think Creed's feeling well."

"I feel fine," Creed answered, and turned the corner hard. "Just fine."

"Wanna tell me what's going on?" I could almost feel the desperation in Nick's voice. "I was supposed to do the school run, remember? You put me in charge, right? You put me in charge after mom died."

Creed flinched at the words and jerked his gaze to the screen. A scowl cut deep before he jerked a frantic glance my way, as though he'd only just realized what was happening. His foot eased off the accelerator and we slowed as the turn to the school came up ahead.

Relief swept through me as Creed finally answered. "Yeah, yeah, Nick. I did."

"Ryth," my brother spoke to me. "You okay?"

"Yeah." I swallowed hard, watching the familiar buildings come toward me. "We're at the school now."

"Okay. Good, and Dad?"

"Yeah?"

"If you take my sister and drive like an asshole like that again, you and I are going to have problems. You understand me?"

Agony coursed across Creed's face as he pulled into the drop-off zone, slowing the car until he braked to a stop. He didn't answer, not for a long time. His cheeks reddened against his pale skin as he nodded. "Yeah."

"Call me when you get out, Ryth," Nick added, then ended the call.

My hands were shaking as I grabbed my laptop.

"I'm sorry," Creed started as I yanked the handle and shoved open the door. I couldn't get out fast enough. *Ryth! I, wait, I—*"

I pushed the door closed, gripped my laptop, and stumbled away. My knees were shaking and the breaths sawed in and out of my chest as I stepped further from the car and called Nick.

"Hey," he answered instantly, that low bass tone spilling through me. "You okay?"

"Y-yeah, I think so." I looked over my shoulder, watching the gray Mercedes pull out and make a U-turn. "He's gone."

"What the fuck was that?"

I stared at the rear of the car until it disappeared. "I don't know. But whatever it was, it wasn't good."

"Just as long as you're okay. Goddamn bastard. Just wait until he gets home."

That flutter came in the center of my chest, like wings expanding, brushing the cage around my racing heart. "Nick."

"Yeah, princess?"

I stopped walking. That's what he did to me...*stopped me cold in my tracks.* "I miss you."

"You want me to come?" His tone grew deeper, *huskier.* "You can skip...I'll take you to our park. Tell me what you want, and it's done."

I wanted that, more than anything. Footsteps crowded in from the other students around me. I caught sideways glances from some of the other females as they passed. God, if they only knew what I had waiting for me. "I can't," I sighed, and kept walking. "But the moment the damn bell rings."

"I'll be waiting," he answered me. "And this time, you're all mine, got that, princess?"

A shiver tore through me. "Yes."

"Good girl."

I ended the call with the words resounding through me and pushed open the door, descending back into Hell. Voices grew louder as I headed for the first class. I scanned unfamiliar faces for Gio, and the memory of our last interaction came roaring back to me.

My cheeks burned, remembering the way Tobias had grabbed my breasts in front of him, the act branding me, just as his body had. But there were things left unsaid between Gio and me, things that included Lazarus Rossi.

I ground my teeth, hating how anger followed. How could Gio have just stood there, knowing what they'd done? My father's bruised and bloody face lingered in my mind, the way he'd hung his head in shame, knowing the position he'd put us in.

Flames blazed under the surface, burning my entire world to the ground. I pushed through a crowd that was gathered outside the classroom. "Let me through."

But they didn't move, leaving me to clutch my laptop and shove through, catching a glimpse of Gio with his back turned to me.

"*Gio!*" I called.

He stood, talking to others already seated.

"Gio," I called again, catching the flinch before his spine straightened. But he didn't turn my way, couldn't even give me the goddamn respect of looking me in the eye.

"Look at me."

The others glanced my way, two guys I barely knew. Anger cut through me like a goddamn razor at their gazes, and I tasted the burn.

"You don't want to talk to me, fine," I hissed. "Goddamn spineless asshole."

"I'm the asshole?" His voice was thick and slurring as he turned to me. He tried to find my gaze, blinking thick tears that he wiped away with a tissue.

"What about what your fucking *brothers* did to me?"

I froze, stunned. He was a goddamn mess. I didn't know where to look. Bloody lips. Swollen eyes. Ugly, deep purple bruises that covered one side of his face.

Knuckles.

That's what had done that.

"You want to talk about *spineless?*" He stepped forward. "How about two on one? You wanna talk about that? No...I bet you don't, you fucking hypocrite."

"Okay, settle down," the teacher called as he strode into the classroom. "Mr. Romano. It looks like your weekend was...*interesting.*"

Gio glared at me before turning and pushing past to take his seat at the edge of the classroom and far from me. I couldn't move, even as others slid into seats around me. All I could see was Tobias' ruined knuckles...and my own cruel words. *Did you hurt him?*

Yeah, Tobias' answer followed.

Good...

Good.

I turned, slipping into the vacant seat in front of me, my movements in a fog. Voices came, the teacher speaking words I couldn't hear. Gio glanced over his shoulder, that squinted, painful stare finding me before he looked away.

They'd beaten him...

Bad.

Because of me.

I sat there in stunned disbelief, unable to hear a damn thing the teacher said, and when the bell rang, I was one of the first to move.

"Gio," I called and pushed my way toward him.

But he was already leaving, shuffling his way out of the classroom in an effort to get away from me. I swallowed hard, catching stares from the others in the class fixed on me. Heat burned in my cheeks and for the first time in days, I tugged my hair down, covering the side of my face, and walked out, desperate to get away from them.

33

Nick

I turned at the sound of the Mercedes pulling into the driveway. The engine died before the *thud* of the driver's door carried inside the house. *Goddamn bastard.* I clenched my fists, waiting for the front door to open before my father walked through, his head hanging low.

He stopped just inside and lifted his gaze to mine before a pained expression cut across his face. "Don't, okay, just...*don't.*"

"Don't?" I cut across the foyer, standing in front of the man I called father. "That's all you've got to say?"

"I'm sorry." He shook his head.

"You're *fucking sorry?*" I closed the distance, grabbed him by the filthy shirt, and glared into his eyes. How I'd ever seen this man as powerful was beyond me.

He wasn't powerful in this moment...he was a scared little boy. I took in the exhaustion in his gaze, then the filthy shirt fisted in my grip. "How about you tell Ryth that?"

"Tell Ryth what?" Caleb asked, stepping down the stairs behind me.

My older brother shot me a glance, one filled with panic, before he turned to dad.

"Tell her he's sorry for almost fucking killing her in the car this morning," I clarified, easing my brother's conscience. "Drove like a goddamn maniac and left her fucking terrified."

"What the fuck for?" Caleb moved to stand at my side. "And why the hell is there blood splatter on your damn shirt?"

Dad raked his hand through his graying hair and shook his head. "Nothing."

"What the fuck aren't you telling us?" Caleb took a step closer, bending to meet his gaze.

Lawyer versus lawyer. I knew who I'd put my money on.

"What the fuck did you do, dad?" Caleb searched his face.

But our father wasn't about to be cornered, not by his own sons. Anger flared deep. "Get the fuck out of my goddamn face, Caleb...and you—" he shot a glare my way. "Stay out of my goddamn business."

But his business was our business...especially now, where Ryth was concerned.

"What the fuck are you still doing here, Caleb?" Venom etched dad's words. He was a viper in that moment. One already bitten and hurting, ready to strike. "Don't you have a home to go to?"

"You want to talk about home?" That darkness rose in Caleb's eyes. "Or would you rather us just ignore the fact you brought a strange woman and her daughter home before the dirt had settled over our mother's coffin? What kind of fucking home do you think that is?"

Heat flared in dad's eyes "It's *none* of your concern."

"It is when you terrorize a young girl, one who's about to be our stepsister." Caleb never budged. When I looked at him, all I saw was mom.

Dad's shoulders slumped, the fire that'd been there a second ago snuffed out in an instant. "It was a mistake, okay?"

"One you won't repeat," I added. "I drive her to school and I pick her up. Me, or one of the others."

Surprise filled him and he scowled, then glanced at Caleb, who just met his stare with stony silence.

"Fine," dad muttered. "Whatever you want. I need a damn shower and some fucking sleep."

He headed for the stairs. I swore I saw him pause for a second as though there was something he wanted to say. But then he was gone, with the heavy thud of steps.

"What the fuck was that about?" Caleb muttered softly.

I shook my head as my phone *beeped.*

Ryth...

I grabbed my cell, opening the messages.

Natalie: Open the door, Nick. I want to see you.

"Shit." I winced as the sound of her damn Nissan pulling into the driveway.

Caleb scowled at the sound, then shook his head. "That's all yours, brother."

He left me...the sonofabitch left as the engine outside died. I frowned, my pulse speeding as Ryth roared to life inside my head. "Fuck." I strode to the door as the thud of a car door sounded.

Her shadow passed across the window as I opened the door. "What are you doing here?"

She forced a sad smile, stepping closer to the door. "Baby."

She reached for me, but for once I pulled away, shaking my head. "Don't."

Her cheeks flushed as she glanced behind me. "You not even going to let me in?"

Why? I wanted to ask. But that familiar ache of sadness wrapped around my heart when I looked at her. I didn't love her, that was easy to understand. I felt...*sorry for her.*

"Come on, Nicky." She stepped closer. "Do you hate me that much?"

God, I wanted to be a cold bastard like Tobias was...just once, I wanted to stand in the doorway and tell her to fucking leave.

"Wow," she wrapped her arms around her middle. "So you do hate me."

"I don't...I don't hate you," I muttered. "Why are you here?"

The flush in her cheeks deepened. "My earrings. I left them here...I need them back."

Shit.

311

"Where, I'll go get them."

She shook her head and moved even closer, pressing her hand to the center of my chest. "Don't be silly. I'll only be a second, Nicky. You can come with me."

It was a bad idea, a *real* bad idea. Each step she took felt like betrayal as Natalie pushed past and stepped inside. I had no choice but to follow her up the stairs and into my room. She turned the moment she was inside, her eyes raking my body. "I missed you, baby." She stepped forward, reaching out to me.

Her hands were warm and familiar. "Don't." But I didn't move, didn't push her away, even though I wanted to.

"Didn't you miss me?" she murmured, moving to press her breasts against me.

In my head, all I saw was my sister, her tiny breasts, smooth and perfect under my hand. "No, I didn't, Natalie," I said as I looked into her eyes.

The savage flinch almost made me feel like a bastard. She stepped back, glancing around the room. "Sure, okay. That fucking hurt." She turned away and lowered her head, fighting back tears I knew were a lie.

Because she was a liar and, as much as I hated it, Tobias had been right all along. She was a traitorous bitch, sleeping around behind my back, making me feel somehow like I wasn't good enough.

She made a move to kneel on the floor, peering under the bed, searching.

I clenched my jaw and forced the words through clenched teeth. "I thought you knew where they were?"

"I do," she sniffled, bending low to reach deeper into the shadows.

"Natalie," I started, watching as she dropped her head, her body shaking as she wept. "Fuck." I stepped closer and knelt beside her. "Move, tell me what they look like," I commanded, peering under the bed.

"They look like earrings," she muttered, turning to me.

She was close, too close.

Closer than what I wanted. Her hands were on me in an instant, her body pressing against mine, pushing me backward until my ass hit the floor. I lifted my hands to push her away, but she captured my wrists, pushing me down until I lay on the floor.

She lifted her leg, straddling me in an instant, reaching for my damn zipper. "I missed you so much, Nick. I can't...can't stop crying, can't stop wanting you."

"Natalie, *no*," I snarled, pushing against her.

Until she kissed me and her scent invaded, soft and familiar. Christ, how many nights had I inhaled that scent, until I she was my air...my world, and my long, endless nights. The button of my jeans gave way and the slow slide of her hand parted my zipper. Something shifted from my pocket, *my damn phone* falling to the floor with a thud.

"I want you, Nicky," she moaned. "I want you."

"Stop!" I barked, grasping her hand as it closed around my cock, and tore free from her grip. "I said *stop!*"

I pushed her off me, but not as hard as I wanted to. Still, she fell sideways on her ass, staring up at me as I pushed to a stand. Her tears still fell, thick and fast. Shit, maybe she was hurting.

I shoved my hand through my hair. I didn't want that...didn't want her in pain.

But I didn't want her either.

Ryth burned in my memory, what we had with our little stepsister. As wrong as it was, it was what I wanted. Every day...every night. I wanted *her*.

Natalie pushed up from the floor as I pulled up my zipper and buttoned my jeans.

"You fucking hurt me, Nick," she blubbered, and sniffled, wiping clear snot on the back of her hand. "You hurt me bad."

Jesus. I turned, searching the nightstand for the damn box of tissues.

"Who is she?"

I froze with the question.

"I know you're fucking someone else," she moaned. "I want to know who she is."

I turned on her, pissed off. "That's fucking rich. You screw half my fucking friends behind my back and now you come here questioning me? We're not even together anymore."

"We are." She just stood there, practically stomping her foot. "We *are* together."

I let out a bark of laughter and shook my head. This was so her...the fucking psycho bitch. "We're *not*." I forced the point. "I broke up with you, remember?"

She lunged, grabbed the glass from the nightstand, and smashed it against the edge with a scream. The damn thing shattered with a *crack,* splintering into shards that fell to the floor. Blood flowed, slipping down to course over the meat of her palm. "Who is she, Nick? *Tell me...*"

"Fuck, Natalie!" I roared, charging forward to grab her wrist. "Stop this...*I said, stop!*"

Her hand trembled, and she dropped the last shard of glass. She looked at me, so goddamn lost, tears still shimmering in her gaze. "Who, Nick? Tell me, I need to know."

My lips curled and, enraged, I roared. *"I just lost my goddamn mom, for fuck's sake!"*

She flinched at my anger. I'd never been like this with her before, never pushed so close to the edge, even after all the things she'd done. But now...now, when she stood there with her lying, demanding eyes, she drove me to clench my grip. Pain carved through her gaze. She flinched as I turned her hand and looked at the gash in the middle of her palm.

Blood dripped to my floor. "Jesus fucking Christ." I threw her hand down in disgust.

My anger cooled far too quickly. When I looked at her again, I wondered how I'd ever thought I was in love. This wasn't love, *this was pity.* "I just lost my mom. I've hardly been out of the goddamn house. You can ask the guys, if you're so fucking convinced I'm seeing someone else, tell me...*how on earth could I find the time?*"

The lie hurt going down.

Still, I swallowed, but instead of the bitter burn, I tasted my stepsister's pussy, salty and sweet. Fucking intoxicating. Christ, I wanted more.

"Nick...*I'm sorry,*" she pleaded.

I took a step away, disgust rolling through me as I glanced at the floor.

"I'm so sorry," she wept, her body racked with sobs again. She looked like a goddamn mess when she gazed up at me. "I'm so sorry I made a mess of this. I made a mess of it all."

I just shook my head. "No, Natalie...*no.*"

She nodded hard as still more tears fell. "I did. I fucked it all up."

I winced, hating how quick the disgust came. "Let me get you a damn towel," I muttered, staring at her bloody hand. "Just...just don't move around and bleed on anything else."

I strode from my bedroom and hurried along the hall. My stomach tightened the moment I opened the bathroom door, barging in as Tobias stood under the shower.

"What the fuck's going on?" he muttered, tilting his head back.

"*Nothing,*" I snapped, grabbing a towel, and stilled.

I gripped the vanity, staring at myself in the misted reflection. It wasn't just Natalie. Wasn't just my father. Wasn't just these fucking lies I told them and my own damn self. I was unraveling on the inside, hating how fast panic rushed to the surface when it came to Ryth.

I was scared when it came to her.

So fucking scared.

I didn't want to lose her.

"Nick?" Tobias called from the shower.

I shook my head, staring at my reflection. The lies were for myself...

I closed my eyes and all I saw was that goddamn birthmark on her cheek, and that vulnerable fucking stare. Christ, she was like a flower blooming for the first time. The shower switched off behind me and my brother stepped out. The weight of his hand on my shoulder forced me to open my eyes.

I lifted my gaze to his.

He knew.

He fucking knew.

Those cold, dark eyes glinted in the mirror. We were fucking falling for her. That *kid* who'd invaded our fucking life with her downcast eyes and quiet, barely controlled existence. She wasn't the aftershock of our pain...*she was the catalyst.*

The one who'd changed everything.

I looked down at the towel in my hand, suddenly remembering Natalie bleeding on my damn floor. "Shit," I snarled, and strode away, leaving Tobias standing there, butt-fucking-naked.

"Here." I shoved open the door and stepped back inside my room.

But Natalie wasn't standing where I'd left her moments ago. She was kneeling, her head lowered and her shoulders curled. I glanced at my phone, not far from her. I grabbed it and shoved it into my pocket before pressing the towel against her hand.

"Your father's getting married," she said quietly. There was something a little unhinged in her gaze when she looked at me. Pain flickered, carving deeper than the gash on her hand. "That's what you told me, right? That your father's getting married. Tell me...*who was she again?*"

I flinched, looking down at her hand. "Elle Castlemaine."

"Elle..." she repeated, her voice empty. "So, you'll have a whole new family, a new sister, too..."

I didn't like this. "Press it against the cut, Nat."

She didn't move. "I want to come," she declared.

"What?" I leaned closer, pressing the damn towel to her hand, then turned to survey the mess on the floor behind me.

"I...want to come. I think I deserved that, don't you? After all, I've been part of your family for the last five years."

It was four...but I wasn't about to argue.

"Invite me, Nick," she demanded.

"Fine," I snapped, panicking inside. If I brought her to the wedding, at least it'd look like everything was back to normal. I'd end it after, whatever this was—I looked into her eyes—I'd tell her to leave me the fuck alone. "If you want to come to the damn wedding, then come."

She nodded, pressed the towel to her hand, and rose from the floor. "Thank you."

Then she walked out like nothing had happened, leaving the damn broken glass behind. I stared at the mess, listening to her footsteps thudding on the stairs.

The front door opened, then closed with a *bang*. I strode to the window and watched her climb back into her car. But she didn't start the engine, not for ages...until finally the faint growl of the Nissan came and she left.

"What the fuck was that about?" Tobias inquired from the doorway.

"Hell if I know," I answered, glancing behind me to where she'd sat on the floor.

I grabbed my phone out, unlocked it, and looked at the video...

The video of my soon-to-be sister.

34

Caleb

There was blood on his shirt.

Blood on his shirt and the same panicked look I'd seen before.

Back when things were bad...

And he was in trouble.

He wanted to pretend I didn't remember those times, the times he'd spent staring into the bottom of the bottle, back before mom became sick. A twitch came from the corner of my eye. Was it a habit or a premonition? Fuck, I hoped it wasn't that.

I turned, leaving Nick to deal with his psycho ex, and listened for my father's footsteps in the hallway before the soft *thud* of his bedroom door closing. *What the fuck are you still doing here, Caleb?*

The words rang inside my head. He didn't want me here...and he sure as hell didn't want me asking questions. Nick opened the front door behind me. "What the fuck are you doing here, Natalie?"

I left that mess behind and made for my father's study in the back of the house. Darkness waited as I cracked open the door. The blinds were drawn, leaving murky shapes to guide my way. But fuck if I didn't know this room as well as my own. I made my way past the towering bookcases filled with law journals.

Journals kept by my mom.

I reached out, my fingers skimming the desk until I found the lamp and hit the button. The desk was bare and neat. It was always neat. But I'd learned long ago what was on the surface was only a glimpse of what was underneath.

I rounded the desk and sat in the chair. The weak amber light barely reached inside the drawer. I reached in, grabbed the stack of paperwork, and placed it on the desk in front of me. Funeral arrangements, a bill, a copy of mom's will. Nothing I didn't expect.

But there had to be something. Something I was missing.

He'd left yesterday out of the blue.

Right after his bachelor party, where he'd been intoxicated as hell.

I hit the keyboard of his desktop, waiting for the screen to come alive. One glance at the door and I punched in the same damn password he'd used for the last ten years.

Incorrect.

The message blinked like a slap across my face. I tried again *Naomiforever85.*

Incorrect.

"What the fuck." I sat back. He'd changed mom's password? My mind raced, trying to fill in the goddamn blanks before I glanced at the open drawer beside me. The papers sat on the desk, revealing a black velvet ring box. I grabbed it and opened it.

A wedding ring sat in the middle.

Crammed with diamonds.

Expensive as fuck.

Not that he couldn't afford it. After all, mom had left him a nice chunk of change, the benefits of him marrying into money. But Elle...Elle didn't have a goddamn cent.

I jerked my gaze to that blinking box on the monitor and punched in the letters, *Elleforever20* and hit enter.

The screen came alive. I fought a wince as a scream carried from somewhere upstairs, along with the sound of shattering glass.

"Nice one, Nick," I mumbled absently, leaning closer to the screen and bringing up dad's planner to yesterday's date.

Mitchelton. "Mitchelton?" I muttered, and that sick, cold feeling rose inside me once more.

I didn't need a fucking map to know where that was.

I scrolled through his calendar, finding more meetings listed there at times when I knew damn well he wasn't there...until I stopped at a specific date about a month ago, with a name attached to it. *Ryth.*

My damn pulse stuttered. I clicked the date, but there was nothing else, just my little sister's name. "What the fuck are you up to, dad?"

Whatever it was, it wasn't good.

I logged out of his computer and shoved the paperwork back in the drawer before I switched off the lamp. The bastard would be sleeping. But I wasn't trusting a damn thing when it came to her. She needed someone to protect her, someone to look out for her.

She needed someone to care for her.

Now she had us.

35

Ryth

"Gio!" I called his name when the break bell rang, but he kept walking, shuffling with a limping gait that only seemed to get worse as the day went on.

I grabbed his arm as he walked out of the double doors and headed for the trees that shaded the tables and seats.

"Get the fuck off me, Ryth!" He yanked his arm away.

"Wait," I barked. *"Gio, wait!"*

He stumbled but kept limping toward a group of others who just watched us with cold, calculated amusement.

"I didn't know."

He stopped dead in front of me, his shoulders hunched, then turned, staring at me through the swollen slit of one eye. "You didn't know..."

I swallowed, fighting the urge to wince at his face. It was even worse this close up. "No. I didn't know."

He stared at me, searching my gaze as a thick tear slid from the corner of his eye. I clenched my jaw. I was going to murder Tobias. Stepbrother or not, he was going to feel my goddamn wrath.

"You know, it's sick what you're doing with them."

I flinched as though he'd slapped me. "What?"

"What you're doing, it's not right. Your mom is about to marry their dad."

I shook my head, glancing to the others behind him. "It's not like that."

"Then what it is like? It looked pretty fucking obvious at the club."

Heat burned in my cheeks as it all came flooding back to me. "They were protecting me from the goddamn bouncers. If they hadn't put their fucking hands on me..."

"You were underage at a bar that's notorious for sleezy assholes, what the hell did you think would happen?"

"I *thought* I'd be able to walk in there, underage or not, and not be goddamn assaulted, especially by the employees!"

The fire burned in me now for a whole different reason. "I didn't see you being manhandled. But then again, I guess it doesn't matter, not with the company *you* keep. But hey, if it makes you feel better about having friends who threaten and maim people, especially those who are inside prison, then go right ahead."

Gio's lips curled in a sneer. "You have no idea, do you?"

"No," I crossed my arms over my chest, meeting his glare with my own. "But I'm guessing you're about to tell me."

There was a shake of his head. He started to turn away, then thought better of it, turning back to tower over me. "First their mom dies, then your dad is thrown in prison. Now you're a part of their sick, twisted family. Seems a little convenient, doesn't it? Tell me, Ryth, are you really that fucking stupid that you're going to play happy fucking family, or do you not care?" I couldn't escape his glare. "That's it, right? You don't care. Have they fucked you, is that it?"

I flinched, my breath catching in my chest. "That's none of your goddamn business, and what do you mean it *'seems convenient'*?"

"You're a smart girl, Ryth. Why don't you figure it out?"

"Tell me." I lunged, grabbing his arm, pulling him toward me as that savage side came roaring to the surface. "Tell me what you mean, Gio, or I'll—"

He saw me then, saw the real me, the dangerous me. The part of me that was a little too much like my father...and it stung.

He looked at my hold on his arm, but he made no move to wrench away. "I felt sorry for you when you came here, that's why I volunteered to show you around." He met my gaze. "I felt sorry for you, being in that house with those fucking assholes. I thought you were different. But you're not different, are you? You're no better than them."

He yanked his arm from my hold, took one last look at me, and said, "Stay the fuck away from me, Ryth. Just stay the fuck away."

"Gio!" I barked as he strode toward his friends. *"Gio! Tell me what you mean!"*

My chest ached, like a strap cinched tighter with every step he took from me. I charged forward as they slid from their seats and left, not once looking my way.

I stared at Gio's shuffling gait as he walked away. My head was spinning, trying to capture the meaning of his words. But they were a jumble, scattered and strange.

Seems a little convenient.

...a little convenient.

...a little...

What did he mean? What did he mean?

I closed my eyes, not even caring I stood in the middle of the grassy area in front of everyone. Creed's driving this morning had shaken me. The way he'd acted...the way he'd looked. Now Gio. A wave of nausea rocked me as I turned, gripped my laptop, and strode away.

By the time the bell rang for class, I'd hit the street. I kept walking, leaving the school behind. I needed to think and I couldn't, not in there, not now.

Cars flew past as I moved, crossing the street, making my way to I didn't know where. Right then, I didn't care.

A little convenient.

The words were stuck in my head and I couldn't get them out, no matter how much I tried. *A little convenient...a little convenient...a little—*

"Stop," I pleaded out loud. "Just stop this."

My steps were automatic, my thoughts stuck in that loop. I grabbed my cell and my finger slid across the screen until I punched in the code to unlock it. But the moment I moved my finger over Nick's number, I froze. I couldn't do it. I couldn't call him...

I couldn't call any of them.

I stopped walking, my heart in my mouth. *First their mom dies, then your dad is thrown in prison...*

Dad thrown in prison.

No. The reason he was in prison was because of the Rossis. I looked at my screen, but instead of calling my brother to come get me, I pulled up the search and started typing.

I was on the visitor list for the prison. I knew that. Dad had said if I needed to talk, he was only a call away. I entered the number for the prison, waiting for the guard to answer.

"Mitchelton Prison."

"My name is Ryth Castlemaine and I was wanting to talk to my dad, Jack Castlemaine."

"Hold."

I stared at the cars as they passed, realising for the first time where I was. Our park was not too far ahead. I couldn't believe I'd walked all the way here...

"He's not available," the guard snapped.

"Not available?"

"That's what I said."

"Do you know when...when he will be available?"

"No."

No? "Okay," I murmured. "I guess I'll call back later."

"Sure," he snarled, then hung up the phone.

Not available. The words sat heavy in my chest. I pocketed my phone and kept walking, only this time every step felt like torture. I stopped at the edge of the park, my gaze moving to the spot where Nick had tackled me to the ground.

An ache tore through my chest and shivers followed, ones that tore a sob from my lips. Anger and pain collided, until they were all I could feel. Tears came, but I didn't know if they were tears of shame or disgust. I didn't know what I was doing...

Didn't know what I was doing with them.

The memory of the heat of their passion died away as my phone gave a *beep.*

Nick: Why aren't you at school, Ryth?

I stared at the message, my thoughts frantic. How could he know? I swallowed hard and typed with shaking fingers, *I am at school.*

Beep. The response was almost instant.

Nick: Lie to me again, Ryth, and it'll end badly. Where the fuck are you...and who are you with?

"Who am I with?" I whispered. *"Who am I with?"*

That anger that seethed so close to the surface boiled over. *"Who I'm fucking with?"* I stabbed the screen, punching out the reply, and hit send. But the moment I did, I froze. "Oh shit...*oh shit.*" I stared at what I'd sent...as that sinking feeling took hold.

I'm with Gio. We're fucking right now and he's brought along his friends, what's it to you?

I was so fucked.

Literally fucked.

I started typing, *Nick, that was a joke* and hit send. But there was no reply. *Nick.* I hit send again.

Still no answer.

Panic gripped me as I pressed his number to call and listened to his phone ring. "Answer the phone, Nick!"

My breaths were a roar in my ears as the call went unanswered. The heat of my anger was slipping away as I pressed the button again, listening to his phone ring, and ring...*and ring.*

Minutes, that's all it took. A faint snarl came to my ears, familiar, *sinister.* Then the squeal of tires, sounding painful. I jerked my gaze up as a dark blur hurtled toward me. I was moving before I knew it, stumbling backwards as the Mustang took the corner sideways and fishtailed before the V8 engine kicked hard and charged toward me.

Terror gripped me as I stumbled, the car hitting the entrance to the park hard, kicking up stones as it came to a screeching stop. Nick was out of the car in an instant, his face full of rage as he scanned the park behind me. *"Where the fuck is he, Ryth?"*

I stumbled, still moving backwards. "Nick...I..."

He was unhinged, savage, rounding the front of the car to come toward me. Fear punched through me as I stumbled, my feet catching in the thick grass.

"I'll fucking kill him!" he roared. *"I'll tear the fucking punk apart!"*

I'd never seen someone so enraged, so completely unhinged, as Nick charged across the grass toward me. My laptop slipped from my hold and hit the grass, but I didn't stop to pick it up...*I couldn't.* I scurried, like the mouse I was...falling backward as Nick lunged.

He hit me hard, tumbling me to the ground, his crazed torment all I could see. "H-he's not h-here..." I stuttered. *"Nick,* he's not here!"

"I'll fucking kill him if he so much as lays a hand on you." My stepbrother glared into my eyes. "Tell me the truth, Ryth...*who the fuck were you with?"*

Violence.

Death.

His possessiveness was a fist around my throat. All I could feel was his cruel fingers digging into my shoulders and the heat of his breath on my face. In an instant, I was back there, prey for them once more. "Get off me!"

Rage burned in his eyes. "I don't fucking think so, princess."

Hard breaths. A look of cold madness. This wasn't the Nick I knew. This Nick was...*dangerous.* He searched my eyes for the lies. "Tell me who, Ryth!"

"No one...*okay?* There isn't anyone..." Tears came as I sobbed. "Anyone but you...all of you."

"You sure about that?"

Through the haze, I saw his misery, his depraved longing, as he lowered his head, his deep voice compelling. "It's too late for you, Ryth...*far too late.*"

The heavy feel of his hand came on my thigh, driving up my skirt, right here...in the middle of the park, in the full light of day.

"Too late for me to let you go...too late for me to forget about you."

His hand slid between my legs and his fingers skimmed my sex.

"Nick...*stop,*" I whispered.

The shake of his head butted against my cheek. "You don't get it, do you? There is *no stopping* when it comes to this. Not with you."

Agile fingers dug into my panties, finding my clit and stealing my terror. I closed my eyes, hating how my body betrayed me. "I was angry," I moaned. "And scared."

"You scared now, Ryth?" he growled, his fingers digging under the elastic of my panties and plunging in.

I jerked with the invasion...and moaned.

"You scared now, princess?"

"Yes," I groaned. "Yes, I'm scared."

"Good." He yanked his fingers away, then grabbed me around the waist before hauling me up from the ground.

"Nick...stop...*my laptop.*"

"Leave it," he snapped, lifting me over his shoulder. "I'll buy you a fucking new one."

The sight of the laptop bounced with each stride, silver glinting in the sun before we dashed into the shadows. Cool air plunged between my thighs as he pulled me from his shoulder and pushed me against a tree.

"You fucking make me crazy, you know that?" he growled, pressing against me, his big hand kneading my breast. "I would've fucking killed him if he'd fucked you. I would've killed them all."

He was a beast in that moment, a cold-blooded savage.

I tilted my head back as he kissed my neck, reached under my skirt to grasp my panties, and yanked them down. "I wouldn't care. I'd go away for the rest of my fucking life."

The thought of that terrified me. I shook my head as he knelt, tugging my panties off and shoving up my skirt. "Don't...don't say that."

"They fucking touch you, Ryth," He slid his hand up along the back of my thigh. "They'll pay with blood."

He pulled me closer and his mouth found my slit. Warmth rushed in, sliding, sucking, finding the part of me that came alive. I slid my fingers through his hair, bowing my spine, letting him go where he wanted. He made me want to fuck, made me want to disappear, Made me want to be nothing more than...*this*.

"Fuck me," I croaked, fisting his hair. "I want you inside me."

He rose, the taste of my hunger on his lips as he worked the button of his jeans, then shoved his zipper down. The door to the Mustang was still open, the keys probably still in the ignition. My brand new laptop lay on the grass out in the open, but right now, there was nothing more important than him.

He gripped my waist and lifted, driving me against the trunk of the tree. His thighs widened mine. His thrust was urgent, driving into me, and I couldn't get enough. "Yes," I moaned, dropping my head forward. "Oh God, *yes*."

"You're mine...you get that, Ryth?" he grunted, driving into me.

Hard friction made me feel raw.

I wanted it...wanted it all. Warmth moved through me and the slick sounds grew more insistent.

"You...belong...to...*me*."

I wound my arms around his neck, holding on as he drove his cock inside me. Everything else melted away until there was just him...just us...*just this*.

The rumble of his growl invaded my hearing.

The scent of his sweat.

The punishing thrust of his cock.

It all brought me undone.

My body quaked, a pent-up moan tore free as stars exploded behind my eyes. "Make me yours," I cried as I clutched him, pulling him against me. I couldn't get enough, not of the feel of him inside me.

Nick braced his hand against the tree, driving his cock deeper and harder, until I jolted with the impact. He lifted his head, his glare brooding, and dangerous, and singlemindedly focused on me.

His pale lips curled against his teeth as he thrust deep inside me and let out a guttural moan. Sweat glistened on the top of his lip. He stared into my soul, invading, searching, leaving a tiny piece of himself in there.

"Next time I call..." he forced through hard gasps. "You fucking answer...*got me, princess?*"

I matched his brutal breaths with my own, my pussy clenching and throbbing as I nodded.

He slid out, leaving me empty and aching before lowering my feet to the ground. His towering presence was threatening as he caught my chin and tilted my gaze to his. "You understand me, Ryth? You make me unhinged like that again and you won't like the consequences. I'll chain you to my goddamn bed if I have to. I'll fuck you until you forget anyone outside our family exists. Because you *are* my family, princess. No one else touches this pussy, get it? Tobias, Caleb...or me. You want to be fucked, you come to us..."

Desire raged with his words. He wasn't letting me go...not until I gave in. "If I'm family, then you better understand I'll hit as hard as I fuck."

There was a tiny scowl.

I jerked my chin from his grasp, and glared. "Did you know Gio was the one Tobias attacked?"

He rocked back on his heels, understanding now...

But I wasn't letting him get away so easy, even if I still burned for his touch. "Answer me, Nick...*did you know?*"

36

Tobias

"Ryth...*wait*," Nick called.

The heavy thud of steps drew my focus. She was pissed...*really pissed*. Not that I wasn't expecting it. I shoved the controller to my desk and rose from the chair as she rounded the landing.

"Ryth, for fuck's sake!"

"Get the fuck off me, *Nick!*" she barked.

A damn hurricane tore into my room, snarling, her eyes wide, and her hands flailing in the air as she screamed at me. I caught that weak-ass prick Gio's name, then something about it being convenient, whatever the fuck that meant.

But the entire time my little sister stabbed me in the damn chest with her finger and screamed up in my face, all I thought about was fucking her.

"You fucking beat him bloody!" she roared. "He walks with a goddamn *limp!*"

"He's lucky he's walking at all," I answered coldly. "He has Caleb to thank for that."

I could still see the blood on my hands, still hear his whiny goddamn pleas. He thought he was fucking safe hiding in Lazarus' shadow, thought he was untouchable. When it came to Ryth, no one was safe...*not even Lazarus' chump.*

"You could've killed him!" She was working herself up.

She wanted to hit me. *Fuck, she wanted to hit me.* I'd let her, too.

Only her.

I lifted my gaze to Nick, who just looked at me with a pained expression and shrugged. His hair was a damn mess...*hers was too.* My brows rose as I narrowed in on her. The way her shirt was wrinkled, the way her breaths deepened. I stepped closer, making her pull her hand back.

"You look pissed, little sister," I murmured. "*And well ridden, too.*"

She flinched, and her breath was snatched away for a second. Then those perfect lips curled in a sneer. "You bastard."

Her venom made that *thing* in my chest flutter. "Now you get it." I stepped forward as Nick closed my bedroom door.

Her fucking mom was still here, still feeling '*under the weather*'. If she was gone, I'd have her daughter on the floor in an instant, her knees parted and her pussy filled. I swallowed a flare of jealousy. I wanted my fucking fill too.

I licked my lips as she stumbled backward and smacked into my brother. That flare of anger met a flicker of fear. I caught the flare in her eyes. She flinched when I lifted my hand...*that, I didn't like.*

"I am a bastard," I said carefully as she glanced behind her, moving to the side until she hit the wall. "I am a mongrel, and a bully. I am a ruthless piece of shit and a goddamn animal." I stopped right against her, forcing her against my chest. I didn't give her room, didn't give her air...*didn't give her a thing.*

Suffocating.

Buried.

Howling with desire.

That's how she made me feel.

That was the fucking beast she triggered. The one who'd invaded her goddamn room and stolen her panties. The one who'd driven his fingers into that sweet little cunt under the table with our parents just a few feet away. The one who wanted to see her ruined by me...and my brothers.

So fucking ruined.

"So you better get your pretty head around that, little sister. Because when it comes to family, there's nothing and no one I won't destroy."

She stiffened, then tilted her head until those blue eyes met mine. The primal urge to protect her corrupted me. My hold slipped, there was no stopping the fall. Because I was falling.

"Stay away from him," she warned. "There'll be no more bloodshed, do you hear me?"

"As long as he stays away from you."

She flinched and swallowed hard, then shoved me away. "Let me out." I moved away, letting her go. *"Let me the fuck out!"* She shoved Nick to the side, yanked open the door, and was gone with the thunder of her steps.

I stared at the open door, listening to her.

She'd calm down...

Or she wouldn't.

Either way, she was safe. That's all I cared about. Nick met my gaze, giving me a wounded smile before he left. Her bedroom door slammed with a *boom!* Loud enough to let everyone in the damn house know she was pissed.

I clenched my jaw, then turned.

She thought her precious little boyfriend was hurt.

But she didn't understand.

It had been a message.

One received loud and clear.

Touch her...and see what happens.

I glanced at the monitor and found that the game was stuck and I was dying over and over again. I stepped closer and hit the button, killing the damn thing cold. I couldn't play, not all fucking day. I'd been waiting for her to come home, waiting for her to explode.

Now that she had, I needed to run.

I grabbed my sneakers, yanked them on, and strode down the stairs and out the door. By the time I hit the end of the driveway, that unmerciful anger was back.

She was safe.

She was protected.

That's all that mattered.

I turned my head, pushing into a jog...trying my best to ignore the gray fucking Audi following me in the distance...and the Rossi hitman behind the wheel.

37

Ryth

"You look perfect, Mom." I smiled when she turned.

Her eyes shone with concern as she reached toward her hair. "You think?"

"I *know*." I stepped closer, grabbing her hand. "Stop fussing... you'll ruin it."

"You're right," she agreed, and dropped her hand. "You're right."

She looked perfect in a simple, off-white dress, the lace hugging her figure. She didn't look like my mom. She looked like someone else, someone young and perfect...someone happy. I wanted to feel that happiness for her...*I was desperate to feel it.* But no matter how hard I smiled, I couldn't stop thinking about dad.

"Mom."

"Hmm?" She turned, looking at herself side-on in the mirror as she slid a hand down her ass.

"I haven't been able to reach dad. I've called the prison like five times, now they don't even try to get him to the phone. They tell me he's not taking calls or visitors, and I don't understand why?"

She froze, her gaze meeting mine in the reflection.

Fear.

That's what I saw. Fear.

"What's going on? Why won't they let me talk to him?"

She turned slowly, stepping close. "You know I love your father. I *have* loved him for a very long time and I'm going to do everything in my power to get him out of where he is. But, honey, your father did some terrible things, cruel things, things that the law just cannot overlook. As hard as Creed and the other lawyers have been working to help him, they just have not been able to find a way to get him free."

I rocked back on my heels. "They...*they can't get him out?*"

All this time, I'd been waiting for the call, hoping and praying I'd at least see him again, even if we were no longer a family. I wasn't a kid...I wasn't naive. I knew we'd never have again what we'd once had, and maybe that was a good thing. It wasn't like it had been happy. But I didn't want this.

Didn't want dad forever behind bars.

"So he took the news hard." She reached for my hand. "And I guess he just needs some time to process this. You understand, right?"

Tears threatened my view. I tried to swallow the hard lump in the back of my throat. But the damn thing wouldn't budge. I nodded slowly, my mind racing, trying to come to terms with the news.

"When he's ready to see us, then we'll go...as a family, because that's what we are, Ry. A family. We will support him, we will love him. We will do everything in our power to bring him home to us, no matter how long it takes."

"You—you won't give up on him?"

She brushed her hand along my jaw and stared into my eyes. "No more than I'd give up on you."

I forced a smile. "Good."

"Good?"

My smile grew wider. "Yeah."

"Alright." She dropped my hand and turned. "You're really okay with us leaving right after, aren't you? I mean, I hate to leave you on your own. But the wineries are apparently calling."

My pulse throbbed. I nodded. "Yeah, of course. I'll be busy anyway with school."

"And you have the boys here if you need anything."

That burn reached higher as she drew me in for a hug. "Two weeks is too long to leave you."

Two weeks...two weeks of them. Avoiding them. Hating them.

"No, it's not too long. It's your honeymoon. Besides, I won't even notice you're gone."

She pulled away, smiling. "Promise?"

"Promise."

She clapped her hands together like a damn schoolgirl. "Okay, so let's do this. Let's become a family."

I grabbed the small bouquet of deep yellow roses, followed her out to the entrance of the lavish garden, and stopped by her side. The last week had been a blur. I hid at school, hanging back in the classroom while Gio still limped away, avoiding me as best as he could. Then I left school, snarling at Nick as he waited at the drop-off point *every morning and every goddamn afternoon.*

Then I came home, to lock myself in my room, furious at Tobias and the other two for treating me like I was a damn possession, something they could control...and use when and how they wanted.

I had news for them...

There'd be no *using*, not by them.

Not since the park.

I licked my lips, heat rising to my cheeks as soft music began to play, and the memory returned. The hard tree against my back, Nick as he'd fucked me like a damn animal. I winced, playing it off as a smile at one of the guests, and followed mom toward Creed.

It was standing room only. The small gathering was only supposed to be close friends and family. The inside of the event center was stunning at night, with masculine gray glass windows and a black floor, but they were balanced perfectly by the white and pink wedding decorations.

The wide open doors gave a glimpse of the dark sprawling gardens. I tried to remember how many acres mom had said it was, but I couldn't.

The music grew in tempo, pulling my focus to Creed. He stood at the end of the aisle in front of some kind of priest in a dark suit. My steps stuttered as the man of God lifted his gaze and I saw the frozen smile on his lips as he looked at me.

Jesus. I swallowed, taking in the hard jawline and cold smile. I'd never seen a priest who looked like that...*ever.* The white collar gripped his neck like a shackle, making my pulse stutter as I moved my gaze back to his eyes. There was something darker lurking behind his brown eyes. Something not quite...*holy.* I shifted my focus to the name stitched onto the jacket of his immaculate black suit.

Hale Order for the Lost.

For the lost?

What the hell did that mean? Creed turned as the music grew. His eyes widened as he caught sight of mom. But it was Caleb who captured my focus, standing at his father's side.

Caleb, whose gaze seemed to burn right through me.

"Doesn't she look lovely, Nicky?" The female murmur from my right invaded my mind, tearing me from my brother's stare.

My pulse sped as I narrowed in on a woman standing next to Nick. She wound her arm through his, pressing her body into his side as she glared at me. I jerked my gaze to his. He looked pissed...*and cornered.*

"My hope is that one day I'm standing there with you," she whispered, her stare like a dagger.

Agony plunged through my chest at the words. Fire found my cheeks as she forced a giggle, pressing harder against him. But Nick...Nick just stared at me.

"I'm so glad you invited me," the bitch continued. "I never thought we'd get back together."

Get back together...

Panic moved in. I forced my feet to move.

Voices crowded in. But the words were slipping away from me as my world spun out of control. *Get back together...GET BACK TOGETHER!*

"I'm honored both Creed and Elle have come back to the Order," the priest's voice began. "We go back a long way...back to college."

I tried to swallow the scream. But my senses were heightened, narrowing in on her cruel fucking voice. "Your new sister is weird."

"Stepsister," Nick snapped.

"So, without any further ado, let's move on to the vows," the priest smiled.

Caleb shifted beside Creed, scowling as his gaze narrowed in on me. He was trying to draw my attention, glancing back at Nick and the woman he was with...*the woman he was now back with*. I was so stupid, so fucking stupid. What had I thought this was...*love?* My cheeks burned even hotter as a small tortured sound ripped free from my throat.

My world kept spinning, but it wasn't the floor or the twinkling lights of the room...it was them.

Tobias.

Nick.

Caleb.

I was such a fucking fool.

"Don't let us stop you," Tobias snarled from the front row.

Their focus was like a razor burn on my skin. I felt the graze as the priest started the vows. His voice droned and seconds felt like hours as Nick's returned girlfriend gushed and whispered, drawing my attention. I couldn't look away from them, didn't want to look at the way she clutched his hand and slid her arm along his, knowing all the things we'd done together.

I'd given them my virginity.

My stomach clenched at the thought. I was going to be sick. I was going to ruin mom's fucking wedding day and be sick all over the goddamn floor in front of everyone.

No...

No, I'm not.

Just hold on.

Just...please.

"Creedence, do you take Eleanor to be your wife?"

Tobias strode across the aisle to stand behind me.

Creed glanced our way, then turned back to the ceremony, nodding. "Yes."

"And Eleanor, do you take Creed—"

"She's trying to rattle you," Tobias murmured behind me. "Don't fucking let her."

"Yes," Mom answered. "Yes, I do."

"Nick," the bitch said loud enough for everyone to hear. "I want us to get married."

"I now pronounce you husband and wife. You can kiss the—"

My stomach lurched. It was going to come up, it was all going to come up. My lunch, my juice. *Everything*. I stumbled away as the crowd erupted onto cheers. They moved away in a blur as I raced from the ceremony and headed for the bathrooms.

Laughter cracked out. I knew instantly who it was. Darkness blurred as I plunged through the shadows, punched open the ladies room door, and stumbled inside.

Shimmering black tiles, and glistening chrome shone. I lunged for the basin and hit the tap as my belly clenched and released. But there was nothing in there, nothing but the champagne I'd drunk earlier.

Footsteps resounded.

The door opened and I jerked my gaze to the sound. "Go away!"

"Oh," Nick's bitch smiled, stepping in. "It's you."

My hands were shaking. My entire body pulsed. The tears I'd staved off all this time came roaring to the surface.

"Ryth," Nick called as he pushed in and shoved the bitch aside. His pained gaze found mine as he stepped closer, reaching for me. "Ryth..."

"Oh, a little family tiff, is it?" Jealousy seethed in her snarl.

"Shut the fuck up, Natalie!" he snarled. "I should *never* have fucking asked you."

I clenched my jaw and leaned against the vanity. God, it felt like my fucking heart was tearing from my chest.

"She's not..." Nick started, his desperation a growl as he came closer.

"Get the fuck away from me!" I screamed, slapping his hand away.

His bitch just laughed.

Laughed.

God, all I could see was them, her big tits in his face. I bet he liked them...bet he liked them more than mine. Tears fell as I unleashed a moan and buckled.

"Nick," Tobias called from the doorway.

"Ryth," Caleb called my name as the crowd out there cheered and clapped, drowning us out.

"Why do you give a shit?" Natalie sniggered. "It's not like she's family. You've only known her a few fucking months."

"Nick," Tobias warned. "If you don't leash that bitch, I will."

"Get the fuck out, Natalie!" Nick turned on her. "Just fucking leave."

She flinched, the smug smile on her face shattering, just like I wished she would. She lunged for me, grasping my arm, her sharp nails driving deep enough to sting. "I fucking know what little sluts like you want. Stay the fuck away from him, you cheap whore, or I'll make you fucking regret it."

"That's it." Tobias charged into the bathroom and grabbed Natalie by a fistful of hair. "If anyone here is a whore, it's you, you cheating, fucking cunt. Now get the fuck out!"

"Get off me!" she screamed, trying to tear from his hold.

My chest snapped tight, the bathroom suddenly full of *them*.

Hungry.

Desperate.

Males.

"Ryth..." Nick started as I lunged, pushing past him. *Pushing past all of them.*

"Ryth!" Caleb called.

But I shoved and fought, charging past to get out of that fucking room. The crowd cheered as my mom called out, *"BYE!!!"*

I tried to look for her, but they were hidden by a wall of well-wishers, those who crowded around the newly married couple, clapping and cheering as they left. I caught a glimpse of mom's dress as she was whisked through the doors by her brand new husband and was gone.

Gone...

Tears blurred my sight as I scanned for a place to hide, catching sight of the darkness outside. I had to get away...had to leave this place and these people.

"Ryth!" the three of them called in unison.

I had to get away from them. I charged for the open doors, leaving the pretty event room behind, and sought solace in the night.

38

Ryth

The sound of a car's engine cut through the dark, coming from the entrance as another, louder one, roared to life. The supercharged engine howled and tires squealed as Natalie's car took off. It had to be her...*Nick's girlfriend.*

I let out a groan and stumbled down the patio stairs, my heels quickly sinking into the grass and the soft earth.

"Ryth...*for fuck's sake!*" Nick roared behind me.

I didn't care. Didn't want to see them...*any of them.*

This pain was too much, too cruel...too...*consuming.* I kicked off my heels as I ran, not even bothering to stop for them. I just ran, gripping my dress and driving my feet into the ground.

The *thud* of heavy steps came behind me.

"Fuck's sake, woman!" Nick was on me in an instant, grabbing my arm and pulling me against him. *"We're not back together!"*

"I don't care!" I screamed, tearing my arm away as Tobias and Caleb came running. My tears blurred their faces. "I don't care. I just...I can't be here...not with you. *Not with any of you.*"

Tobias' lips curled in a silent snarl.

Caleb's dark eyes flashed with concern.

Then there was Nick. Nick, with his pleading fucking eyes and his outstretched hand. He shook his head, denying my words. I stumbled backwards, losing sight of the event room and all the guests as they partied inside.

"We're not back together," Nick insisted, his voice breaking. "I fucking used her, thinking I could shield what we have."

"You...you fucking hurt me." I shook my head, tears continuing to stream down my cheeks.

"I know."

"No! *YOU DON'T KNOW!*" I screamed. "You don't *fucking* know!"

He didn't get it...*none of them got it.* I was in too deep here, too dark. All three of them stepped closer, crowding in. I couldn't get the feel of them out from under my skin. Living with them...sleeping with them. I was open and raw. I was becoming more broken with every kiss and every touch. I was falling for them...*hard.* I *knew* that. I wrapped my arms around my body, feeling the cool air against my skin.

"You fucking hurt me...*you all hurt me.*"

My breaths sawed through my chest. Agony carved deep...until that coldness broke through.

"I know we hurt you," Nick whispered, inching closer.

The warmth of his hand felt like a brand. I flinched, looking down at the way his thumb instantly caressed me, like he knew exactly what I craved.

But he didn't...none of them did. They didn't know that I ached. I ached so fucking bad. I wanted to tell him. I wanted to scream my pain into his face. I wanted to hurt him like he'd hurt me.

I froze.

No. I wanted to *use* him. I wanted to use all of them.

My breaths deepened as that torture inside me turned dangerous. His honey eyes looked almost black as Nick whispered, "Please, Ryth."

"Get on your fucking knees, Nick." The words were cold, stony, not my own. They couldn't be. They belonged to someone dangerous, *someone in control.* His brows furrowed with a look of surprise. I was the one who stepped closer this time, lifting my gaze up, and up, to meet his. "Just shut the fuck up and get on your knees."

The agony inside me mingled with something sinful, something stained and tormented. Something that howled with conquest as the towering male in front of me did that, dropping to his knees.

"Fuck me," Tobias murmured, his gaze riveted on his brother.

But Caleb...Caleb knew.

I met Nick's focus as he tilted his head up, his hands moving to my thighs. I slapped them away. "No. This isn't for you."

His frown deepened like he didn't understand.

Because he didn't.

"You treat me like *her*." I slid my hands down my thighs to the hem of my dress, that newfound power like a fucking drug, going straight to my head. "You give me what you want...and yet you take all, every inch of me, every sigh, every tremor. You take and you take...*and you take.*"

He licked his lips as I pulled my dress higher. My fingers found the thin strap of my G-string before I bent and slid it down. I didn't feel the stab of the cold grass on my feet or my racing heart as my panties hit the ground. I felt powerful.

He didn't lift his hand, didn't pull away. This powerful male who'd filled me with terror just days ago, now let me slide my fingers through his thick hair and clench my fist.

He jerked at the movement and his head snapped backward, that dangerous spark igniting in his eyes as I guided his head lower, pressing his face against my sex. "No more," I snarled, meeting Tobias' stare, then Caleb's. "No fucking more."

Tobias just watched as I stepped forward. Nick's hands flew back, catching his fall as I held his face against my pussy and drove him down to the ground.

My knees hit the cold grass, until his hand slid underneath one, a barrier of warmth. Déjà vu slammed into me, taking me back to that night when my mom and Creed had announced their engagement.

It was Nick who'd pinned my hand in place, Nick who'd yanked my dress aside to watch Tobias' fingers slide into me. It was Nick's warmth I took now as I ground myself against his mouth. A shudder ripped free as I yanked my own dress aside, lifting one knee to ride his mouth.

Tobias reached for his cock, his hand gliding over the bulge in his pants as Nick's tongue slipped along my crease and then plunged inside me. I dropped my head backward and moaned, grinding and fucking his mouth. "You so much as look her fucking way, and this is done." I looked down at him. "You get me?"

He curled his tongue, gliding deeper, his other hand sliding out from under my knee to grip my thigh and grind me against him harder. I met Tobias' gaze, then Caleb's. "You so much as text, touch...kiss another woman and this is done. I'll leave. I'll fucking leave and you won't ever see me again. Do... you...understand?"

Tobias was a fiend, watching how I thrust against Nick's face until I blocked his air. "Yeah," he answered.

"We understand," Caleb moaned, yanking down his own zipper. "But you're suffocating him, princess."

Caleb stepped closer and lowered himself to the ground next to his brother, his cock hard and ready. "Maybe I can be of use?"

I lifted my knee and climbed from Nick, who sucked in hard gasps, watching as I straddled Caleb, guiding that big cock inside. I shuddered, my orgasm so close as the head pushed in.

"Jesus fucking Christ," Caleb moaned. "Use me...use me however you need, little sister."

"Use all of us," Tobias urged as he stepped closer. "However you want, whenever you want, day or fucking night."

"There's no one else," Nick repeated, his lips glistening. "Not anymore."

I reached for Tobias as I rocked my hips, working Caleb deeper and deeper inside. A snarl tore free from me as Tobias reached for his zipper. I pulled away, stopping his hand, until he dropped them to his sides, catching on real quick.

Heat coursed through me as I bucked, slamming my hips down. I fucked them, tugging Tobias' cock free. "Your hand around my throat," I demanded.

He moved, clenching those cruel fingers around my neck as I rode his brother. It was always Tobias. Tobias with his needy fingers and his caustic love. Tobias who'd bullied me, who'd attacked me. I moaned, that thought drawing my end even closer.

I guided his cock to my mouth. "Tighter."

His lips curled and his eyes flashed to Caleb's thick cock sliding in and out. I could still hear the celebrations, hear some cars leaving, hear the music blaring. Hear it all as I bent, taking him into my mouth.

Tobias' fingers clenched, choking me as I slid him deeper, working my tongue along his shaft. His cock flinched inside me as he closed his eyes, letting out a moan. "Keep doing that, little mouse, and I'll give you whatever you want."

I pulled free. "I told you what I want. I gave my demands."

"She wants us," Caleb groaned underneath me as I drove down, riding him hard. "That's what she wants."

"Look at us, princess," Nick urged. "We're here, cocks out, desperate for a fucking touch, a fucking taste. We're desperate for *you*."

Tobias' hand slid from around my throat, his fingers pressed together as he held them against the birthmark on my cheek. "You might wear our brand on the outside, but we wear it in our chests. Believe me. Name your goddamn demands. Whatever they are, they're yours, little sister." He looked down at me. "They're yours."

39

Ryth

We left in a blur of fingers and mouths. I clawed Caleb, riding him until he'd stretched me wide. When my body shuddered and that feeling of euphoria finally moved on, Nick left us long enough to run and get the Mustang, pulling the car around the back of the event center.

We left with the throb of the engine, stealing away from the last of the partygoers, me in the backseat, Tobias on top.

"Fuck me, little mouse," he groaned. "Where the fuck did that come from?"

I reached between us, fisted the hard bulge in his pants, and lifted my head to kiss him. His jacket was discarded, the black vest opened against his unbuttoned white shirt, and those dark, brooding eyes staring at me. "Right where you weren't looking," I answered. "So turn me the fuck over, Tobias. This time I'm on top."

He chuckled as the car cut along the quiet, darkened road that would lead us to the highway, then to the city and back home.

Home.

What would that be like without mom and Creed? My heart couldn't handle the image of that. Strong hands gripped me as he shifted his body, turning us over in the seat. My dress caught, but Caleb reached through the seat, tugging it out, only to slide it higher, leaving his brother to take over, shoving it further upwards.

"Caleb stretched you, princess?" Tobias murmured. "You still hot from my brother's cock?"

I let out a moan at his words, my body already aching. "Yes," I answered, sliding the strap of my dress lower. "Does that upset you?"

"Fuck, no." He reached between my thighs, finding the crotch of my G-string I'd tugged back on in a hurry. "Not when it comes to you, little mouse. We get all of you, every goddamn night and day."

They were insatiable.

Hungry and desperate.

The car swerved.

"Eyes on the goddamn road, Nick," Tobias barked under me. "You fucking crash before I get to fuck our brand new sister and I'll be pissed."

Sister.

The word rolled through me. What we had was sick...twisted. We were family by marriage now. There'd be people watching us, making sure we were being proper.

Tobias' fingers slipped under the edge of my G-string. "This pretty little cunt of yours desperate for more?"

Aftershocks turned hot under his touch. My pussy clenched. I wanted this all day, every day. All of them claiming me, riding me. I wanted them to want me as much as I wanted them. "Yes," I moaned.

"Jesus Christ, I want to pull the car over," Nick groaned.

"Just get us home, brother." Tobias slipped his hand free from my sex and reached up, gripping the back of my neck to draw me against him.

Soft, pouty lips. His heat of desire.

"The next two weeks are going to be fucking incredible," he moaned.

I kissed him, pulling away to stare down at him, catching those glittering dark eyes staring back at me. Everything had changed tonight. They'd thought they were the ones who called the shots, that they were the ones in control and I was nothing more than a little mouse at their mercy.

They were wrong.

They were at mine.

I was lost in Tobias' mouth and the feel of his hands on my body. He held onto me as the car swerved and bright lights from the intersection invaded, splashing across his face as we hit the highway. The Mustang's V-8 engine throbbed as it ate up the miles to get us home. By the time we pulled into the driveway, the frenzied desire we'd had between us had cooled, leaving something deeper, something slower in its place.

This place felt like home, more of a home than anything else I'd had before. The front gates slid closed with a bang as we climbed out of the car. I pulled my dress down as Tobias adjusted himself. I'd never been more thankful of rich people and their towering hedges. Could you imagine what our old neighbor, Mrs. Cromwell, would've thought?

I stifled a smile as Nick climbed out, then pulled his seat forward for me, his intensity meeting mine as I climbed out. "Princess," he murmured, closing the door behind me.

That's exactly how I felt, lowering my gaze to the ground, that shy smile blending with the heat that crept into my cheeks. That's how they made me feel. Like they didn't just see me... but they craved me.

Caleb stood by the open door when we stepped inside. He lifted his hand, waiting for mine. I was captured in an instant and my bare feet left the floor. Nick had my shoes in his hand as Tobias locked the front door and engaged the alarm.

There'd be no leaving tonight.

Not for them.

I wound my arms around Caleb as he carried me up the stairs. His long, muscled body flexed under me as he moved. He carried me into the bathroom, and the others followed. My zipper was pulled low by expert hands. Caleb's lips found my shoulder, then moved to my neck. "Need to take it slow, princess," he murmured. "Pacing is important here, we don't want to hurt you."

His words hit home.

They wanted to fuck me all the time.

My body needed to keep up.

I nodded, leaving him to slip my dress off. My heels were dropped to the tiled floor as Nick undressed, and Tobias followed. "Mine." He staked his claim, shoved his pants to the floor, and stalked forward, his cock hard and bobbing as he moved.

God, I'd never seen someone so beautiful.

Predatory and cruel and yet, as he reached me and gripped me around my waist and lifted, he was tender. I wrapped my legs around him as he hit the taps and adjusted the spray. We melted into the warmth, until my back hit the cold tiles, making me flinch, then he turned, pressing his own back against the cold.

"Whatever you want, Ryth," he growled, staring into my eyes. "Whatever you want."

I reached down and slid my hand along his length. Power rippled through me as I stared into his eyes. He'd beaten a man to send a message. He'd do more if he needed to. This bully who'd made my life Hell was more than he portrayed. He was a bastard, but he was my bastard. I angled my hips, guiding him inside. "Fuck me, Tobias. Fuck me."

He gripped my ass and angled my hips down as he drove inside to the hilt. A moan ripped free. My hands slid on slick skin. I was lost to the feel of him, vaguely aware when Nick and Caleb joined us in the shower.

Hands over my breasts. Lips against my neck.

I melted.

We found ourselves in Nick's room later, all three of us in his bed. There we slept, me in the middle, surrounded by their heat. I closed my eyes, waiting for sleep to claim me, unable to think about anything other than how perfect this felt.

I wanted this forever.

Just the four of us.

Slept crept closer, with my body already numb, just my mind to follow. A hand slid over my hip, a steel band of muscle around my waist, before I was yanked backward until I pressed against a chest.

"Mine," Tobias murmured, his voice already heavy with sleep.

The scent of him invaded as I closed my eyes. I shifted against him as Nick's leg moved under the comforter, pressing against mine. The only one not touching me was Caleb. But he was here, staying with us, and that said more than anything.

I gave a sigh and slipped under sleep's hold, more contented than I'd ever felt before.

⬡

"LITTLE MOUSE."

I surfaced at the low murmur in my ear. Something warm pressed against my back. The hard erection pushed between my thighs. I reached behind me, touching a warm thigh. "Tobias," I sighed.

He rocked against me, his hand cupping my breast. "Is it too early?"

I kept my eyes closed and lifted my knee, sliding my foot lazily along the outside of his leg as he entered me. God, this felt good and right. Nick lifted his head and watched through half-slit eyes as his brother took me from behind, then dropped his head back to the pillow.

But he didn't close his eyes.

Instead, he watched, reaching out his hand for mine. Our hands collided and our fingers slid between each other's into a clasp as Tobias thrusted, his heavy breaths growing deeper and more urgent.

I closed my eyes and arched my spine as that heat rolled through me. A guttural snarl and he drove deep, grunting as he came. This is how it'd be with them, always touching, always wanting. I couldn't get enough.

"Food," Nick muttered as Tobias stilled, his hand still on my hip. "It's your turn, little brother."

With a mumble, Tobias pulled from my body and rolled, climbing from the bed with far too much energy for this time of the morning.

"Eggs and bacon?"

"With toast," Nick added.

"Wasn't asking you, dickhead."

I smiled and lifted my head, meeting my stepbrother's stare from the end of the bed as he tugged on Nick's sweats. "Ryth?"

I smiled. "Eggs and bacon sounds perfect." My belly let out a grumble, drawing a scowl from him before he turned and headed out of the room.

I tracked his steps to the bathroom, then all the way down the stairs.

"You sure you're okay with us?" Caleb murmured from behind Nick. "Not sure you know what you've gotten yourself into."

"Not sure myself, to be honest," I answered as I pushed up from the bed. "But I guess we're about to find out."

40

Ryth

"You know," Nick muttered, shoveling a mess of bacon and eggs into his mouth, then stabbing the air with his fork. "This is probably your best, little brother. I'm impressed," he said, giving me a wink.

Tobias stood there, scowling at his brother's plate still piled high, then looked at mine, sitting empty. "I didn't fucking cook them for you."

"I know...which makes this the best," Nick smiled, triggering a growl from his brother.

I looked from one to the other as Caleb strode into the kitchen, yanking on a soft black t-shirt, oblivious to the fight about to break out.

"Better eat, princess," he suggested. "Before Tobias has a damn fit."

I dragged the plate toward me and slid an egg and two pieces of bacon onto the plate, earning a sideways glance from Nick. "Are you gonna eat all that?"

Tobias started around the island as Nick let out a bark of laughter and threw his hands in the air. "It was *a joke.*"

But Tobias wasn't playing, lunging to grab him around the collar as Caleb casually poured his coffee, then lifted his cup to his lips. Violence followed as the two men wrestled and swore. Nick laughed harder, which only incited Tobias even more... and I just ate my damn breakfast.

"Sunday," Caleb murmured, closing his eyes and enjoying his coffee. "How I love thee. What's the plan today, princess?"

I just shrugged, wincing as the squall of possessive idiots went to the floor, throwing each other around. "Assignments, I guess. I have plenty to—"

Caleb snapped his eyes open. The fight stopped behind me in an instant.

The hairs on my arms stood on end. I swallowed a mouthful of food as Caleb shoved away from the island and strode toward me. "I don't think so, Ryth. It's our first day together. We're going out."

"To the beach?" Tobias asked as he shoved upwards. "So I can finish kicking Nick's ass in the water."

"To the gym," Nick recommended.

But Caleb glared at the two men as they pushed to stand, their hard breaths surrounding me. "What do you want to do, Ryth?"

My two stepbrothers looked my way, wincing, both dragging fingers through their hair.

"Yeah," Tobias muttered. "Anything you want, little mouse."

I'd hardly been out...like at all. Ever since I'd moved in with them, it'd been rushing to get enrolled at school, and then the wedding...*yeah, the wedding*. I'd almost forgotten all about that. I stared at Caleb, knowing right now, in this minute, we were kin.

"You're my brother" I whispered.

"Stepbrother," he corrected.

My breaths came hard and fast. I knew that...I understood that. *But it hadn't hit home until just this moment.*

"Princess," Nick started, coming closer. "Easy."

"We can take care of you," Tobias reassured, a little quieter. "Better than anyone else can."

"Take care of me?" I repeated, meeting his gaze.

He nodded. I thought about the breakfast on the table, the way they stopped on a dime when I needed something.

"No one will dare touch you, not with us at your back," Tobias added. "Not now that you're a Banks."

I was a Banks.

"Jesus," I whispered. "You all must think I'm sick."

"Sick?" Caleb placed his cup on the counter and came around to me. "No sicker than we are. You want this, right?"

A cold ripple of fear came from behind me. Nick flinched and jerked his gaze from Caleb to me.

"Little mouse?" Tobias murmured, so damn quiet.

And the entire time, that voice in my head howled what I'd always known. "I want...." I turned to glance at all three of them. "I want to go to the damn mall."

Tobias let out a groan and turned away. "I fucking *knew it.*"

Caleb's lips curled into a slow, careful smile. "Then the mall it is."

It was under protest, I *knew* that. Which made it all the more enjoyable. I let out a squeal, slid off the chair, and lunged for the stairs, until I stopped and turned back, rushed to Tobias to wrap my arms around him and stare into his eyes. "Thank you for breakfast. It was my second favorite thing this morning."

I kissed him, tasting the salty bacon on his pouty lips. His arms went around me, pulling me hard against him. He was already fucking horny, already hard, the bulge rising as I deepened the kiss, then broke away. "I'm so fucking excited."

It was every woman's dream. Three hunky guys at my side, even if they didn't enjoy themselves as much as I did. We took Caleb's Lamborghini and parked close to the front doors before we climbed out.

I'd never felt so alive, so excited. I'd been living in my school uniforms and the few things Creed had bought me when I'd arrived almost two months ago.

"Okay, where first?" Caleb hit the button and locked the car.

"VS's," Tobias piped up, earning him a glare from Nick.

"You gonna walk into Victoria's Secret with your damn sister, are you?"

"If she's Ryth, *yeah,*" Tobias acknowledged.

"We need to be careful about this," Caleb muttered, rounding the car, staring at Tobias as he passed. "It can't get out."

"I don't give a fuck," my moody stepbrother snapped.

Caleb stopped, anger flickering in his eyes as he glanced my way. "It's not about you, idiot. It's about *her*."

Tobias flinched, then followed his brother's stare to me as it hit him. He licked his lips. "Yeah. You're right."

"So, whatever she wants, she gets, and we'll stand outside the store and play the dutiful older brothers, grumbling and complaining like you do so well. Got it?"

It was the first time I'd seen Caleb pull rank like that.

And it worked.

"Sure, of course" He grumbled. "Whatever you want, little sister."

"Now that's settled, let's go," Nick said as he motioned toward the entrance of the mall.

I walked past them, reaching out to grip Tobias' arm. "Come on, big brother, let's see what we can get with the whole two hundred dollars in my account."

He just scowled, then glanced behind us to Nick.

But I didn't care, I was so ready to spend my money a hundred times over. First, bath bombs, 'cause I hadn't relaxed in a bath since moving in with three fully grown men who had no comprehension of personal space or time alone.

Tobias let me drag him inside, past the food court, even though he resisted then and headed for a shop called Bath Elegance. I relaxed and spent time sniffing each one until I was almost dizzy on lavender and rose.

Tobias picked up one, sniffed it, then walked over to me. "This one."

I glanced at the chalky white ball in his hand. "Yeah?"

He nodded. "Yeah."

I grabbed it and lifted it to my nose. The scent of vanilla hit me. It was exactly like the perfume my mom had given me last year for Christmas. "Oh, you like that one."

"Yeah." He glanced at the woman behind the checkout, then gave an obvious shrug. "I mean, it's fine...if you want it."

I grabbed three and headed toward Nick, who stood at the counter. Caleb had disappeared the moment I stepped into the store. I hadn't expected them to hang around. To be honest, I was more than grateful for the car ride here and back home.

"Eighty-three dollars," the cashier said, busy staring at Nick, who leaned casually against the counter, oblivious to the way she seemed flustered.

"For bath bombs?" I muttered, my stomach dropping hard.

Nick just chuckled and handed me his black American Express card. "Yes, for bath bombs, Ryth. Keep it." He motioned to the card he'd shoved into my palm. "That one is yours anyway."

My heart leaped as I looked down at the card in my hand, my name printed on the front, *Ryth Castlemaine.* "You can't be serious?"

He shoved off the counter and stepped so close he could almost kiss me to murmur, "As a fucking heart attack, little sister."

Then he strode away, leaving the woman behind the counter with her brows rising and her jaw dropping. "Holy shit.," she whispered, glancing at the card in my hand. "Did he just almost...*kiss you?*"

"Of course not," I forced the words as I handed her the card. "He's my brother."

I left the store, my cheeks burning and my head giddy.

Shop after shop they took me to, Caleb joining us an hour later. All three waited patiently, usually beside me as I browsed, then picked out new trainers under Tobias' guidance. "I thought we might start to jog together."

He stilled, elation widening his eyes. "You want to run with me?"

There was no way I'd be able to keep up, still I shrugged. "Why not? I need to improve my stamina."

His grin was instant, and the lip bite that followed hit me right between my thighs. "Damn right," he answered, smiling as he cast not one, but two, pairs of shoes onto the counter with a devilish glint in his eyes.

He was gonna run me to death, I just knew it.

We spent hours shopping and there wasn't a grumble, not even when the bags piled up and I'd bought an entire wardrobe of the most beautiful things I'd ever seen, dresses, jeans, a soft cashmere sweater that Tobias said matched the ugly mark on my cheek. I looked away when he said that, standing in front of the display with the soft fabric pressed against my cheek.

I smiled and tugged my hair lower.

"Uh-uh, little mouse." Tobias gently pulled my hand away, staring at my face before meeting my gaze. "You don't shy away from us...*ever.*"

Heat moved through me, closing in around my heart.

"We'll take these to the car and come back," Nick said, hefting the bags into the air.

Caleb followed, carrying his own purchases as well as mine.

I grabbed the sweater, feeling the burn of Nick's card as I swiped it once more. I'd owe him money for the rest of my damn life...but I was sure we'd be able to come to some kind of agreement. My pussy clenched at the idea of that, trading money for my body. I stopped dead, watching as Nick walked out of the store. Then I'd be *his* whore.

"You good here?" Tobias asked.

I glanced his way, finding a bemused expression on his face before he stepped closer. "Or do you need to try something on in the dressing room?"

I knew *exactly* what he meant. "We're in a shoe store, there are no dressing rooms."

"There's a back room, isn't there?"

I couldn't hide the smirk. "You can't wait?"

His intense stare was answer enough.

"Tobias," came the deep, familiar murmur behind us.

My stepbrother stiffened, then slowly turned. Lazarus Rossi stood behind us, flanked by his bodyguard. He took one look at me, then at the bags in my hand. "Out shopping?"

A.K ROSE & ATLAS ROSE

Tobias took a threatening step forward, putting himself between Lazarus and me. "How is that any of your goddamn business?"

"Just strange is all." Lazarus shifted his focus to me. "That you're not concerned at all about your father, seeing as how he's missing."

My stomach sank. "Missing? What do you mean, missing?"

Those icy blue eyes gave me nothing but a sinister glare. "You're really going to stand there and tell me you know nothing?"

I didn't need to stand here. I pushed forward, stepping around Tobias. He grabbed my hand, pulling me against his side. "He's not missing, he's upset after the news he's not getting out."

"Upset?" Lazarus took a step closer, coming chest to chest with Tobias, but still holding my gaze. "That's what you want to believe, then go right ahead."

"You know what?" I snapped, my face heating. "Fuck you, you piece of shit. Fuck you for putting him in there in the first place!"

"Putting him in there?" Cold, hard rage flashed in his eyes as he leaned closer to spit, "He's fucking lucky he's still breathing. You have no idea how close we were to putting a bullet in his goddamn brain. You steal from us, and you deal with the consequences. *He* knew that...and he did it anyway."

"Steal?" I couldn't see straight. "*Steal? Steal what?*" I hissed. "What the fuck did he steal, fresh fucking air?"

"Ryth," Tobias warned like he knew I was stepping across a line.

But I didn't care, not anymore. "We have *nothing!* Why the fuck do you think we're living with the Banks?"

"Because your mom knows the truth," Lazarus replied as he glanced at Tobias. "And so does your dad. Jack isn't in prison, Ryth."

"Then where *is* he?" I barked.

Lazarus searched my eyes for the truth. "That's a very good question. Your mother is lying, and I want to know why."

He met Tobias' glare before turning away. But I couldn't let him go, not yet...

I lunged and grabbed his arm. His bodyguard reacted instantly, grabbing my wrist and twisting until I cried out. Tobias lashed out, driving his fist into the guy's chest. "Get the fuck off her, Freddy!"

In an instant, my happy day dissolved into chaos. A gun was drawn and pointed at Tobias.

"Back the fuck off, T," Freddy warned.

My wrist throbbed, and panic moved in as I stared at the gun. "No...*no!*"

"Freddy," Lazarus called his attack dog off. "Let's get out of here."

But Freddy didn't move, not until Lazarus turned and left, leaving the rest of those in the store staring at us.

"I've called the police," the shop assistant called.

"Don't bother," Tobias growled, staring after Freddy as he left, following his damn master. "We're already leaving."

41

Ryth

"Ryth!" Tobias barked, shoving aside onlookers as he pulled me out of the store.

But I couldn't feel his hand, nor their stares. I couldn't feel anything but that empty feeling in the center of my chest.

"What the fuck happened?" Nick charged forward, quickly looking around.

"Lazarus happened," Tobias answered, glancing my way.

Rage exploded in Nick's eyes as he scanned me. "Did he hurt you?"

He's fucking lucky he's still breathing. You have no idea how close we were to putting a bullet in his goddamn brain. Lazarus' words resounded, hollow and strange in my head. "He said mom's lying," I muttered as Tobias dragged me toward the front doors of the mall. I turned to look right at Tobias. "He said she was lying."

"Yeah, well..." he muttered.

I flinched. "What's that supposed to mean?"

He said nothing, just lengthened his stride, forcing me to step faster to keep up. Caleb was striding toward us as we hit the automatic doors and made our way outside. "What happened?"

"Lazarus," Nick answered. "Seems the mouthy bastard had plenty to say."

Caleb focused on Tobias' hold on my arm, then the pained look in my eyes. "You're hurting her."

"What?" Tobias growled.

Caleb moved toward me. "Let go of her arm, T, you're hurting her."

His grip eased instantly before he looked down at the reddening marks on my arm. "Sorry."

We went straight to the car, climbing in amongst the mountain of bags. I stared at the bags beside me on the rear seat. I didn't want them anymore, *any of it*. I leaned forward and put my face in my hands.

"Ryth?" Caleb called my name from the driver's seat.

"Ryth, talk to us," Nick urged in front of me.

But Tobias said nothing. I could feel the chill coming from him and the memory of that gun aimed at him turned the panic inside me cold. He could've been killed...*all because of me*.

I opened my eyes and turned to him.

He stared straight ahead, those dark eyes growing darker as Caleb started the Lamborghini and pulled out of the parking lot.

"He said dad stole from them." My gaze drifted as Laz's words came back to me. "What the fuck did he steal, it sure as hell wasn't money!"

The car grew uncomfortably quiet...*too quiet*. "What did he steal?" I repeated, and turned to Caleb first, then Nick.

"Drugs," Tobias answered beside me, his glare burning a hole in the back of Caleb's head. "Your father ran drugs for the Rossis."

"Drugs?" I whispered, and slowly shook my head. "No, that's not right."

Caleb met my gaze in the rear-view mirror. "It's the truth."

"Drugs?" The word slammed around in my head. "My dad stole drugs?"

"Drug *money*," Caleb answered as he changed gears and punched the accelerator. The sleek sports car didn't feel heavy and throbbing like the Mustang. Instead, it charged forward, tearing around corners under expert hands. We flew back home, hitting the driveway with a jolt until the Lamborghini's engine died.

Drug money...my father stole drug money. *Jesus...this was bad... this was really, really fucking bad.* My brothers climbed out and Caleb headed for the door, leaving Nick and Tobias to carry my bags inside. But there was a difference now. Nick stayed back, scanning the street as Tobias hustled me inside.

Did they think Lazarus was going to come for me?

Jesus. It hit me like a punch to my chest. They did...they thought Laz or the Rossis were coming for me! This was all because mom had lied to me. I hurried inside and headed for the kitchen, yanking open the refrigerator door. My bags were dropped on the kitchen floor before Caleb turned to us. "I want to know exactly what Lazarus said, word for word."

"What the fuck does it matter?"

Caleb braced a hand on the counter and directed his laser focus at Tobias. "It matters."

Tobias scowled, but then repeated what Lazarus had said, word for word, exactly how Lazarus said it.

"Jesus," Caleb swore as he turned away, pacing the kitchen floor.

"What?" I whispered, narrowing in on his face.

He stopped halfway across the floor.

"Spit it out, brother," Nick snapped. "What the fuck is it?"

"I knew he was a lying piece of shit," Caleb snarled, staring at the ground. "I just fucking knew it."

"Knew *what?*" Nick snarled, turning to him. "Tell us!"

"The day he came home covered in blood splatter and took Ryth on that goddamn joyride, I knew something had happened. So I went to his study. I logged into his computer and I found where he'd been."

My breaths stopped, and my heart hammered.

"His diary had the name Mitchelton."

My stomach sank. "Mitchelton...*as in Mitchelton Prison?*"

No one answered. I guessed that was answer enough. My mind raced, trying to piece it all together.

"It could be nothing," Caleb said, but he shook his head.

"And it could be *everything*." Tobias took a step closer, a savage look burning in his eyes. "I told you what he was fucking like. I told you what he was doing when the three of us were here with mom the day she got her test results. I fucking *told you,* and still you kept telling me it was a goddamn mistake. He broke her heart...*he broke her fucking heart.*" Tobias looked at me, and something shifted behind the darkness in his eyes. "While we were holding mom as she fell apart, he was cock deep in some woman's pussy...three of them, to be exact. I fucking beat the shit out of Lazarus when he told me, when he'd done nothing more than have my goddamn back. Because it ruined our fucking friendship, all because dad couldn't handle the fact his wife was dying."

I couldn't speak, couldn't look away. Not from the agony that flared in his eyes, or his words that practically bled. "Now do you believe me?" He turned to glare at Nick. "Brother?"

The muscles of Nick's throat clenched. "Yeah," he answered. "I believe you."

"The study," Caleb growled. "There has to be more information, something I didn't see before."

Tobias nodded, his lips curling into a sinister smile. "Then let's rip it apart."

Nick looked my way. "Down to the fucking concrete if we have to."

"Princess." Caleb reached for my hand. "Let's get to the bottom of this."

My knees shook as I stepped forward and took his hand. We all headed for the study, and Caleb threw open the door and hit the button for the blinds. Sunlight flooded in, revealing all those dark corners and filthy secrets. I glanced at the rows and rows of law books on the shelves and felt sick to my stomach.

What the fuck was Creed up to? And why the hell was my mom involved?

Caleb rounded the desk and hit the button, bringing the computer to life. I'd let Creed buy me things, let him treat me with kindness, and all the while...

Nausea rolled through me again.

All the while he was planning, what?

Nick leaned over Caleb's shoulder as he unlocked his father's computer and set to work opening and scanning every file he could. Caleb knew what he was doing, knew what he was looking for, hitting all the commands the computer needed to search through files and files of documents.

"Where is the money?"

Tobias jerked his gaze to me. "What?"

I met his stare. "Where is the money? The feds took everything, surely if they'd found something, we'd know, right?"

Caleb lifted his gaze from the monitor. "Not necessarily, not if they're building a case."

"A case against who? They already have my dad in prison."

Caleb glanced at Nick as Tobias let out a harsh bark of laughter. "They're coming after us, is that it?"

"Who else could it be?" I asked. "First dad is gone, then that very same night mom drags us here...to be a family."

Caleb pushed up from the chair at the same time as Nick whirled.

"That's what this is all about, isn't it? It's not just a marriage, it's a pact, a pact between your father and my mom," I declared as some of it became clear to me.

"Jesus," Nick whispered. "She's right."

Electricity hummed in the room, standing the hairs on my arms on end.

"Now all we need is to find out why," Caleb stated, glancing at the monitor.

"And what happened to my dad," I added. "That first. That first and everything else after."

"Agreed," Nick said. "Everything else we can figure out, but family is priority."

My chest lightened with his words. Something fluttered against my heart, or it could have been my heart. Nick held my stare and I knew for the first time that this was what true loyalty felt like.

It didn't bail. It was true and grounded.

It was raw and hungry, just like this thing we shared between us...*all of us.*

"Then let's get to work," Tobias urged. "You go through the computer and I'm going through these damn books. Something has to be here, somewhere."

Tobias stepped over to the bookshelf and grabbed the middle book on the shelf nearest his hand, tugging it free. The gold edged navy blue tome weighed down his hand. The look of disgust on his face grew as he flipped through the pages and dropped it to the floor. It hit with a *thump*. Nick and Caleb stared, like that was sacrilegious, the breaking of a spell. Maybe it was...maybe I had a spell to break, too.

I moved toward another shelf and reached out.

"Not those, little mouse," Tobias warned, stilling my hand. "Those are mom's."

I pulled my hand away, glancing at the few journals. The spines were creased and the covers were worn. I didn't know why I hadn't seen it before. The divide in books was so damn obvious. This section was small and messy, filled with journals and thick, softcover books, whereas the ones that Tobias had yanked free, only to flip through the pages and drop to the ground, were crisp and new almost.

Thud.

Thud.

Thud.

Book by book, Tobias pulled the bookshelves apart. We searched the rest of the day. Caleb grew frustrated searching the computer and traded places with Nick, only to yank open the drawers of Creed's desk and search every space he could.

Thud.

"There's nothing here," Tobias growled, yanking another book from the shelf.

"Keep looking," Caleb muttered.

Tobias yanked the next one free without even searching the pages. *"There's...nothing here."*

I bent, grabbed the book on statute law he'd dropped, and flicked through the pages, my fingers shaking.

"Then we damn well keep looking until we find something." Caleb upended a drawer and knelt amidst the contents.

Tobias was right.

Deep down, I knew it. It was what I was afraid of.

"Fuck this!" Nick shoved the keyboard across the desk. My back ached as I shoved up to a stand, looking around at the desolation. We'd moved from one side of the study to the other, searching every book...all except the small section of their mom's, left untouched.

There was nothing here.

Nick leaned forward, resting his head in his hands on the desk.

Silence.

Strained silence.

Underneath that, hope sounded like the scrape of screws coming undone.

"We need a break," Caleb muttered.

I glanced out the window at the fading sunlight. We'd been searching most of the day with no breaks, no stopping, our frustrations growing by the hour.

"Food, shower, and we make a better plan," Nick stated.

"I need to fuck or fight. I need..." He glanced my way, then winced. "Forget it."

He was gone in a blur, making for the open door and disappearing. The heavy thud of his footsteps on the stairs sounded, then faded.

"I'm going to get food." Caleb turned from the window. "I'm goddamn starving."

"You going to be right here?" Tobias turned to me.

I saw the hunger in his eyes, the caged, seething anger that needed release. "Go," I murmured. "I'm fine."

A nod and he turned away. I didn't need to ask where he was going. It was where he always went when he was riled, running.

Caleb left the study, with Tobias not far behind, leaving me alone in the middle of the destruction. I looked around at the mess of books and upturned drawers, my gaze drifting to the untouched shelves of their mother's journals.

Ones they didn't want to touch. I stepped closer, the urge to pull them apart just to make sure still in my mind. But the moment I touched the cover of the first journal, I knew I couldn't do it. Naomi Banks lingered like a ghost in this place, leaving behind far too many memories and wounds that still bled. I pulled my hand away and left the study, listening to the front door thud as I stepped out.

The house was quiet. Too damn quiet. "Nick," I called softly, and climbed the stairs.

But there was no answer, then, as I hit the landing on our floor, the grunt of sex spilled out under his closed door. I flinched, pain flaring as I was drawn to the sound.

The sound of fucking.

"Nick?" I murmured, and cracked open his door.

The slick slaps of flesh on flesh sounded. Nick lay on the bed, his cock hard and ridged in one hand, and his phone in the other. I flinched as though I'd been slapped. My insides clenched as it hit me.

Porn...he was watching porn...

Pain flared through my chest until the familiar female groan came to my ears.

"What the fuck?" I exclaimed.

Nick wrenched open his eyes. "Ryth," he groaned, his phone dropping to the bed.

On the screen, the sex played out. Only it wasn't the kind of sex I'd expected.

It was him and me...with Tobias standing naked in the background.

Nick's head was buried between my legs before he rose. His cock filled the screen before the camera angled in, following the movement as he entered me for the first time.

On the screen, I bucked, moaning as that thick head slid inside me. My body was quivering, my moans ringing louder. "More," I whimpered in stereo. "More Nick."

I couldn't think. My mind was racing. "You recorded us?"

Shame and hunger moved across his face. "Yeah."

I stepped closer to the bed, my gaze divided between us on the screen and that same thick cock in his hand. "And you watch us?"

He licked his lips. "Yeah."

Surprise, jealousy, and satisfaction collided. He was still hard, still aching. Déjà vu hit me. He'd watched me on that first day when he took me to the park. He'd watched my clumsy attempt at pleasuring myself.

Now I wanted to see him.

"Keep going," I ordered, meeting his gaze. "I want to watch."

There was a flare of surprise before his hand went back around his cock and slowly moved up and down. Only this time, he didn't watch the screen...he watched me. The real me.

I forced myself to stay where I was. Heat moved through me as he clenched his fist around that hard length. My mouth watered, watching the vein under his shaft pulse with the pressure. Firm, strong. Corded muscles flexed on his arm as he slid along that smooth length, stroking all the way to the head, and then fisted hard back down.

A tiny clear teardrop formed at the tip.

I stepped closer, unable to hold myself back anymore.

"How many times have you watched it?" I murmured.

"A...*lot*," he groaned, his brows furrowing.

"Do you have other recordings...of other women?"

"No," he answered, his hand never stopping working that hard thickness as it blushed at the head. "Only you."

"Because I was a virgin the night you fucked me?" I reached out, grazing my finger along the heat to capture that bead.

He let out a deep moan, part animal, part man. "Yes."

I sucked the taste of him from my finger. "And because I was to be your sister?"

His body quaked, his cock spasmed at the words. He didn't need to speak. I saw it all.

"Your sister," I whispered, "who you drove to the park. Your sister who you made spread her legs in your car and fuck herself."

He closed his eyes and dropped his head backward. "Fuck, yes."

"You want that again, Nick?" I whispered. "You want to see me in your car, my legs open, my white panties yanked aside?"

He came with a long groan, cum shooting to splash against his stomach.

Fuck, if my own body didn't pulse and tighten with the image. I'd never seen anything so carnal.

Beep. A text splashed across the screen.

Natalie: Baby please...

The sight of her name hit me like a slap. I flinched and stepped backwards as Nick opened his eyes.

"What?" he groaned, and pushed upwards, concern flaring in his eyes.

I couldn't stop the jealousy from stealing me away from the moment we'd just shared. "It seems your *girlfriend* didn't take the hint," I snarled. "Maybe you weren't as clear as you said you were."

Then I turned and stormed out of the room as my own phone vibrated in my pocket. I reached for it as pain stabbed through my chest.

"Ryth!" Nick called as I slammed his door closed. *"For fuck's sake, Ryth!"*

But I didn't want to speak to him, not now. I headed for my bedroom, the only place of sanctuary I had, and slammed the door behind me.

"Fuck off, Nick," I growled as the heavy thud of his footsteps rang out. "I'm warning you, just leave me alone."

I gripped my phone and sat down on the end of the bed. Deep down, I knew I was being irrational, that if she was pleading with him, that he'd made it more than clear he was done.

Still, I couldn't stop the pain, or that overwhelming feeling of helplessness.

Beep.

My phone sounded again. I dragged my thumb across the screen and unlocked it.

Gio: *If you want the information, then you need to see me.*

What?

I scrolled down, reading the previous texts.

Gio: *Lazarus held back the truth about your dad. He's alive. He's asking for you. But I'll only talk to you, Ryth, not your fucking asshole brothers. So, if you want to know, then it needs to be done in secret and tonight.*

I reread the message, my pulse thundering as my phone *beeped* again.

Gio: It's now or never. Come to the address I sent. I'm waiting right now.

Nick's heavy steps sounded before the *slam* of his bedroom door. "Fuck you, Natalie!" he screamed. "Fucking *bitch!*"

My brother raged as I shoved upwards, my heart in the back of my throat. I couldn't stop staring at the text. *If you want to know, then it needs to be done in secret...and tonight.*

Dad...

If he was out there, I had to know he was safe. I went to my door and quietly turned the handle. But if I told Nick, there was no way Gio would talk. Not after what they'd done. I could be there and back before they knew.

Only then I'd know where dad was...

That thought drove me as I crept past Nick's door and headed for Tobias'. I stepped in, hurried to his desk, and grabbed the keys for his Jeep. I'd be back within the hour. They'd never even know I was gone...

42

Ryth

I gripped the steering wheel of Tobias' Jeep, wincing as I ground his gears and glanced at the map on the screen of my phone. God, if I broke his damn car, he'd never forgive me. I shoved my foot against the clutch and forced the gear until it clunked.

My phone gave a *beep*. Tobias' name flashed across the screen. I ignored it, and the two more texts that came after it. When Nick's name followed them, I swallowed a flare of pain and drove my foot harder against the accelerator. I'd call them as soon as I got there. Once I explained, they'd calm down. Would they be pissed? Yeah, especially knowing it was Gio, but if I kept the call open and they heard everything he said to me, then they'd know I wasn't going without a plan.

I knew they didn't like Gio, knew they'd rather put him in the hospital than allow him any kind of contact with me. But if he was in a coma, he couldn't tell me what I needed to know, and right now, the need to find out where my dad was outweighed their possessiveness.

My phone started to ring, and Nick's number flashed over the map Gio'd sent me. "Shit." I swiped the screen.

"Ryth—" Nick started.

"Wait," I snapped, still a little pissed from earlier. "I can explain."

"You'd better," Tobias growled in the background as I punched the clutch and geared down around a corner. *"Jesus...is that my damn gearbox?"* He shouted.

"Yes, and if you don't stop talking, I won't be able to tell you I know where my dad is."

"You do?" Caleb broke in. "Where?"

"Well, not right now. But I will—"

"Ryth," Nick's voice grew cold. "I want you to tell us exactly what the fuck is going on?"

I tried to concentrate on the unfamiliar roads and the fact this was only my third ever attempt at driving a stick shift...and I used the term *'attempt'* loosely. "Promise you won't get mad?"

Nick let out a growl. "Not as mad as I will be if you don't tell us what the hell is happening."

"Gio sent me a message—"

"Sonofabitch," Tobias snapped. "Goddamn *bastard.*"

"I'm trying to tell you and not crash here," I yelled.

"Tell us." Nick sounded panicked.

"He said that Lazarus was lying," I explained. "He said that he knows where my dad is."

"And he wasn't going to tell you with us there," Nick added.

"Not after what Tobias did, no."

"Goddamn piece of shit," Tobias growled. "You know he's lying, right? There's no way Laz would tell him a goddamn thing."

"Are you sure about that?" I glanced at the red blinking light on the map, then lifted my gaze to the flickering lights as they broke through the darkness. "Because I'm not, and right now we have nothing else. I can't take that risk, I just can't."

The Jeep barely jolted on the lonely dirt road I'd been driving for the past ten minutes.

Tobias' growl grew louder. "I don't trust him."

"I know." I geared down, slowing the Jeep. "Which is why I was going to call you anyway so you can hear everything he says."

"You were?" Nick broke in.

"Yes, I was. There was no way he was going to tell me anything with any of you there, so right now, this was our only option, unless you'd rather I talk to Lazarus Rossi instead."

"Over my dead body," Tobias practically howled. "Send us the coordinates, we're on our way."

I slowed the Jeep a little more, gripped the phone tight, and took a screenshot, sending it to Tobias' phone with one hand. By the time they caught up, I'd have the information I needed. "Done."

A stampede sounded on the other end of Nick's call. The *boom* of the front door came barely a second before the Mustang's engine growled to life.

"Just hang back," Nick ordered. "Wait for us to get closer."

I sought out those glittering lights, sure that if Gio even suspected they were on their way, he'd clam up. There's no way he'd talk to me then. I glanced at the phone, listening to the Mustang's squealing tires as Nick drove it hard.

I couldn't take that chance, not when what I needed was so close. I eased my foot off the brake and let the Jeep pick up speed.

"We're right here," Nick's voice came through the speaker, as though he knew on instinct that I needed him. "Twenty minutes from you."

"Okay," I whispered, scanning the darkness as the front door of the building opened and Gio limped out, leaving others behind. Laughter and voices spilled through the window.

I lowered my hand, hiding the fact that my brothers were listening to every word. Gio looked at the Jeep, then scanned the darkness. "You came alone?"

"You told me to."

"Yeah, well." He massaged the back of his neck.

He was nervous, still nervous after I'd told him the truth. I got out of the Jeep in front of the house and climbed the wooden stairs, glancing through the window. "I'm here. Tell me what you know."

"Inside." He motioned with his head.

I shook mine. "That wasn't part of the deal."

Hate flashed in his eyes as he turned on me. "Neither was three broken ribs and a bruised splayed neck, but I guess we get what we get, don't we, Ryth?"

I froze at the sudden savagery, the others inside would hear us... they'd come, wouldn't they? He stilled, sucked in a hard breath, and glanced over his shoulder to inside the house. Goosebumps raced along my skin and my instincts were on fire, telling me not to go in there.

"Tell me what I want to know," I demanded, not moving an inch. "Tell me and I'll go."

"Come in the house, Ryth." he turned back to me, but his once kind eyes now held no warmth. There was just stony anger. "Come in and I'll tell you what you want to know."

I looked toward the doorway behind him, catching one of the jocks from school peering out and narrowing in on me before turning away. There had to be at least five others partying inside. Gio wouldn't do anything, not with a crowd, would he?

"Don't fucking do it," Tobias' voice came from my phone in my hand. "Ryth...."

Time froze as Gio stared at me. My pulse thundered, sending a chill down my spine before fear finally kicked in.

I spun and lunged, stumbling down the stairs as Gio let out a snarl.

"Get the bitch inside now, Gio!" a female screamed.

I knew that voice...knew that fucking cruel bark. I glanced over my shoulder, seeing Natalie standing in the doorway as I flew across the front of the house. No...God, no.

I drove my boots into the ground, the Jeep all I saw.

"Get the fuck out of there now, Ryth!" Nick roared from the phone as I ran...until I was hit from behind.

Gio grabbed me by the hair, wrenching me backwards. "Fucking bitch!"

I kicked and punched, trying to get away. *"Get the fuck off me!"*

"Goddamn cunt." He yanked me back as I tried to shove forwards, pulling me so hard I fell and hit the ground. "Think you're too fucking good for me?"

Fire lashed my scalp, his fingers entangled in my hair as the others from inside began to spill out.

"Get her inside, Gio!" Natalie screamed as she ran toward us.

No...no, please no! I lashed out, driving my fist into his side, watching as he buckled with pain.

They'd hurt me...if I went in that house...they'd hurt me.

I shoved upwards, tearing free from that vicious hold, my boots finding purchase on the hard ground. Voices came from those inside as they stumbled out of the house. But they made no effort to help. I knew deep down they wouldn't. The Jeep glistened in the moonlight...like a beacon.

Get there...that's all I had to do. I shoved up and ran with all I had.

"No, you fucking don't!" Natalie screamed.

I caught the blur of movement, then a heavy *smack* that lashed my face, snapping my head sideways, and my body followed. I stumbled and fell, hitting the ground hard. But before I could think, she was on me.

Sharp nails clawed my face, dangerously close to my eye.

"Fucking cunt!" she screamed. *"You think you can take MY boyfriend?"*

I fought as hard as I could, slapping her hands away. Tears instantly filled my eyes, blurring her as she came for me again. My phone...*my phone.* I jerked my gaze across the ground, finding the glint.

I tried to shove upwards as she slapped my face once more. My head rocked with the impact and my ears rang, burning with the blows as I roared, *"He's not* your *fucking boyfriend!"*

"You fucking *bitch!*" She lunged, her eyes wide and wild.

Gio held his side as he limped closer, glaring at Natalie. "You said you weren't going to hurt her!"

I pressed my hand to the sting of my cheek. My fingers came away glistening in the night. Blood...that was blood. I jerked my gaze to her as she came closer.

"She thinks she can take my Nick from me?" she spat. "I'll make it so he never looks at her again."

I moved, stumbling sideways toward my phone. Muffled roars grew clearer as I bent on trembling legs and grabbed it.

"RYTH!" Nick screamed. *"FOR FUCKS SAKE, RYTH!"*

I lifted it to my throbbing face, my voice trembling as I spoke. "I-I'm here. I'm here. Nick, I'm scared."

"Hold on, princess. I'm on my fucking way...just hold the fuck on."

She took a step toward me, her curled lips baring her teeth as she focused on the phone in my hand. "He's mine...*you got that, you stupid, ugly cunt?"* She dropped her hand to her waist and drew something long and silver from her pocket. "He's always been *mine."*

The knife flicked open with a *snap,* the long blade glinting as she stepped forward. "I'll make it so no one looks at you ever again."

My stomach clenched, and fear rooted me to the spot. "No...*please no."*

"NATALIE!" Nick's roar boomed in my ears. *"NATALIE, DON'T YOU DARE FUCKING TOUCH HER!"*

She jerked her gaze to the phone in my hand. "Is that him?" Her breaths stilled as agony carved across her face. *"Is that my Nicky?"*

She didn't need to cut me with that damn knife. Her words did it for her. I swallowed the agony, forcing myself to play her game. I nodded and lifted my phone. "Yes. Yes, it is. He wants to talk to you."

She licked her lips, the knife still shining in her hand. "Put him on speaker."

I tried to see the button, praying I hit the right one, my finger trembling violently. But the moment I did, Nick's voice filled the air.

"Natalie," he snarled. "You fucking hurt her and you're *dead* to me."

She winced, her breath catching.

"You hear me?" he barked, his voice filling the phone, smothering the roar of the Mustang's engine.

"I'm dead to you now anyway," she murmured, lifting her gaze to mine, her face brightening. "You never cared this much about me."

"You fucking cheated on me." His deep voice was etched with agony. "You fucked other guys behind my back and you didn't give a shit when I found out."

She shook her head, the knife trembling in her hand as her face grew brighter and brighter.

For a second, it didn't click. But Nick kept talking. "You're the one who ruined what we had, Natalie, no one else."

"I did it because you stopped wanting me." She took another step closer, desperation making her clench the knife in her hand tighter and direct that unpitying violence at me. "Now I see you won't want me ever again."

I waited for him to answer.

Waited for anything as the others from the party crowded around.

But as my pulse grew louder, I caught the sound of tires skidding. The Mustang's engine roared as the car kicked up dirt and hit the shoulder with a thud. Doors were thrown open as my brothers charged. Gio's eyes widened as they came for him.

"Banks!" someone screamed. *"Fucking bastards!"*

In a blinding blur, the fight broke out, but it was eight against three. I jerked my gaze to Natalie as she let out a feral scream and lunged toward me, the blade slashing in the air.

"Ryth!" Nick roared, throwing out a fist, driving it into some asshole's face.

Headlights lit up the fray. Fists and blood. Tobias was a fucking animal, charging forward to take down the biggest of them there, unleashing his blows with sickening savagery.

Still the sound of cars grew louder behind us. There were more coming, more against my brothers. Fear chilled me to the core.

I leapt backwards as Natalie slashed the knife through the air, coming for me. "Fucking *slut!*" she howled as my brothers fought all around me.

Their yells drove me forward. I dodged the slash, stepping to the side, then lunged, driving my pathetically small fist into her stomach. It barely made an impact, but it didn't matter, I was already swinging with my other fist, only this time, I drove it into the side of her face.

The blow hit hard, crunching my knuckles.

She stumbled sideways.

Nick divided his focus, desperate to get to me, but there were two of them on him, two who drove their fists into his face and his stomach. He left out a grunt and swung his savage glare back to his attackers.

"Nasty fucking cunt," Natalie punched out the words at me, her fingers cradling her bleeding nose. "I'm going to hurt you for that."

"The fuck you are," I snarled, and stood my ground, my brothers fighting at my back.

The *crack!* of a gunshot came a second after cars skidded to a stop behind us. But I didn't dare take my eyes off her, not for a second.

"Enough!" Lazarus barked, striding forward.

But punches were still being thrown by Gio's asshole buddies. Freddy moved fast and charged forward, then raised his gun and took aim. *"We said enough, asshole!"*

Lazarus Rossi carved a line through the middle of the melee, sparing a glance at Gio, who was under Tobias, his arms outstretched, his mouth bloody and ruined once more.

"You," Lazarus snapped. "You stupid fucking idiot. I fucking warned you." Lazarus looked to Tobias, who was filled with brutal frenzy.

Something passed between them. A kind of unspoken loyalty... or maybe it was the fact that Lazarus knew a few minutes more and Gio wouldn't need to worry about his injuries because Tobias would kill him.

"Freddy," Lazarus called his bodyguard. "Get him the fuck out of here."

Freddy moved instantly, striding forward. Tobias didn't fight when Gio was dragged out from under him, just held the asshole's glare. "The next time I see you, there won't be anybody to stop me, you got that?"

Gio spluttered, bloody flecks shooting in the air as he coughed and tried to breathe.

"I will end you," Tobias promised.

"You won't need to." Lazarus stepped closer, meeting Gio's stare. "Because I'll do it for you."

"Uh-uh." The bark came from behind me.

I jerked my gaze to Logan as he strode past me. His movement was just a blur as he lashed out, grasped Natalie's wrist, and twisted until her knees buckled and she cried out in pain.

"Let go of me!" she screamed.

I sucked in a hard breath, watching the merciless male as he twisted harder. The knife dropped to the ground before he shoved her away. She stumbled, cradling her hand as she shot a tearful stare toward Nick.

But he was sickened by the sight of her. His lips curled, hate burning in his eyes. He didn't need to say a thing before she broke down and sobbed. "You hate me. You really hate me."

"Come near any of us again and you'll find out just how much." His voice was stone cold.

Her shoulders slumped as she wrapped her arms around her middle.

"Get her out of here," Lazarus snapped.

"You heard him," Logan barked, jerking his gaze to a car still idling behind us. *"Move."* He took a step toward her. She flinched, fear flaring through the pain in her eyes.

She stumbled toward the car, leaving us behind. Still, I couldn't help but watch her leave.

"She's gone now," Lazarus murmured, his gaze on me. "She won't be bothering you again."

The way he said it, I knew she was about to have the most terrifying ride of her life. They might not hurt her, but she'd know just what would happen if she tried to come after us again.

"The rest of you better clear the fuck out, unless you want to find yourselves on my goddamn shit list."

Movement broke out in an instant, the rest of them shoving up from the ground and stumbling away, racing back to the house.

"You wanna explain this?" Lazarus glared at Tobias.

I knew who he was, knew his reputation as being dangerous. Yet Tobias just turned on him, meeting his stare with his own. "Explain? Sure, Lazarus. Let me lay it out for you, *brother*. This asshole decides to call Ryth and tell her you're holding out on her, that you know exactly where her dad is, and the only way he was gonna tell her was if she met him face to face. But it wasn't about her dad, was it? He wanted to lure her here alone."

Anger ripped through those blue eyes of the Mafia asshole. "That true?" He jerked his gaze to Gio.

But the spineless asshole didn't answer, just swung his glare to Natalie as the car doors closed. "It wasn't my idea."

Lazarus stepped toward him. "But you went along with it. You lured a young woman out in the middle of nowhere at night. A young woman whose father works for me."

Gio flinched. "He stole from you."

"That's not *your* business, now, is it?"

Gio paled under the wash of the Mustang's headlights. "I thought..."

"You thought," Lazarus repeated. "Next time you *think*, Gio, you'd better be far from me." The Mafia Prince's voice grew dangerous. "Don't go back to school. In fact, don't go anywhere in this city. Go home, pack your shit, and leave. I see you and you're done, feel me?"

Gio's eyes widened, but there was no getting out of this. His shoulders slumped as resignation hit home. "Yeah, Laz."

"Mr. Rossi to you." Freddy made sure the point was driven home. "And I'll personally make it my mission to drive by your place tomorrow...you know, just to make sure you got out of the city. Might check on your mom, too, just to ensure she's okay."

I hadn't thought Gio could look any sicker...I was wrong.

He left, his head drooped low, slinking away like a beaten animal.

"He's not coming back," Lazarus reassured as he looked at me. "I'll make sure of that. But I don't know where your father is, Ryth. If I did, I would've told you. I might be a bastard, but I value family."

"You wanted to kill him," I answered, there was no way I'd believe him.

"Is he dead?"

I stiffened at the question. Panic flared as I glanced at Tobias, Nick, and Caleb, then slowly answered, "No."

"Ever ask yourself why that is?"

I met Lazarus' piercing stare. "No."

"Maybe you should." He turned and strode away toward his bodyguards. "If I find your dad, Ryth, believe me, you'll be the first to know."

He left me stunned, my mind reeling, as Nick stepped close. His fingers trembled when they grazed my cheek. "Jesus, Ryth."

"Are you hurt?" Tobias grasped my hand, as his gaze searched my body for cuts or blood.

"No," I whispered, leaning against them. I wound one arm around Nick, then the other as far around Tobias and Caleb as I could reach. "Thank God."

Their hands held me, pulling me against their warmth as I shuddered and shook.

"Let's get you home," Nick murmured in my ear. "Then we can work out what the hell this all meant."

43

Ryth

I climbed into the backseat of the Mustang and Tobias drove the Jeep behind us all the way home. By the time we pulled up in the driveway, my entire body was shaking and my head was pounding viciously. Nick opened the door and I tried to climb out, but my knees buckled.

He lunged, grabbed me around the waist, and lifted me. "Easy," he whispered, pulling me against his chest.

I took in his warmth, clutching him, and let him carry me inside. We were through the door and climbing the stairs before I knew it.

"It was for nothing." My tears fell as I lifted my head. "It was all for nothing."

"No." Tobias shook his head. "It wasn't for nothing. I knew Lazarus wasn't behind any of this, but at least now we know for sure."

I lifted my head as Nick carried me into his bedroom and gently placed me on the foot of his bed, bending over to part my hair. I hissed with the sting of his fingers.

"You have a gash," Nick said, pulling back.

But Tobias peered closer, smoothing my hair down. "No. That's a goddamn tear."

"He had me by my hair."

All three of my brothers froze, then turned their gazes sharply my way.

"He did what?" Tobias asked carefully.

A chill coursed through me as I lifted my gaze to theirs. I swallowed hard at their dangerous gazes. "He...he had me by the hair."

Tobias glanced at Nick, then Caleb. "Did he."

But it didn't matter, not anymore. Gio was gone, exiled from the city by Lazarus. There was no way he'd come back.

"I'll get some antiseptic," Caleb said quietly, and left, making his way to the bathroom.

I pressed my fingers to the burning area and winced. "So, it has to be Creed, right? He has to know something."

"Whatever it is, he's not telling us," Tobias muttered.

"I tried to call him before." Nick turned, pacing the floor. But the moment he turned, I caught the blood on his cheek.

"You're hurt." I shoved up from the bed. "Nick, you're bleeding."

I crossed the room, forcing my knees to hold me. He touched his cheek and stared at his fingers when they came away bloody. "It's not mine." He met my gaze. "It's okay, Ryth. It's not mine."

I grabbed his hand, looking at the mess. He'd lunged, beating them down with unmerciful blows. He'd fought for me...*they all had*. My heart swelled. "You came for me."

He stared into my soul. "And will again, princess."

"Every fucking time," Tobias added.

"Until the goddamn end," Caleb finished as he strode into the room. "And beyond. Now, sit. We need to figure this out."

Nick walked me back to the bed, sitting me back down. But I couldn't look away from the blood on his cheek, or the unsatisfied danger in his eyes. I shoved thoughts of Gio aside and tried to think. "How do we find out what he knows if he won't tell us?"

"We make him," Tobias growled, clenching his fists.

"He's our dad." Nick shook his head. "No matter what, we have to trust he has our best interests at heart, and Ryth's."

He and mom were married now.

"So, we have no option but to figure this out on our own...and wait for them to return," I said, wincing as Caleb gently applied the antiseptic cream to my scalp, then touches the deep scratch on my cheek, his dark eyes turned menacing. "Fucking bitch." He growled. "The next time I see her."

"I have some guys I know," Tobias said quietly. "I can get them involved."

"T, no." Nick shook his head. "I'm not going down that road, not again."

I looked from Tobias to Nick. "Going down what road again?"

"Nothing." Tobias shot a glare at Nick.

But I wasn't having it. "Uh-uh," I said, sounding exactly like Lazarus' bodyguard. "No secrets, remember?"

Tobias clenched his jaw and that same broody expression I'd come to love settled in. "I know them from the Rossis, okay?"

I pushed up from the bed, feeling a little stronger now. "How deep were you in with him?"

"How deep?" Nick let out a chuckle and shook his head. "Tobias was his best fucking friend."

"Was," Tobias muttered. "Past tense, brother."

It all made sense now, the way Lazarus had looked at Tobias, the way he'd come charging in tonight had less to do with me than it had Tobias. Lazarus loved him...like a brother.

Had I had Lazarus all wrong? "He said my father wasn't killed for a reason. If he's not the one after him, then it has to be someone else."

"And it all comes back to the missing drugs," Nick said.

"And the money," Caleb added. "Always the goddamn money."

"But who?" I asked.

No one had an answer for that. We stood there, those words heavy in the air, then I moved forward, opening my arms. They held me for a while, until someone's stomach howled.

"Food," Caleb muttered. "Is in the kitchen."

We went downstairs, to where the discarded food still sat in the carryout bags. It was still warm and delicious. After we ate, I showered under the watchful gaze of Caleb, who helped dry my hair and applied fresh antiseptic to my stinging scalp and clawed face.

I hurt all over.

My arms, my head, my thighs.

My heart, more than anything. I climbed into bed with Nick. But this time we were alone. Caleb had gone to his room, Tobias to his.

"Are they okay?" I lay down against the pillow next to his.

"Yeah." He pulled off his boxers and climbed into bed naked. "They'll work through it in their own ways."

So much had happened tonight. Too much.

"Roll over and press against me. I'll hold you."

I did as he said, shifting my ass back in the bed until it rested against his cock. His arms went around me, one hand clasped my breast. Even when he grew hard, he never went any further, content to embrace me.

I closed my eyes. I didn't think I could sleep, but then exhaustion moved in, taking me into the darkness.

"I thought I'd lost you tonight," Nick's voice drifted to me. "We would've killed them. Natalie, too, if it came to that. They hurt you again and it'll be done."

"I'M GOING." I stood my ground. "I'm not missing out on passing my final year because of them."

"It's too dangerous." Tobias braced his arm across the doorway, blocking my way out of the bathroom as he eyed me up and down. "But you can keep the uniform on. I can relive my high school days."

"And fuck anything with a skirt?" I snapped, then froze at the outburst.

"Ouch." Tobias gripped his chest. "That fucking hurt."

"Sorry," I muttered as a pain stabbed through my abdomen. "I think I'm getting my period."

"Heat pack and chocolate, yeah? Or what do you normally go for?"

I froze. "What do I go for?"

"Yeah, little mouse." He stepped closer, grazing the back of his fingers down my cheek. "What's gonna make you feel better? You want to fuck? That might help. I know some women get more...needy."

Heat drove through my body.

"You needy, little sister? You can ride us all damn day if that'll help with the cramps."

"What cramps?" Nick muttered as he walked by, yanking on his shirt.

"Ryth's getting her period," Tobias explained, but never looked away from me.

Nick met my gaze. "Oh. You want to fuck, or do you want to be left alone?"

"What is it with you guys?" I grumbled, stepping back. "What I want is to go to school and pass my final year."

"So you can leave us?" Tobias' gaze narrowed, that thunderous look taking over.

"No, you idiot." I gave him a playful slap. "So I can get a damn job and actually be, you know, worthwhile in society."

"Fuck society," Tobias growled.

"On that, I tend to agree," Nick added. "Fuck society."

I gave a deep sigh and crossed my arms. "That's fine for you to say. Now, are you going to drive me to school, Nick, or do I have to drive your Jeep again, Tobias?"

"Christ, no," he snapped, then winced and corrected himself. "If you're determined to go, then Nick will take you. But one fucking glimpse of Gio or any of those fuckers, and I want you to call me instantly. You got that?"

I nodded.

"I mean it, Ryth. No more fucking stunts."

"I got it," I muttered as a cramp clenched once more.

Nick drove me in silence, pulled up at the drop-off zone, and scanned the nearby cars before nodding. "I'm going to be close anyway," he said. "So, anyone gives you a hard time, I want you to message me."

"I understand." I gripped my laptop and yanked the door handle.

"And Ryth," he added as I climbed out. "I'm proud of you, princess. You handled yourself well last night and now today."

I gave him a small smile and nodded, closed the door behind me, and turned to the school's entrance. I wouldn't buckle and I sure as hell wouldn't fall. The deep throb of the Mustang's engine echoed behind me as I strode to the front doors. The students hanging around outside stared as I walked, like I knew they would.

But this time, I held my head up.

After all...I was now a Banks.

44

Ryth

No one spoke to me. Not in first period, at least. I glanced at the empty seat where Gio usually sat, with my heart in the back of my throat. Flashes of memories came roaring back to me as the teacher called for quiet. The attack last night. Mom's wedding. I pressed my hand against the sting on my head as mom's voice echoed.

He just needs time, that's all, honey. He's fine...you trust me, right?

She'd lied to me.

But why?

She had to know about dad stealing...

Is he dead? Lazarus' words came rushing back to me.

No. No, he wasn't dead and I wasn't naive enough to think the Rossis didn't have reach in prison. I forced the panicked thoughts aside and tried to concentrate on class. I had my last year to finish, that's what I could control right now, even if the rest of my life was chaos.

Someone cleared their throat. *"Bitch."*

I stilled with the word.

"Brother fucker."

My throat turned arid as heat crept into my cheeks.

"Filthy fucking cunt."

"Okay," the teacher snapped his head around from the board. "That's enough. Who said that?"

Fire lashed, burning all the way to my stomach. My phone let out a *beep,* and for a moment, I was thankful.

I held my phone under the desk, hiding the movement as I swiped the screen.

Creed...

I flinched as my heart leaped into my mouth. We'd been trying to call him and mom for the last few days. Every time the call went to voice mail. At first, we hadn't been concerned, but then after yesterday...after yesterday, the messages left for them turned from frantic to demanding.

Creed: Meet me out front of the school. I'm waiting to take you to your dad.

I read and reread the message, my heart pounding as I lifted my gaze to the teacher.

"Well?" He glared at the other students. "Who the hell said that?"

I shoved up to stand, drawing every gaze my way. "Excuse me." I grabbed my bag and my laptop and hurried for the door.

Dad. He was all I thought about as I raced along the hallway and shoved through the front doors. Creed's dark gray Mercedes sat parked against the curb, the engine idling. I gripped my laptop tighter and raced for the car.

The window rolled down. Creed looked at me from behind the wheel. But instead of finding the calm, relaxed man who was still on his honeymoon, I found the frantic Creed.

"Get in," he demanded.

I yanked the handle and opened the door, then caught the bright blood on his shirt. *What the...*

"What is that?" I froze, standing on the curb. "What happened?"

"I don't have time to fucking explain, Ryth. Get the fuck in the car now."

The way he spoke.

The way he looked.

Those dark eyes were growing colder. This wasn't the man who'd taken me shopping, or the man who'd joked as we shared pizza. This man was trembling, shaking with rage or fear, I wasn't sure. My stomach tightened as I reached for my phone. "I'll just call Nick and let him know..."

"Don't bother, he's already waiting for you, with the others."

"He is?" My hand stilled.

"We don't have time for this, Ryth. Just get the fuck in. We need to leave *now*."

He looked into the rear-view mirror, making me glance at the street behind him. "Is someone following you?"

"What the fuck do you think?" He shoved the car into gear and slowly rolled forward. "Stay the fuck here if you want, but we're all leaving...*now*."

"Wait!" I lunged, throwing myself into the passenger seat.

Tobias. Nick. Caleb. They were all that drove me. "They boys...they're leaving?"

"We all are, it's not safe here. Not anymore." He punched the accelerator and jerked the wheel, tearing the car around in a U-turn before accelerating hard.

I scrambled for my seatbelt. "Why, what the hell happened?"

He was stony, his gaze fixed on the road ahead. Panic moved in...my mind raced, conjuring images I didn't want to believe. All I cared about was them...

"Are they hurt?"

"Who?" Creed jerked that hard glare my way.

"The boys, Nick, Tobias, and Caleb?"

He just shook his head, but it wasn't convincing. I looked at the mess on his shirt. The smear was too big to be just a cut...but a stab wound? "Whose blood is that, Creed?"

He didn't answer.

"Creed." Terror moved in, clenching my belly, making my mouth dry. "Tell me now."

I grabbed my phone, thumbing the screen, but he lashed out and snatched it from my hand as he stabbed the button for his window.

It was gone before I knew it, sailing through the air to hit the road behind us.

"What the fuck, Creed!" I screamed, shoving up in my seat.

"You don't need it." He clenched his fists around the wheel and kept driving, taking us where, I didn't know.

I snapped my gaze to him. "What do you mean *'I don't need it'?"*

He just drove, pushing the Mercedes harder as we took corners, the tires squealing. I shoved my hand against the seat, pushing myself as far away from him as I could. "You're scaring me."

"You'll understand," he said, and braked hard.

I searched the street, seeing a large metal warehouse hurtling toward us, the towering security gate open, the roller door already up.

"Tell me what's happened. Are they in there? Is Tobias in there?"

"Yes," he answered. "They're waiting for you."

I was desperate to call them, desperate to understand as the car hit the entrance and headed to the open door of the warehouse. Darkness swallowed the car, blinding me as Creed switched off the engine.

I had no choice but to follow as he yanked open his door and climbed out.

"Nick?" I called, stepping out. *"Tobias?"*

My head still throbbed, but fear burned inside me as I left the car door open. "Caleb...*Caleb, where are you.*"

"In here, Ry," mom called.

"Mom?" I surged forward, searching for her in the dark.

Something shifted in the shadows, black on black.

"Over here, honey," mom called, tearing my focus to the left. I moved carefully forward, still not seeing well in the darkness. "Mom, what's going on?"

"It's okay," she said as she stepped forward.

But she didn't open her arms to hug me. Instead, she just stood there, her arms by her sides, gripping her phone in one hand.

Creed's footsteps rang out as a chill raced along my spine. I glanced at my stepfather as he stared at me.

"We had to come back early," mom said, her gaze fixed on me.

"We left you messages," I started as she lifted her hand.

"We know," Creed admitted. "But we were...busy."

The blood smear on his shirt drew my focus again.

"We were sent a recording, Ryth," mom murmured as she swiped her thumb across her phone's screen. "A disturbing one. One that will confuse a lot of people, and ruin our plans."

"Plans?" I questioned as a deep moan ripped through the darkness.

I jerked my gaze to the sound coming from her phone. There was something familiar about that moan. Something that hit me in the chest like a fist.

Moans played out in stereo. The sounds of fucking made my stomach clench. I knew...I knew instantly. It was Nick's recording. The one he watched over and over again on his phone. The recording of all of us.

"Mom," I whispered, my gaze finding hers as that moan in the darkness came again.

"Ryth," Nick's low groan reached me.

"Nick?" I started forward as that shift in the shadows came once more.

Three men stepped out of the darkness, coming from where Nick moaned...and in the middle was the priest. The one from the wedding...I jerked my gaze to the name stitched onto his black jacket *Hale Order of the Lost.*

"We can't have this messing up our plans," mom murmured as the priest and his men stepped forward.

They surrounded me, closing in with menacing, stony stares.

"You're coming with us, Ryth," the priest declared, nodding to the two others with him. One of them grabbed me, his hold like a vise around my arm.

"No..." Nick groaned.

I wrenched my arm from my attacker's hold and tore away from them, stumbling backwards.

"It's for the best," mom answered, her voice cold and unfeeling as she glanced at the screen of her phone. "You'll be safe where you're going."

"Nick!" I screamed, tearing my gaze from her and frantically searching the dark.

But they were on me in an instant, yanking me back as I lunged. I caught the dark outline of my stepbrother, his arms bound behind him...a dark patch soaking through his white shirt.

"Take her," Mom commanded. "Take her to the Order...keep her away from the truth."

Panic roared. I fought, lashing out with all I had, until a hand clamped over my mouth and my nose was filled with the pungent, bitter sting of chemicals.

The warehouse swayed. I kept trying to fight, bucking in their hands, my gaze fixed on my brother.

"Nick..." I cried, my voice strange and warped. "*Nick...help me...*"

Until I plunged headfirst into the darkness and knew no more.

Epilogue
TOBIAS

"Answer your fucking phone, asshole." I snarled, listening to my brother's voicemail for the tenth goddamn time. I winced, hating that sense of foreboding festering inside me. I couldn't shake it off, no matter how hard I tried.

The damn thing had haunted me since I'd left for a run, and with each mile I ran, it only grew darker...until I cut it short and came home. I sucked in hard breaths, sweat sticking my shirt to my back as I downed my water.

"Problem?" Caleb stepped into the kitchen and glanced my way.

"Just Nick, the goddamn prick," I answered, watching as Caleb rounded the counter and poured himself another coffee. "Find anything?"

"No," he sighed and braced his hands on the counter. "Nothing we don't already know."

Fucking hours. He'd told me he'd text the moment he dropped Ryth off. "I think something's—"

The sound of the front door wrenched me from my thoughts. I hadn't heard the Mustang. But still...

"About fucking time, asshole," I snapped, striding out of the kitchen. "You said you'd text after dropping Ryth—"

Dad stood in the foyer, dressed in a bloody shirt.

"What the fuck! Whose blood is that?" I was riveted on the stain as I stepped closer.

Elle stepped in behind him. She looked from me to Caleb.

"Dad?" Caleb spoke, stepping past me. "Want to tell us what's going on?"

That dark feeling grew inside me, opening like a gaping pit.

I stood on the edge of that chasm...the ground falling away under my feet.

"Nick," I whispered, that blood connection roaring to the surface.

"He's fine," Dad answered, stepping closer. "He's at the hospital."

But that thundering in my heart said otherwise.

"Ryth?" Caleb asked.

As though he knew...

"She's gone," Dad answered, that same unflinching fucking stare fastened on me.

"What?" Caleb stepped closer. "What do you mean, *gone?*"

"She's been sent to the Order," Elle said, stepping closer, her gaze fixed on me. "We saw the recording, we know what you've been doing."

But the way she said it held no flicker of disgust.

No, this bitch was calculating.

Right down to the goddamn bone.

"You fucking cunt," I roared as I stepped closer. "I'll kill you... *I'll fucking kill you!*"

I lunged, hurtling myself through the air toward them. "Give her back to me! *GIVE HER BACK!*"

Ryth

DARKNESS...DARKNESS held me down. I tried to surface, tried to kick to get free. A hard breath sucked fabric against my mouth. My senses clouded...until a low moan tore free, triggering a memory.

I cracked open my eyes, feeling the bounce and jolt of a car. But I couldn't see anything. I jerked, pulling my hands. Steel links snapped taut.

"Stop moving." The command came from beside me. "It's no use."

I let out a moan as the memory moved in. Nick...Nick was hurt, lying on the floor of a warehouse. "What did you do to him?"

"Nicholas is fine," my captor answered. "But you, Ryth...you better be ready to be saved by the Order."

"Nick!" I screamed, even though I knew it was useless. I bucked, my senses roaring now, carving through that murky shroud in my mind. *"NICK!"*

Grab this hot as hell scene with Caleb for free as a bonus!

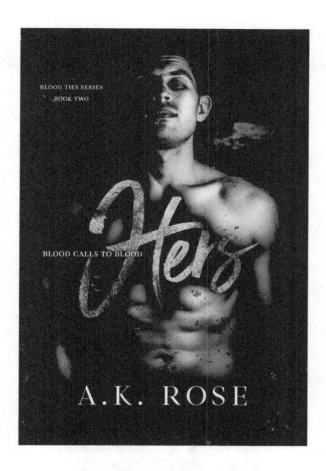

BLOOD TIES SERIES
BOOK TWO

Hers

BLOOD CALLS TO BLOOD

A.K. ROSE

Preorder your copy here!

My brother is bleeding.

My stepsister is gone.

The ones responsible called themselves family.

By blood, and now by marriage.

I want to destroy them for what they've done.

Burn everything they have to the ground.

But first I need to find her.

Ryth.

The pathetic, little mouse that scurried into our lives and made a home.

I can't forget her, can't get her out of my head.

She unleashed something dangerous in me.

Something that drove me to ruin her.

And ruined myself in the process.

She was once a game to me...

She still is...*only this time it's for keeps.*

Want NSFW (Not Safe for Work) Pre-release Digital Versions of my books? Join my exclusive club on Patreon and be the first to read *all the steam...*

- What you get by joining:
- Pre-release copies (limited to the next release before it goes live on Amazon)
- Discrete ebook covers
- NSFW Art
- Exclusive content
- Teasers and new chapters of upcoming releases

- Monthly short stories based on your favorite characters and more...

Click here to join

Made in the USA
Monee, IL
27 October 2024